FLYTE
OF THE
CENTURY

FLYTE
OF THE
CENTURY

RICHARD FENDRY

NORTHPAW PUBLISHERS

2021

Northpaw Publishers LLC
www.northpawpublishers.com
Printed in the United States of America
Publisher's Cataloging-in-Publication data
Fendry, Richard.
Title : Flyte of the century / by Richard Fendry.
Identifiers: ISBN 978-1-7364416-0-2 (print edition);
    ISBN 978-1-7364416-1-9 (ebook)
1. Spy thriller — Fiction. 2. Technothriller — Fiction. I. Title.

First Edition
10 9 8 7 6 5 4 3 2 1

OVERTURE

"I am not a good man. I am a vile man. I am a disgusting, filthy man! I am a gross, ugly worm, a horrid stinging vespid! I am the snarling, hollow-cheeked face of bitter, merciless despair, the wan, hemorrhaging miasma of the devouring shadow of the vortical void!"

"You perhaps exaggerate a bit?"

"Yes, I am a shrieking goony bird, an implacable dudgeon, the ravaged, crumbling hull of a disintegrating vessel, the most craven and virtueless of insidious betrayers!" He creaked. "Of this there can be no dispute – somewhere in this stunted, beguiling burst pustule of a world, there exist a full eleven, perhaps thirteen, disabused, chin-stroking paladins who are in some significant way superior to me!"

"And you could slash that number by conquering the proclivity to mix metaphors. But seriously, Doctor, as a three-peat Nobel Prize laureate, you and your life must count for a little that glitters."

The spry, old quondam king of the plasma scientists laughed maniacally. "Yes, my prizes! They decorate my existence. They allow me to prevail in asinine petty squabbles by crowing, 'I don't see *you* winning any Nobel Prize!' I submit, budget-wit, that if you are impressed by the three wreathes of a man of no account, then you are simply of no account by a factor of three!"

The celebrity scratched and stretched. "Dr. Shalom, the corona of your intellectual heritage expands to stoke the scientific ascent of untold future generations. To get down to tacks with such an unvarnished idol would be my supreme honor."

"A supercollider was my hammer." Shalom smacked the celebrity in the shoulder, and the car swerved slightly. "You could get yourself elected to serious high office, scout, without ever spinning whoppers that heavy on the fulsome scale. Or is it your slick point that I illuminate the crepuscular sky like the halo of a burning tire pile?" He pulled a panpipe pack of test tubes from his breast pocket and produced a calibrated shot glass from beneath his doomsday thermometer necktie. He unstopped two of the tubes, carefully poured a mixture and swished it around his palate before swallowing. "Ahhh!" He smacked his lips. "Laureate's proprietary blend of nitroglycerin. Try talking *your* way aboard El Al with this!"

The celebrity patted the Planck-walking stretcher of the spatial gauze on the stomach. "I didn't realize you could eschew the cash prize in favor of merchandise. Is there a tip you'd care to share on munitions futures?"

"A uranium speculation boom is always imminent." Shalom returned the tube set to his pocket but placed the glass over his eye like a loupe. "Invest first in what alarms you most." He scrutinized the prominent pipeline curl which divided the golden-brown waves adorning the celebrity's scalp from forehead to cowlick. "I'm rarely afforded the opportunity to tease someone else about his hair. But in risible rejoinder to your nagging contumely, my dishwater blond drainage-ditch-comber, is that fedora filler you're ferrying the escape tunnel for your pet tube worm or a keratin conduit for your shock therapy cable?" Thrumming his own elegantly unkempt locks, Shalom continued surveying the scalp of the celebrity the way a jeweler might review the surface of a paragon pearl.

The celebrity considered Shalom's gnarly snow-white down with a distinguished patina of grey which lay matted in split-end entropy on one side and puffed in convex complexity on the other. "What do you call your coiffure: heavy water and high voltage?" He smiled archly. "I'm sorry, I'd just resolved it's beneath my semiprecious dignity to upbraid you on your apparent penchant for falling asleep with your head out the window, but since you seem bent on rambling like a tornado in search of a trailer park, I had to make an exception."

Shalom shook as he laughed. "Yes, I no longer drive because all the horn honking kept waking me up." He shifted the glass to the other eye and squinted as if wielding a monocular microscope. "Perhaps that coastal California gnatcatcher nest on your oblate poll was inspired by some piece of hideous neo-post-modern suncatcher art in one of your rancho ramshackle specialty museums, where a lucky patron is afforded the opportunity to visit an antique potato grater."

"Check your aggression, Charlton." The celebrity filliped the glass from Shalom's face. "Where hostilities escalate, my wave doubles as a rocket launcher." He smiled complaisantly. "Don't compel me to shoot the curl."

"Oobops, don't get your neutrinos in a bunch!" The legendary slayer of subatomic hydrae hiccuped and sat back. "I am resigned to being effete and defeated; I am a totally spent and discredited sauropod! I no longer conduct scholarly research! I am something akin to senile. I spend my twilight hours captivated by the form of a tea leaf or the structure of a frost flower, mesmerized by the inner force and outer smoothness of a magnetized river stone or a buffed woman's bottom."

The celebrity made a quick right turn. "The fact is, thunder lizard, we cannot accept your resignation. Veteran informants have recently observed you in a research setting. They're as certain as hailstones sting that you were cracking more than your knuckles."

"You're confident it didn't merely appear that way to observers who drag theirs?" Shalom swept his fingers over the celebrity's pipeline curl in a crisp glissando. "How does your fizzing ossicle of a brainpan configure it, Oobops? Should Saturday night find me in the basement of the university library up to my axillae in gamma ray burst charts, pausing only for the side amusement of juggling ancient dictionary volumes with beleaguered dust jackets straining to find a word that rhymes with 'orange'?"

The celebrity forced a diplomatic chuckle. "The only word you can't fathom, Charlton, is 'quit.' King physics is your irresistible force, and to the extent you're not buried in work you feel like you're buried alive. Cadres of concerned scientists may have dismissed you as a turbulent high-altitude wind menace, an odious digger of loosely strung dimensions of dementia, but our net assessment leaves us confident these smackdowns are struck in the same flat key as expert opinions that the first nuclear blast would set the entire planet ablaze or that supersonic travel would trigger implosive vibrations-"

"Heed the warnings of the brontophobes, hodad-head." Shalom buckled his safety harness. "The experiments they halted could throw rivers and children alike out of their beds and cause the Earth's atmosphere to escape into space like a magician's dove!" He clapped his hands sharply. "I spent most of my star-crossed career pressing against the tendentious grain of miscalculations about the ionosphere and the magnetosphere in establishing new standards of cosmic repulsion. Yet, here and now, you have captured the realm and made it your own. You, buzz-saw-breath, have summarily eclipsed me."

The celebrity offered the grin of a man being garroted. "Flattery will get you nowhere except possibly dumped on the curb a long crawl from the tower suite of your luxury hotel."

"Hah!" Shalom snorted sardonically. "The consensus of society's yawing vultures is that I am trapped as a philosopher, that I have painted myself into a corner with a coat of heavy nihilistic latex." He unbuckled his harness. "You overlook the possibility that I might raze the parameters of the universe and step outside the labyrinth without hazard to my soles."

The celebrity nodded. "You and Buber both. Concede that cosmic being recurs as human becoming, and we'll toss popcorn in the centrifuge, kick back and enjoy your home movies of the big bang. In your sparks and histrionics, Dr. Shalom, I smell the blood of a super-heavyweight idealist, a conscientious priest of profound inquiry compelled to devote his full might to preventing degradation of the environment. Or if not, we have the preternatural resources to support you in any effort you'd care to make toward heading up that platinum-paved causeway of high-end humanitarianism and personal heroism."

Shalom fidgeted with the handle of the glove compartment and opened it. "What are you suggesting, wheedle-wright, that my fundamental motivation should lie in fixing my legion of jackleg detractors?"

"Absolutely not!" The celebrity pounced like a chess prodigy. "Petty behavior from the universal unifier lacks a certain coherence of style. Consider these sage words which still echo throughout the Stockholm Concert Hall in the afterglow of your stellar acceptance speech upon receipt of your first Nobel: 'Although we can't quite yet grasp it, we are at the inception of the opportunity to touch the power to change the nature of nature. And grasp it we must or forever resolve to dwell in mind caves of our own self-imposed obtuse impotence.'"

"How thick you slice your hubris to quote me as witness against myself!" Shalom produced the jar of astringent fireballs that the celebrity had stored behind the false back of the glove compartment. "In my near eighty years, haven't I uttered virtually everything, including 'I'm even more fun now that I'm married'? What you're alluding to there, deadwood dick, ignited my big rip with Club Standard Model." He shook the fireballs. "So what might these spook-house staples be?"

"Extremely dangerous!" The celebrity attempted to snatch the jar but the top-card topologist refused to relinquish his hold. "If you're a smart laureate, you'll leave fingerprints off, please!"

"I haven't seen jumbo atomic sootballs in years!" Shalom struggled to remove the lid. "The classic cinnamon candy dipped in a delicious licorice slurry? You might score major points by not being so stingy!"

The celebrity gained a firmer hold on the jar. "You're cradling heptane-based sludge pellets! They'll melt in your mouth and take your gums along for the ride!"

The jar vibrated as Shalom laughed. "How frustrating when we can touch something that we can't grasp, hmm, kibitz chip?" The celebrity grabbed a wrist, but the wielder of the polar shield resisted the force of the hold with astounding strength. The celebrity intensified his grip for an instant but vacillated. Shalom's wrist slipped free and the sprung tension slammed the jar against his chest.

Shalom dropped the jar and lifted the test tube pack out of his pocket. A steady cadence of drips emanated from some of the tubes. "Determined to make me break my diet, Oobops? Now I must storm the university pharmacy barn and petition the dispenser to re-vial me."

The celebrity eyed the doctor earnestly. "In the familiar refrain of our leading gurus and mentors, perhaps it *is* time you switched to a more effective program."

"Yes, booster-shot, why don't I try the parabolic flight-pattern diet?" Shalom allowed the tubes to continue dribbling into his pocket. "There are reputed to be periods of complete weightlessness."

"Another ingenious idea." The celebrity patted his pipeline curl and rubbed his neck. "Let's start thinking about what we want to do for dinner. If I envision roughly what our working relationship might be with my mouth full, maybe I won't be able to talk either of us out of it."

Shalom patted his power pocket protector and rubbed his wrist. "Yes, Oobops, I foolishly forsook the bonus bourgeoisie breakfast I was offered earlier, so with your gracious blessing, I would atone for that mother of bureaucratic sins now."

The celebrity nodded. "I know a little place that's unsurpassed for both talking business and celebrating afterward. It's a ramshackle tavern beneath the Salton Sink that specializes in genetically altered crustaceans. The place has no atmosphere so I've tabbed it the Mars Bar, but if you like your whiskey straight and your waitress curvy, it's a red-hot ticket."

"I prefer my waitress genetically altered." Shalom produced his calibrated shot glass. "Yes, Oobops, seafood! My body does not tolerate salt and I detest myself, so it's the perfect combination! It should save me the trouble of preparing my bedtime emetic." He exhibited a regal glower and offered an empty glass toast. "May the slow downhill slide of your life accelerate smoothly."

"Here's wind in your face, governor," the celebrity countered with a bent elbow, "and salt in your wound as well."

Here's a little tip: Bake day-old bread;
Add a dash of brash right-leaning spread.
If you want to save some dough and keep your family fed,
Here's a little tip: Bake day-old bread.

Never ride a northbound camel south;
Ship stuck in arrears puts foot in mouth.
So please reverse the verse: I think iamb therefore I shout!
Never ride a northbound camel south.

Sticky-fingered grips steal your best scenes;
Allied they shall stand with ways and means.
Let your life inform your craft and the pork provide
the beans,
Sticky-fingered grips steal your best scenes.

1ST MOVEMENT

Inbound. 1055 PST Friday 17 March.

"Stick this in your diplomatic pouch, California!" Having lost his authorization chip, the celebrity crashed through an eighth-floor window on the western face of the O Building at the Prosecution Complex in Santa Monica. More precisely, the vacuum climber pads attached to his feet crashed, crudely enlarging the pilot hole initiated by his California Gull replica UAV kite. The celebrity gingerly squeezed the goo-filled flak packs which girdled his double-layered body armor and his compressed-air chestpack tanks through the entry portal and found himself five meters above the floor of the mock school gymnasium in the Urban Warfare Training Center. He descended the inside of the glass-and-steel curtain and turned to face the dimly lit bleachers.

"Halt!" A security guard rapidly approached from the opposite end of the pseudo-structure. *"Freeze!"*

"More options?" Sweating profusely in his strong-suit, the celebrity opened the tinted vent flaps of his helmet visor with a double head bob. "Training test exercise!" he bluffed.

The security guard continued charging and raised his double-barrel directed energy launcher. The celebrity leapt back onto the wall and climbed. "Final warning!" the voice below echoed. "Stop and drop!" The celebrity hustled more intently toward his breach hole. The guard fired his weapon in active denial mode, shooting a wave beam that induced a sensation of intense heat throughout the celebrity's body. The blast hindered his voluntary movement but he continued upward. "Don't do it!" The guard fired his cannon again, further restricting the celebrity's neuromuscular thrusts. "Quit before you fall and hurt yourself, crampon-head!" The celebrity gritted his burning teeth and kept climbing. He reached his escape hole without absorbing another blast. The guard appeared to be experiencing equipment trouble. The celebrity hastily guided his pad-clad feet and legs through the lacuna. He endured a blast of energy in the form of a shockwave ring, which blew him the rest of the way through the hole and nearly off the building. He lost his right-hand suction pad and dangled against the outside of the wall.

He regained his equilibrium and employed a spasmodic three-point mambo motion to descend diagonally toward the northwest edge of the building. His shorter-beaked Swainson's Thrush UAV kite had breached a commissary window on level six and hovered outside the hole diligently pecking to enlarge it. As he approached, a blast from inside the building demolished the kite. Another security guard poked his head outside. "That's an endangered species!" the celebrity screeched.

The guard pivoted to situate the celebrity in his respective lines of vision and fire. "So are you!" He extended his directed energy launcher. The celebrity raised his right elbow and pulled the trigger ring, discharging a faceful of sticky foam from the nozzle lashed to his triceps. The guard fired his weapon wildly and staggered backward. The celebrity enlarged the ingress with his ped pads and swung his feet into the hole. Leaving the tanks and vacuum pads parked on the outside wall, he propelled his body inside the building. He found himself in a recessed corner of the commissary. He fired a refresher volley of itchy goo at the guard, punched him in the ribs and tossed him to the floor. He kicked the guard's cannon aside and confiscated his combatant's lapel badge and sourcerer.

The celebrity leaned against the probiotics vending machine and caught his breath. A female security guard appeared at standoff distance brandishing her directed energy launcher in high-energy laser mode with heat-seeking antipersonnel precision guidance system. "Hands up!" she commanded. "On your knees!"

The celebrity raised his arms and dashed past the vending machine. The guard fired, and the beam acquired the body-temperature bacteria-product dispenser as its target. Before she could pulse another shot, the celebrity reached the partition which demarcated the hospitality staff work space and vaulted it. He landed on a counter, vaulted another divider and another after that. Leaving a chorus of panicked shrieks in his wake, he raced up an aisle. A *BANG HEAD HERE* sign complete with brass gong hung outside a corner cubicle. An associate poked his nose into the aisle beside the sign to investigate the commotion, and the celebrity impulsively swatted the man's head into the gong as he turned the corner of the grid. He hustled down the border aisle and entered the commissary proper, which was beginning to fill with diners.

The celebrity lost his pursuer but gained an interceptor. "Get down!" Another security guard brandished his 9-mm service pistol, presumably loaded with rubber slugs or similar low kinetic impact specialty munitions. The celebrity ran wide to maintain the protective shield of dining table clusters between them. "Everybody down!" The guard fired a shot which penetrated one of the celebrity's goo packs and sent a cascade of sticky foam under pressure over the commissary tables. The guard fired another shot which punctured the other goo pack and released another sticky foam wave. Most of the diners abdicated their seats in favor of the floor space beneath the tables. Running in a radical crouch, the celebrity angled toward the nearest emergency exit. An associate made a swipe at his ankles, and he high-stepped through the tackle attempt. A bullet shattered glass in the exit door as he approached it.

The celebrity slid and kicked the latch to open the door. He rolled and bounced back to his feet on the other side.

He staggered against one of the deluxe bins of recyclable waste with which the narrow corridor was cluttered. He situated his helmet to protrude out of the top of the next bin and squatted beside the door. The guard started through the door, and the celebrity sprang, pinning him against the jamb and twisting his right wrist until he dropped his firearm. The celebrity elbowed the guard in the jaw, pummeled his gut and yanked him into the corridor. He treated him to a waning stream of sticky foam and forced him to the floor with a pert kick to the knee. He reclaimed his helmet and flipped the waste bin onto the supine guard. He retrieved the pistol and leaned on the upended bin. "You stuck-up dragoon, you must know that penetrant munitions are prohibited inside the bullet-free zone of the Prosecution Complex."

The security guard who'd blasted the vending machine appeared at the door ready to fire another laser pulse. The celebrity jumped behind the upended bin and donned his helmet. The guard shot a beam through the door and bin, and her downed colleague screamed. The celebrity trained the pistol on her, and she vacated the area.

The celebrity shoved the adjacent bin into the door and sprinted to the emergency exit at the end of the corridor. He unloaded his spent flak packs and opened the door. He found himself a step outside the kitchen. He ejected the magazine from the pistol into the compost caboose. Beneath the disconcerting red strobe light and P.C. emergency alarm that shrieked like ancient cartoon figure Betty Boop being quartered amid a tetrad of angry tractors, he re-entered the commissary proper and slipped behind a decommissioned counter. Moving on his knees, he labored to breach the communication application of the Qilroy he'd lifted from the guard. He attempted to broadcast a message to all P.C. security personnel: "Deploy fog generators on level six from commissary through bridge to U Building! Repeat: Deploy foggers on level six in commissary!"

The celebrity reached the end of the counter. He appeared to have a clear path to the alcove through which he'd originally entered the commissary. He stood and started walking. "There he is!" A security guard charged and raised his directed energy launcher. "Hands! Now!" The celebrity shielded himself behind a pair of undeterred diners. "Drop!"

The celebrity waved the pistol, the guard backpedaled and the doughty diners hit the floor. "Fetch!" The celebrity heaved the handgun at the salad bar and bolted for the alcove. He endured an overall burning sensation as he dodged another confused diner. The female security guard charged from the periphery struggling with her weapon. He would beat her to the alcove, but he resolved that if any security personnel remained stationed at his hole in the wall, he would seriously reconsider surrender. He ducked around another couple standing blithely ignoring the floor show, raced into the alcove and found it empty except for the sparking, hissing probiotics vending machine. He knocked the machine onto its side, nudged it beneath his exit hole and leapt onto it. He withdrew a handful of slicker-capsules from his fanny pack and flung them onto the floor. The guard arrived, slipped and fired her weapon. The laser locked onto the bacteria dispenser and induced an eruption of light smoke and crackling sounds.

The celebrity leaned out of the hole, grabbed his top suction pad and pulled his body outside. He tossed the chest-pack tanks over his shoulder. The barrel of a directed energy launcher protruded through the hole, and he kicked it out of the hands of its aspiring shooter. He jammed his feet into his ped pads and moved laterally toward the edge of the wall.

Another security guard leaned outside the hole with his directed energy launcher. "We're not playing anymore, asshole!" The guard aimed his weapon. "Give it up!" The celebrity descended. The guard fired. The celebrity felt as though he'd been plunged into boiling oil as the waves excited the molecules of his hypodermis. He emitted a scream and worked downward. "Stop and save yourself a lot of pain or worse!" The guard fired again. "Upping the payload! Would you rather lose your eyes or your genitals?" The celebrity wasn't pleased to trust his vital organs to the reflective surfaces of his armor, but he was in no position to bargain, and he continued to the edge of the wall as rapidly as pain would permit. He felt engulfed in energy as he negotiated his turn onto the northern face of the building. A heat-seeking laser pulse followed him around the corner but couldn't penetrate his armor.

He moved inward on the solid ocher brick surface and allowed himself the luxury at level four to stop and cough violently. He detached the vacuum climber pad from his left foot. He withdrew the inflatable carpool dummy from his fanny pack. He lowered himself another body length, lashed the dummy to the discarded ped pad and set it to inflate in five minutes. Once deployed, the dummy would respond to the slightest vibration with the calm voice declaration, "Yes, officer, I want to cooperate."

The celebrity beat a hasty two-point ascent to the roof of the O Building. He encountered the P.C. asset protection drone straightaway. "Lie flat on your belly!" The drone hovered a meter over his shoulder. "Fingers interlocked behind your neck!"

The celebrity disengaged the vacuum climber pad from his hand. "That sounds refreshing, but I can't stay!" He swung the pad around on its compressed-air-line like a lariat noose and whipped it into the drone, knocking the surveillance vehicle to the roof. He crushed it beneath his ped pad. "How'd that go down with you, spotters?" He removed the ped pad and hustled to a roof position directly above his original eighth-floor Urban Warfare Training Center entry point. He unwound a segment of the black rope wrapped around his waist and rigged the forward end to both suction pads. He affixed the pads to the roof as a double anchor. He produced the requisite slack and leapt off the roof.

His soles bounced twice on his descent over the glass wall, and he stopped at the entry hole. He let himself in again and surveyed the mock gymnasium below for activity. He seemed to be the lone occupant. He lowered himself to the full extent of his rope, which left him hanging two meters above the floor. He released the terminal end of the rope and landed on his feet. He scrambled from the gym to the mock principal's office.

Trainees frequently deserted the Bureau personal tank on one of the Training Center sets to save themselves the tedious chore of returning it downstairs to the armory. The tank was painfully difficult to enter, problematic to steer and a plodder at full throttle. The celebrity found the tank in the closet. "Luck of the Scots-Irish," he crowed. On the peg beneath the turret, he hung the lapel badge he'd confiscated from the first security guard he'd sauced. With a moderate struggle, he awkwardly crammed himself into the vehicle and shut the hatch.

The celebrity started the engine and reviewed the control panel. Operation of the telescoping "heavy hand" mounted on the bumper guard promised to be particularly tricky. The vehicle jerked, balked and started forward. He tried to swerve around the principal's postmodern desk but couldn't maneuver sharply enough. The tank pushed the desk until it was wedged against the door. The celebrity toiled frantically to open the door with the service hand and finally succeeded. He further employed the hand to flip the desk onto its side. He raised his treads and crushed the desk as he traversed it. He rattled through the doorway down the hallway and out of school.

The personal tank rumbled past the mock hospital ward to a real emergency exit. Opening the door with the service hand, the tank advanced to the freight elevator. The celebrity switched on the scratchy loudspeaker and attempted to summon the elevator with a voice command but ultimately accomplished the task by pressing the button with the hand. The elevator conveyed the tank to level six. The vehicle proceeded to the central hallway and speed-crawled past the commissary toward the Plexiglas-covered bridge to the U Building.

A rhythmic pounding permeated the tank. A security guard lugging a thermal fog generator appeared in the scope and checked the lapel badge. The celebrity opened the audio filter. "Cameron!" the guard exclaimed. "We heard you got slimed!"

"Shut up!" the celebrity snapped with a sheepish rasp.

Another security guard equipped with a directed energy launcher charged out of the skywalk. "About face with the armor!" He twirled his forefinger and pointed upward. "Threat is on the O roof!"

"Update, conflicting reports!" The tank resumed its sluggish advance, and the guard skipped aside. "Checking U roof! Spread out!" He pushed onward, crossed the twenty-meter skywalk bridge and passed the vacant guard post at the U Building entrance. He pivoted the vehicle to ensure that neither of the guards who'd confronted him was shadowing him.

The celebrity guided the tank to the elevator bay. "Do not," a prerecorded announcement warned, "repeat: Do not use elevator in emergency." The hand pressed the elevator button. As he waited for the dilatory lift system, he observed the passage of the ninety-minute mark from the scheduled time of his missed appointment.

Forty-nine and a half hours previously, the celebrity had been encamped under the robust Latin American sun in Leon, Nicaragua, wielding the stick in Operation Foxhound to exact moral payback from the last pair of former California legislators to loot the state treasury. He'd approached what several analysts labeled a vanity op with pride and extreme prejudice. And he felt satisfied that he'd succeeded in reducing the two wayward lawmakers who'd manipulated the state public employee pension system for the obscene benefit of themselves and a cadre of fellow marauding opportunists to an abject lesson. Any near-future expatriates hoping to retire comfortably in Nicaragua courtesy of American tax dollars would now be well-advised to reconsider. The California Intelligence Bureau had rewarded his efforts by notifying him of his termination effective immediately with cause classified and reminded him that CIB bylaws required him to appear in the office of the Director of California intelligence within 48 hours if he wished to appeal the action.

Scrambling to return home in time to arrange an appeal, the celebrity had grown increasingly agitated about his discourteous dismissal. When circumstances forced him to re-enter the country under cover of the radar-corrupting massive arrays of wind turbines off the Monterey County coast, he'd become obsessed with the idea of conducting an incursion into the Prosecution Complex to keep his appeal appointment. He'd continued toying with the idea to the point that he'd prepared himself mentally and physically for the protest assault. However, he'd left his North Hollywood home in his strap-on Buick Skylark with ample time to reach the P.C. on schedule provided he elude traffic by taking an unsanctioned air route over Beverly Hills.

A minor rotor explosion had forced him aground on the sinuous eastern Bel Air portion of Sunset Boulevard. The full significance of being stranded in this area had quickly become apparent after he abandoned the craft unable to summon roadside assistance. There was no sidewalk. Hedges and plantscapes extended to the curb, rendering pedestrian space as artificially precious as the surrounding real estate, and forcing anyone on foot to scamper from side to side of the thoroughfare with eyes vigilantly cast over shoulder to dodge the torrent of terrestrial vehicles which zipped blindly around the curves. He'd finally contacted a car service from a bus stop in Beverly Hills. But before he could be rescued, a bug flew under his helmet and into his eye, scratching his cornea. There was still irritation.

The elevator conveyed the personal tank up to level ten. The floor had been designed in an open concept with long, communal tables and few dividers. Incredibly, the open concept had proven disruptive and grossly inadequate for a compartmentalization-obsessed spy agency, and the level remained under redevelopment. The tank moved invisibly through the dark, unoccupied work space. The celebrity parked the tank in a special-needs lavatory. With some struggle and strain, he propelled his body out of the vehicle and shed his strong-suit.

He strode to the stairwell and started toward the D.C.I.'s level twelve office. Two associates descending the stairs eyed him suspiciously. He realized that his helmet still sat atop his head. He yanked it off as he arrived at level twelve and a man stepped out of the door. "We got him!" He waved the helmet and grabbed the open door. "Here's his headgear!"

"Got who?" the associate queried.

The celebrity smiled politely. "Sorry, I'm not allowed to divulge." He stepped inside. "But we got him." He slammed the door behind him and proceeded to his work area. He hustled through the hive of cubicles in the Subdirectorate of World Free Visions & Operations and opened the door to the anteroom of the top echelon offices. He took a deep breath and approached the high desk of the three-headed secretariat. He took an abrupt detour and checked his helmet in the closet. He inspected his sandy blond waves in the door mirror and adjusted his pipeline curl so it divided his scalp into perfect hemispheres. He fluffed once more and continued to the secretaries' desk.

The three secretaries all entered voice-over-digital data at their respective computer terminals and ignored him. Still breathing and perspiring heavily, he stood before Head Secretary Radmilla Eisenstadt, an attractive middle-aged woman wearing oversize rose-colored Jatakar aviator glasses and a smart salmon-and-charcoal power business unigarment. When two solid minutes passed with no acknowledgement, he boosted his upper body onto the edge of her desk. He slowly leaned forward until she recoiled with a tight-lipped glare and squared her shoulders with an authoritative panache. "Ahab Oobops," he announced, "here for my ten o'clock with Mr. Aldred."

"You missed your appointment, Mr. Oobops," Radmilla snipped. "You missed the grace period that followed. You'll need to make another appointment, and the earliest we could squeeze you in, if he'll allow it, is next Tuesday."

The celebrity returned to the floor. "You know I'm required to appear at his office within 48 hours of my termination notice in order to lodge an official appeal, Rad, which leaves me exactly four minutes." The wall clock displayed *11:41*. "You're further aware that Bureau bylaws stipulate he must see me in a timely manner once I appear, 'timely' meaning immediate." He smiled deferentially. "Even if I was technically tardy, I'd expect you to bend the rules for me because skirting regulatory red tape *is* one of the fundamental themes of our departmental mission."

Raddy emitted an astringent hiss. "I'm not even sure if he's still in his office." She activated the command link phone on her desk. "Your reason for being late?"

The celebrity exhaled with gale force. "Tell him I had to pace the hallway for two hours to work up the nerve to interact with *you*." He attempted to smile disarmingly. "The truth is I had to make an emergency repair stop. The wax button holding up my pants melted."

Over the top of her frames and beneath her long lashes, she rolled her violet eyes. "We'll check his exasperation threshold."

The celebrity bent forward and offered a small salute to the pinprick cyclops cam embedded in the bridge of her frames. "My button failed when the bomb that blew me and my Buick out of the sky detonated."

Pazzionette, the statuesque African-American undersecretary who'd formerly ruled the collegiate volleyball court, eyed him curiously. "Oobops, did you say you had an explosion in your pants?" Amber, the crimson-haired undersecretary on Radmilla's right wing, chortled conspicuously.

"Yes, Mr. Aldred," Rad snarled into the mouthpiece, "Ahab Oobops is here in full hostile mode spreading his negative energy." The celebrity leaned closer. "Today he's combining his verbal thuggery with an attempt to intimidate through physical proximity. Shall I require him to reschedule?"

"Madam Secretary knows I can't reschedule, D.A.!" The celebrity retreated to the floor. "Tell her to sheathe the attitude."

Radmilla cupped her mouthpiece loosely. "Hmm, I see, yes, sir, very well." She deactivated the circuit, removed her Jatakar and twirled the specs peevishly. "Mr. Aldred says you should have a seat and wait." She displayed a predatory smirk enhanced by her fabulous cheekbones. "He's having a tantrum because you're late, and he'll summon you when he's consolable."

The celebrity tapped nervously on her desk. "Explain to me, Raddy, how a man with a lobotomy has a tantrum."

Rad slipped her Jatakar back over her nose, put her head down and resumed her data entry. "I suggest you direct any question regarding Mr. Aldred to Mr. Aldred or to Mr. Aldred's immediate supervisor, per California state policy."

"All right, canvass the detox centers and see if the governor's phone privileges have been restored." The celebrity bent forward, stretched his neck and tilted Radmilla's monitor upward. He swiped her screen so he could peruse the hidden borderline contents. Although it was encrypted, *The Washington Hollywood Observer* tabloid could be identified in the lower left-hand corner.

"Go sit at a visitor's terminal!" Raddy emitted a hiss of intolerance and returned her monitor to its original position. "They're loaded with patriotic state literature for your professional enrichment!"

"Ahab, if offensiveness was a disease, I'd send you a get-well bouquet." Amber fanned her nose. "You could use it."

The celebrity stared down the barrel of her sneer. "Oddly

enough, Amber, it's my understanding that your sisters are quite attractive." He strode to the farthest visitor's terminal and utilized it to display the current edition of *The WHO.* The cover story offered the complete hacked psychiatric file of actress Mimi Pinkerton. The banner read: *"I want to be known and loved by more people than I have the time to meet."* In other stories, a natural algae bloom had turned a stretch of the Potomac River emerald green overnight, and an elementary school principal, who'd been ambushed and beaten over the head with wooden rods by three of his 7-year-old pupils, was charged with striking back by lacing the boys' school lunches with erectile dysfunction drugs.

A window featuring Radmilla's head popped into the center of the screen. "He's calling for you, Mr. Oobops," she advised.

"He has a loud voice, doesn't he?" The celebrity sprang to his feet, hustled up the aisle and pounded on Rad's desk as he passed by.

She held her gaze on him. "Your mother had a loud bark," she muttered into the mouthpiece of her phone.

"Yours had a loud rattle." He proceeded to the blue ion curtain which separated the anteroom from the inner sanctum and waited for her to remove the electrical charge. She nodded subtly, and he pushed open the heavy metal double doors, sustaining a light shock.

He slinked past the door of A.D.D.O. Montoone's office plus the unmarked door and strutted into the office of Director of California Intelligence Danforth O. Aldred. The uber-spacious domain provided an opulent contrast to the cheap fixtures of the anteroom. The chartreuse walls and quaggy, aquamarine carpeting inspired images of early morning in a manicured Sherman Oaks country club golf course rough. Turgid artistic furnishings including a life-size redwood Minotaur and a mushroom cloud composed of shiny pennies lay strategically inserted amid modern furniture fit only to challenge the intelligence and insult the taste of the observer. A bronze abstract bust behind Aldred's huge desk depicted the Great Martyr of nearly one hundred years before and on the wall above it hung an enlarged reproduction of *The Wreck of the Hope* by Caspar David Friedrich.

The willowy Aldred descended the mysterious carpeted mound in the corner of the room toting a putter over his shoulder. As he approached in the filtered light, his prominent temporal scar clashed with the rest of his soft, gentle features. He flipped his putter aside and extended his right hand. The celebrity extended his right hand and quickly withdrew it in tandem with the director. The two men ceremoniously clipped each other's chins with sneaky left hooks. "How now, Unique Agent Oobops?"

"I'm sorry I upset you by arriving late, Handsome Dan." The celebrity followed the D.C.I. to his desk. He rubbed the scuffed underside of his left forearm. "Someone planted a bomb-"

"Don't even bother to apologize." Aldred seated himself in his wingback curule. "I turned your impertinent tardiness to my personal advantage." He patted his short brown hair. "I amused myself by alternately persuading my psychiatrist to commit suicide and then counseling him to refrain from it. Finally, we compromised and he settled for self-mutilation. Off the record, I was practicing my putting while speaking with him and I did become vexed at my inability to sink one."

The celebrity smiled complaisantly. "You mean you only missed one or you missed them all?"

The D.C.I. cleared his sinuses. "You were a collegiate golfer, weren't you, Oobops?"

"No, Big Sir, my sport was hooverball." The celebrity thrummed his washboard abdominal muscles. "I was the captain of the club hooverball team."

The director produced his granny glasses Jatakar. "Only golf will break your heart."

The celebrity nodded. "Hooverball will only break your nose and neck."

Aldred gestured to the visitor's wingback curule beside his desk. "Please don the family jewels and take the electric chair." The celebrity wrapped himself in the electrode-studded headband, necklace and bracelets designed to monitor his brainwave activity, eye and lip movements, heart rate and perspiration level. In what was the Studio's second-worst-kept secret, the biometric tell app of the D.C.I.'s Jatakar would apply the behavior algorithm stored in the quantum computer to the celebrity's physiologicals and verbiage in order to gauge his evasiveness quotient and semantics. "You bring with you the stale uric after-scent of one who's been too long on the road."

"You recalled me from Nicaragua, D.A." The celebrity seated himself. "I was only able to make my deadline by infiltrating the coast through an offshore wind-and-solar matrix to avoid radar."

The director situated his Jatakar on his face. "Remind me what you were doing in Nicaragua." A garish yellow light issued from his lenses.

"I was in the process of winding down Operation Foxhound." The celebrity surveyed the twinkling ocean whitecaps that rolled across the D.C.I.'s desktop from real-time satellite imagery. "I submitted my concluding fustian."

Aldred stared stoically. "Ah, yes," he uttered ten minutes later, "Operation Foxhound." He pressed his thumb and forefinger against his brow. "Much of your fustian is written in the present tense with sentences that have no subject. Here I find an instance of where you've twisted a noun into a verb. 'Tasked,' Ahab? 'Transcripted?' Turns out such a tortured report reads like something cheap and disposable." He pointed to his red Queen Mary leaning smokestack wastebasket. "Not the stuff of a permanent record. Moving forward, please express yourself as though you've been exposed to formal higher education."

He stretched his collar. "In substantive terms, what activities does 'winding down' entail?"

The celebrity shaded his eyes. "Having exceeded my target in Foxhound, I turned my attention to planning and preparation for my next assignment in Operation Desert Sponge."

"Operation Desert Sponge." The D.C.I. steepled his fingers. "Would you like to refresh my memory on what that is?"

"Are you joking?" The celebrity slapped himself. "Er, I'm so sorry, D.A. It's our groundbreaking enterprise, the Bureau's most ambitious project to date." He leaned forward. "Basically, we're going to send an unmanned spacecraft out to capture an Apollo asteroid, and the harvest will be systematically pulverized, analyzed, sorted and stored as the craft returns to Earth. While it is occulted by the moon, the craft will split into two. The module carrying the mineral-rich payload will park itself in orbit around the moon for future retrieval. The other module, designed to pass for a meteoroid, will hurtle straight to Earth on a trajectory to strike the western Sonoran Desert in Mexico. Our hi-def ground-penetrating radar has detected a field of ancient artifacts here beneath a popular trail used by undocumented immigrants to cross into the U.S. Our spacecraft will explode in the sky into a fireball pattern that suggests recently canonized St. Juan Soldado. A common motif among the artifacts seems to be the twisted 'Z/7' form of a wounded runner." The celebrity felt a proud grin spread across his face. "The shockwaves will only begin when the meteorites hit the ground. As investigators uncover the artifacts, Marian apparitions can be expected. Anthropologists will carve out careers around this event. But primarily, a tourist destination boomtown will result, and people who would aspire to enter the States illegally will find better opportunity in the desert hot spot."

Aldred pressed his thumb and forefinger against his brow. "I have the *cojones* to appreciate a mission design fraught with a bit of risk. But that sounds more like a bit of a reach, not least from an engineering standpoint. It also strikes me as an extreme remedy for a chronic social disorder that is something less than dire. It's a tricky proposition when one attempts to play a class of people vastly more intelligent than himself."

The celebrity winced mightily. "The dedicated *secutors* who dominate the scientific community have proven that they're every bit as susceptible as anyone else to interpreting events in a way that supports their preconceived notions." He dropped his elbow heavily on the desktop. "This is a veritable cloak-and-dagger symphony. And the general idea originated with you, D.A."

The director removed his Jatakar and traced his temporal scar. "Radmilla is vying frantically for my attention, so please excuse me, Ahab." He clasped his ultra-secure golden leadership finger phone. "Yes, Rad?" He paused intently. "An assault on *this* building? Penetrated through the wall glass? Please hold." He gazed at the celebrity and jammed his sourcerer back over his nose. "Do you have any knowledge, Oobops, of a lone wolf commando raid on this facility, in which the perpetrator scaled the curtain of the building like some deranged comic book mutant, executed a forcible entry and brutally waylaid security?"

"Don't you love a good storm, Handsome Dan?" The celebrity smiled complaisantly. "I thought I knew a shortcut to your office."

Aldred reactivated the leadership phone. "Radmilla, cancel the global alarm and advise asset protection that it was indeed an exercise." He paused. "The incident will be fully reviewed. Discipline will be decisively administered." He paused and hiccuped. "The drill was conducted with the expectation that we'd find security at its laxest on St. Patty's Day. Apologize to everyone for the exploitation." He terminated the connection and eyed the celebrity menacingly. "She reports that you created a diversion with a carpool dummy, you terrorized the commissary and you commandeered a personal tank."

"I admit it was aggressive, D.A., but I felt no small sense of betrayal when I was terminated." The celebrity sat rail straight. "I was humiliated, and I needed to make a statement of personal protest. I also had a tight deadline to meet in order to formally appeal my dismissal, which is what I'm registering right now. Someone planted a bomb in my Buick and I lost my authorization chip, so I had to enter the building by extraordinary means. Otherwise, security might have detained me downstairs and I'd have forfeited my right to appeal."

"Your appeal is duly noted." The D.C.I. patted his hair. "I'm relieved that you weren't injured further in the blast than to have your chip jarred loose, but that's why you're trained in survival skills such as negotiating a low-altitude crash. Produce the dislodged chip and place it on the desktop."

The celebrity tapped nervously on the rolling waves. "I didn't lose the chip in the blast, D.A.," he confessed. "Or even when my boots hit the boulevard in Bel Air. After the vehicle was incapacitated, I beat my forearm against it in disgust. In my agitation, I guess I didn't recover the chip."

"So we must now change our authorization code because there's a loose chip floating around the streets of Los Angeles?" Aldred cleared his sinuses. "Ahab, I can appreciate the need for a release when one's personal comfort level is disturbed. I could use a release myself right now to occlude the dishonor of the trite alibi I had to channel through Radmilla to protect you." He stretched his collar. "It's a level of comfort erosion which hadn't beset me since I was a young man fixed up on a blind date with a girl who was patently pregnant. I spent the entire dinner dreading the possibility I'd have to forgo dessert to assist in a tabletop delivery."

The celebrity decided to build a bridge of parallel digressions. "I recently invited a neighbor into my house to discuss philosophy. The man identified himself as a card-carrying member of the Flat Earth Society. The conversation culminated in him chiding me for my naivete." He surveyed the floor. "Why was I terminated, Handsome Dan?"

"You know that information is classified, Oobops." The D.C.I. produced an ice pick. "Only the quantum computer knows for sure." He traced his temporal scar. "In response to your official appeal, the select tribunal of review will convene by a year from the end of the current state assembly term to consider your case for reinstatement. Until then, you will perform your standard duties on speculation of being reinstated. The only effective change is that you'll now be officially designated as a contractor and you'll notice the temporary cessation of your medical and retirement benefits along with a twenty percent reduction in base salary. You will receive a compensatory award, of course, should your appeal be upheld." He hiccuped. "In the meantime, we need to issue you a contractor title. Are you disposed to work in an environment of drones and dominions?"

The celebrity shrugged. "As long as I'm not pushing anti-personnel buttons."

"Far from it." The director bared his teeth. "Drones and dominions are angels, and you're the new Studio chaplain. I'm advised that your personal habits include regular attendance at church services. So congratulations. Congress and each of the military branches have chaplains. I've always felt deprived that the intelligence service lacks one."

The celebrity rose. "I honestly must question whether I'm a suitable choice for that position, Handsome Dan. A lot of the loggerheads milling around the P.C. would tell you I'm something short of holy."

Aldred gestured to the visitor's chair. "In your personnel file, you're listed as a 'dissident Catholic.'"

"Too dissident." The celebrity reseated himself. "For a time, I engaged in a one-man crusade to heal the Catholic and Protestant schism by alternately attend-"

"Then you're perfectly nondenominational," the D.C.I. interrupted. "Your cover duties as chaplain will obligate you to offer a vaguely reaffirming spiritual message at certain Bureau functions such as our National Day of Outrage observance." He enabled a desktop keyboard and entered data. "I'll request that the secretary formalize the contract on your way out. I'll also instruct her to issue you a new authorization chip."

"Might we first revisit my loss of job benefits, D.A.?" The celebrity rubbed his fingers over the whitecaps. "It's a rather disturbing situation."

Aldred pressed his thumb and forefinger against his brow. "Ahab, if you're denied a company vehicle, then you rely on your own." The director grabbed his leadership phone. "Pardon me, Radmilla is signaling again. Yes?" He paused. "It has little to reconcile with environment ministry." He paused. "Are you contesting the position itself or the candidate chosen to fill it?" He paused. "Therefore, they complete each other. The less obvious he's been in the past, the more successful his missions have generally been." He paused. "That's correct. It had been implanted in his forearm, but he dislodged it while delivering a blow. Perhaps he could be strategically tagged in a sensitive area." He paused. "Thank you for reminding me. Sanction him with both." He terminated the connection. "Did you overhear any of that, Oobops, or are you beyond rehabilitation as a spy?"

The celebrity smiled complaisantly. "All the world's a power grab?"

"Any merit accumulated before your appeal is heard may be presented as voucher points for reinstatement." The D.C.I. traced his temporal scar with his ice pick. "As acting office medic, Radmilla reminded me that we wish to replace the outdated RF chip system with an experimental biometric blood marker. Volunteers will soon be injected with crystals so tiny they're not filtered by the liver or kidneys and provide the individual with a blood signature identification." He bared his teeth. "I just designated you as a volunteer, so Rad will insert you into both systems. She implied you're a wuss-bag, but I trust you'll refute that notion when you prove the blood marker is safe and effective."

The celebrity hissed. "How many points short of reinstatement could I be after Desert Sponge?"

The director cleared his sinuses. "More than if the event were staged on desert real estate owned by some honcho to whom we owe a political favor. In fact, Ahab, I'm squeezing you out of Desert Sponge and passing the boondoggle to Unique Agent Teretsara Tohnyin."

"Tess?" the celebrity objected. "How does she rate, D.A.? I've been taking on Desert Sponge research and development for months! I can't imagine how the dirty girl got herself attached to the project, but I hope it didn't happen right on this desk!"

Aldred twirled a long, manicured finger. "Thar she blows, Ahab!" He jabbed his ice pick into the desktop. "I like a go-getter, and that's Tess to a T!" He roared. "Tohnyin's performance on her current assignment implementing a successful plan for the forcible removal of a hideous piece of civic art plus the gratuitous window-breaking legacy you left upon arrival at the P.C. today occasion this switch." He removed his Jatakar. "But don't die of envy yet, Oobops. I have something else nearly as meaty for you, and it shouldn't require half the delay for a gratifying resolution." He eyed the celebrity squarely. "Operation Shalom."

The celebrity felt the biological need to complain further. "I guess this shatters the urban myth that a clear desk equates to a clean mind, hmm, or is it a clean desk equates to a clear mind?"

The director traced his temporal scar with the ice pick. "Ahab, you're surely familiar with the expression: Everyone talks about the weather but no one does anything about it."

The celebrity inhaled deeply. "No, D.A., I never talk about the weather."

"Then prepare for a low-pressure system to alleviate the

stress of your intellectual drought." The D.C.I. rolled the ice pick between his palms. "Oobops, what do you think you'd have if you could bottle the sun?"

"That's a hot one, D.A." The celebrity smiled complaisantly. "You'd have one hell of a container."

Aldred moved slowly but leapt out of his chair. "Please reassure me I'm not engaging a total troglodyte by admitting you've heard of Charlton Shalom."

"I know the name." The celebrity tapped the desktop irritably. "He's some news correspondent, isn't he?"

The D.C.I. stretched his collar. "Through what spinning wheel of delusion do you filter your world news?"

The celebrity chafed. "I'm generally too busy pinsetting the news to worry about how it's interpreted. Wait, I have it! Shalom is a weatherman!"

"That's affirmative." Aldred turned his body and studied the celebrity out of the corner of his eye. "The best kind of weatherman, the kind whose predictions are never wrong because he exercises control over the atmospheric forces."

The celebrity studied *The Wreck of the Hope*. "He must make inaccurate forecasts every once in a while just for the sake of appearances."

"This individual is no tree-ring-tracer, Ahab, so get over yourself and pay attention." The D.C.I. patted his hair. "He's been regarded as the first man to truly comprehend the meaning of time. He theorized a wave particle – the softon – and developed a mathematics which at least temporarily explained the dark energy of the universe."

The celebrity clicked his tongue. "He sounds like no ordinary genius."

"Not by intellect or ego." Aldred smacked the celebrity in the pipeline curl with the ice pick. "Recipient of an unprecedented three Nobel Prizes in physics for his work with ball lightning, gravity waves and magnetosphere fields, Shalom was being hyped as the grand slam scientist by pundits in their zeal to make him the first to get a fourth, but eleventh-hour research contradicted his findings about dark energy and stymied the progress of the movement."

The celebrity shook his head. "You're only as good as your last experiment, Handsome Dan."

"The Nobel committee was not deterred." The director broadened his sneer. "Buckling to the pressure of the extreme media buzz, they decided instead of backtracking to move diagonally and they awarded Shalom the Nobel Prize in literature for a novella he'd authored while institutionalized titled *The Sun Is Cold*, which depicted the ultimate revenge mission of the victim of a botched abortion."

"Shalom developed the habit of wandering off, didn't he?" the celebrity recalled. "After his wife dumped him, his daughter shoved him into a sanitarium."

"His capacity issues involved problems chilling, socially and physiologically." Aldred rolled the ice pick between his palms. "When he was awarded his literature prize, Shalom felt abjectly patronized. And he was immediately sued for plagiarism by best-selling author Bryce Horshboro-Kohluey over *A Cesspool Assessment*, the latter's early tome about a horrifically injured man who only wanted to die and his subsequent revenge against the interloping medical, political and religious establishment. Now doubly humiliated on the world stage, Shalom threatened to drive a monsoon through Sweden into the heart of Europe. Fortunately, a crack team of counselors calmed Shalom and prevailed on him to transfer his rage to climate change."

The celebrity smiled complaisantly. "I took a stiff measure of Horshboro-Kohluey in college: *Cohen's Koan*. He writes well about bodily secretions."

The D.C.I. donned his Jatakar again. "When Hurricane Joy made an inconceivable pivot in the Atlantic Ocean and dumped on Europe, many wondered whether Shalom and the U.S. government were somehow responsible. When Shalom expressed outright glee over the freak summer ice storm which paralyzed Potsdam, some became convinced." He knit his brow. "And yet, the scientific community in general believed he'd terminally discredited himself with his work on dark energy. Today, most consider him no more than the 'Charlatan' rainmaker pursuing the 'theory of absolutivity.'"

"They consider him trash because he called the global warming phenomenon an 'environmental fart in the wind' just before his last disappearance." The celebrity gestured that the director should return to his seat. "As you've undoubtedly deduced, D.A., I'm familiar with the Shalom situation and have been taking neurotic pleasure in forcing you to rehash it." He smiled archly. "It's difficult to determine exactly when he started and stopped working for the federal government, but his public outbursts fueled an investigative feeding frenzy, in which his entire life was scrutinized, and he was ultimately charged with having violated conflict-of-interest laws for accepting consulting fees from a geoengineering company while conducting research funded by a government grant. Then the Real Deal legislation passed and all charges were dropped. Lincoln Worbley used him as a prime consultant in erecting the Arctic shield and stated afterward that it wouldn't have been effective without his input. Does that about cover him?"

Aldred reseated himself. "The polar shield worked as intended to achieve enough negative radiative forcing to restore the atmosphere to pre-industrial conditions for over three years. But no sooner did Shalom dismiss the effort and disappear than the numbers began betraying the projections of the standard climate model." He stretched his collar. "The experts at such widespread concerns as the National Oceanic and Atmospheric Administration, the World Meteorological Organization and the Intergovernmental Panel on Climate Change are as baffled as we are. The polar shield is no longer diffusing enough sunlight to effectively counterbalance our greenhouse gas overload. If original chief project engineer

Worbley hadn't been conveniently killed building the Western water pipeline, perhaps we'd have more answers. But as it is, we are left to speculate that an actor with intrinsic knowledge of the shield has become a sell-out to civilization and joined a faction that feels threatened by our technologically elite barrier. Shalom is the prime suspect who cannot account for himself. There is no record of him engaging in any commercial transaction or utilizing any government benefits in more than two years."

"Sabotage?" The celebrity clicked his tongue. "If his life doesn't display on the grid, you have to conjecture that he's not living, don't you? Failing that, perhaps he's thrown in with some futures investor dedicated to capitalizing on climate change. On the brighter side, he might have connected with a good-natured group of little green men who's determined that the polar shield should fail because they're threatened by geoengineering tech in general."

Aldred pressed his thumb and forefinger against his brow. "There are sinister forces that wish to see the shield fail because they believe that climate change can bring short-term benefits to certain local areas such as the Great Lakes region of the U.S. They benightedly continue to dismiss our warnings that the only real warming winners will be weeds, insects and rodents. Hell, the increase of ultraviolet radiation penetrating the atmosphere combined with a fluctuation in air pressure can leave people more susceptible to diffuse axonal stretch, and as you might guess, I am particularly sensitive to the prospect of brain injury." He cleared his sinuses. "We have extensive networks of sympathizers stationed in the Upper Midwest, where statistical incongruities and variations purport to be most robust. These Earth patriots are sensitive to the future worldwide ravages that will occur with the continued uncountered accumulation of carbon and other greenhouse gases. Our Alice network in Wisconsin is particularly sedulous, and we've had several Shalom sightings in the area of their Madison stronghold."

The celebrity nodded. "You want me to find the shrinking snowpack where our traitor laureate is couching?"

Aldred jabbed his ice pick into the desktop. "You'll fly to Chicago, where you'll contact your retinue agent. As you'll ascertain from your Operation Shalom treatment, the reagent has performed most of the preliminary heavy lifting. He's established a Chicagoland safe house from which you'll stage your incursions and conduct your forays into Wisconsin. Prepare your sourcerer for file transfer." The celebrity opened his Qilroy, rolled his shoulder forward and received the director's vital intel stream. "You are to locate Shalom and determine whether he is being stashed against his will. If so, you are to arrange an exfiltration so he can be resettled under the friendly flag of California. If he is voluntarily aiding interests hostile to planetary sustainability or he refuses to adopt a less than cooperative disposition, you are licensed to reason with him. Persuade him to return to our side and make him believe it's his idea. Otherwise, you will order a stunt man to execute an extraordinary rendition and provide support so this polarizing figure may be thoroughly grilled and removed as a threat by any means necessary."

The celebrity coiffed his pipeline curl. "I've never been the most practical man, D.A., but I resist the notion that the best place to initiate a hunt for a superior mind is in flyover territory like Wisconsin."

Aldred brandished his ice pick. "Where under the sun, bright boy, would you suggest starting the search for a wizard who's gained a reputation for being able to control the weather?"

The celebrity smiled complaisantly. "How about the temple in Jerusalem?"

"Starting already with insider microaggressions, chaplain?" The D.C.I. steepled his hands. "Shalom has tax problems in Israel, and his daughter who's twice committed him to mental institutions lives there. He's considered an eco-terrorist in

Europe and is subject to being fined on sight for the devastating weather patterns which have gripped that continent. He's currently being tried in absentia in regions of India for crimes against the environment because the polar shield hasn't protected them as advertised from their escalating tropical depression." He hiccuped. "The temple in Washington might be a logical spot to commence a search. After all, the Weather Service originally operated under the auspices of the Department of War. But all indications are that the feds find him even more feckless than he finds them. No less an authority than his first wife relates that during their world travels, he chronically complained about 'alien culture and cuisine' and lamented his separation from the 'comfort and familiarity' of home."

"You allude to his family." The celebrity eyeballed his Operation Shalom treatment. "I'd recommend that we focus on personal links who are probably serving as angel benefactors."

"He's an only child with a reclusive history." Aldred stretched his collar. "He's always been suspicious and aloof from colleagues." The D.C.I. removed his sourcerer and anxiously looked around. "He's endured two bitter divor-" He sprang to his feet. "Where's my ice pick?" He circled his desk. "Oobops, locate my stress tool!"

The celebrity dropped to his hands and knees. He combed the area around the smokestack wastebasket and beneath the director's desk. He opened the bottom drawer and withdrew a folded blue polyethylene item with a black D-shape zipper that proved to be a body bag. The D.C.I. hopped back behind his desk and kicked the drawer shut. "You never go through my desk," he decreed.

The celebrity rose to his knees. "I'm sorry, Handsome Dan."

"You ought to know better, Oobops." Aldred jammed his Jatakar over his nose. "Stand and review the display on the desktop." The celebrity climbed to his feet and observed glamour photos of five attractive women. The director spread his hands over the images. "Click your pic, Broderick: my two ex-wives, my current wife, Unique Agent Addie Meyer or Unique Agent Tess Tohnyin. Indicate the babe that you find most desirable." The celebrity pointed to Tohnyin.

"My wife isn't your type?" The director patted his hair. "Deception should be your strong suit. You're not contrite about invading my privacy – or the Prosecution Complex. You don't regret that I've misplaced my ice pick." He fired his sourcerer at the celebrity. "You weren't really involved in an air traffic accident on your way here, were you? Strip to the waist so I can examine your body for fresh scrapes and bruises."

"You're not serious! Er, excuse me, D.A." The celebrity removed his biometric monitors and Qilroy. He hastily unbuttoned his shirt and tossed it onto the desktop. "You see my forearm and shoulder are a bit scuffed." As the D.C.I. evaluated his torso, the celebrity espied the tip of the ice pick protruding between the splat and cushion of the Big Sir's wingback curule. "Maybe this'll bag your pardon." He snatched the implement and handed it to the director.

"You seek to make amends?" Aldred exerted downward pressure on the celebrity's shoulder. "You're a student of ancient history. Offer the Greek gesture of supplication where the transgressor kneels before the aggrieved with an arm wrapped around the latter's knees."

The celebrity winced mightily. "Come on, Handsome Dan, how many times have you insisted you'd never compel a member of your team to do something you wouldn't do?"

Aldred sank to his knees and hugged the celebrity's thighs. "Atone!" The D.C.I. produced a parachute-cord cutter. He severed the celebrity's belt, clipped off the pants buttons and sliced deeply into the material. The celebrity's pants fell to his ankles, his protective cup dropped onto his toe and his genitals spilled out of his butchered briefs. The director returned to his feet. The celebrity replaced his groin guard and hiked up his pants.

"Ahab, I don't feel comfortable trusting you." Aldred

leaned over his desk and attacked the celebrity's shirt with the parachute-cord cutter and ice pick. He halted abruptly. "I must request your indulgence. A power struggle for control of my motor cortex among disintegrated neuron clusters spurred tyrannical behavior."

The D.C.I. reunited the celebrity with his shredded shirt and Qilroy. "What's next, D.A.?" The celebrity produced his Lahnzhitude Pin-Up flexicuffs designed to resemble a cream-tone thong. "Will it be me who goes bad?" He attached one cuff noose around his wrist and the other around a belt loop to hold up his pants.

Aldred pointed to the door with his ice pick. "It'll be you who goes to Chicago." He returned behind his desk and mussitated.

The celebrity saluted and tottered out of the director's office with wrist held high. He hustled down the hallway and waited at the ion curtain for the secretary to extinguish the electrical field. He finally punched the emergency override button, absorbed a light jolt and pulled open one of the doors. Radmilla stood before him leveling a long-barrel squeeze-handle punch. "Drop anchor, Ahab." She jammed the barrel of the instrument into his solar plexus, and he instinctively parried the punch with a lateral forearm thrust, which ruptured the belt loop holding his flexicuffs noose and sent his pants to his ankles followed closely by his protective cup. Rad lowered her aim. "You want it between the buoys?"

He kicked his cup. "What do you think you're doing, you nut-job?" He pulled up his pants.

"You're the deviant who felt compelled to expose himself in the middle of the anteroom." Radmilla accommodated the celebrity's navel with an authorization chip. "Mr. Aldred sanctioned me to tag you in a sensitive area."

"He was exaggerating for effect!" He retrieved his cup.

"Mr. Aldred does not exaggerate!" She pointed to the ion curtain. "If you believe I failed to properly execute his instructions, return to his office and request to file a complaint." She followed his gaze toward the unoccupied secretarial desk. "The other secretaries have left for lunch, so after all that, your modesty is still intact."

The celebrity eyed the overhead surveillance camera. "At least we fed Sacramento an eyeful, hmm?"

"I don't believe that would be possible." She dragged her latex-glove-covered hand over his abdomen. "You have a tiny, superficial cut." She displayed her blood-tinged finger. "As office reserve safety director, I must insist that we treat your wound in the infirmary, so let's finish our business there." She stepped back. "What did you do to yourself to tear up your clothes? Are you concocting some workman's comp strategy?"

The celebrity smiled complaisantly. "Direct any question about Mr. Aldred to Mr. Aldred."

"Mr. Aldred did that to you?" Rad laughed incredulously. "Meet me at the infirmary door." She tucked the long-barrel punch beneath her arm and headed back to her desk.

The celebrity clutched the front of his pants and followed. "Where is the infirmary?"

She stopped and eyed him over her shoulder. "How long have you worked in this building? Seven years on this floor?" She hissed. "It's through the cloak room."

"What cloak room?" He nodded. "I've heard there's a panic room off the executive closet."

Radmilla rolled her eyes and placed the punch on her desk. "Come this way." The celebrity clutched the front of his pants and followed her into the closet. "This, Mr. Oobops, is the cloak room." She pointed toward the hatrack. "That's your space helmet, isn't it?" She slid a cache of jump suits aside and exposed a wall designated by a large green cross. She tapped the wall and demonstrated that it was actually a door by opening it. She gestured that he should precede her into the darkness. He chivalrously returned the gesture. "Do you really think I'm unacquainted with your basic tricks? You go first." The celebrity expelled an aggravated breath and entered the panic room. Rad locked the door behind him. The stuffy, smoky atmosphere overwhelmed him. A heavy cannabis haze hung oppressively in the air. Orange LED floor lights were activated and provided minimal illumination. He groped around and discovered a massage table and row of lockers.

"If you resent having to submit to this procedure, Mr. Oobops," Raddy's voice obtruded through a speaker, "consider how objectionable I find it. I appealed to Mr. Aldred to send you to the nurse, but he insisted that I remain practiced as floor emergency medical tech." The celebrity sustained a coughing jag, and a soft lavender argon light added substantial illumination to the limited confines. He discovered a toilet and beside it a sink containing a warm bong. He endured another coughing fit, and the argon light disappeared. He hacked violently again, the argon light returned and the door opened.

Radmilla entered and coughed. "What do you think you're doing in here?" She fanned the air.

"You tell me!" He windmilled the air. "You're the one who stranded me in this-" He struggled to squelch more coughs. "Foul environment."

"Check your alibi, Mr. Oobops." Rad shook her finger. "Some of us keep personal belongings in here, and the other secretaries just picked up their purses before they went out." She placed her arm in front of her face and attempted to suppress a series of coughs. "I'm quite positive they would've reported a situation like this!" He clutched his pants and strode toward her. She retreated outside the room and slammed the door shut again.

"Mr. Oobops," Raddy's voice pierced the room through the speaker, "I'm going to vent the infirmary for twenty minutes. The air better be pristine when I return, or I'll trouble Mr. Aldred with the matter." She coughed weakly. "I'm going to need access to your lower abdomen to inject the blood marker by puncturing your inferior vena cava. So lie on your back on the table with pants down, shirt raised and wrists in the restraints."

The celebrity flipped the bong into the toilet. He found a bag of organic buttery caramel corn atop the lockers. He reclined on the table per Rad's instructions, relaxed and munched himself into oblivion.

"Ew, he's practically nude!" He awoke to find Amber and Pazzionette hovering over him. "Mr. Oobops!" Amber blushed and giggled. "We expected you to be bigger up close!"

"Mr. Oobops, baby!" Pazzionette contributed. "He could still be a doll, just not as anatomically correct as you'd like." The celebrity readjusted his pants. "You jacked my snack?"

"Ladies, we're pleased you're here." Radmilla entered brandishing a huge needle. "Mr. Oobops has an allegation that he'd like to bring against you. Don't you, Ahab?"

"Against *us*?" Pazzionette glared. "We caught *him* with his pants below his knees."

Rad scrunched her nose. "Mr. Oobops is in the infirmary to receive his scanner-detectable bloodstream signature security tagging, and he believes that one or both of you recently employed the room as a recreational smokers' lounge."

Pazzionette hissed. "I don't want to trade wild accusations."

The celebrity tittered. "Can we please just complete my bodywork before I lose my buzz?"

"Ladies, please excuse us." Raddy pressed a hand into the celebrity's solar plexus. "If you're afraid of the restraints, interlock your fingers behind your head." She impaled him with the needle the instant they were alone. "I realize you have the pain threshold of an 8-year-old, but it takes a moment."

The celebrity coughed. "Where do you get the idea that I can't tolerate physical pain?"

"It's in your personnel file." The needle quivered in Raddy's hand. "I vaguely recall entering the information myself."

The celebrity laughed. "I hope you have some demonstrated level of skill."

Rad sneered. "I'm a licensed medical technician. I've capably performed countless procedures. I administered the placebo anesthetic at Dan Aldred's precision lobotomy and handed the surgeon the ice pick when his scalpel broke."

"All so D.A. could never go back and deprogram the quantum computer?" The celebrity pressed his palms against his face and unleashed a coughing jag .

"It was mood surgery to remove the element of surprise from his psychological reaction set." Radmilla peered over her Jatakar lenses. "Didn't your mother ever teach you to cough into your elbow so your germs don't contaminate your hands and everything your hands subsequently touch?"

The celebrity tittered. "Mom was remiss in pedantry on pot party etiquette!"

"As long as we both understand the outrageousness of your conduct, I won't report you for smoking in the building." Rad sneezed into the crook of her elbow. "I sent you the standard contract to engage you on behalf of the Bureau as spiritual director. Just sign and send it back."

"Did your mother teach you to blow your nose on your sleeve, too?" The celebrity howled.

She withdrew the needle and he moaned. "To best manage your pain, tuck your chin into your shoulder, firmly plant your tongue against the roof of your mouth and apply firm pressure with both pinkie fingers against your brow directly over your nose and do the same with your index fingers at the base of your temples."

The celebrity was overtaken by exhaustion and lapsed into a short period of unconsciousness. When he regained a degree of lucidity, he found Radmilla walking him out of the closet and around the anteroom. Somehow his briefs had become reversed so the major crotch hole exposed his glutes. With each giddy step, he felt himself melt further into the carpeting until he sprawled over the back of a visitor's chair. Rad flipped his pants and groin guard onto the seat. "You understand now you mustn't donate blood." He blacked out again. He reawoke when he tumbled to the floor.

A dapper man and woman with visitor's tags strode up the main aisle and stepped over him. "Mr. and Mrs. Edie Collier for our three o'clock with Mr. Aldred."

From the secretarial desk, Mrs. Collier pointed at the prostrate celebrity. "What's *that* supposed to be?"

"Some art students from the university are coming over later to carve gargoyles that'll be placed on the exterior of the building to scare away birds," Raddy explained. "He's serving as the model."

"Good casting," Mr. Collier agreed.

Pazzionette marched past the celebrity and tossed a towel over his pelvis. "Throw another over his head," Amber advised.

The celebrity rose to his hands and knees. "Get yourself out to wherever you're supposed to be, Oobops!" Radmilla commanded. "We're tired of covering your butt up here."

Outbound. 0110 CST Saturday 18 March.

"This quidnunc, the gutter-ball who's assigned to serve as my local guide, has a name like 'Wintergreen,' but it's German – *Vintergrun? Rinnenkugel?* – and we're supposed to tryst in his 'working hangout,' probably the locker room of some yoga studio where they wear green 'tards." The celebrity drove south on California Avenue in Chicago searching for the site of his prearranged meeting with his Midwest reagent. He had dutifully arrived at LAXXX International Airport nine hours earlier to discover that he'd been booked on a non-existent flight. A California closet optimist, he'd elected to believe that the phantom booking error was airline in origin rather than Studio undersecretary and booked himself on a moderately priced alternative High Speed Civil Transport. He'd subsequently planted himself in a corner lounge chair of the boarding gate to dissect the Operation Shalom files he'd received from Handsome Dan Aldred as he awaited his new 1900-hours departure time. He'd ascertained that he would contact his retinue agent via the official agency drill bit broadcast to all Studio personnel by Radmilla Eisenstadt in conjunction with the global code word of the day. The reagent, a self-proclaimed "macro-surgeon, as sharp-edged in a back alley as at a computer terminal," would then convey him from the neutral point of introduction to the safe house he'd recently procured in the Chicago area.

The celebrity's Shalom study had been interrupted by a gate-wide groan and collective tumult the likes of which he hadn't witnessed since P.C. security started shooting in the commissary. The H.S.C.T. flight had been cancelled, forcing passengers to scramble for a substitute. The next viable option to present itself had been a red-eye flight on which he was in the process of securing his reservation when his Qilroy alerted him of an opening on a space plane scheduled to depart from LAXXX at 2000 hours for a polar transfer orbit landing in Chicago. Preapproved for space travel by his physician, he'd raced to the far end of Terminal Five and claimed the last seat on the spacefarer.

The celebrity surveyed infrequent pockets of activity on California Avenue from the Ford Escort he'd rented at Chicago O'Hare XX Lowball Auto Traffickers. "No, the treatment described this hangout as an 'alco-hall,' chosen because it's so Midwestern." As a space tourist, he'd experienced no short-age of diversions: from the rocket burst at twelve kilometers through floating untethered along the curved walls of the nautilus-shell-shaped cabin to the salad bar attended by live rabbits. He'd found the progressive charts of arctic polar ice cap shrinkage presented for comparison with the real-time scope view below an instructive footnote to his upcoming mission. The same was true for the high-altitude drones he'd sighted seeding the stratosphere with sulfuric acid vapor for radia-tive forcing as the season for fortifying the polar shield with reflective particles commenced. He'd seized spare interludes to further review the Operation Shalom legacy and peruse trending global surface temperature models. Sometime during the space plane captain's narrative on craft design and super-alloys which rendered travel through the radiation of the aurora safe, he'd developed the distinct sensation that his files were being exposed to unauthorized eyes, inducing him to relocate the treatment in the best hiding place within his sourcerer. By the time the space plane seats flipped to take G-force pressure off in re-entry, he'd lost the treatment. Contact specs were paramount among the missing information, although he did recall a few details such as a California Avenue location "around back from" some gentleman's club.

A phalanx of twelve lean individuals in skeleton costumes with glowing phosphorescent bones provided an eerie display as they glided along the street on their scootboards. The celebrity recognized his beacon in the glowing brick tower of XXX-Ray's Strip Mine. He turned onto the first cross road and gleaned a parking spot on a quiet, narrow side street a few blocks away. He locked the Escort and headed toward the club.

Two boisterous men staggered through the shadows and paused beside a parked compact truck. The shorter man emitted a raucous whoop and stamped his foot against the passenger's door of the vehicle. The two men leaned against each other in a fit of revelry, and the celebrity surveyed the depressed door as he approached the truck. The two men straightened their postures, and the kicker expanded his chest with a low roar. The celebrity might've sidestepped them with the deferent regard they expected, but he chose to continue on a path that intersected them. When they neglected to separate, he lowered his shoulder slightly, planted it in the chest of the door-crusher and knocked him to the pavement.

"Crazy son of a bitch!" The flattened perpetrator attempted a leg-whip as the celebrity walked over him. "Is that your toy truck?"

"Bad mistake, asshole!" The taller, lightly stubbled one whirled snake hands and shambled in a reasonable imitation of a pay-per-view ultimate pugilist. "Come on, wimp." He threw a pair of jabs. The shorter, stockier one climbed to his feet and reached into his jacket pocket. Both thugs had dyed blond hair with dark borders. The celebrity kicked the vandal's hand before it could secure what it sought. The taller brawler threw a punch, which the celebrity returned, accenting the impact of his fist with his elbow. The shorter scrapper threw a roundhouse punch, which the celebrity caught. He whipped the perpetrator into the concave truck door. The taller thug faked a kick to the knee, circled his leg and thrust his foot at the celebrity's face. The celebrity blocked the brunt of the blow with his shoulder and grasped the truculent work boot. He twisted it over, sending the taller brawler to the cement, and he stamped his heel into the center of the idiot-savate's hamstring.

The shorter scrapper confronted the celebrity with a large knife. The celebrity backpedaled.

"Keep that in your pocket, and it won't end up in your colon." He stole a glimpse of the taller thug struggling to his knees. "Otherwise whip out your fork, and you can both eat me."

"Let's go, slit-slut!" The shorter thug jabbed with the knife repeatedly. "Let's see how hot your blood is."

The taller brawler regained his feet and produced a set of nunchucks. The celebrity smiled deferentially. "Does your wife know you borrow her necklace?" He charged the knife-wielder, skipped aside and exchanged a slash for control of the weapon. He elbowed the perp in the jaw and engaged him as a shield from the taller thug as he rained blows on him. The shorter scrapper crumpled to the sidewalk. The celebrity brandished the knife as he circled the stick-twirler. He slipped inside prime swatting range with a stutter step and blocked a blow from the weapon but lost the knife in the process. He exchanged a kick to the groin for a punch to the face and possession of the sticks. He smashed both thugs in both knees with the nunchucks.

The celebrity coughed and caught his breath. The street remained deserted. He produced his pair of rainbow sparkle ruffle-and-lace V-string Lahnzhitude Pin-Up flexicuffs and locked one of the nooses around the shorter scrapper's wrist. He dragged him behind the boot-customized truck and knotted the V-string around the ball mount of the trailer hitch. He dragged the taller brawler behind the truck and locked his wrist in the other noose of the Lahnzhicuffs. A mass of stickers on the rear bumper of the vehicle included *REAL MEN DON'T HARM ANIMALS.*

The celebrity retrieved the knife and nunchucks and headed to XXX-Ray's Strip Mine. An interactive midget pitchman hologram stood outside the front door. The celebrity smiled complaisantly. "Hey, brother, is there another tavern or cabaret close by?"

"Why would you want to go anywhere else, man?" The artificial persuader displayed giant teeth. "This is the center of the Milky Way! There's state-of-the-art airport scanners inside to underscore all the other mind-blowing equipment."

The celebrity withdrew the knife and nunchucks from his pockets and dropped them at the interactive pitchman's feet. "I have headway to make with impulsivity issues."

The pitchman hologram pointed. "Around the side of the building and up in back is Triple Axel's High Dive, but it specializes in private affairs, family stuff."

The celebrity nodded. "I'm meeting a henchman who I suspect is another one of my boss's relatives." Triple Axel's High Dive rang a mission bell of familiarity. He followed the narrow path to the rear of the building. He hiked up an extended flight of dark, squeaky stairs to a landing with a modest sign which read *Caution Stairs Treacherous.* He trekked up another extended flight of stairs to a door bearing a weathered sign that stated *Chicago Historical Preservation Society Treasured Land-*

mark. The door creaked when he opened it, and he found a hall with a large sign suspended overhead turning in the breeze. It proclaimed *TRIPLE AXEL'S HIGH DIVE AT THE TOP OF CHICAGO'S TALLEST THREE-STORY BUILD-ING*. Plaques commemorated significant events in Chicago labor history such as the Haymarket Square Riot of 1887. The only doors that were marked were the three restrooms. He advanced through the half-open doorway at the end of the hall and entered a quiet, hazy cavern of a room with a long bar and a warped wooden floor. In another life, the area might've served as a chronically bottlenecked practice ballroom.

Three men sat huddled on stools toward the center of the bar across from the apron-clad bartender. Two solitary individuals occupied tables on opposite sides of the dingy, windowless room. The celebrity recognized that cuts on his hand and forearm were still bleeding and retreated with the intention of pampering his wounds in the men's room. But he found his path ostensibly blocked by an off-the-wall mural hologram of a picket line. "Scab!" the horde chanted. "Scab! Scab! Scab!"

"That's what we're looking to develop as soon as you scullions let me shove through and clean up." He opted to dispense with the medical care and approached the bar. He stood over the shoulder of the nearest stool patron, drawing a chain of irritated glances. He locked glowers with the taciturn bartender, a veritable werewolf of a man with thick, wavy brown hair, scraggly beard, bushy brow and deranged eyes. "Greetings, toastmaster." He saluted. "What are the odds of sporting a cold one?"

"What do you need?" the bartender uttered.

"A preferred beer?" The celebrity smiled complaisantly. "I don't imagine you carry Mayday, so my first draft choice would be a Pacifico or Sierra Nevada. Unless, of course, you have S&M Head Light, a welcome relief for the calorie-conscious tourist."

"Are you asking for a Mexican beer?" The bartender sounded as irascible as he looked. "We only serve domestic."

"Those are California brews," the celebrity instructed. "Any on hand?"

"Wipe the shit out of your ears, sunshine," the patron stooled between the others advised. "Harry told you there's only domestic."

The celebrity grabbed some bar napkins. "Bah chillbilly." He pointed to the tallboy bottle of craft brewery megastar Teddy Fillabuster that sat before the closest stool patron. "I'll settle for a Teddy, ambassador."

Harry exchanged disparaging looks with the middle stool patron in the V-neck sweater vest and turned back to the celebrity. "You'll settle." He shook a cup of dice, slammed it on the bar with a punctuating vehemence and sauntered several strides down the line. As he blotted blood with the bar napkins, the celebrity noticed the large *Municipal Smoking Permit #15437* sign and a manikin head and torso wearing a battered Cubs cap behind the bar. Harry returned with a Fillabuster tallboy and opened it. "I would've figured you for a narghile head."

The celebrity located the expense account in his Qilroy and established a tab. He snatched the bottle and shifted his gaze from the wall mural to the stool patrons. "To you and your respective lynch mobs, your magistrate." He took a swig, trembled and coughed. He set the tallboy on the bar and wiped his watery eyes. The stool patrons provided the bartender with a chorus of raucous guffaws. "As a super suds sommelier, sir, kindly afford me a wedge of lime and a pinch of pink mountain salt."

"Yeah, Harry'll give you a wedge," V-neck gibed, "and a pinch."

Harry bent down behind the bar. He flipped the celebrity a small lime chunk. He snatched a shaker of Himalayan salt from the shelf and spilled a micro-dune on the bar. "Happy, camper?"

The celebrity added the condiments to the bottle and inhaled deeply. He returned the Teddy to his lips and chugged it. "Sunshine soldiers eschewing shoulder surgery should surely salute sharply." He saluted. "Fetch me another Teddy, will you, Harry?"

The bartender indolently dealt another tallboy. The celebrity discarded his napkins. He saluted again and carried both the full bottle and his empty bottle away from the bar.

He proceeded to the tables in his quest to identify his retinue agent. He silently rehearsed Rad's official drill bit of the Friday 17 March work day and weekend. The sounding line "I'm into leather" would trigger the keynote comeback "I'm into iron." The follow-up solicitation "Pumping or packing?" would be answered with the deal closer "I'm flexible." He resigned himself to the probability that if his contact was indeed in the bar, he was the sage grouse in the V-neck sweater vest. He'd return to the bar when he eliminated the two lone table-sitters as candidates.

The nearer patron wore a blue turban with stud earrings and sat in a trancelike state focused on a vanity mirror facing him on the table. His left arm was supported in a sling. The celebrity bypassed him and approached the other man, who promptly stopped chattering into his sourcerer. He wore a green corduroy coat and chrome watchband wraparound Jatakar. "Excuse me, I don't mean to intrude, but I wonder if I'm in the right place. I'm into leather." The man gestured, and the celebrity seated himself. "Did you say you're into iron?" He offered the full tallboy. "Pumping or packing?"

"PartisAnn," the man invoked the name of America's militantly bisexual pop diva noted for maintaining half her body in perfectly unkempt fashion. "PartisAnn sang it on Pulaski Day."

"Sang what?" The celebrity realized that the man's wraparound glasses weren't a sourcerer. "Wintergrinder?"

"*SangFreud.*" The man sampled his complimentary Teddy

Fillabuster. "Your being is mind and body. If you eat and read nothing substantial, you're half-junk and the other half of nothing."

"That's rather incisive for her." The celebrity strongly suspected that he wasn't in the company of his contact.

"Her lawyers will explain the rest, and then who'll be sorry?" The man in the watchband glasses gulped more beer.

"I'm sorry already." The celebrity rose.

"You undulate and ululate and then you wonder why you late," the chrome-glasses man honked the lyrics to the PartisAnn hit "Ovulate".

The celebrity lugged his empty beer bottle past the man in the blue turban. "I'm into leather."

"Fuck the official agency bit, wick-head," the patron snarled.

The celebrity backtracked. "I.B. Winterhocker?"

The man in the blue turban snorted with contempt. "I heard you're a regular retard with names and numbers."

The celebrity seated himself at the table. "You don't earn 15 college credits in ancient Greek and Roman history by holding a loose grasp on facts and figures." He smiled complaisantly. "It's I.B. Winter- Ah, Winter-"

"You don't have it on 190 proof I'm me, razhipux, don't be banging my name around like a tin vibrator." The young man in the blue turban had soft, deep-set eyes and Ralph Waldo Emerson mutton chops to the jugular. "You think you're some fancy-ass scholar, Greece-spot?"

The celebrity chuckled politely. "I have plenty of core credits in the humanities and natural sciences to support my degree from U.C. at Irvine in Drama and Music." He consulted his Qilroy. "If you're irritated by the late hour, put on some PartisAnn and get past it. I had travel complications. I believe I've found you in my handy database, I.B. Winterhalter. Pumping or packing?"

"Get the goddamn name right if you're going to smear

it all over!" The man in the blue turban drained the last few drops from his mug. "I.B. Maundermacher!"

The celebrity tapped the table rhythmically. "I'd appreciate it if you'd swallow the expletives."

I.B. slid his mug into the celebrity's chest. "I'd appreciate it if you'd swallow my cum."

"How would you like to swallow your teeth?" The celebrity smacked the reagent in the forehead with the heel of his palm. "So your monogram is I.B.M.?"

"Thanks for finally showing up, wuss-pipe." I.B. rubbed his brow. "Take care of my next drink."

"What does the 'I.B.' stand for?" The celebrity clasped the mug. "'International Brotherhood'?"

Maundermacher sneered. "'Ibbity Bibbity,' bub."

The celebrity waved his empty tallboy until he garnered Harry's attention. He gestured with two fingers for another round and received a less gracious gesture in return. "Come on, Harry, make my Teddy a double!"

Harry leapt over the bar. "Am I showing any thigh, Malibu?" He took three steps toward the table. "You want something, you come to the bar and order it. You want nothing, then get out of here!"

The celebrity snatched the tallboy bottle and rose. "Hey!" I.B. snapped. "In Sickinois, the midpesterners call that brewy brandy a Filly, not a Teddy." He burped. "And while you're up for it, Bruce, order me a Chicago-style fat pretzel with mauve Dueseldorf mustard. Got it?"

The celebrity returned to the bar. "High-Hat Harry." He summoned the bartender with a pleasant smile and wave. "Would you please set me up with a pair of Fillies: one tapper and one under glass? I'd also like a Chicago-style fat pretzel with Dueseldorf mustard, mauve Dueseldorf mustard, if that's available."

Harry curled his lip menacingly. "What the hell kind of whack-job are you? A Chicago soft pretzel with moss dookie mustard?" He ripped a package of pretzels off the rack, flipped it onto the bar and pulverized the contents with his fists. He demanded full payment as the two remaining members of his stool chorus howled derisively.

The celebrity transferred funds and nodded to the stool gallery as he waited for his beverages. "If the proprietor of this establishment were a machinist, would he be a screw-machine jock or a boring bar operator?" Harry presented the Fillabusters. The celebrity oscillated his forefinger between the bartender and the manikin in the Cubs cap before collecting his drinks and bag of crumbs. "I see *custody* of the brain you guys share is designated by who's wearing the 'C' cap." He turned and strode away.

"Bring those back here, chief!" Harry roared. "I forgot to spit in them for you!"

Maundermacher smirked as the celebrity returned to the table. "You're a real smoothie, aren't you, Oobops?" The celebrity pitched the pack of pretzel bits into the reagent's face and provided the beer. "No Dueseldorf?" He cackled. "You are such a knob."

The celebrity reseated himself. "Kudos for picking this lovely nightspot on the periphery of civilization."

Maundermacher sneered. "Hey, shove it, snarftro! This environment you can count on having space to talk privately."

"I'll concede a master barroom for racketeer interns promotes a mind-your-own-business vibe." The celebrity expelled an aggravated breath and gulped Fillabuster. "So is Dan Aldred your uncle?"

I.B. took a protracted swig of beer. "What's it to you, kindling? He ain't my sugar daddy."

"Skip it, skip it." The gaunt man in the chrome watchband wraparounds approached. "Skip what? Skip lunch? Skip rope?" He turned blankly and headed toward the exit. "Skip turn. Skip town."

The reagent snickered. "Aren't you going to try to grab a

ride with your friend Skip, Ahab?" The PartisAnn fan skipped into the interactive picket line hologram.

The celebrity smiled complaisantly. "I was a far more optimistic man when I walked in and presumed that he was you."

Maundermacher patted his turban. "What kind of clue do you need? A flashing sign on the ass that says, 'Down over here, douche-bag'?"

The celebrity leaned forward. "Okay, Ib, you've worked the rant act to death. I don't know if you're sacrificing other opportunities to be here like the rest of us, but regardless of how paltry you've decided the pay is or how demeaning you think your duties are, you should appreciate that you're in a unique position to positively transform the quality of life in widespread regions of the world. The great Roman orator Cicero called government service the highest human calling and a sublime moral duty to the public trust." He clenched a fist. "Rise like the sea and boldly ride the challenge! Serve!"

"Yeah, you know so much, history-bluff." The reagent sipped his Filly. "Without stroking your Qilroy, tell me which got its statehood on first: California or Wisconsin?"

"Illinois." The celebrity chuckled. "I'll always go with California."

"Guess again, sawdust-head." I.B. guzzled more beer. "You're wrong by two years. But I'll give you another chance to reduce yourself from such a big lunk-sack. Who was president when Wisconsin was admitted to the union and the California territory was annexed? Get it right and I'll hop up to the bar and hit up Harry for a bottle of Chablis." He smiled archly. "I'll even give you a double hint." He flashed and waved the peace sign.

The celebrity smacked his lips pensively. "Buchanan, James Buchanan?"

Maundermacher jabbed his fingers into the celebrity's eyes. "Polk!" He hooted. "President lucky number eleven."

The celebrity gasped. "You miserable bastard!" He covered

his burning eyes and groaned. "What the hell's the matter with you?" He kicked the reagent beneath the table.

"Aughh, you steaming pile of pig shit!" Maundermacher snickered sardonically. "You threw the first one!" He grunted. "You're lucky the prez wasn't Pierce."

The celebrity opened his eyes and observed the coruscating scene through a lachrymal blur. "Are you working for Wisconsin, you psycho?"

"Stop overreacting, tear-jerk." The reagent took a swig of Fillabuster. "I only blipped you a glancing blow." He gulped more beer. "Listen, Oobops, I'm here because I had to choose between the Midwest and the Middle East. You know I was working on my tan in a program to infiltrate rich mosques around Orange and San Diego Counties. And I couldn't wait to take down the underdeprived little pukes jamming to jihad." He ripped open the bag of pretzel crumbs. "You wish you could grow a beard half as perfect as the one I layed in." He snorted. "Hell, you wish you could grow a beard as god-awful as Harry's, but I worked up a full wool jacket. I had babes beg to touch it." He shook his head. "But then the keepers got it in their shorts that I should learn to speak Arabian and even hunker down with the camels and asses over in the Stans, like I could really use that rap."

The celebrity sipped his Fillabuster. "For future reference, Nazmul, I don't take my drinks with a detached retina." He rubbed his eyes and guzzled more beer. His vision had cleared but considerable agony lingered. "So now that we've finished exchanging pleasantries, let's discuss the accommodations you'll provide and consider what use you can be as a backup."

"Hold on, Hazel, we still have pleasantries left to cover." I.B. gestured to his disabled left arm. "Aren't you going to ask how my arm feels?"

The celebrity punched the biceps of the limb in question. "How-"

Maundermacher flung his arm out of the sling and backhanded the celebrity across the left temple. "You tell me!" A tiny, glistening blade that extended from a ring on the reagent's pinkie finger parked itself at the celebrity's right eyelash. "Ready for your close-up, scuzz-face?" He bared his teeth. "If you ever try to bash me again, I'll take your eyeball. They might morph you a functional replacement in a year or two, but see how you like being without your stereo for that long." He emitted a perturbed breath. "Better quit while you're still even." He retracted the blade with a flip of his wrist.

"I'm not transcendental enough to bash you, Waldo." The celebrity drained his tallboy and opted to dismiss the reagent's adjustment-period hostility with extreme clemency. "Besides, I could use your assistance with a funny thing that happened on my way over. I lost my op treatment files. I need to copy yours."

"Hell no, those are proprietary access, not to be shared." Maundermacher smirked. "This is a trap. You'll go running back to D.A. and tell him I flunked my screen test." He reinserted his left arm into his sling. "Why not just ask Aldred to copy you again?"

"Confidentially, it'd make me look a little less professional than I'd like." The celebrity smiled complaisantly. "A CIB field agent has ultimate discretion to share any information on a need-to-know basis."

"Like a nipple on that beer over there?" The celebrity turned to find Harry addressing him from the near side of the bar to the amusement of the multiplying stool gallery.

"Keep humping for that performance bonus, Harry!" The celebrity turned back to I.B. and tapped his tallboy on the table. "Prove you're a performer talented enough to make clutch field decisions, and star material savvy enough to be a unique agent."

Maundermacher nodded. "Maybe I can lend you a peek at what chestnuts you're missing to get this gig growling. Maybe I can land some extra compensation for it." He emptied his mug. "It's your job to suck up people's dirty secrets, Oobops, so if you have any idea of what you're doing, you must have a regular cistern of sludge on Aldred." A wry smile flickered across his lips. "I want enough stick to give me real-time leverage. I want the means to manipulate."

The celebrity laughed rumbustiously. "The mercenary shamelessness of that proposal is so egregious I'm tempted to consider the possibility that it's not your attempt at a setup." He leaned closer. "You'd confide in me if you were doubling for Wisconsin, wouldn't you, Ib?"

The reagent sneered. "You don't want to consider a means that you could sweeten a menial transaction to your mutual advantage, dill-whistle, you can file any favors you want from me up your ass sideways."

"Have you been able to finagle any leads on 110328A/404?" the celebrity whispered. "Charlton Shalom," he clarified. "Any theories on his whereabouts? Any hunches?"

I.B. spun his mug. "I have a hunch it's time to talk about the safety shack, snoodihink. There's three bedrooms, so you get your own. I will share the bathroom with you because there's only one, and it's a luxury flash'n'flush with a temp-control directional power-mister shower."

The celebrity smiled complaisantly. "King-size tub? I could use a good soak."

"No shit, honeysuckle rose." Maundermacher fanned the air. "There's a tub, but I don't want any other dude dunking his junk in it. There's a hot tub on the observation deck for you to boil your booty, and there's a community pool." His gaze intensified. "The kitchen is a real trip. It comes with an actual coal-burning oven."

The celebrity chortled incredulously. "Seriously, Maundermacher?"

"Hell no, numb-nuts!" The reagent shook his head. "And the name is really 'Winterhalter.' Is there any sheet of shit you won't crawl beneath?"

The celebrity watched two obstreperous men emerge

from the hologram picket line. "You're a walking wilderness of mirrors, Ib." He placed I.B.'s vanity mirror face-down on the table. "A veritable carnival curiosity parlor." A taller man with a limp crossed the picket line and joined the other two. The closest man wore his hair in a bushy, frizzed squirrel tail, and his blond companions had black streaks delineating their hairlines. "I predict you'll score big bonus points gaming the system." The celebrity popped an astringent fireball capsule into his mouth.

"There he is!" The shorter truck vandal pointed at the celebrity. "That's the motherfucker!" The squirrel-master led the march of doom to the table.

The celebrity gripped the tallboy bottle. "Hold on to your mug," he instructed Winterhalter.

"Where do you get the idea you can mess up my truck, jerk-wad?" The squirrel-master patted the celebrity's shoulder with the bottom of his plump fist. "You'd seem to owe me a door, a hitch and maybe a side-order of pain and suffering."

The celebrity nodded. "Let me guess: Dag and Chuckie here told you that they tried to stop *me* from kicking in your door?"

"How else would he know that?" The shorter scrapper leveled a fierce kick into the celebrity's chair. "I want the knife back you took off me, too, shit-head!"

"So!" The reagent sprang to his feet. "That's why you dashed in here, sat your sorry ass down and asked if you could pretend you know me!"

"Scrutinize the dent in your door, inspector," the celebrity advised the squirrel-master. "And I'm certain you'll find that the imprint matches the pattern on the bottom of this choir-boy's clown-size clodhoppers." He winked at the perp.

"Bullshit!" The shorter thug slapped the tallboy out of the celebrity's hand and to the floor.

"How dare you?" Winterhalter screeched. "To act like punks in my holy hour?"

"Hey, settle down over there!" Harry's voice resonated from behind the bar.

The taller brawler shoved the reagent. "Go purify yourself-"

Winterhalter threw a wicked punch from his sling into the taller thug's face. The squirrel-master and the shorter scrapper wrestled the celebrity and his chair to the floor. The shorter thug delivered an energized elbow to the celebrity's groin. From beneath the table and the squirrel-master, the celebrity watched the reagent scramble through the picket line hologram. His face oozing blood, the taller brawler plunged to his knees. "First I want to break his fucking nose!" He grabbed the tallboy bottle and slammed it against the floor but it didn't break. He punched the celebrity in the eye. He successfully smashed the bottle against the floor. He stabbed the celebrity under the chin with the jagged neck piece. An electric slurp sounded, and he lapsed into a spastic fit.

"Nobody pulls a weapon in my bar!" Harry squatted beside the table with a baton-style stun gun clutched in each fist. He simultaneously stunned the squirrel-master and shorter scrapper, sending both into spastic fits.

The celebrity separated himself from his ragtag inquisitors. "Hat-Trick Harry mixes it up!" The bartender stunned the celebrity, and the jojoba coating of the astringent capsule dissolved as he flailed.

The taller brawler and the shorter scrapper both rose to all fours. "Give the son of a bitch a boot-bottom facial!" Dag suggested.

"You can all stay down while we wait for the cops." Harry clapped his batons. "Or else I'll put you to work in the back keeping the ice cold with some previous bad-apple customers."

"How many times do I need to be victimized tonight?" the squirrel-master protested.

The taller brawler crawled closer to the celebrity and kicked him in the ankle. Harry stunned the idiot-savate again.

The celebrity rocked and sprang to his feet. "One last round for all three of them, Harry!"

The bartender approached the celebrity brandishing the batons. "What part of hugging the floor didn't you understand, Westwood?"

The celebrity dodged Harry's baton thrust, grabbed him by the arm and whipped him into the shorter scrapper. He seized control of both of the bartender's wrists and pulled him close. "Harry, hand Homer here a hemlock highball, ha ha ha!" The noxious fumes of lachrymatory aerosols and airborne toxins in the phlegm-buster pitched Harry into a paroxysm of coughing and wheezing. The celebrity shoved him over the taller brawler, dropped to his knees and grabbed the squirrel-master by the collar. "He who heeds hearsay humors hate." The squirrel-master tore out of the celebrity's grasp hacking and choking.

The shorter scrapper retrieved the baton that Harry had dropped and employed it to smash Winterhalter's mirror. He advanced against the celebrity with the baton and a vanity shard the size of a carving knife. Harry staggered back to his feet and approached the celebrity ahead of a patron toting a half-full pitcher of beer. "You're going down, whore-hound," the truck vandal decreed.

"You're the horseless headman." The celebrity broke wide for the exit.

The High Dive posse lent chase. "Throw him off the roof!" The shorter scrapper's pursuit angle placed him squarely in the celebrity's path. The celebrity grabbed a chair and plowed over him. The patron with the pitcher heaved it but missed everything except the floor. The patron in the V-neck vest hurled himself at the celebrity's legs but a crafty kick and little leap thwarted the tackle attempt.

The celebrity burst through the picket line hologram, sprinted to the outside door and darted down the first extended flight of stairs. He reached the landing and started down the lower flight. The stairs suddenly shifted into a smooth ramp, and he tumbled and slid the remainder of the way, hitting the pavement like the original birdman. He bounded to his feet shaken and scraped, and he raced down the alley without looking back. He turned several corners and hustled down more dark side streets. "How d'ya like my Houdini, Harry?" He laughed until he realized that he'd lost his bearings and his Qilroy.

Hug a she-quoia at Altamont,
Ply courtship tactics that I gleaned from my aunt:
Stage a fight, then treat her right, stay out all night;
Allow her high carbs but control the last bite.

Recurring nightmare in Corcoran:
Wake up each morning and I scream, Not again!
Too many cowgals out to prove that they're men.
Restore what's sideways to how it's never been.

Clam-dig deep secrets at Pismo Beach,
Post nasty antics that nobody can teach:
Slap their thighs, then poke their eyes and claim your prize;
Works for behemoths up to clean half your size.

2ND MOVEMENT

Inbound. 0555 CST Sunday 19 March.

"Were you born in a crab tank, cluster-cluck?" Again attired in his trademark blue turban, I.B. Winterhalter revved the engine of his rainforest green Jeep Glory Roadster. "Get your bedwetting ass packed in the rear so we can shut the damn door!"

The celebrity checked his facial contusions in the passenger-side mirror. "Next time, if you wouldn't mind, you dune-dodging Daeshiree, give me a heads up before you give me a heads off."

"What is he bawling about?" A woman in a homburg with a shaved brim tilted her seat farther forward so the celebrity could squeeze into the backseat.

"Pay no attention," the reagent snarled. "That's just Oobops."

With no available leg room, the celebrity occupied the backseat on all fours. "If Ib ever bails on me again-"

"What?" The woman slammed the Jeep door twice.

The celebrity shook like a dog. "I.B. better believe he'll absorb some brutal blowback if he abandons me in action again."

Winterhalter snickered sardonically. "I don't know what the hell you've got to be chafed about, Zig. You boost me into your dicey, little personal squaddle, and I punched out an escape opening. I trusted you'd have the survival sense to be on the stairs right behind me."

The celebrity sneezed and snorted. "In the first place, that frizzy-tailed bristlecone would've been more amenable to a peaceful resolution-"

"In the second place," the reagent snapped, "you fire off your distress signal in the middle of the night, and we have to turn out and drive all the way back into the city in this downpour!"

The celebrity rubbed his drenched hair. "You're sitting with your feet up, and I'm clinging to the dark side of the world with no Qilroy!" He pointed to Barbee's Bassment Blues Bakery nightclub several doors down Sacramento Boulevard. "We're lucky I was able to cajole the waitress into sending the Studio helpline my extraction location. Her name's Travista or something. Remind me to send her a little extra when I cover my tab."

"Nice you were thirty meters off the tags of your Code Orange, you tripped-breaker." I.B. guided the Glory Roadster into northbound Humboldt Park traffic.

"I left the club in a hurry – something you should appreciate – and I've stayed on the move in the rain the past three hours to stay out of trouble." The celebrity inverted his body and leaned his head against the passenger-side window. "I spent the last two nights and all day yesterday hanging around in parks and behind businesses in between searching for my rental car, which I'm convinced was stolen." He hissed. "But head south and we'll try looking for it some more."

"Mr. Oobops." The woman fixed the celebrity with a glower. "Why don't you have your rental car?" Her voice was raspy. "Whose fault is it you don't have your Qilroy?" She scratched her hat. "So what is the reason you have to talk to us like a piss-head?"

"I'm sorry." The celebrity wiped his face. "Are all those questions rhetorical?"

"Oobops, this is my friend Madelyn," Winterhalter

announced. "I've invited her to live with me at the safe house, and she's trying it on for size."

Madelyn produced a muslin pillow case. "Shouldn't Oobops wear a sack over his head so he doesn't try to track the location?"

I.B. grimaced affectionately. "He's supposed to know where the sanctuary is. And we need his help to scare up his wheels first."

"I believe the sack accessory," the celebrity advised Madelyn, "would serve you better."

"You're some bitter disappointment, Oobops," the prospective lady of the safe house grumbled. "I'll assume your mood suffers when you're a wet hen."

"The safe house location is posted on my Jatakar." The reagent glanced back and pointed to the sourcerer clipped to the back of his turban. "Read it out loud three times so you don't forget it!"

The celebrity patted his hair. "Instead let's just become inseparable."

Madelyn turned completely around. She extended her left hand and ran her pinkie over the inflamed area beneath the celebrity's right eye. "You should try a cucumber slice on that." She smiled sweetly. "You're going to have a big scar." She probed his pipeline. "They ringlet radically when soggy, hmm?" She slid her hand across his scalp and rapidly withdrew it, extracting a hair.

"What's the brainstorm, play-pal?" The celebrity rubbed his head.

"I have an Irish Claddagh ring with a red moonstone Kells knot heart." Madelyn presented the jeweled band with a crisp twist of the wrist. "And I have the disease."

"Disease?" the celebrity challenged.

"I can't help it." Madelyn removed her homburg to reveal a sparsely covered pate with a Himalayan-grade widow's peak. "Trichotillomania." She tore out one of her own hairs. "I pull."

"There isn't a sedative somewhere with your name on it?" The celebrity smiled complaisantly. "Look for a user-friendly narcotic with a hair restorative property."

She punched him firmly in the shoulder. "You think I'd do this if I had a choice, you creep? You think I'd still look this good without meds?" She hissed and turned to face forward. "Wanker."

"You really are a soulless dick, Oobops." Winterhalter turned the Jeep south. "You probably get jollies galore mimicking people choking in the commissary."

The Glory Roadster prowled the streets around Douglas Park searching for the misplaced Ford Escort. The celebrity commandeered the reagent's Jatakar to ascertain the license number and official color of the vehicle he'd rented from O'Hare Lowball. No city block looked more familiar in the hazy initial light of the day than it had when he'd hunted on foot the previous afternoon. He verified with the Chicago Police that the Escort hadn't been towed. Numerous beige Escorts appeared parked along the road but none had the essential plate number. "Ian, can we quit crawling around?" Madelyn demanded. "If we're not getting some breakfast, let's go home!"

The celebrity sighted a beige Escort on 25th Street with no license plates. "This must be it." He hopped out of the Jeep and contacted Lowball again. The VIN on record was invalid. "The only personal items that would identify it," he conceded, "are my suitcase and briefcase in the trunk." The rental agency pinpointed the location of the vehicle to within a kilometer of where the celebrity stood and attempted without success to unlock the interior and open the trunk remotely. The rental company tried to start the engine and activate the panic button. The ignition and security systems of the Escort on 25th Street remained unengaged. The celebrity climbed back into the Glo-Ro. Winterhalter cruised through the streets of the neighborhood again. The precipitation ceased, extending the search a few more minutes, but the Escort wasn't recovered.

The Jeep hit the Eisenhower Expressway and headed west toward the safe house in Batavia. "Did you start the coffee, Ian?" Madelyn turned to the celebrity. "I love my coffee slow-filtered, and I hate walking in with it not perked."

"How short have you known Ib?" the celebrity inquired.

"We connected in the checkout counter line a few weeks ago," the reagent blithely recalled.

The Sunday morning traffic flowed fairly freely, and the Jeep closed the distance on a Duryea Avenger in the adjacent right lane. The Duryea overtook a semi and executed an abrupt lane change in front of the Glory Roadster. Winterhalter braked, vented a protracted note on the horn and passed the impertinent motorist on the right displaying an extended medius. "You couldn't anticipate he'd move to pass the truck?" the celebrity admonished.

"I should watch out for *him*," I.B. scoffed. "You may be too much of a simp to stand up for your right to the road, but I'm not!"

Madelyn eyed the celebrity intently. "Did no one ever teach you to be a man, honey?"

The celebrity banged his head. "A quiet, inconspicuous diplomacy is always the preferred course. And all it takes is a bit of gravitas and maturity."

The Jeep exchanged the expressway for a highway which ultimately ran past Fermi National Accelerator Laboratory and led to a narrow, meandering road on which the Whispering Willowwacks condominium complex was located. "Yes, unsettled boarder, this is the safe house," Winterhalter wearily acknowledged, pulling into the courtyard behind a cream brick structure with brown trim and round, maroon shingles.

"It has a rustic pretentiousness," the celebrity allowed. He climbed out of the Glo-Ro into the damp air after I.B. and Madelyn. As they approached the Studio hideaway, they encountered a man and woman tending a utility vehicle with both cab doors and rear hatch wide open.

"What the hell are you looking at?" the man snapped.

"What the hell *are* you?" Madelyn answered.

"That must've been one hell of a fart!" the reagent surmised.

Madelyn led the procession up the steel stairway to the second-floor unit. Several jagged gouges decorated the door, which Winterhalter opened by removing his Jatakar from his turban and providing a standard security guard-card with biometric signature. The celebrity followed his hosts inside and was momentarily throttled by the effluvium. He coughed and staggered as if he'd been kicked in the face by a weighted boot. "Are you drunk, Oobops?" Madelyn inquired.

"Ah, there's a slightly musty smell, isn't there?" The celebrity struggled to squelch an extended coughing jag. "A certain acrid pungency?"

"It should smell like coffee." Madelyn viewed I.B. through narrowing eyes. "Didn't you activate the machine?"

"*Putain.*" Winterhalter gestured to the celebrity. "I was about to when this scrote distracted me with his moaning about my scary driving." He tossed his turban onto a threadbare davenport.

Madelyn redirected her moue to the celebrity. "Thank you so very much, honey." She strode to the kitchen, stimulating motion lights along the way.

The celebrity surveyed his surroundings. "Keep up the fight against volatile organic compounds." The receiving room was painted in banana clip camouflage yellow, and a blue plastic tarp served as curtains. Heaps of rumpled clothes and paper garbage seemed strewn with abandon, and a worn Persian carpet ran diagonally across the scraped wooden floor. He relied on his fireball conditioning to tolerate the harsh environment.

"You're suspicious, Oobops," the reagent asserted, "of how I could procure such a comfy cribby on the pitiful acquisition fund they gave me." He smirked. "You recall Hubbell the hacker?"

"The name is familiar." The celebrity eyed the giant entertainment screen framed by computer command towers. "He's that secure software company officer that licensed wormhole access-"

"Piss up a rope, whipworm!" I.B. scoffed. "I thought even you'd know he was the grumpy, old crossbow who cleavered at least eight people in the Chicagoland area. He lived and hung himself in this unit, and we're the first occupants in three years. It's not believed that he murdered any of his victims here, but there's still a small swell to level the complex. The aftermath is we're still standing, and I dealt us a hell of a bargain!" He grinned smugly. "*Whispering Willowwacks.*"

"The world would love what you've done with it." The celebrity placed a finger under his chin. "The absence of axes is an absolute asset."

"Who's your woman, Oobops?" Madelyn returned. "What's her hair like?" She squeezed the celebrity's elbow. "Got a special partner?"

The celebrity shook his head. "I'm kind of fragile for a relationship, and I really haven't had the time."

"Great then, you're a domesticated animal!" Madelyn exchanged discerning glances with Winterhalter. "You must cook. 'Awad,' is that what you go by? Cleaning is a common courtesy but you can schlep your keep around here in the kitchen."

The celebrity eyed the reagent intently. "Ib, can I please examine your operation treatment?"

"Don't be intimidated by the modern platform," Madelyn persisted. "Even if you're a complete dork, the auto-chef next to the Sous Vide can guide anyone. And I just shopped in recognition of your visit, so the pantry is stocked with everything."

The celebrity coughed. "If there's a cold plasma generator, I might fry up some mite medallions with a side of mildew salad."

"That's funny, honey, the moment we met I could tell you'd

make a great jerk chicken." Madelyn exhibited a perplexed smile. "And along with that a mean little pesto."

"Save the gourmet shit for supper." I.B. groped Madelyn's buttocks. "Take advantage of the warm snap to fix breakfast on the grill on the observation deck." He slid his hands upward, and she pushed them away from her ample bust in what appeared to be a perfunctory preliminary rebuff. "But don't mess with my weather instruments out there."

"We'll take our coffee in the bedroom, Awad." Madelyn pointed to a doorway and imparted directions to the bedroom and deck, respectively. "Don't be a premie. Wait for the custom café to finish each cup before you grab them off and bring them in." She smiled pertly. "Then you can take some time to learn your way around before you really get to work."

"Get in the mood for some seafood, dude." Winterhalter took Madelyn's hand and led her through the doorway to the bedroom. "It's '*Ahab*,' but just call him 'Oobops.'"

The celebrity refrained from objecting. The instant his hosts disappeared he awakened the house computer, and he began exploring closets, desk drawers and the narrow spaces behind the furniture. A veritable haystack of shredded paper stood in a recessed portion of the front room. Initially attracted by the sheer magnitude of the mound, he hid his pleather pouch of fireball capsules at its bottom.

After an extended examination of the bathroom, he ventured into the kitchen and completed a cursory tour. A stainless-steel cabinet held a veritable arsenal of serious cutting and chopping tools. The toaster on the counter island beeped and ejected a pair of pastries that on closer examination proved to be monitors. Madelyn's image appeared on the one facing the coffeemaker. "How's it brewing, Oobops? You've identified the Big Dripper? How far along is the payload?"

He smiled complaisantly. "I replaced your grounds with some tar sands, and we're waiting for the oil slick to disperse evenly."

Madelyn furrowed her brow beneath a carnation bandanna. "I'm thinking thicker *is* better. Increase my foam-to-milk proportion by ten percent. Is it obvious how to do that, or not so much? Press the white frother button and follow the prompts. The Bister Brown mug is mine. Take it off as soon as the machine says it's ready. But leave Ian's vaporizer mug on for another minute to build better foggage. He likes his coffee with a cloud, and we don't want to disappoint the boss."

The celebrity finished the orders as requested, pleased to exchange a few household chores for the scarcity of his hosts' company. He conveyed the coffee product in the Bister Brown mug along with the steaming decoction in the faux crystal vessel up the hallway. The bedroom door wasn't shut tight, and the pulse of moaning, creaking and inspired respiration easily transcended it. "Take two." He knocked softly with his elbow. He waited and knocked again. "Coffee break." He stooped to leave the delivery on the floor when the sounds of satisfaction subsided. "Coffee."

"Then bring it, Joe Pervert!" Winterhalter directed.

The celebrity pushed open the door with his shoulder. The room featured the furniture centerpiece of a king-size mattress on an attractive wood frame suspended from the ceiling by heavy, blue chains not unlike those favored by zoo administrators to serve lower primates. I.B. and Madelyn nested on the bed wrapped to their axillae in a luxurious fur blanket surrounded by pillows of assorted sizes, shapes and colors. The obligatory ceiling mirror crowned the arrangement. Madelyn accepted her foam-rich beverage in the Bister Brown mug. "How *long* were you in the hall listening, sicko?" She savored a sip.

"I hope you don't mind that I spiked it with depressants as an experiment." The celebrity surveyed a bureau painted in diagonal blue, violet and white stripes that matched the wall pattern.

Winterhalter yanked the blanket to Madelyn's waist. She

snickered and backhanded the reagent in the groin. The celebrity grudgingly conceded that the woman possessed the most parabolically perfect breasts one could hope to encounter, as pleasingly plump as possible without looking a touch overinflated. He handed I.B. his vapor-spewing mug. "So was that Hubbell's bed?"

Winterhalter sneered. "You don't know what scientific process causes the continuous fog, do you, hall-monitor?" He raised his mug. "Hydrodynamic cavitation." He imbibed liquid and inhaled cloud through the slotted straw.

"That research will prove invaluable if I'm ever up for the role in a musical of coffee-quaffing Bud Frump." The celebrity slapped the chain.

"I got some fabulous cod yesterday," Madelyn declared. "We'll be ready for breakfast in a little over an hour."

The reagent snorted. "And I just reconditioned the grill, so you can go cook your cock off."

The celebrity turned and headed for the door. "Hey," Madelyn called after him, "if the little dripper in the sink drives you crazy, fixing it can be your next project." He shut the door tight and proceeded back to the house computer in the receiving room. He disabled alarms and conducted further maneuvers to breach Winterhalter's file security. He plateaued quickly and relayed the hacking effort to a crew of nimble bots.

He returned to the kitchen and defrosted the cod fillets. He provided the auto-chef with a remoulade-thick French accent and enlisted its aid in preparing grilled fish tacos. He cut the cod into strips and left them in a vacuum-sealed chili-citrus marinade. He marched out to the deck accoutered with a twelve-piece set of grill-master gadgets and found a reconditioned oil barrel of a grill freshly painted electric purple beneath a former-shower-curtain drop cloth. The makeshift grill contained a grate on wobbly legs over a slightly used pile of briquets, a pair of cylinders and a cracked hardwood post. The briquets were conservable, and he broke the end off the post. He wasn't certain whether the reagent employed the post as a poker or a source of smoker chips. It had probably once served as part of the footboard for Hubbell's bed. He tightened the mound of briquets, lit paper towels in a cylinder to create a chimney and lined the edge of the mound with post wood chips.

He retreated to the kitchen and prepared a fresh fruit salsa along with avocado and jalapeno garnishes. He returned to the grill and cleaned and oiled the grate to bar clinging. He heated the tortillas. When the grate grew sufficiently hot, he replaced the shells with the cod strips and pineapple slices. He tented the array with foil until the fish had browned and fruit had caramelized.

Winterhalter appeared on the deck attired in orange jump-suit pajamas cinched at the waist with a bow. The celebrity began flipping the food chunks with a spatula and encountered considerable sticking, flaking and breaking. The reagent approached agape, his fists jammed against his hips. "Were you raised in the dump?"

The celebrity smiled complaisantly. "It'll taste just as bold shredded." He employed the tongs to maneuver a tortilla beneath the grate and catch cod fallout.

I.B. pressed his palms against his temples. "Oh my god, what a dumb-ass!"

"What's happening out here?" Madelyn arrived on the deck in orange jump-suit pajamas.

Winterhalter jabbed the celebrity in the head with his medius. "This idiot is cooking our breakfast in the trash can!"

"Eewww." Madelyn approached, holding the celebrity in her pitying gaze while clutching her stomach. "How often did your mother drop you on your head, honey?"

I.B. hissed. "Twice just last week."

The celebrity surveyed the deck. "Then where's the grill, Crassus? And what's this thing with a grate filled with charcoal briquets?"

"What you got here, bonefish-head, is the remains of the frame of someone's patio stool and the rest of their refuse." Winterhalter kicked the barrel. "It's a courtyard receptacle that got tagged with graffiti, and I just repainted it because I do odd jobs around here." The reagent sauntered to a large black box on the other side of the hot tub. "You aren't allowed to use charcoal on the wood deck, dipshit." He unfolded segments and flipped down legs. He rolled the smokeless electric grill into the center of the deck and pounded on it. "This, squad-oosh, is a grill!"

"I assumed it was a hot tub accessory." The celebrity gestured abashedly. "I expected it would generate freak waves and bizarre rhythms in the water."

"Fetch some water and put out your fire," Madelyn instructed. "Let's save the gills and grills for later and whip up something simple in the kitchen."

The celebrity ingratiated himself to his hosts by adding blueberry pie filling to instant oatmeal for breakfast and introducing date scones, California salad with queso blanco croutons and Pinot Noir wine alongside peanut butter sandwiches for lunch. He fully redeemed himself by advising I.B. and Madelyn that his arrival constituted a state visit, which qualified for a sumptuous dinner in an elegant restaurant at company expense. The trio accordingly spent the evening at Tulles Fine Dining & Cocktails on Chicago's northwest side.

An hour after returning to the safe house, Madelyn invited the celebrity to join her and I.B. for late night aquatic maneuvers in the Whispering Willowwacks pool and fitness center. As a goodwill gesture, he accepted a pair of tattered trunks and agreed to party dip with his hosts. "I don't swim so well," he initially excused himself from heavy frolicking. But he survived multiple laps and a collision with the reagent before resting on the recliner-top flotation pad in the deep zone of the pool.

Smartly endued in matching pink cream bathing cap and bikini, Madelyn swam gyres around the celebrity and treaded water beside him. "Ian!" She nodded toward the *12:02* display on the wall clock.

Winterhalter hopped out of the pool, hustled to one exit and appeared to lock it. He turned and headed to the opposite end of the aquasphere. "Conspiracy to drain the pool as a joke?" the celebrity inquired.

Madelyn stared blankly until I.B. had locked the other exit. "You have a wild, breezy mouth," she observed. "We need no snitches nor hitches when we snuff you."

The celebrity scrambled out of the pool. "You are such a yuck, Oobops!" Madelyn laughed raucously. "You should've seen your eyes bug out! You're such a pushover, such a fall-for-anything guy!" She swam to the edge of the pool. "At midnight, we attach an entry code to the doors, and the pool space becomes an adults-only swimwear-optional rec room, just like the five-star commercial spas." She removed her top and exhibited her full, heaving breasts. He seated himself on one of the poolside chaises. She hurled both pieces of her bikini at his feet, giggled and dived under the water.

Winterhalter thrust his trunks over the celebrity's head and flopped onto the adjacent chaise. The celebrity shed the obstruction, and the reagent flipped him a spare towel. "Is that a bodacious speciwoman?" I.B. emitted an ecstatic chortle. "CIB wishes it had a pair of high-magnitude turbocharged bazumas like that working on location! I'm trying to get Madelyn etched on the Studio payroll pad because we have an incredible lack of solid American showpiece babes in the field, eh, toots-sweet?"

"It's alarming." The celebrity managed his sensory overload with a series of short breaths. "Haven't you had a brush yet with Addyson Meyer or Tess Tohnyin?"

The reagent scoffed. "I didn't say CIB has nobody who *thinks* they're hot." He wiggled his tongue and waved to Madelyn. "The closest Tess can relate to a radical racketeer is her double same-letter initials. I recall the real winchesters from high school were like your Barb Babcock and Stacy Stackhouse and your Kris Koytus." He smiled wryly. "If Tess is double anything else, it's agent." He grunted. "She's a cusp girl."

The celebrity eyed Winterhalter intently. "Are you speaking to a specific disposition or are you evaluating her in astrological terms?"

I.B. wrapped his towel around his waist. "Tess sticks her nose in the air and puffs herself up like some D-va but that's a real stretch. You can declassify her to C-grade easy."

Madelyn emerged from the pool dripping and approached the chaise row. "What are you two snookers jabbering about?"

"You're so busted, I.B.!" The celebrity smiled archly. "We were evoking cherished high school mammaries."

Winterhalter hissed and rose. "I need to lay some lava." He dropped his towel, strode to an unmarked door on the opposite end of the pool and slammed it behind him.

Madelyn flagellated her wet body with a wet towel. "A little too shy, Ahab, to lose the trunks and wade in with the adults?"

The celebrity nodded. "Someone should remain on guard against the total breakdown of civilization."

She straddled the chaise beyond the one that the reagent had vacated. "I started high school shy and elusive. I had a thing for this guy, a real player. I learned that he put it out there how he was going to do me, referring to me all over as his 'sophomore project.'"

"He was writing a position paper," the celebrity inferred.

"I decided to play along." Madelyn wrapped the towel around herself provocatively. "There are few activities more exhilarating than bringing a schoolboy to climax with no genital contact." She moved to the closest chaise. "One of those is boosting him over the threshold of climax and squelching it so he can't. Ever been treated to that experience?" She clamped her hand on his knee. "Did it burn like a son of a bitch?" She giggled. "I finally let my crush take me the way he wanted, but I choked it so he couldn't finish. I apologized and invited him to replay the down, and when he did, I choked it again.

He cracked me across the mouth hard enough to draw blood." She laughed and parted her lips amorously. "When Ian and I retire to the swing tonight, you want to come with and give us a little push? If you have a fear of heights, I'll bet I can cure it."

The celebrity chortled. "You've got quite a grip there, pardner." He patted her wrist. "I like the gentle fury that accompanies your urge to lead a man on, but that's how tortured souls start wildfires."

"What does that mean?" She sneered. "You're uninterested?"

"I have an emotion deficit." He smiled complaisantly. "I'm all business."

She assessed her pink cream nails. "Maybe you should spend a little less time developing your body and a little more developing a personality."

Winterhalter returned, and the floating party folded. The threesome tramped back to their condo, and the celebrity proceeded to the lopsided mattress in the makeshift guestroom provided by his co-hosts. The accrued fatigue from his day of displacement in Chicago enabled him to realize his ambition of falling into a deep sleep the moment he covered his neck with the plastic tarp blanket. An intractable spring, however, pressed against his ribs with enough force to inspire him to abandon his bed at 0330 hours and resume his attempt to access Winterhalter's files at the main computer in the receiving room. He remained unsuccessful in the effort and returned to bed after an hour. He was officially reawakened at 0800 hours by the reagent. "Madelyn thinks you owe us a fancy breakfast, but we're tolerant fucks, and we'll settle for eggs."

The celebrity rose, meandered to the kitchen and gathered eggs. Under the tutelage of the auto-chef, he carefully cooked three omelets with persillade, queso quesadilla and asparagus tips. He prepared coffee drinks to order and blended citrus juices for a morning punch. He brought the first omelet to the table, folded it in the pan and flipped it onto Madelyn's plate. "It smells heavenly," she conceded. "Spy's secret spice?"

The celebrity retrieved the second omelet and adroitly transferred it to I.B.'s plate. "If these don't work out, I have a phalanx of reserve eggs standing by ready to be scrambled."

The reagent sneered. "If you're taking the back-up-system approach, double-doable, why not go for poached and settle for hard-boiled?"

The celebrity smiled complaisantly. "I curiously find myself this morning entertaining a slight aversion to water."

Madelyn sampled her omelet. "It looks fluffy but it's a bit dry." She took another bite. "A little tough and rubbery." She eyed the celebrity. "You used too much heat, honey."

Winterhalter tasted a chunk and chewed noisily. "A *little* rubbery?" He tossed his utensils onto his plate. "He must've found a 'vulcanize' feature on the stovetop."

Madelyn nodded. "It has a heavy chemical aftertaste, like it came from a vending machine." She tried another small bite and spit it into her napkin. "You really expect people to eat this crap?" She sprang to her feet. "I'll make us scrambled eggs." She headed into the kitchen, and the celebrity followed her. He returned to the table with the third omelet and deposited it on his plate.

The reagent shoved his plate aside. "If we were at your house, cheese-whiz, I'd heave this dish against the wall, and we could lay bets on how long it'd stick."

The celebrity voraciously consumed his omelet and licked the plate. Ten minutes later, Madelyn served scrambled eggs. The curds were mealy, moist and lumpy, but the celebrity picked at them without complaint. "Will you aid Ian," she submitted, "in removing the glaze finish from the cabinets in your room and replacing it with a muted umber acrylic varnish?"

The celebrity chugged his citrus punch. "I'm not here as the skating bear in your workaday ice follies."

Winterhalter scoffed. "I guess when failure is routine, you limit your activities to minimize your exposure."

The afternoon proved more productive. The two backup

sourcerers that the celebrity had requisitioned from Santa Monica arrived by special delivery, and he began the process of loading the appropriate software into the Qilroy and Jatakar, respectively. He felt relieved to command financial resources again, but the Operation Shalom cache remained top secret with official file access available only with personal authorization from the director or deputy director.

The celebrity assisted Winterhalter in grilling a select variety of German wursts for dinner. Afterward, the unlikely triad settled in the receiving room to watch the Hugh Milliter thriller *The Feast Of Fists*. Amorous activity between I.B. and Madelyn erupted on the davenport and escalated. The celebrity rose to leave the room.

"Stick around, Ahab," Madelyn suggested. "Next we'll put on a rom-com."

"I thought you'd already begun one on the sectional." The celebrity placed both hands over his heart. "It pains me to see live theater adulterated."

Madelyn leapt to her feet. "Pardon me, honey, I admit I could use a gaydar-aid. You at the very least play both ends of the court, don't you?"

The celebrity smiled tartly. "I'm going to invest the energy I'd expend debunking that idea on procuring some Zinfandel." He trudged to the kitchen, located a bottle of Stirrups Value Added brandy and continued to the guestroom. He tapped the bottle for a single exploratory belt and loaded more apps into his sourcerers. He attempted to hack into Winterhalter's files remotely but encountered additional security obstacles. When he was certain that his co-hosts had retreated to their romper room for the night, he returned to the computer in the receiving room and conducted further assaults on the reagent's Shalom files. He grew weary and suddenly sensed I.B. and Madelyn behind him practicing strategic shoulder-surfing.

"You think I'm not tracking where you're trying to tread, truditz?" Winterhalter poked the celebrity in the back of the head. "There's a pinhole cam in the desk lamp, a zoom nanny cam in the pendant light and a breach alert on the command recorder, just for starters!"

"I'm sorry if I got too personal before, honey," Madelyn interjected. "But you could help me out if you're versed in specialized crafts like sewing."

"He's just a *seemstress*." I.B. slapped the celebrity in the shoulder. "One more breach binge, beach-bitch, and I'll report you to C.I."

The next day brought prosperity in the form of two famil-iar packages. Lowball Auto Traffickers had located the missing Escort semi-submerged in Hegewisch Marsh and recovered the celebrity's briefcase and suitcase. Santa Monica had received and rerouted the items to the safe house. Following a joint lunch effort which produced jeweled rice with barberries, Madelyn sat with the celebrity at the dining room table as he opened his briefcase and inspected the avian replica California Thrasher kite. "This is surveillance."

"What the hell do you do for your job exactly?" she demanded. "Hide in the bushes and sniff for some untoward act you can pass back home to someone who believes his stink-ing opinion about it is important?"

"It can be a trace more interactive." He smiled complai-santly. "Yet why is it that every time *I* question what *your* professional activities entail, you whip up a slurry of obfusca-tion and subterfuge?" She snarled and plucked a pair of hairs. "Hand of the spyder." He exhibited his mechanical spider. "Eye of the snayke." He displayed his mechanical snake. "In a recent op, we swapped a subject's clothes for a duplicate outfit with a particular superpower. So the snayke bored a tiny hole through the corner of a basement window, crept up to her bedroom and camped for surveillance undetected."

Madelyn hissed. "You watched her undress."

"We watched where she kept her running gear so we were able to make our substitution." The celebrity replaced his items in the briefcase. "The snayke had previously neutralized the home security system. When the family ventured out, the snayke opened the bedroom window. The spyder climbed in carrying the smart knockoff athletic apparel and exchanged it for the original. The spyder then exited carrying both the original outfit and the snayke." He closed the briefcase. "That's what we doves call a coup."

Madelyn rose. "I'm employed as an activity planner for the group that owns Ray's Strip Mine." She exited.

The celebrity conveyed his two reclaimed luggage pieces to the guestroom and opened his suitcase on the mattress. He suspected that a set of fresh clothes would please his housemates no less than himself, and he donned a baggy pair of tan pickpocket-proof cargo pants along with his faded coral University of California at Irvine Anteaters *Eater Nation* T-shirt. He spent the remainder of the afternoon combing the internet for obscure links to Charlton Shalom.

Winterhalter announced that Madelyn had left for the evening, and the celebrity treated him to dinner at an outrageously inexpensive restaurant. When they returned to the safe house, the celebrity withdrew to the guestroom and nuzzled I.B.'s file safeguards in what had become a contact sport. He conducted another inconsequential grand foray on the internet for clues to Shalom's whereabouts, sustaining himself through the undertaking with intermittent gulps of Stirrups Value Added.

Sometime after midnight, Madelyn returned to the house and rumbustiously leaked her intention to decompress in the pool. Packing a headache which only promised to grow more severe, the celebrity accompanied her and the reagent to the Whispering Willowwacks spa. He hadn't noticed the message in flashing red letters on the door during his previous visit: *No Sourcerers & No Sex.* A nude middle-aged couple standing beyond chaise row quickly reclaimed their swimwear and departed. I.B. shed his yellow *Up For Grabs* T-shirt, Bermuda shorts and skivvies. Madelyn shed her black satin robe and blue floral pattern bikini. The hickey on her neck appeared fresh, and the celebrity wondered whether she'd acquired it within the purview of the reagent. He removed his *Eater Nation* T-shirt and cargo pants, and he reclined on a chaise in his borrowed trunks. The hormone-happy couple joined hands and dived into the pool.

I.B. and Madelyn surfaced at the recliner-top flotation pad. They traded light, teasing pecks and caresses. Madelyn fixed her gaze on the celebrity. "Ready yet to join us in the altogether club, honey?"

"Perhaps in a strictly advisory capacity." The celebrity kneaded his scalp. "I'll teach you to perform bastinado on each other."

Madelyn snickered peevishly. "You're still too tight-toed to get birthday suit raw?"

"He's as spineless as his inflatable lover," Winterhalter speculated.

The celebrity stood, slipped out of his trunks and waved them overhead. "Here's to the total loss of privacy."

I.B. and Madelyn shared a long, hard, steady working-stiff's kiss. At its conclusion, she chewed on his ear and looked back at the celebrity. "Don't you ever get lonely, honey?"

"He thinks outside the box," the reagent explained. "He's a do-it-yourselfer."

Madelyn giggled. "Maybe if his conk and his cock had exchanged growth rates, he'd be beating off the girls."

The celebrity nodded. "I take it, topolotta, you're considered fairly well-proportioned on your home planet?"

Madelyn scoffed. "I'm so sorry if your little feelings are hurt again, honey." She scratched her bathing cap. "You didn't seem to have such a short fuse about any of your other inadequacies." She smiled sweetly. "You have a mini-tip you wanted to share before?"

Winterhalter glowered. "Mind your own small business,

peanut," he cautioned the celebrity as he tickled and groped Madelyn. "You're hardly equipped to offer any make-out tips!"

"Ian is the consummate sexpert!" Madelyn whooped and embraced the reagent. "As the sports dweebs say, he can fill it up! He can score it! He's a magic man!"

The celebrity clapped lightly. "Maybe for his next trick, he'll put a baby in your belly and disappear."

Madelyn snickered sardonically. "Oobops, your father impregnated your mother with a wet sneeze!"

The celebrity nodded. "How do you know my brother?"

"I love it!" Winterhalter cackled. "'A wet sneeze!' The next time I code in, I'm going to spread that one around the office!"

The celebrity smiled complaisantly. "From the mouths of boobs come gems."

With echoes of expletives suspended in the air, the celebrity dived into the water and swam laps around his co-hosts. He climbed back onto his chaise and quickly drifted into unconsciousness. He awoke to find himself naked on the davenport in the safe house condo receiving room. "Oobops, you're alive!" Standing over him in her jump-suit pajamas, Madelyn bounced a button off his abdomen. "You were so out of it when we dragged you back up here, do you even recall the bumps?" He covered his lap and sat up. "You should learn to hold your liquor better, jazz-hands." She smirked. "I'd expect that talent to be one of your business basics."

"Something besides Value was added to my Stirrups." The celebrity rubbed his sore left underarm. He recognized that the hair had been removed from his left axilla and the right side of his chest.

"We took the responsibility to meet some of your manscaping needs." Madelyn extracted one of her own hairs. "I tried like all ripshits to lay in a funky pattern but you didn't have enough body hair so I just cleared a pit and a pec. Anyhow now it's your turn to go to work, Aclops." I.B. arrived at her side in his jump-suit pajamas. "I think we'd all profit from a strong cup of coffee before breakfast."

The celebrity held his head and strained to read the time display in the corner of the giant entertainment screen: *7:40.* "It's Wednesday morning?"

Winterhalter clapped his hands. "But what month, crondyke? Get some clothes and get a move on!"

The celebrity strode to the guestroom. Forty minutes later, he arrived at the coffeemaker in his *Eater Nation* T-shirt and cargo pants. The brewing process had already been initiated. "Finally, Oobops, there you are in the flesh!" Madelyn appeared on the toaster monitor. "We hoped you didn't scamper off shame-faced into hiding." Her fuzzy pate and shoulders glistened in the aura of the shower mist. "I designed and started our cups, so all you have to do is serve them up when we sit down at the table. In the meantime, do you feel up to breaking some more eggs for breakfast strudel with ham, scrambled eggs and hash browns? There's a puff pastry pack-"

The celebrity crammed the monitor into the toaster, inadvertently knocking the ersatz appliance off the counter and disabling it. "She's already honked off at your slack-assing, herniglud." I.B. arrived in the kitchen wiping his soggy body with a towel.

The celebrity stiffened his neck. "I'm still a bit overwhelmed by her pluck in violating me last night. Beneath that, I trust she spiked my brandy with a narcotic. I would've never made it through the Mission if I passed out from a few jiggers-worth!"

Winterhalter snickered. "Blame me, prehab. She disputed how easy it'll be to swab Shalom off the street once we find him, so after you dormed out I treated you to a blast of chloroform to demo we could lug you back up here without any muss or fuss." He buffed the wiry top of his head. "Of course, then she couldn't resist testing what it would take to wake you."

"So she knows the purpose of our presence here and our operation objective?" The celebrity winced mightily. "Did you ever think you might not want to spew specs in front of an outsider because she might prove to be a valve lifter in the enemy machine? Did you ever think?"

The reagent scoffed. "Relax, Yousef Yesser, she's kosh."

"You mean you've given her a security clearance?" The celebrity proceeded to the cabinet and snatched a box of Frosted Beasties breakfast cereal. "You're running her?"

Winterhalter leered. "I'm handling her."

"Did I hear my good name slammed, babe?" Madelyn appeared in her jump-suit pajamas with a towel wrapped around her head.

I.B. snapped his towel into her buttocks. "Oobops confessed he's scared of you."

Madelyn gazed at the celebrity with a pouty curiosity. "Aw, honey, is it that you're afraid of all women?" She displayed her hands. "Don't be in denial. Give us a show of hands so we can compare your finger lengths."

"Here it is in a nutshell," the celebrity snapped. "Nothing has been more antithetical to the ascent of civilized man than the desire to impress empty front-loaders like you."

Winterhalter scoffed. "Don't go off half-cocked, Oobops."

"He's a bladder of hot gas." Madelyn grabbed I.B. and imparted a whispered observation.

The reagent cackled. "Mad says you're a self-service pump with a micro-nozzle."

The celebrity nodded. "The Mad seismologist? There's nothing more delightful than sloppy tits. If you're still around in five years, you'll watch her chafe her nipples when she hitches up her belt." He took the Frosted Beasties to the dining room table, seated himself and poured a mound of cereal over his plate.

Several minutes later, I.B. and Madelyn carried their respective coffee blends to the dining room table. "You've spent a fair amount of time in the kitchen, bohunk," the reagent observed, "so you've seen the shitload of shiny hotspots on the walls, and you can't deny that seamless no-skid countertops are a must-have."

"The walls could be painted flat renaissance blue to match the tarps." The celebrity shoveled two handfuls of cereal into his mouth.

"I've been grinding it out in these whacked-over conditions for two months now, cud-raiser." Winterhalter dropped heavily into his chair. "Even you complain that the dex-defying air stinks like sweaty feet, although that might just be you." He inhaled his coffee vapor. "I want you to squeeze your juice with Santa Monica and set us up with funding for a major refurb project."

"We apologize, Ahab," Madelyn submitted, "if we haven't been sympathetic that your body image leaves you slightly undone."

I.B. emitted a protracted eructation. "Yeah, we didn't figure a scud-wafer in your position for the snap-and-go-spaz type."

"Your prime responsibility since establishing this haunt," the celebrity reminded the reagent, "has been to bird-dog for Shalom contacts and connections." He tapped on the table with increasing intensity. "Now it's crunch time. I need to examine your files-"

"I can hook you up with people who call Charlton by his first name," Madelyn trumpeted. "I recall 'Charlton Shalom' coming up every time Junior would go name-dropping."

"Junior?" Winterhalter challenged. "Jason Padata?"

Madelyn fixed her smug gaze on the celebrity. "You ready to put in an encouraging word for us with the lip-farts at the home office, set-dresser?"

The reagent hissed. "His word means jack-shit. Let's see him put up some solid material improvements first."

The celebrity smiled complaisantly. "I can give you black teeth and purple urine."

"Jason Padata used to be Henry Padata," Madelyn disclosed, "a lobbyist who wallowed in the wild life before he met the right woman to reform him." She giggled. "Well, she wasn't me, and he *is* still a lobbyist. But he remained a bachelor into his forties, and then he married a woman umpteen years older than him."

The celebrity expelled an impatient breath. "That indicates what?"

"Oh, Oobops baby, I'm sorry." Madelyn dug beneath her head towel and plucked a hair. "You're single and forty."

"He'll turn 28 in September," I.B. reported with intrusive accuracy. "He thinks acting old makes him look dickstinguished." He clutched Madelyn's hand and eyed the celebrity intently. "She switched me on to this transducer, and I did some body-checking. He worked for the Commerce Department and mangled a hedge fund, and now he's a lobbyist with ties to the Sickinois Intel Agency."

"I don't like the idea of involving Illinois Intel." The celebrity rose and rubbed his brow. "They're less likely to aid us than sell us out to Wisconsin, and they're certainly not going to appreciate our encroachment on their turf."

"Suck on your lead pacifier, hacklemesh." The reagent scratched his chest. "Neighbor agencies equal natural enemas. Plus this kwink owes Madelyn personal favors."

"Jason's nowhere near as dark and spooky as you, honey." Madelyn blew the celebrity a kiss. "I've met his wife Jacinth. She's a properly fussy little lady who'd retch if she knew her hubby's past. But Jason is prone to deeds of pitiful sentimentality, and their perfect union is cemented by their son and their contrary personalities."

"She's a toy virago, and he's a walking marshmallow?" The celebrity squelched the impulse to hold his sore underarm. "What sort of favors?"

"I'll call, and you can ask him." Madelyn sipped her coffee and consulted her Qilroy. "Junior always did make it a habit to drop in at his office late, so this should be the ideal time to contact him." She engaged the speaker function and placed a call. "Jacinth must be flirting with age 60, and Henry was so flippin' blown over by the arrival of their son that he cleaned up his lifestyle and changed his name to 'Jason' to match the boy's. So Senior became Junior, and Junior is Senior." The call failed to launch, and Madelyn placed it again. "Beware of throwing shade on the wife or son, cuz Junior don't much tolerate anyone going off on his family."

The call reached an answering machine. "That's fine." The celebrity reached over the table and punched the call abort button. "We'll take some time and formulate a more elaborate pitch to pique his interest and gain his confidence."

"Fuck that." I.B. clasped Madelyn's Qilroy shoulder. "Jerk his chain back." She replaced the call, and the reagent smiled implacably for the automated prompt. "Jason Padata, this is I.B. Winterhalter of emerging energy start-up Fickle Flicker here with vogue California physicist Abe Obispo, who's messing with a measure to combat climate change based on work Charlton Shalom did with electric fog." He cleared his throat. "Before our people scale-up our investment on further R&D, we'd like to run some uncertainties by Shalom up-close-and-personal. I have a source who swears you know someone with a source who can direct us." He emitted a hoarse cough. "Obviously, this is urgent, so call me back as soon as you get my message. You've got my number, but in case it got lost in your system, I'm attaching it in text, and in case you lose the attachment, we'll call you again every five minutes until we hear from you." He smirked and terminated the connection.

Five minutes later, Junior returned the call. "Sorry, I'm not sure who you are." He contorted his lip anxiously. "How are you getting ahold of me?"

"How are we getting ahold of Charlton?" Winterhalter pointed Madelyn's Qilroy cam at the celebrity. "Here's Abel Oobisp, who I mentioned. Now where's Shalom?"

"How's that?" Padata gasped. "I have no idea. And I can't imagine why you'd think I'd know anyone who would."

The reagent snickered sardonically. "I'm calling in a favor. Reliable sources insist you and Shalom used to mix freely in mudrooms for the empowered with keepers of the mushrooms."

"I don't know what you're talking about." Padata scratched his crop of bright orange hair. "Anything that bizarre must've been a long time ago in a land far away." He furrowed his brow. "I'm not sure what your interest is, but I can't help you, and I'm too busy to look back-"

"Jason sweetheart owes everyone a favor." Madelyn turned the cam on herself. "Padata, how art ya?"

"Who the hell-" A bright strawberry blush permeated Padata's pudgy face. "I really have to go."

"Not so fast, master." Madelyn scowled. "Don't treat me like some old jar of yick at the back of your fridge."

"Shalom?" Jason scratched his nose. "Shalom to the extent of my knowledge has dropped off the edge of the Earth. His family probably tucked him in another out-of-the-way loony bin. Maybe he's depressed about Worbley's tragic death. They got along fiendishly."

"Then how's your wife, Junior?" Madelyn rose. "My friend Selene is sponsoring an occult objects party, and we'd like to invite Jacinth for the evening."

"Yeah, she's busy." Padata pursed his lips. "I'll see if I can scrounge up anything fresh." He terminated the connection.

Madelyn's hands alighted on the celebrity's shoulders. "As a way of thanking us, honey, why don't you wander back into the kitchen and fix us a special treat like lemon bars?"

Winterhalter displayed a wry smile. "Those would kick ass with beer-can chicken."

Madelyn sighed. "I just spied some flurries, so we won't ask him to step out to the grill and expose his tenderloins to the cold, even though that's probably what he deserves." She extracted a hair from the nape of the celebrity's neck. "Angel hair pasta would rock our brunch, hmm?"

The celebrity returned to the kitchen, preheated the oven

and boiled a large pot of water. He donned a waxed apron and processed three large lemons in the citrus press. He procured a set of bowls and a crust pan. He received a call on his Qilroy from the reagent. "Go to ComCon-4, fuddle-head; Padata's back and I'm putting him on with us."

Jason dandled a little scarlet-haired boy on his lap. "Do you fellows propose to impact the vapor chemistry itself, or offer a more economical, more easily deployed, injection method? I gather you're aiming at aerosol cloud consistency, maybe the component droplet size, or do you believe you have some additive that'll increase reflectivity or provide more protection against ozone damage?"

"Get real, Junior," Winterhalter snarled, "we don't hand out free samples."

The celebrity smiled complaisantly. "You appreciate the sensitive nature of intellectual property, Mr. Padata, but I can confirm we'd be materially appreciative for any assistance you'd provide in arranging the audience we seek. We've arrived at a crucial juncture in moving our research forward."

"It's your move, Jason," Madelyn asserted. "Step up to it."

Padata exhaled heavily. "You're familiar with the Chicago-based environmental group Parallacts Associates? It originated as a consortium of business, political and academic decision-makers for advancing the conversation about improving the water quality of Lake Michigan by restoring the ecological balance threatened by invasive species, waste treatment issues and shifting climate. It has evolved since, of course, into an expanded network dedicated to taking advantage of the economic opportunities presented by situations, events and policy solutions throughout the Great Lakes region related to climate change and the hype surrounding it." He stroked the tot's hair. "For a short time, the late Lincoln McGuay-O'Toole Worbley sat on the board of directors, and if anyone I know has a clue to the whereabouts of Charlton Shalom, it would be them. Once a month, they sit down and entertain a pitch to sponsor a project with potential major environmental impact, usually on a Friday morning so they can start their weekend party afterward with lunch downtown." He began tickling his Qilroy. "They're willing to show patience and play long shots, so I'm texting you their office info, and you can send them whatever prospectus, patents, cover letter or resumes you care to lay on the line." He grinned. "If they find you a fraction as fascinating as you seem to find yourself, you can probably expect a motion to meet in a couple of months."

"How do we send a more powerful signal, Mr. Padata?" the celebrity demanded. "We need to expedite the effort. Perhaps if you could vouch for us-"

"I recall the padrone was always *thrilled* to be of service," Madelyn contributed.

Padata emitted an awkward chortle. "I'll explore putting in a much-needed personal plug for you, Maddy."

"I suppose these crap-happy Parallacts deer-licks are absolute aments to deal with?" I.B. speculated.

"I have to go help little Jase." Padata patted his son's head. "But don't burden the board with charts or power graphics. I'll give you another tip on opening a business presentation to a hostile audience. It reduces the speaker's social discomfort and grabs everyone's attention." He paused to let the anticipation mount. "You survey the room, break into a nasty, little ironic titter and declare, 'I am sooooo evil.'"

"I am sooo evil," little Jason cooed, upending his father's grin.

"Uh, the boy has differential equations to get to." The lobbyist terminated the connection.

The celebrity clicked his tongue. "Whenever money talks, it sounds a lot like him, hmm? I felt more of an airflow toward optimization than metanoia." He returned to his brunch preparation but the lemon bar filling ultimately became contaminated with seasonal greens, and the angel hair pasta failed to rise above the consistency of goop. He patched together macaroni and cheese as a surefire stopgap. Afterward, he retired to his guestroom and treated himself to the guilty listening pleasure of Hap & Conway Sutherland's *Ain't Nobody Better Bother Me Tonite* as he perused the uniformity of outlooks on the shifting climate by CIB analysts and their sources.

Winterhalter prepared a vegetarian dinner of barley couscous. "You impressed Jason," Madelyn advised the celebrity as he seated himself at the table. "Really, I think it was your apron that impressed him. It made you look like a gonzo scientist, and it rattled him to the point that he called back to say you have an appointment with the Parallacts pricks Friday." She plucked a hair. "The day after tomorrow. Don't bother to gush with gratefulness. Anything that gets you out of the house has to be classified a win-win."

"A separate peace." The celebrity attempted to savor the broth.

Outbound. 0920 CST Friday 24 March.

"Here to wreak havoc on the planet is a dense sprawl, snags of decadently dirty old-growth, on display daily underheeding and overheating to the appropriation of a peril." The celebrity drove across the south branch of the Chicago River in I.B. Winterhalter's Jeep Glory Roadster. He conducted a brief reconnaissance of the Loop and successfully inserted himself in Empty Suitland Clothiers Outfit. As a standard precaution, he declined the salesman's invitation to submit to a fitting-booth body scan, lamenting that he couldn't let an online sartorial service record his measurements because he coached the dodgeball team for the Death Valley Chapter of the Federal Witness Protection Program. He purchased a tan hemp power suit with burnt chili Lord Clarksdale business loafers and arrived 70 minutes early at the Wacker Drive skyscraper which housed Parallacts Associates. Jason Padata had exhorted him to appear one full hour before his 11:50 appointment, and he prided himself on covering the cushion with extra padding. He passed the security checkpoint and proceeded to the 14th floor Parallacts office suite to find two young women seated at desks behind a partition. An embossed cherry wood *Reception-ist* sign situated in front of the ethereal blonde induced him to approach her. "Ahab Oobops," he proclaimed, "here for my appointment with the Parallacts board of directors."

The receptionist had a vibrant, sparkling smile accentuated by finely honed dimples. Her soft eyes were sheltered behind a Jatakar with lavender-tinted ovate lenses which veiled her in an aura of mystery as they shielded her from glare. Her hair spilled to her shoulders in subtle waves of variegated gold. "Very good, Mr. Oobops," she replied with ample felicity, "I'll inform them you're here. Please make yourself comfortable in the welcome center. My name is Tiffany."

The celebrity backtracked to the plush, overstuffed black mohair davenport, seated himself against one of its flared arms and placed his briefcase behind his calves. Tiffany smiled as she engaged some remote authority in a soft, terse conversation. She rose, opened the Dutch door and approached the davenport. Clad in a teal blazer, short skirt and sandals, the woman possessed a physical perfection of unsettling proportion. "It'll be a while, so please allow me to offer you the enriching amenity of a massage to unclutter your mind, relax your body and sharpen your focus."

The celebrity heard an insipient chortle escape from his throat. "That's an idea! Particularly if you'd be the masseuse, it'd be a splendid idea, but I'm already focused-"

"Yes, I will be your masseuse this morning." She seated herself beside him, her knee lightly brushing his.

"No, really." He recognized the futility of any effort to erase the awkward grin which had commandeered his lips. "That won't be necessary. I, ah, couldn't."

She removed her Jatakar and stared into space. He allowed

himself the indulgence of lightly patting her wrist. "I'm sorry," he whispered, "is something wrong?"

"I don't know." She scrutinized him. "No one ever declined before. If you'd prefer, I could arrange for an Asian woman to give you the massage. It wouldn't be quite as long, but she'd be here within 30 minutes. Or a man. There's an African-American bodybuilder – Mercury – with arms like metal bands-"

"No, please." He patted her knee in sweet surrender. "What's wrong with me?" He anticipated pondering the question later with some intellectual vigor. "I'd be delighted to receive your stimulus package."

Tiffany grinned and ensconced her lavender lenses in her hair. "I trust it'll be an invigorating, empowering experience." She took his hand and drew him to his feet. "Let's go to the fulfillment center." He grabbed his briefcase and she nodded. "We can put that in the safe."

He shrugged. "It's not much more than my lunch."

She looked askance at the other receptionist. "Removing temptation provides everyone with relief." She led him through the partition door and behind her desk. She took the briefcase and stashed it in a wall safe. She guided him around a couple of corners and into a cramped room containing a massage table adorned with aquamarine sheets. A fluorescent lamp in the shape of a pair of hands commanded space on the far side of the room and a pair of toothy primitive tribal masks divided by a diagonally positioned spear decorated the wall at the foot of the table. An oval credenza holding a collection of conspicuous objects such as crystal pyramids, xylophone mallets and tuning forks stood against the near wall.

He took the mallets and drummed lightly on the surface of the credenza. "The mystic power of the indefinite pitch, hmm?"

She motioned for him to follow her beyond the credenza around a corner into an alcove, the inner wall of which was composed of a bamboo screen bordered by a column of three primitive head carvings. He clicked his tongue and patted the top head. "I have a kitschy totem in my kitchen with faces that possess integrity of form independent of which end faces up."

She eyed him dubiously. "The tiki gods are pleasure spirits, more lighthearted than the rest. I continue to lobby for a tranquility fountain accessory." She swept the screen aside to reveal a closet. An extra-tall stool with tubular foot-ring occupied the center floor space while sundry cassock-style garments shared the right side of the wardrobe rod with some empty hangers. Tubs and jars populated the overhead rack. "Place your clothes in here." She faced him squarely. "You'll need to remove all your jewelry, including your Qilroy, and any prosthetics or temporary extensions. Remove everything, unless you have an issue with that."

"Nah, ah." He felt his pulse quicken. "Where one's not nude, massage is dressage, nay?"

She chuckled politely. "Great, I'll give you a couple of minutes." She left him with position directions and the promise of a refreshing cup of cardamom tea at the conclusion of the massage.

The celebrity stepped into the closet and doffed clothes, irked by the alacrity with which he'd allowed a sensuous woman to confound his confidence and wilt his wit. He strode to the massage table naked and acutely self-conscious. Framing an oval mirror on the inside of the door was a wood carving which depicted a pair of lizards attempting to swallow each other's tail. He climbed onto the table buoyed by the virility suggested in his upper body musculature. He covered himself and lay on his back anxiously, trepidations about the meeting with the Parallacts board hanging over him. He resented Winterhalter for infecting him with a ridiculous sense of inadequacy. Who needed to be impressed *that* way? Some of the sexiest women were fairly flat-chested. He preferred a toned athletic body to an hourglass figure any day of the week, or at least no less than six out of seven. Perhaps the exception was Friday. Tiffany knocked softly. She entered and stood over him in a sleeveless midnight blue jersey, her hair constrained in a loose ballerina bun. Light, subtle island music splashed throughout the room. "Any health condition or tender areas I should be aware of?" She seemed to notice the scratches, cuts and bruises on his face for the first time. "Ooh, what happened here?"

"I'm from California, and there was a slight earthquake during my last facelift." He failed to upend her frown. "It was just a clumsy domestic accident roughhousing with a giant squirrel."

She caressed his chin and pulled the sheet up to his neck. "You're not allergic to Number Eight Heavy Duty Rubbing Compound, are you?"

"For a hand-rubbed crackle finish?" He lifted his head and shoulders off the table. "What's in it?"

"Basic rust or paint remover, I imagine." She snickered and pressed his shoulder against the table. "I'm joking. You have your choice of an unscented linseed-oil-based unction that's great for your skin or a Tahitian lime fragrance body lotion."

"Mnh," the celebrity purred, "on behalf of the remnant California growers, I'm inclined to resist any sort of citriculture competitor."

"The oil it is." She smiled and disappeared around the corner.

The celebrity considered the gritty, uncomfortable sensation of oil on his skin. "Tiffany," he called after her. She reappeared unscrewing the cap of a bottle of amber liquid. "I'm so sorry, but could I have the tropical topical instead? I might be allergic to linseed oil."

"Of course." She whirled and proceeded back around the corner. He heard a dull thump, and she returned momentarily carrying a hefty tub under her arm. She set it on the credenza and removed the cover. She glided to a position at the head of the massage table and rubbed her hands over the sheet atop his shoulders. She began slowly caressing his cheeks and neck.

"I'll be careful not to muss your hair." He closed his eyes as she cosseted his head. She slid the sheet to the bottom of his chest. She slathered her hands with lotion, and her fingers fluttered across his shoulders like angel-wing butterflies.

He moaned softly. "Some remarkable people must've been handed over here."

"Excuse me?" The pressure became more intense as she explored his trapezius.

"I expect many captains of industry have landed on this table, and a few might've found a rub from a big, muscular guy handy in smoothing over their transition to prison life." He opened his eyes. "A little pre-gallows humor there."

"Okay?" She widened her eyes and he reshut his. She stretched his neck and kneaded his shoulders. "If you talk a lot, you won't maximize the benefit of the massage." She took control of his left arm and rubbed it with a scrupulousness. "Make a muscle." She squeezed his biceps and paused. "Oh, that's interesting."

He beamed shamelessly. "I try to take care of my body."

"I'm noticing the depilation of your underarm." She moved to his right side. "Your right pec also presents a contrast to your left."

"My business associate's woman, a snake with kneecaps, sheared me while I was sleeping. It's not like I'm sucked into the PartisAnn vacuum."

Tiffany's fingers froze on the celebrity's forearm. "And you have a problem with someone who is?"

He drew a deep, uneven breath. "This moment I have absolutely no problem."

Her face became poutier, and her soft hands resumed their measured undulations. She neatly folded his arm across his abdomen and exposed his leg. She explored the area with feathery strokes, and he recognized his elevated level of arousal. "Your thigh muscles," she whispered, "are knotted like a twisted rope." She completed her sally against his right leg and foot.

She exposed his left leg and worked more lotion between her fingers. "This is just a therapeutic exercise," she purred as she kneaded his thigh. "There's nothing more to it."

"Mnh." He swallowed hard and shuddered with pleasure as she slid her hands from his hip to his knee. "I guess the prospect of facing the board has me worked up."

Her smooth, meandering palms swirled down his shin and clasped his foot. "They're only human, just like you."

"Or at least," he murmured, "no more than a shade or two beneath."

She manipulated his toes with delicate force. "I'm here to disembarrass you from all of your negative premonitions." She pressed and caressed his entire leg. "Stiffness is my sworn enemy and the last thing we want for you." She covered his leg and returned to the head of the massage table. As she elevated the face cradle, he attempted to focus on his imminent presentation. Above all else, he was a performer trained to elicit a calculated response from his audience.

Tiffany lifted the sheet. "Okay, Mr. Oobops, roll onto your stomach and creep up a bit, if that's possible." The celebrity slid his body so his face was framed by the cradle. She rearranged the sheet. "You *do* have quite an athletic body. Are you a runner?"

"Only in the face of danger." He snickered without accompaniment. "I'm sorry it's not obvious, but I suspect my fitness regimen incorporates many of the same moves as Mercury's. I like to unwind throwing a heavy hammer."

"I guess I see it." She pounded his right hamstring. "It's just not something that really fascinates me. Muscles are so previous century, wouldn't you have to concede?" She pressed her hands into his calf. "Eating healthy and keeping trim are important, but the mind is what's potent."

He winced. "What's on it, or what's in it?"

She plied her fingers vigorously over the bottom of his foot. "Use me as the conduit to your personal revitalization.

Confidence is there to be picked like a fruit. Wear it like a shirt." She repeated her routine on his left leg. "Mr. Oobops, resolve to be free of anxiety. Immerse yourself in cool, positive thoughts."

She replaced the sheet over his leg and whisked it off his back and buttocks. She slathered more lotion on her hands and kneaded the deep tissue of his shoulders. "There's so much tension in your body. Highlight your strengths: your inscrutability and your resourcefulness. Whatever power structure you represent believes in your ability, and you wouldn't be here now if you weren't prepared. You crave the spotlight, and you've lobbied for this opportunity." She ran her hands down his spine. "You're smart, and you're in command. You will deliver your presentation without apologizing your way through, making excuses for yourself or harping on your deficiencies." She stopped and sighed. "Mr. Oobops, we're making minimal progress. Your back is still so tight. Can I interest you in a little G.I.?" She smiled when he lifted his face. "Guided imagery?"

"Satellite photography?" He rolled onto his side. "Of what?"

"It's a directed relaxation technique." She pressed his shoulder to the table. "Hypnotism's baby brother. As I work over your physical being, I'll suggest a tranquil setting, like a woods or a beach. It's a great way to purge anxiety and empower you without leaving bruises." She snickered. "Like to try it?"

He felt little motivation to resist. "I've always considered the beach my ultimate refuge."

"Let's hit the beach." Tiffany strutted to the head of the massage table. "We're first going to lower your blood pressure by synchronizing your breaths and your heartbeats." She rubbed his back lightly. "Relax, relax totally." Her strokes became even more feathery. "From here we take deep, cleansing breaths." She led him through a brief routine of breathing exercises, and with a rich, vivid depiction of the scenery, transported him to an ocean beach. "As you float, you immerse yourself in cool, clear, positive thoughts. Your subconscious mind is not a saboteur but a servant." She wrapped an electrode-studded thick leather band around his head. "One more device to help you." She connected cables to the electrodes. "You'll hear your pulse and learn to control its rate through biofeedback." A series of bright blips charged the air. "This is your place at the edge of the sea. Breathe in its life, breathe out any troubling cares. Sunbeams dance across your body and kiss and caress your skin, penetrating to the center of your being. You find a small shell swept in by the tide. You pick it up, breathe all your troubles into it and hurl it into the sea, watching it skip across the tranquil, placid water: plop, plop, plop. You continue along the beach, feeling the sand between your toes, warm and nurturing on the soles of your feet. You've never felt so free, nearly weightless. You see a fish surface on the water, see a child's red balloon on a string, floating over a cluster of rocks. You easily hop from a low ledge to a higher ledge, and you leap from the highest rock and retrieve the balloon in your outstretched fingers. You press the rubber skin-"

A bang jolted the room. The celebrity snapped to attention, and the resistance of the cables attached to his headband wrenched his neck. A sharp pain shot through the area of his right trapezius. He removed his headband and rose to all fours.

"Mr. Oobops, please stay down!" Tiffany rode the celebrity's shoulders back to the massage table and pinned him there. "Just a moment, please!" She released him and disappeared around the corner.

The celebrity rose to his elbows. He rubbed the side of his neck, grinded his teeth and rotated his head. Tiffany reappeared. "Oh, Mr. Oobops, I'm so sorry!" She displayed a pair of white briefs besmirched by a massive stain. "The overhead shelf in the closet collapsed, and somehow the bottle of oil spilled all over your suit and clothing pile." She possessed a gorgeous flustered smile. "We can send them all out to be cleaned, and they'll be back in two hours. Your presentation can be postponed until then."

He collapsed to the massage table. "I'm always willing to trade favors."

She rubbed his head. "You are so appreciated." She returned to the closet. "We'll get you a shoeshine, too." She exited with his laundry bundle and remained absent for ten minutes. She knocked vehemently when she returned. "Again, Mr. Oobops, my sincerest apologies!" She stroked his neck and withdrew the headband. "At least this'll give us more time to work out your kinks." She stopped abruptly. "Excuse me, I have to leave again for a moment." She exited and remained absent for another ten minutes. She knocked softly, re-entered and seated herself beside him toward the foot of the massage table. "Mr. Oobops, do you feel that you're a sophisticated individual with a progressive sense of humor?"

He emitted a deep, cleansing breath. "I laugh frequently, but I'm a regular at the asylum."

She snickered politely. "They just informed me that your presentation absolutely cannot be delayed. A couple of the board members will be traveling this afternoon, so if it doesn't get done now, you'll have to reschedule for some time in May or June."

The celebrity considered the prospect of life with I.B. and Madelyn for another two months. "I can't come back; I'll have been fired by then." He propped his head on an elbow and looked back at her. "Tell them I'll be visualizing them all naked anyway, so if you could see that they peel off their outerwear and then rustle me a towel, we'll call it even, and the show can go on ultra-casual."

A concerned grin flickered across her lips. "There's not much chance they'll approve that plan, but you may have noticed there's theatrical garb in the closet. Someone recently addressed the board in a kimono. It broke the tension, and everyone loved it." She darted around the corner and returned with a yellow Japanese robe and brown burlesque tuxedo. "You could borrow either of these and expect a fabulous result." He hesitated, and she furrowed her brow. "Confidentially – Ahab, is it – my job here is in some jeopardy because of attendance issues, so if you'd go through with this without mentioning that your suit got soiled through my carelessness, I'd do just about anything for you, up to and not including the obvious."

The celebrity sighed. "I'll look for a sophisticated way to take advantage of your offer." He examined the garments. "They open in the back like a hospital gown." He thrummed the tuxedo.

"I'll cinch you up nice and tight." Tiffany laid the tuxedo on the massage table. "And I have large feet so I can fetch you a pair of my androgynous slippers to save you from going bare-foot." She hustled out of the room, and he pried himself off the table. He donned the one-piece tux and found the sleeves and legs only slightly excessive. She returned and crammed his feet into her burgundy slippers. She tied his laces and fluffed his tails. She moved around him for the full-frontal view. "I didn't notice before. Are you a natural mouth-breather?"

The celebrity nodded. "I get extra medicinal carbon credits from my doctor." He rubbed the side of his neck. "I pulled a muscle when your closet imploded, and now my jaw doesn't want to lock."

She cocked her head. "Your head seems to be listing a bit." She leaned closer. "A tiny bit of spittle is collecting at the corner of your mouth, too, so you'll want to concentrate on correcting for that." She brushed his hair. "Otherwise, I believe you're ready for the idea center. Will you require technical assistance to set-up and deliver your audio and visual effects?"

He wiggled his mandible. "I intend to propose an idea beyond embellishment by whistles and crayons."

"Remain conscious of smoothing over that arrogant edge, too." She offered a tender smile of encouragement. "You're going to kill, Ahab."

Tiffany left the room for several minutes, and the celebrity spent the time rotating his head. She returned and took him by the hand. "They're ready for you." She led him into a wide, shallow room with wood-paneled walls, and he found himself facing a refectory table populated with seven face cards who constituted the governing board of the consortium called Parallacts Associates. The two wing seats at the table were vacant. The lights remained comfortably dim, and a dull alpine scent further enriched the atmosphere. On the wall behind the board hung a trapezoidal abstract painting which suggested a chef wrestling a python into a steaming pot. Shalom didn't appear to be present. One of the governors was definitely a woman. Five of the seven members eyed him with the affability of irked crocodiles. The man on the right wore a wide, permanent, avuncular grin. The man in the center, a menacing figure with a large frame and gravelly voice, introduced himself as Chairman Fletcher Weikert and rapidly identified each of his cohorts.

Tiffany hauled the celebrity to a lit *X* on the plush red carpet perpendicular to Weikert and left him. "Due to the eleventh-hour nature of your scheduling and its proximity to the noon hour," the chairman stated, "I hope you don't mind, Mr. Hupops, that we ordered a catered lunch, which should arrive momentarily. If we like what you have to say, we might invite you to stick around for it." Everyone tittered.

"Did you enjoy your massage?" The African-American man seated on the far left had been presented by Weikert as a former pro football or basketball player. "If you have something that interests us, it's on the house."

A conveyer belt on the table held a simmering coffeepot, frosted pitcher and cup stacks. The avuncular man on the right summoned the vessels, poured himself a cup of coffee and continued smiling. "That's a unique outfit," the gender-neutral panelist observed. "May I inquire what your thought process was in choosing it?"

"Opportunity loves originality." The celebrity speculated

that Tiffany's confidential appeal was some sort of loyalty test and straightened his collar rather than the record. "Delving deep into the dreary, abstruse science behind the emerging discipline of solar radiation management, I'll do what it takes to energize my personal magnetic field." He forced a grin. "The option was a yellow kimono."

"I fancy a fancy kimono," the man with the avuncular grin remarked.

"That's a ninja robe you're referring to," Weikert rasped. "Geishas wear kimonos."

The celebrity snickered. "I stand sans samisen."

The chairman eyed the celebrity intently. "Do you have a problem with the Japanese?"

The celebrity chuckled heartily and drooled on his sleeve. "Why no, I'm a huge fan of female sumo wrestling, and I fancy that Japanese rapper, the one who touts himself as the new Sinara, uh, what's-his-name, Hiawatha."

The apple-cheeked young man with deep-set eyes and thick, dark, wavy hair seated to Weikert's right snarled audibly. "His name's Hiakawa, bright Bart."

"Mnh, right," the celebrity conceded. "*His* name ought to be Kimono." Wired with anxiety in need of an outlet, he began pacing. "As in a Japanese wrapper?" He pointed to the abstract painting. "I hope that's not your caterer's specialty of the day." The board turned in unison and eyed the painting as the hollow strains of the celebrity's laughter strafed the room. The seven pairs of supercilious eyes fixed him with a fresh irritation, and he panicked. "Excuse me," he snickered maniacally, "but I am soooo evil." The grin of the man on the right dissolved, and the celebrity awaited the palpable transformation of the governors from allied skeptics to prospective bedfellows.

"What do you have for us, Mr. Oobtops?" The man on the right regained his grin. "Lob your presentation."

The celebrity inhaled deeply. "Basically, how much money are you interested in making?"

"Basically," Weikert snarled, "how much money exists?"

"Here's a puzzle," the celebrity delivered his planned opening thrust. "If I asked you to consider a package, and I told you it has a molten core and a thin crust encompassed by a gaseous envelope, you'd probably all imagine pretty much the same entity, wouldn't you?"

"A fresh-baked chocolate éclair," the woman cooed.

"Your panty liner," the young man with the cheeks and curls suggested.

The celebrity smiled complaisantly. "I recall you were presented behind an opaque title." He approached his fresh-faced lampoon-chucker. "Some insider parlance for executive straight man?"

"Kevin is our tobslar," the chairman rasped. "Tracker of bullshit laws and regulations." He gestured like a quarterback sending his receiver deep. "Mr. Hupops, you are kindly directed to remain on your mark."

"I don't know how anyone with any connection to energy solutions could be unfamiliar with my post," Kevin asserted. "The landscape is so dominated by subsidies, tax breaks and credits and loan guarantees, it's a bigger merit ghetto than the intelligence and defense industries combined."

The celebrity returned to his lit X. "Let's consider that our planet has a specific hum, a distinct resonance, a harmonic constitution defined by the dynamic interrelationship of the electrostatic charges of its component particles."

"Hopefully, Mr. Oopgobs," the woman urged, "the dynamic interrelationship of a tight schedule and valuable time finds some resonance with you. Please select a goal and orient yourself to it."

The celebrity envisaged frolicking on Pismo Beach. "I hoped to designate as a point of departure the observation that the fortune of any energy startup is somewhere between ambiguous and tenuous and requires a timeline horizon longer than people in your position are generally willing to give it.

Every time a formidable clean-tech challenge arises, a cheaper, more ostensibly efficient source of dirty-tech is improbably reconditioned. I'll leave it to you to pick the particular competing interest on which to lay your bets, but I exhort you to treat the moral imperative of climate crisis as more than an afterthought to economic concerns. Commercialization value has a bad habit of leading where it should follow. This problem demands a region-by-region analysis which will identify varying aspects as more pressing drivers, but any lack of consensus on emphasis shouldn't negate-"

"Am *Iah* hearing you wrong," the man to Weikert's left interrupted in a slight drawl, "or are you working up to *not* lecturing us on eco-ethics?"

"By no means." The celebrity stretched his neck. "A prevailing sentiment seems to have arisen that the grand scheme behind the polar shield is flawed, and as movements splinter the scientific community advocating reversion to the basic measure of seeding the stratosphere with sulfate aerosol or an alternative means of radiative forcing such as increasing cloud reflectivity with sea-salt, I boldly proclaim my belief in the impeccable integrity of the science of Charlton Shalom!"

"Super, Mr. Oobops," the man with the drawl replied, "advise us on the geosciences. Give us something rock solid."

The celebrity wiped drool from his chin. "Based on atmospheric indicators that I've studied, I believe the principle of the electric fog is sound, or it would be with some adjustments."

"You believe you understand the plasma principle behind Shalom's shield?" Kevin scoffed. "Lincoln M.O. Worbley, the man who built it, used to sit on this board, and he confided that he didn't quite understand it."

The celebrity rubbed his neck. "Of course, the basis of the structure is a latticework of levitating particles oriented to the Earth's electric field-"

"That's supposed to be a state secret, isn't it?" the woman asserted.

The celebrity smiled complaisantly. "That's why I need to verify my design theory with Charlton Shalom personally, so I can establish if I've independently derived different disc particles but am still measuring the same signals-"

"You want us to introduce you to Shalom?" Weikert rasped.

"I've met Shalom," the celebrity peevishly bluffed. "He might not remember me, but I attended his symposium on the Hutchison Effect at Caltech."

"You know Charlton Shalom?" the androgynous figure challenged. "Isn't he insufferable?"

"Ah, he's not there that much." The celebrity snickered nervously.

"What we're concerned with here," Weikert decreed, "is not science but science management."

"Remember how your science profs used to preach that the final answer to a problem isn't so important as how you arrived at it?" the avuncular panelist offered. "Here we're just the opposite."

"Just a few weeks ago a man favored us with a lavish presentation," the woman related. "He explored the intricacies of the photophoretic force on his digital whiteboard. He invoked equations replete with Greek symbols to define climate sensitivity as the ratio of temperature change to flux of energy. By the time he finally worked around to his design of high-altitude ionization clouds, he'd created a restive, hyper-skeptical audience." She chortled. "It didn't end well for him."

"You must be *awayah*, Mr. Oozlops," the man with the drawl prevailed over one or two other voices, "that the prime game-changer in system design is the little mattah of scale. It's the key reason why most desktop climate change models prove themselves to be so half-assed." He and Kevin held the celebrity in mutual glowers. "If you're augmenting a sulfur or selenium particle so it scatters more sunlight or remains aloft longer, that's wonderful. But we have no impetus to evaluate the potential of any incremental system upgrade ourselves or help you gain the ear of visiting scientists who might have an abiding interest. We're impressed by something bright and shiny with the ability to anticipate the social and political ramifications that are inevitably bound to follow."

"If I could mix or match certain properties I've discovered with what Charlton has," the celebrity persevered, "we can verify the viability of a cooling blanket of another sort inasmuch as the electrical energy to sustain it is derived from the Van Allen belts."

Kevin groaned. "Not another warmed-over ionospheric heater. The idea of the 'solar tap' was promulgated as far back as the 1960s by physicist Walt Richmond, who cited its potential to discharge global consequences at least as dire as those imagined by the most radical green-backed guerilla."

The celebrity hissed. "Follow me for a moment, Kevin."

"You're not allowed to call him 'Kevin' until you earn his respect," Weikert admonished.

The celebrity nodded. "How about if today we just call him off? Unless sucking the lifeblood out of a prospective new system is in the executive charter, let's turn down the high-beams." He wiped away drool. "Let's consider what happens if we treat the planet like a living organism and try to utilize its own defense mechanisms."

"Achh!" the chairman scoffed. "You sound ready for your *batsu* parting gifts. *Batsu*, a precocious cultural illiterate should stand advised, is a genre of Japanese gaming where contestants endure pain and humiliation."

"Mr. Woopops, do you enjoy golf?" the associate with the perpetual grin inquired. "Are you good at it?"

The celebrity coughed and cleared his throat. "I struggle on defense."

"Of course you would because you're trying to make an awkward pitch off a terrible lie." The avuncular grin grew broader. "We couldn't connect with Universidad Cabo de Montana Profunda in Leon, Nicaragua, but we pursued the reference you provided from Leif Greenland Atmospheric Physics Research Laboratory and reached a 'Radmilla,' who curtly informed us that you're a failed California state spy trying to leverage his way back into the business."

"You mean the game?" The celebrity tittered. "Cabo is part of a military installation behind razor wire on a street with no name, but Radmilla is an incorrigible practical joker."

"Is she?" Kevin snapped. "Maybe you are. What are you attempting to accomplish?"

"Mr. Oobsops," the woman uttered, "please assure us you're not really here to try and sell us some tax-free carbon credits?"

"I'll buy a box of energy bonds, little girl," the gender-neutral individual contributed.

"You've been called, fraud," the black associate interpreted, "sunk, punk – busted, shot down, blown away, nuked."

"You got no bombs left there to play with, Noguchi?" Weikert chided.

"The final act delivers no disappointment!" Overwhelmed by audience feedback, the celebrity recalled how his destiny had been altered during a theatrical performance in college when a spectator heaved a live skunk on stage. "The real marvel in my permutation of the cooling blanket is how the particulate substrate is introduced into the atmosphere with no energy outlay." He exhibited a wicked smile. "Several near-Earth meteoroids are captured and then released on a trajectory which results in a series of controlled strikes above the Arctic Circle in Greenland. The dust rises and is held over the pole in the electric fog."

Kevin stood and applauded. "That has to be the most reckless, environmentally irresponsible proposition I've ever heard. A crock of shit for the ages!"

"Controlled strikes?" the man with the twang scoffed. "The uncertainty of the volume of dust and debris you'd be spewing into the atmosphere is staggering!"

"You're liable to overblow," Weikert rasped, "and plunge

the planet into a mini ice age." He chortled. "The geo-anthro-pological record, Ludwig, shows that during warming periods, human civilization generally finds ways to flourish whereas during cooling periods, it struggles for survival."

"The last act proved to be anti-climatic," the man with the perpetual grin remarked.

The hulking black panelist rose. "Time to give you the hook, show-dog."

The celebrity waved his arms. "Before you ask me to leave, please, let's submit my plan to Charlton Shalom."

Weikert sprang to his feet. "We've been asking you to leave, muck-jaw, for two minutes now."

"Do we need to call security?" the woman threatened.

The African-American man started around the refectory table. "He'll leave quietly." Weikert bulldozed after him, and with the predictability of a wave of falling dominoes, every Parallacts associate except the woman followed. The black board member approached the celebrity. "You don't require assistance." He peered over his shoulder at his shadow convoy. "I'm going to the bathroom." He continued past the celebrity.

"We'll escort him to the door ourselves!" Weikert grabbed the celebrity's right sleeve. "Take an arm!" The panelist with the drawl clutched the celebrity's left wrist.

"Sorry your *coup de theatre* catastrophized." The associate with the perpetual grin guided the flying wedge toward the exit.

"Mr. Osboots," the man with the twang asserted, "you never did come around to citing the exact scientific principle by which your protective gaseous electric shell is locked in place over the North Pole, did you?"

"Hydrodynamic cavitation," the celebrity gasped.

Kevin gripped the celebrity's collar tightly. "You mean what hangs the haze over your hookah, you dope?"

The celebrity shook and shoved Weikert away. He whirled and punched Kevin in the chest, the intensity of the blow knocking both men to the plush, red carpet. The androgynous panelist dumped the pitcher of ice water on the supine celebrity, spattering the pants and erasing the grin of the avuncular board member. Weikert dived onto the celebrity, and the man with the drawl flopped aboard the chairman. "Here's a terrible parable on conflict resolution, peers," the avuncular associate admonished. Material ripped as the celebrity rolled and twisted. He bridged and squirmed out of the pile. He tried to spring to his feet but the gender-neutral board member clung to his right leg. He snapped his left foot into the individual's ribs, breaking at minimum the hold. He returned to his feet with the tuxedo beneath his knees, hopped and dodged a roundhouse punch from Kevin. "C'mon, folks, that's a wrap."

"Call Mercury!" Weikert bellowed.

The celebrity stomped free of his bunched garment and slippers and dashed naked into the Parallacts welcome center. Tiffany wasn't at her desk, but the other receptionist emitted a semi-shriek. The celebrity reached the main door and scrambled into the empty hallway. He sought refuge two doors down in the office of *Mittler & Owen LLP* but the door was locked. The next door was propped open, and he ducked inside the office. A woman cradling a large box dropped it and screamed. The celebrity roared with distress. "Where the hell's the locker room?" He hustled out of the office and sprinted to the stairwell at the end of the hallway. He charged down one flight of stairs and streaked unobserved into the "XY" room. It was unoccupied, and the motion-activated lighting engaged. He noticed that several ceiling tiles had been slid partially back. He rushed into the corner handicapped stall, hopped atop the railing and leapt to dislodge the two overhead ceiling tiles with his head and hand, respectively. The tile he struck with his cranium proved to be bolted in place. Stunned, he dropped to the floor, leaned against the stall wall and counted stars as he clutched his aching head. Security would probably conduct a sweep of the building, and he didn't want to face questions about his identity and intentions. He mounted the railing again and dislodged the fixed tile with his fist. He pulled his body into the dark, dusty space above the false ceiling and nimbly employed his feet to replace the tiles he'd dislodged. He curled around a thick padded pipe and wedged his body against a brick ledge. He squelched a coughing jag and rested his throbbing head.

At some point, he became aware that the stall beneath him was in use. Legs cramping and back aching, he considered the state of Operation Shalom. Notwithstanding its hasty improvisation, his presentation couldn't have resulted in a more miserable defeat unless a disguised Shalom wielding an alias had actually been one of the country club monsters he'd just faced. He snickered giddily. The board had gone so far as to assault the poseur. He rotated his head. He couldn't recall entertaining such a severe headache.

His mind transported him through his life's other outstanding washouts, notably the loss of his beloved Tina. Having pursued his high school sweetheart to the drama department at the University of California at Irvine, he'd devoted three years to treating her like a princess. In the end, she'd countered his declaration of eternal love with the contention that he was too available and too effusive for a man. Eight years later, he still couldn't purge her from his system. And if their paths never crossed again, his memory would indubitably favor her with the gift of incorruptible youth. Was he nothing but a puppet manipulated by the strings of his genetic hardwiring? Was he no more than a punctuation mark at the end of a biological imperative? If humankind was simply a product of evolutionary factors, why hadn't such self-effacing baggage as romanticism and sentimentality been extinguished long ago?

He cackled maniacally. He'd been inadvertently launched to a higher calling which left him suspended over a public lavatory. Upon hiring him, the Bureau had opened the vault and shown him the mission statement. The Studio was designed to enforce the idea that the law should be the servant, not the master, of its citizenry, with officers who were "invisible guardians of the crystal fountain of justice." Director Handsome Dan Aldred had modernized Aristotle's roadmap for the sublime life as an appeal to become a spy in the service of good government. If porky chunks of gobbledygook spiced with the taint of lobbyists were the ingredients of the law as currently constituted, serious rehabilitation was needed. His faith in government, like his religious faith, often ran on an awfully lean formula. But as the book of Ecclesiastes averred, "All life devoid of passion for something greater is only vanity and misfortune." He hoped Tina had found what she was seeking and married herself a slab of rare granite.

The celebrity gingerly dislocated a ceiling tile and observed darkness below. Having lingered at the top of the restroom long enough to foment an overall calm, he sought to procure clothing and leave the building. He dropped back into the handicapped stall. As he availed himself of the facilities, he considered whether to remain stationary and arrogate the next set of clothes that wandered into the "XY" or scrounge for garb around nearby offices. The latter option struck him as more expedient and humane. The door opened as he approached it, and Kevin entered. The celebrity opportunistically hugged the wide-eyed tobslar and ripped the Qilroy from his shoulder. Kevin clipped the celebrity's chin with a sneaky uppercut and clinched like an armchair predator. The two men exchanged grunts and expletives. The celebrity hooked the tobslar's arm and guided him to the floor in a hammerlock. He occupied Kevin's back and pressed his face into the floor. He maintained control with an oppressive knee and pulled up the tail of his blazer. "No belt, Kevin? You complicate everything."

The celebrity searched the tobslar's pockets. He confiscated a pouch of aromatic melon-scent snuff, a lighter and two handkerchiefs. "Cooperate in perfect silence, you testy, pushy corporate hack, and I won't reduce your chiseled features to a craggy ruins." He released him and rose. "Stay on your knees. Undo your tie and doff your blazer."

Kevin removed his necktie and blazer, respectively. He dangled the tie, flung the blazer and lunged to apply a furious elbow to the celebrity's knee. "*Help!!*" the tobslar wailed. "I'm being attacked by a lunatic!" The celebrity pounced on Kevin and muffled his outburst with his wadded blazer. He landed a triplet of punches to the scapulae and securely bound his wrists behind his back with his necktie. He yanked Kevin's pants and boxers down to his ankles. He leapt to his feet and continued pulling the tobslar's pants until they were inverted, the bottoms were stuck over his shoes and they'd been stretched their entire length.

The celebrity towed Kevin by his pants to a position in front of the handicapped stall. He affixed the pants buttonhole to the garment hook inside the door, propped the pants over the door and locked it so Kevin hung upside-down against the front of the stall. The celebrity gagged the tobslar with his handkerchiefs and donned the blazer.

The lavatory contained two paper towel dispensers, and the celebrity snatched the wastebasket beneath each. He retrieved Kevin's Qilroy, demanded the security code and sent Winterhalter an urgent message: "Cannot talk. Lost Qilroy. Need you to run commando raid on parking garage at Washington and Wells and pull me out. Put tracer on Glo-Ro and meet me at Level 2 with starter app. Confirm."

"You mean like now, Oobops?" the reagent grumbled. "*Face* up!"

The celebrity ensconced Kevin's head in one of the wastebaskets and stepped outside the "XY." He switched his communication mode to voice. "I.B., the Parallacts power-play went sideways, and I need you to extract me from the Loop." He verified the time as 1536 hours. "Shoot for 1700 hours."

"Goonter, Goonter, you gormless two-time loser." Winterhalter hissed. "Mad's about to go out and I have to fix my supper. Call me back after 1900 hours and peak traffic peters off."

"Winterhalter, wait!" the celebrity pleaded. "I'm about to go black so I can't be traced-"

"Blow it out your downtown ass, blue blubber clubber." I.B. narrowed his eyes. "If Mad ain't back and I got to charter another chariot, you don't want to be looking for me before eight, do you?" He terminated the connection.

The celebrity returned inside the "XY," where Kevin squirmed against his restraints. The celebrity produced a flame with the lighter and held it at the tobslar's crotch. "I'm still here, Kevin. You count to a thousand and one before you try to wiggle free. Otherwise, your loins are going to burn like they do for the masseuse, what's-her-name, Tiffany – and then some." Kevin stopped struggling.

The celebrity examined Kevin's Qilroy for anything that resembled a Shalom contact. Finding none, he smashed the sourcerer against the wall, hurled it against the floor and stomped on it. He collected the pieces and successfully flushed them in one of the toilets. "You need never go looking for pain and humiliation," he instructed the tobslar, "because enough is bound to find you naturally. If that's not in the Greenpeace manual, it ought to be." He snatched the wastebasket that Kevin wasn't wearing and carried it to the stairwell. His knee ached and he'd acquired a hitch in his gait. The guards at the security checkpoint on the ground floor were probably watching for him and intended to detain him.

Clad entirely in his borrowed Parallacts executive jacket, he took a deep breath and bolted down the steps as briskly as his tender knee would carry him. When he reached the fourth floor, he produced the lighter and set the contents of the wastebasket on fire. He added melon-scent snuff and emerged from the stairwell on the ground floor exhibiting the smoking receptacle and shouting orders to the security post. "Live fire! Open the door! Chemical fire!"

Adroitly producing a fire extinguisher, a security guard sprang to his feet. "No, no!" the celebrity screeched, waving his arm. "Class D!" He tapped his nose. "Fumes!" He hobbled past the security checkpoint. "Take it outside!" The guard with the extinguisher hustled to intercept the celebrity at the exit. He opened the inner door, and the celebrity squeezed past. "Guy tried to set off sprinklers for wet shirt contest!" The guard opened the outer door, and the celebrity scurried onto the sidewalk. He plunked the blazing wastebasket on the cement and slalomed between two groups of pedestrians. He heard the guard shout after him as he broke into a diminished dash down Wacker Drive. He turned the corner, crossed the street and continued hobbling until he was certain he wasn't being followed.

The celebrity returned to the parking garage where he'd left Winterhalter's Jeep Glory Roadster and located the locked muscle car. He took refuge in the box of a truck parked several vehicles away and waited. An hour or two later, he was forced to leap from the moving vehicle he'd adopted. He looked out at the dark sky and repositioned himself against the concrete barrier in front of the Glo-Ro. The reagent finally arrived. He started the Glory Roadster and dismissed his transport service. The celebrity approached him. I.B. shook his head. "With a partial clothing allowance, Oops, and after we supplied you with all that juicy intel, too." He climbed behind the wheel. "Were your legs too stubbled for their taste? I should've pitched those benders myself."

The celebrity retrieved his original pants of the day from the backseat. "You're bound to be a famous spy someday, Ib." He put on his pants and settled into the passenger's seat. "Only the most defective spies become famous."

"You're not a spy." The reagent gunned the Jeep out of its parking spot. "You've merely taken part in clandestine ops." The car zipped through the parking structure and onto the street. "That was the word from Uncle Dan even before you scored no schematic success scaring up what corporate closet Shalom is stashed in."

The celebrity kept silent until Winterhalter roared blindly around a corner and barely missed a pedestrian. "Drive like me," he gasped, "and I'll never ride with you again!" Apparently irked by the critical analysis of his motor skills, the reagent transferred full vehicular control to the auto-navigator guidance system until the Glory Roadster spun out on a winding section of the expressway.

Winterhalter intermittently switched between automated operation and manual override, and the celebrity lost track of what lights indicated which command mode was active. The celebrity experienced a wave of relief as the Jeep approached the Whispering Willowwacks condominium complex, but when I.B. displayed no inclination to avoid a collision with a Honda leaving the premises, the celebrity jerked the steering wheel, sending the Glo-Ro crashing into the fence supporting the *Whispering Willowwacks* sign. The Honda driver continued onward with horn blaring, while the celebrity and Winterhalter exchanged glares over deployed airbags. "You can drop me here." The celebrity climbed out of the vehicle and waited for the reagent on the stairs of the safe house.

Mah baby can take a contusion.
Our love is nuclear fusion.
Your life holds one grand delusion,
And that's that pain's an intrusion.
So there should be no confusion,
That crazy ol' baby of mine
Can-can take a contusion.

Mah lady gives me adulation.
Kick-start to fire big ovation.

You're rolled by rough stimulation,
But that's her balanced equation.
To guard against deviation,
That jaded li'l lady of mine
Wow-wow gives adulation.

3RD MOVEMENT

Inbound. 1105 CST Monday 27 March.

"Due to heavier-than-anticipated call volume, you're receiving a courtesy disconnect." While I.B. Winterhalter toiled in the parking lot to record his daily atmospheric measurements and repair the fence, the celebrity replaced his call to the secure line of D.C.I. Handsome Dan Aldred at the Santa Monica Prosecution Complex. Secretary Radmilla Eisenstadt answered again. He identified himself again. "Our call is important to you; please hold." Her voice message expressed regret for the delay at the top of each minute. Finally, she returned to the line. "Pardon me, is your call complete?"

"Exactly what," he quizzed her, "was the idea of blowing my cover, you perfidious, shell-headed fart of a woman?"

"Excuse me?" she challenged.

"You're beyond excuses!" He hissed. "You're a witless wonder, a xyster, a prion-riddled fried egg stalagmite! If you want me slaughtered, have the decency to do the dirty job yourself!"

Radmilla exhaled arrestively. "Mr. Oobops, you're a special pleasure. But please don't ask if I appreciate the snippy tone that accompanies your little salvos of insecurity."

"You undercut me flatling, and you can't appreciate the trouble you've caused! You're a punctilio toad, a mewling tocsin, a nettle bush pandour Pandora!"

Rad discharged a more exasperated breath. "I won't stoop to swap spitballs, but I really must wonder why you'd wish to be regarded as no more than some disgraced outlier who's only functional in the most undiplomatic of environments. How's the search for a new position progressing?" She placed him on automated hold, and her voice message expressed regret for the delay at the top of each minute.

A warning beep tone finally supplanted the recording, and a video-enhanced feed introduced Danforth O. Aldred. "Hello, Unique Agent Oobops, how go things on location in Chitown?"

"Inconsolably!" The celebrity stiffened himself with permafrost-grade professional detachment. "How's this for progress? Beyond the mud puddle of Shalom's past associates I've been able to drain through link-analysis, I have nothing. I tried to infiltrate a power brokerage think tank with alleged ties, and I invented a set of false references to support my assumed identity. When they made their routine background check, Raddy not only refused to validate my cover story but informed them point-blank that I was a state of California spy who'd been terminated!"

"Ah, the dangers of deceit." Aldred cleared his sinuses. "Rad's not required to extend reference amenities to a former asset. Even though you're our agent, the official records show your current status as post-employment entitlement recipient retained as minor independent contractor in the disposition of the duties of perfunctory ethical consultant. I realize this policy has the potential to not only threaten the integrity of our operation but also to become a legal quagmire. When the select tribunal of review convenes to consider your reinstatement appeal, you might raise the point in hopes that they petition the council of censors to revise and clarify the facade protocol for future cases."

The celebrity felt his jaw grow lug-nut tight. "In this case," he finally uttered, "Raddy's facade protocol resulted in a boardroom brawl which accorded me the physical safety of a piñata, accorded me a fair degree of personal humiliation and compromised our efforts to the point that our mission may have been rendered impossible to accomplish."

Aldred rubbed his temporal scar. "That's not an appropriate attitude for an operative at any level of this organization, particularly one with due regard for the honor and sacrifice which have preceded him. To be more evergreen, when your teammate dribbles the ball, you pick it up. Embrace one of our baseline best-practices: It's generally more expedient to borrow a facade than to build one. Either way, I'm as personally fond of Rad as I am of you, so would you propose that with dyspeptic paroxysms of gastrointestinal complaint I endorse her discharge as the Q.C. sanctioned yours? Perhaps Radmilla felt that in forcing you to confront a resistance, she was furnishing you with the grist to retool a greater legend. But even if she'd had no moral footing for her improvident initiative, I refuse to direct an office full of assets who've already been terminated."

The celebrity began pacing and patting his marbled abdominal muscles for reassurance. "Throw your full weight into the role of the bully pulpiteer, Handsome Dan. Perhaps you could conduct an unofficial pep rally with Raddy wherein the two of you discover some other proviso which might compel her to promote the success of our operation."

"Oh, don't be such a sadist." The director patted his hair. "I'm cocksure there's nothing Rad wouldn't do for me. If you have an issue with the woman, finesse her to the marrow. Unless you are in fact in the wrong profession." He bared all of his teeth in what could loosely be termed a grin. "At any rate, Ahab, there's exciting news back here in Santa Monica. I've been grappling with a special project and it's come to fruition. I'm changing my name – from Danforth Oakleaf Aldred to Philander Taboo Ledbetter. You may reference me with the unofficial appellation of 'National' or 'Natty.'"

"You're wha-" The celebrity rubbed his neck. "But why?"

Ledbetter hiccuped. "It's so unexpected it's brilliant. There's no reason for it, and that's the whole point. Our enemies will exhaust their resources trying to determine who Philander Ledbetter is. If it's the same individual as Danforth Aldred, why the change? Shhh, Ahab, listen."

The celebrity hesitantly broke the silence. "What is it?" he whispered. "Do you think a collector has decrypted our conversation? Should we switch to elevated code?"

Ledbetter hissed. "Oobops, you galloping galumph-in-the-night, my conversation is always laced with elevated code. Listen." Another minute elapsed. "That's the sound of our enemies' A.I. analytics systems crashing in frustration at their inability to unravel the logic of the name change."

"So is that 'Leadbetter' with or without an 'a'?" The celebrity squelched the compulsion to punch the screen. "A partial name change would cost the same in administrative fees and contain even less potential strategic advantage, so wouldn't it be even more senseless and hence more insidious? You could be Danforth Oakleaf Augustus, but instead of 'Handsome,' you might dub yourself 'Pretty Officer.' Or how about a cutesy name like Roman Homan or S.P. Espy or Casper Wyoming? Or how about a tough, streetwise name like Jimmy Pondscum? Better yet, how about a singular name with no vowels like Tj? The sound of the tide crashing against the rocks on the Monterey County coastline: Tj! Tj!" A silent hiss emanated from the D.C.I. "You're a maniac, Handsome Dan. Er, I'm so sorry. Why the name 'Philander'?"

Ledbetter exhibited a smug, tight-lipped countenance. "The mellifluous progression of syllables recalls the indomitable nomenclature of my chic college coterie like Claire Dieringer, Morgen Tillinghast, Pim Watchorn-"

"Toby Bilderberg!" The celebrity drew a glare from the director. "A chapter of dashing elitist glowworms destined to run the world through names that ring with androgyny. Who can imagine what any one of you might've become with a name exclusively suited for a Type A mega-bull dripping with predatory testosterone? Of course, there's excellent precedent for a name change in the intelligence industry. When President Truman ordered the abolition of the OSS in 1945, the enterprise was only able to survive by changing its name to the Strategic Services Unit." He chortled. "Hell, the Real Deal reminds us that no unpopular government program has to end if it can just acquire a new name."

"In reply to your last relevant logomachy, Oobops, there is no 'a' in 'Ledbetter.'" The D.C.I. cleared his sinuses. "My wife and I have been experiencing some marital discord, so the name selection became ironically appropriate, the by-product of a harmonic convergence."

"At the risk of upsetting the cosmic equilibrium," the celebrity confided, "I could use a harmonic convergence or two myself. I'd also like to lodge a complaint against my *reagent*. Is he really your nephew? His unfavorables crest abnormally high; he's been something on the dark side of cooperative."

Ledbetter scowled. "Yes, I.B. contacted me earlier this morning while you remained undercover in the roll of a sleeper agent. He indicated that you spent the better part of the weekend under the influence of a mind-altering anodyne, that you've unsuccessfully tried to infiltrate his personal files, shake down his female attache, and you commandeered and crashed his vehicle."

The celebrity waxed irate. "With all due respect, Handsome Dan, er, Phil, your nephew is a cockle, a guttersnipe, a lowlife punk, a tin soldier, a schlomo, a saddle-burr duff-wart. So far he and his gamy girlfriend have been about as beneficial as a bar-soap-bottom boat with a rubber rudder."

The director's gaze became glassier. "I recently received a cell-powered sailing pleasure-craft which utilizes a hard rubber rudder to superb advantage. I assured Winterhalter that you're famous for being straighter than a laser and if you ever sucked rock it would most definitely be in the interest of achieving a Bureau objective. I find it deplorable, however, that you've deigned to repay the kindness he extended in opening his safe house to you after hours by betraying him with scurrilous allegations. Don't oblige me to remind you that he is a vested employee of the Bureau and you are not." The D.C.I. produced the ice pick and traced his scar. "I.B.'s a rat terrier; he's an earthy, conniving, unscrupulous son of a bitch."

"Your sister's boy?" the celebrity inferred.

Ledbetter mussitated. "If I were you, I'd keep him upwind from word about your termination from the Bureau, but he's a good man to have at hand. He'll no doubt prove invaluable if you channel him properly. Treat him as your little black-bag life preserver."

The celebrity nodded. "And his safe house as a halfway house to a row house, an environment where even a distinguished spiritual director might find himself reduced to hurling vulgar invectives. We could work around I.B.'s inspired incompetence, but it's his insolent unreliability that really concerns me."

"You could trust him with your sister, provided her jaw is as square as yours." The director sneered. "I'm becoming extremely disappointed in you, Oobops. You've suggested that virtually everyone in the Studio has intentionally thwarted your efforts. Are you gunning for a retroactive paranoia-related disability discharge? Frankly, your entire report equates to a scabrous personal cowardice and laziness."

The celebrity snatched the central backup remote unit off the table and whacked the image of Natty Phil Ledbetter on the screen. The transmission popped. "I'm too scared to bring it up and I'm too slack to look it up, but wasn't it the Great Martyr himself who said, 'Just because you're paranoid doesn't mean they're not out to get you?' Are you suggesting, P.L., that I needn't alert you to problems affecting the success of our operation which you could remedy, particularly when those problems are systemic in the working core of the Bureau?"

Appearing blind with frustration, Ledbetter fingered his scar and repeatedly jabbed the ice pick into his desktop. "Hello," he snarled, "hello, Oobops, hello! Display some of the finely-honed leadership skills to which you bear close witness! It's entirely your responsibility to foster the instrument of your organizational resources in the field, secure the submission of your support personnel and arrange for the expedition of your project objectives. It's a fool who circumvents betrayal by never embracing trust; death by water is just as inexorable as death by fire. Operation Shalom provides you with unparalleled opportunity to expropriate merit you could present before the select tribunal of review to bolster your case for reinstatement."

Ledbetter stopped speaking but continued stabbing his desktop. The celebrity sought to extend a mollifying branch before the director misinterpreted his own fury and arranged to have one or both of them harmed. "I'm reminded of the days organizing my rock band, Natty Phil. It was our first big gig, a packed house, and we go into the intro for 'Liquid Hammer', the trickiest surf song ever attempted, and nobody but me plays a note because they're frozen with fright. So after alerting the lads that as a progressive rock movement, petrified wood was a gateway to stomped fingers and crushed genitals, I kept them positively honest for the rest of the show with frequent shouts of encouragement like 'Whet your razors, stick-men!' and 'Take off the mittens, axe-grinders!' and 'Blow your fuses, pop-tops!'"

Ledbetter patted his hair and the ice pick disappeared. "Ah, to shred the tracks of swell legends with three chords and some attitude. I would infer that your insolent nature ordained you a superb flautist as well but you're aware I've received complete medical immunity to musical influence." He bared his teeth. "Do yourself a favor, Oobops, and recognize that you're not on tour back there."

"I've experienced a technical problem with a chunk of

my Operation Shalom treatment," the celebrity progressed to the original reason for his call. "Certain modules are indecipherable, interlaced with *Diplomatic Clearinghouse* Tagalog or Yappese language course drills." He paused to allow the D.C.I. an opportunity to recall that cases of Bureau files containing corruption in the form of *Diplomatic Clearinghouse* Series language crash courses had recently been reported. "If Winterhalter's information packet is the same as mine, could you instruct him to give me full access to his treatment? I want to make certain I'm not missing a beat-"

"Instead of soliciting a new cane and catheter, Ahab, just lick your thick pick, wet your stomp box and moisturize your sound." Ledbetter pressed his thumb and forefinger against his brow. "Wasn't a guide to the establishing shot of the operation presented in the subliminal incubatory preview to which you were treated while still languishing in Nicaragua? The rest is nothing but logistics." He launched a coughing fit. "I'll expect your fustian in exactly 46 hours, embedded with decryption-thwarting chatter of classical Oceanian buzzwords. If at that time you still believe that you personally or the mission itself are in jeopardy, I'll send a makeup artist to cover your ass."

The celebrity winced mightily. "That's not the standard Studio threat that precedes your order for a critic to shut down operations, is it?"

"No, this is." The director hiccuped. "Complying with all applicable regulatory requirements, Oobops, do whatever it takes to get the job completed." He terminated the connection.

"May your whammy bar always be at odds with your wah-wah pedal, Tj-head." The celebrity allowed his frustration level to supersede any concern that the standard Studio phone burp trap would provide the D.C.I. with his post-conversation salutation. He commanded the computer to call Jason Padata. He felt demoralized by P.L.'s impromptu harangue even though the director was likely to have already forgotten most of it. He'd been given until Wednesday to put Operation Shalom on course for a favorable resolution or he could expect another operative to wrest control of the mission. He left an urgent message for Padata to return his call.

The celebrity wondered what Ledbetter had meant by advising him that all of his conversations were laced with elevated code. Was the statement itself a ploy on the unlikely chance that they were being monitored or had Natty Phil been imparting a cryptic message? Had the name change provided the key necessary to decode the communique or was each time he touched his scar or produced the ice pick a signal? "Big Sir" was the only elevated code name by which the celebrity had ever heard the director refer to himself. He replayed the entire conversation and worked into the afternoon analogizing it against the Black Chamber cryptanalysis software from the Bureau library in an attempt to decipher deeper meaning in the D.C.I.'s transaction. He garnered gibberish and noise, and he moved onward with brute force against the strong encryption of Winterhalter's files. He staged a sham hostile takeover of the quantum computer and borrowed some of the Q.C.'s own unprotected qubits to turn the processing unit against its own private key. He believed that he made progress, but when the incursive smoke of the yottaflops cleared, his backshaft mining operation had been repulsed. He shook out of the clammy grip of a lost battle and camouflaged bot subsets in preparation to strike again.

When Winterhalter returned inside, the celebrity took a break and confronted him. "Did you tell Uncle Ph-, er, Fancy-Dan-Sir I spent the weekend on a drug bob?"

I.B. removed a ray gun from his toolbox. "Hey, I don't deceive the guy unless there's something in it for me. You want to profess that the back room of Barbee's Blues Bakery is a church or a college laboratory, that's ricochet, but if you want me to fluff your fakery, you ought to start by clarifying where the half-day you lost Friday afternoon is." He pointed his gun at the celebrity and the trigger buzzed harmlessly.

The celebrity laughed with exasperation. "You're going to find out exactly where." He retrieved Evans's slightly worn blazer and presented it to the reagent. "Toss this inside the Parallacts Associates conference room door on your way out." He imparted specific instructions on how to ask the Parallacts receptionists for his briefcase and his new suit and shoes. I.B. reacted with startling amenability and left the condominium immediately. The celebrity left another urgent message with Padata. Madelyn had mercifully excused herself earlier beneath a full morion of pitch-blue curls to run a series of "involved errands," and the celebrity found himself completely unencumbered with distractions. He labored intently into the evening trying to hack into Winterhalter's operation files and crack Ledbetter's chat code. He remained perfectly unsuccessful at both endeavors and developed a high-tension headache. Shortly before 2300 hours, a house phone announcement proclaimed that Governor Tierney Roache was calling from the California State Prison at San Quentin. "Maundermacher," the celebrity answered in a mumbled croak.

"*Ja*, muscle tov?" The granular video transmission appeared to present a naked female with arms stretched overhead. "Have you advanced to speaking German, Oobops?" The male voice rang vaguely familiar. "Upon failing to infiltrate a dark shadow facilitator group with foreign ties, you've decided to settle for a dank one – like DANK." The resolution of the image improved to the point that the body of a dark-haired woman with her back to the cam could be discerned. "*Wahr*, the Deutsch Amerikanischer National Kongress is headquartered here in Illinois, but you're trying to wedge your way into Wisconsin lederhosen." Suspended by the strap connecting her wrists, the woman hung from a stout pipe. "Pity." She seemed to be clad exclusively in a leather halter and twin garters. The end of a long belt whipped her superb bare buttocks. "This is Jerry Mercowitz." The camera backtracked at the statement to reveal a horrible creature wielding the belt. "*Ich bin ein Milvaukeean.*"

The fiend looked something like a cross between a camel and a dragon, and he lashed the woman's buttocks again. "So how do you like who you're messing with?"

The camera zoomed in for a close-up. The celebrity knew that he'd heard the name before, but the chimera's large, furry nose, scaly pointed ears and cruel, opaque eyes stymied his already fatigued cognitive abilities. "Jerry Mercowitz?" he required further identification.

"We enjoyed fisticuffs over coffee on Friday." A hairy hand with long, twisting claws removed the head of the frightful beast and revealed the older man with the perpetual smile from the Parallacts Associates board. "Jason Padata requested that I contact you and suggest you stop pestering him before he reports you to the police. But I'm also calling because we control something of yours, and I'd like to arrange an exchange."

The celebrity winced. He should've anticipated that even the lightest task would provide *Wunderkind* Winterhalter with ample opportunity to maneuver his way into captivity. "Congratulate the jar-witted chock trooper on the unadulterated mutilation of the assignment. He should knit a coat of mail out of the tripwires he's collected around his ankles. If you're assaying his value against a stockpile of California's strategic reserves, you're looking at cigarettes, nylon stockings and chocolate bars."

Mercowitz's smile grew a lumen brighter. "As a man who brokers deals for a living, let me advise you that you're at a significant disadvantage-"

"Not having brought," the celebrity interrupted, "a beekeeper's mask or a bullfighter's cape to the bargaining table?" He considered the ethics of a situation where one secretly desired to forfeit a hostage. He strained against the temptation to grossly lowball himself out of an agreement but reasoned that he should attempt to warp such a natural bargaining advantage into a more favorable settlement. "Since my passion to toss him out of your office window will only consume me until I'm driven to strong drink, let me offer you a case of Chardonnay vintage ought when conditions for growing the trophy grape in the Napa Valley were still ripe."

"I recognize that L.A. tops poll after poll as the meanest and most mind-numbing place in America." Mercowitz's shifty look might've fazed a fainter bridge-builder. "But you should realize two things before embarking on a bare-assed streak of bargain-striking embarrassment: one, the fair market value of the object that we covet – Kevin Evans's blazer – is far exceeded by not only your own suit coat itself but your pair of pants, shoes and briefs, not to mention the person who'll model it; and two, we could all probably profit by publicly remaining foes while quietly cooperating with each other. No one need toss in a giant wooden horse full of anything else."

The shot deepened to show the woman slip her wrists from their ties and nimbly drop to the floor. She grabbed a tan hemp power suit coat from the back of a chair and slipped into it. She turned to face the camera, which zoomed in to capture the radiant head and cleavage of CIB Unique Agent Teretsara Tohnyin. "How did you like my Quentin call announcement spoof, Ahab?" Tess pointed at the camera. "After your fade, I was nominated to follow your trajectory into downtown Chicago's finest luxury suites, where you see Jerry and I are currently pursuing extraordinary back channels to restore trust and repair relations."

"Tess!" The celebrity staggered and murmured. "Tess," he pressed Mercowitz, "not I.B., is what you have? That's not mine."

The camera swung back for a more panoramic view as Tohnyin gave Mercowitz a light peck on the cheek. "Ahab has an open option on my heart the moment he destroys himself to prove worthy of it." She plunged her tongue into Jerry's ear.

"He could surely earn an urn by turning that sharp wit on himself." Mercowitz's smirk endured as Tohnyin tugged on his fuzzy mitts to aid in removing them. "The lady got your I.B. to spill his guts upon enticing him to chug a pitcher of Yosemite Jack." Jerry sucked air as Tess peeled the costume pelt from his bare, tanned torso. "He's now recuperating off-camera."

"Yes," the celebrity attempted to conceal his dismay, "men who mess with Tess tend to require recuperation. She could fill her own I.C.U."

The camera captured a medium close shot of Tohnyin against Mercowitz's smooth belly. She had the perfect countenance for a spy. Her high, arching eyebrows accented penetrating jade orbs, and the corners of her mouth curved naturally upward, so she always appeared as though she'd caught the individual in the crosshairs of her focus in a compromised position. Her raven hair, now nape short, possessed irrepressible poof and an almost iridescent luster. At their introduction, the celebrity had found himself continually checking his fly and shoe heels for improprieties. "Fold my hands behind my back, bondage girl," Jerry instructed her.

"You were saying, Tess," the celebrity interjected, "you brought your heart-shaped bedlam into town under the guise of a floating penal institution in order to take down some hard targets?"

Tohnyin sneered. "Pay attention, Ahab." She moved behind Mercowitz. "It seems the little huddle you had with the erstwhile Handsome man this morning upset him immoderately. He called me away from my civic art project to come up here and bail you out of your snafu. I.B. informed me this afternoon that *Uncle Dan* called him and directed him to sneak away from you and meet me. I pumped him for the situation underground but the well quickly ran dry, his recalcitrance superseded only by his fatuousness." She kissed Mercowitz on the neck. "So I took the scant scuttlebutt he spared out to the street and to the Parallacts office. I introduced myself as a Nebula Foundation endowment committee rep investigating your disappearance, and they delegated Jerry to give me an eyewitness revision."

"I volunteered." Mercowitz ogled Tohnyin. "Kevin Evans is still under the weather." He lightly caressed Tess's lips.

"Is that the Skull Nebula, Tess?" The celebrity stood with fists on hips. "It's amazing what you can accomplish when you waste no sweat on guilt and shame."

Mercowitz smirked. "Ahab, that sounds like the prebabble to a monorail of considerable beration. Our desire is that you'll assist us in conducting a longitudinal study measuring the impact of inconceivably clean government policy on inconceivably clean energy potential." He squatted and Tess straddled him. "The lady is on the urge of seizing the patriotic moment with knowledge shared on a need-only basis to test liquidity in a high-yield-curve environment with wide bid spreads."

"Don't beguile Ahab." Tohnyin cackled. "We worry about how much he gets ass-backwards. He's trying to make it through life with a rigid rear and a flaccid front." She squeezed Jerry's head between her thighs. "People with a diminished capacity to experience sensual pleasure generally compensate by trampling the downtrodden, gobbling up the property of the vulnerable and starting wars."

Mercowitz grunted and chuckled. "I thought that prognosis was the province of people with common sense of humor deficiency."

"He has that condition working for him, too." Tess ran her hands through Jerry's hair. "I don't buy it, but a prevailing trade-wind of office gossip theorizes that Ahab wears his protective cup too tight and he's had his kumquats pickled." She hopped forward and faced the camera squarely. "I.B. informed me you wasted the entire weekend in a chemically induced nimbus of heightened detachment."

"And you believe it?" Ten minutes with her always brought him to the precipice of ranting. "How overprivileged I am to have friends in low places. Tess, I need to speak with you privately."

Mercowitz slipped out of his handcuffs and swept Tohnyin

out of viewing range in a bear hug. "Oh, yes," she purred. "Being unable to perform equates to extreme frustration, maybe to a lifetime of silent and unhealthy rage. Never, never suppress it!" Their mutual off-camera giggles and groans forged a fuliginous harmony. "Breathe deep, so deep, stretch, oh, yes; full, powerful range of motion."

"Strong, long strokes!" The passion in Mercowitz's playfully plaintive reply probably peeled some paint.

"Tess!" the celebrity demanded.

Tohnyin's refulgent short haircut and buttermilk smooth left scapula finally crept into the lower right corner of the frame. She cast the classic furtive glance over her shoulder. "Still there, Little Bo Peephole? Did you want to bloviate some sensitive information regulations about Jerry's security clearance? Possibly remind me that he might not be overly trustworthy, and that thanks to your inadvertent tutelage he could now know too much?" She planted a kiss on her fingertip and relayed it to some strategic point on the Parallacts associate's body. "If Jerry knew too much, we'd have to eliminate him as an imminent threat, wouldn't we?" She flashed a frosty grin. "If he refuses to cooperate, I'll have to imprison his precious heart, maybe place him under cardiac arrest."

"See that I'm hung for high crimes!" Jerry reappeared in the picture. "Infuse your campaign with transformidable execution! Electra-cute me!"

"Tragic Tess continually suffers breath-taking lapses in judgement that ruin those around her." The celebrity smiled complaisantly. "I'd calculate my margins accordingly."

"As artificial sweeteners go," Mercowitz riposted, "she's on a punsch-roll to be a *tour de force* of nature."

Tohnyin rewrapped her torso in the celebrity's suit coat and approached the camera. "Jerry doesn't know too much, tinkle-head; he only knows what you should." She drew claustrophobically close. "He knows where we can locate Charlton Shalom." She blew a kiss.

"I knew it!" The celebrity smacked his fist into his open hand. "Shalom's the one who grabbed me on Friday; he's the understated transvestite!" A tremor of dread overtook him. "Oh no, I kicked him in the gut! Is he all right?"

The exuberant laughter of Mercowitz could've filled a wing of luxury suites. "You didn't kick Shalom," he hooted. "That was Frank Marasculco, but thanks for asking about her!" Jerry shoved his head beside Tess's. "She's fine; she thoroughly enjoyed herself; would you like her address?"

Tess smiled like a big sister. "She sounds like the one, Ahab, you unnatural man. It's going to be real."

"Just," the celebrity grumbled through his humiliation, "give me Shalom's address."

"Charlton Shalom has never been affiliated with Parallacts Associates," Mercowitz submitted, "but before some of us revitalized this group a few years ago, it went by the name of Perigee Analysts and maintained a loose connection with Lincoln Worbley, who you're aware was Shalom's adaptive geo-engineer for pet projects like the polar shade. When Perigee melded into Parallacts, Worbley drifted off to an alternative group since disbanded called Paradox Partners, which you're probably aware provided convenient cover for another unrelated group with a nearly identical name practicing extreme organized medical fraud. But in the ashes of Paradox's implosion, some of the personnel reshuffled themselves into a green projects hub consortium named Pedigree Consociates Ltd, with coastal spokes known as the Paramount Players in the West and the Pentagon Players in the East, respectively." Jerry and Tess rubbed cheeks. "The larger the galaxy, the faster it spins. Tell me when your furrowed bean stops revolving and I'll continue circumnambulating."

"Thanks for the confusion, Padata." The celebrity patted his Olympic-sized triceps. "So now I need to go before another board and cultivate more carnage?"

"Try incorporating a little finesse into your arsenal, rumble-muffin." Tohnyin swept her hair back and held her hand on her occiput like a fashion model. "Save some money on physical therapy."

"Jason likes to play tiles he doesn't hold." Mercowitz's meandering fingertips slid across the shallow slope of Tohnyin's shoulders. "Charlton wouldn't sit for any board of directors. He's also reputed to be bitterly estranged from his nuclear family, so your best odds of sinking your eager tentacles into his esteemed matzos ride not on cornering him in a board-room but in a barroom. There's a floating club haunted by the shady diaspora of legal, military and academic intelligentsia in Lake Geneva, Wisconsin, where he's said to be no accidental stranger, and you might have a loaded chance to mix mitzvahs. I'll *whisk* you up there and *once in* you can pinpoint and pin-wheel him." Tess pinched Jerry's cheek.

"So you've actually met the quintessential man?" the celebrity challenged. "You know him?"

"Know him?" Mercowitz beamed. "As fortune would have it, we served together on the same jury just last month. False witness injury case. Are you *shlumpf* enough to believe that, Oobops?" He snickered. "But honest onus, you once-bitten, ball-busting balkanizer, I encountered Shalom light-years ago as a student at the University of Wisconsin. He was supposed to be the teaching postdoc in a Gravitation, Cosmology and Astrophysics course, and I was one of the stable flies yawing about the pions, WIMPs and show particles that kept the physics fizzing. Me and old Chuckles once even shared a unilarity in a warped effort to make some space-time with a pair of swimsuit models, but I'm confident he wouldn't know me from Isaac now. He couldn't recall a proper name to save his monads *then*. He was simultaneously enrolled in multiple universities, but in researching his history for Tess, I couldn't find evidence that he ever spent more than three successive semesters at any particular institution of higher learning or was awarded a traditional Ph.D. by anyone."

"He's an irrational numbers guy," the celebrity theorized, "and four seems to be his sore one. Would you describe him as a free radical?"

Jerry's grin grew almost pensive. "Observing him over an extended period led me to conclude that he had one leg planted squarely in another dimension." He wrapped Tess's arm around his neck. "For your sakes, I hope he hasn't yet slid all the way to the other side."

"That would present a definite conflict of interest," the celebrity conceded. "And you've actually encountered Shalom at this club in Wisconsin?"

"It's not a trap, Oobops." Mercowitz winked. "It's a lead."

Tess offered an innocent smile. "We'll tie Winterhalter to the carriage as our jaunty hood ornament, and we'll be around to pick you up in front of your safe house around four tomorrow afternoon." She turned back to Jerry, and the shot widened. "That is, unless you're sleuth enough to uncover our whereabouts tonight and rescue me from the clutches of this bad, bad man."

Mercowitz and Tohnyin giggled. He dipped her, flipped her and drew her over his knee. "Bring Evans's blazer," Jerry directed the celebrity.

"And prepare to share your Shalom dossier," Tess commanded, "so I can review it before we redeploy."

"Don't sully my suit!" The celebrity emitted a silent growl as the Parallacts associate spanked Tess. "You can't beat old-fashioned child-rearing practices, huh?"

"I'm going to give her such a moonburn, we can fill the tub with her tears!" The camera tilted upward. "*Auf Wiederhoren*, Oobops!" The conversation was terminated.

The celebrity considered whether Mercowitz had intended to convey a warning by ending the communication with a crisp spanking. He pondered whether Tohnyin had attempted to convey a surreptitious message, or whether the entire transaction had been a charade for his or Jerry's benefit. Tess liked to project the bawdy image of a wanton seductress, and the celebrity wondered how often the role engendered consequences detrimental to herself and the Studio. He weighed what he'd just discovered about Shalom. He now had a search epicenter, but the source of Jerry's information needed to be vetted.

The celebrity toiled diligently into the morning to decrypt the conversations he'd had with Ledbetter and Tohnyin but his efforts only yielded more snags and bumps. He fell into a cold, uneasy sleep at the computer terminal, tormented by anticipated complications of Tess falling into enemy hands. The day's exchanges had scrambled the total picture as much as they'd resolved it.

Outbound. 1645 CST Tuesday 28 March.

"*Achtung*, anathema-breath, take a seat and take a stand against ecological chaos." The cut-lip helicon stylings of Homeless Twede Pringo surged from the Ford Passenger Pigeon cabin when the eagerly awaited ground-effect craft arrived beneath a silver lunar cuticle. The crimson-and-chrome gref's peg-edged sawtooth wings and dual tail, which had all remained tucked in pike position for its side-street-legal crawl along the Whispering Willowwacks development, were extended and lowered. "Step up and put your foot down, sod-tamper." The celebrity slipped as he started barefoot up the slick wing ramp, and he halted outside the cabin to adjust his candy-striped seersucker zoot suit with metallic maraschino cherry buttons. Tess Tohnyin at the designer control pedestal with personalized instrument cluster directed him to the backseat beside I.B. Winterhalter. Seated next to Tess in his red crushed velvet dinner jacket with black lapels, Jerry Mercowitz surveyed the celebrity from head to toe. "Jay Gatsby, I presume?"

"Let's hope not." Tohnyin winced. "I've always considered Fitzgerald the great overrated twerp of the early 20th century literocracy."

"Oobops has a trashability that extends beyond any particular time and place," Winterhalter volunteered.

The celebrity flipped Kevin Evans's blazer onto Mercowitz's lap. "I.B.'s accompanying us?" He nodded and dropped heavily into his seat, eliciting an obscene salute from the reagent. "My briefcase?"

"Seersucker is never out of style with the southern gentleman, is it, Ahab?" Jerry turned to face the celebrity, his hand anchored on Tess's shoulder. "It's cool. It radiates a loose, laissez faire leadership expectation and an understated integrity." He passed the celebrity his Lord Clarksdale loafers and black socks. "It's folksy yet genteel. It's edgy." He winked at I.B. and smirked. "And they consider attractive, affluent homosexual couples quite cute at the club as long as they remain the novelty and not the norm."

"Up your square, terminally puckered ass, partner." Winterhalter reached beneath his seat and produced the briefcase. He sported an open patchwork madras jacket over a gossamer shirt and fuchsia leather pants that conformed to the overstated articulation of his lower body.

"Thank you, I.B." The celebrity clutched the briefcase. "I apologize for the mixture of dread and dismay with which I've been regarding you." The reagent maintained his hold on the briefcase until the celebrity wrested it from his grasp.

Tohnyin leveled a cordial smile. "Your suit is safely nestled in my garment bag." The Pigeon canopy bubble locked shut. "Why are you wearing so much body armor, Ahab? Anyone who gets a glimpse of you is going to figure you're some self-styled suburban desperado out to go pounding on trouble's door."

"A thick, slow-walking peppermint stick of maelstrom-spuming, head-thumping proportion," Mercowitz commented, "with something noxious to conceal."

The celebrity flicked an imaginary speck of dirt at Winterhalter. "If I'm squiring I.B., you better believe I have something noxious to conceal." He placed the briefcase beneath his seat.

"By day some prima domo's dungeon-dwelling dust bunny," the reagent snarled, "after dark he's Sir Caltrop Hoo-Hah Cartouche – the Knobshire knight spy."

"Shuck the shields," Tohnyin exhorted. She wore her fashion goggles and a salmon Ultra-Chic trench coat, one of the closetful of trench garments in assorted colors she seemed to carry wherever she traveled.

I.B. draped his arm around the celebrity. "Tess, stop nutrolling my ruggedly scrumptious suite matey."

"Make sure he's strapped in as the last thing before you make sure you are." Tohnyin upgraded the view beyond the cockpit bubble to an infrared display. The engine rumbled, and the Pidge shook as it lifted and rotated on a pocket of air. The gref reseated itself on its belly-pan rollers, the wings and tails returned to pike position, and it haltingly headed to the condominium parking lot exit.

"Shalom, shuddering shrubbery," Mercowitz bid as the Passenger Pigeon clipped the *Whispering Willowwacks* landscaped rock and forfeited a mirror. Tohnyin adroitly fishtailed the vehicle so wing damage was averted, and the craft successfully engaged cul-de-sac traffic. "Oncoming headlights look pretty dull and cool in infrared mode, hmm?" Jerry produced a cigarette.

Winterhalter leaned forward and scrounged a smoke. "Does this scow you're shooting us into sponsor any roughhouse activities to hold the attention of a healthy, young man while he's scouring around for an old sundog?"

"They do offer light jousting at the casino," Mercowitz advised. "Often, combat is joined in drag." He winked at the celebrity. "Knights in white satin?"

"An unsuitable idea for someone with a seasonal affective disorder." Tohnyin eyed the celebrity with irritation. "You have sundown syndrome, don't you, Ahab?" She turned back to Jerry. "He becomes habitually agitated at nighttime. Adding padding only serves to remove suppression."

"I presume the Pidge is a lease," the celebrity threw a subterfuge counterjab. "If you thought we really need a gref, Tess, why didn't you select a more maneuverable, more invisible and less pricey Gurnard or Corsair?"

"I selected this model," Mercowitz confessed. "Enviro-Tess insisted on a gilded glider with a biodegradable future, and this is the only green gref that doesn't come standard with bobsled-style cramming in the cockpit." He extended his arm in a promotional gesture. "Once inside the lightweight composite vehicle body, feel the mesh velour fabric seats, check out the walnut trim and savor the rich ambient 3D virtual sound with perfectly tuned crosstalk cancellation. The current voice-controlled cabin temperature is a perfect 21.5 degrees." His grin tested the elasticity of his skin. "Hopefully, comfort, prestige and stylishness may find some *resonance* with you."

"Flatboat Ahab finds such banausic refinements as swagger and attitude vile." Tohnyin cast a peremptory glance over her shoulder. "And I.B. informed us how invisible the vehicle *you* rented proved to be."

The celebrity smiled at the back of her head. "Don't be overeager to iterate every gossip oik that skitters across your chatterbox index, Scheherazade. Take a lesson from the finer country music divas, and give us more image and less sound."

Tess hissed. "Make yourself clubbable, Oobops. If nothing else, fix it to fake it."

The celebrity sat back and gazed through the clear bubble top, contemplating the vapor streamers that emanated from the fluffy violet cirrus sash which cut a ribbon through the orange-grey dusk. The Pidge reached its Highway 31 objective and its ordered grooves settled over the shoulder causeway on a "solid cushion of air" speeding past terrestrial vehicles with what Mercowitz termed "easement and ascendancy."

Tohnyin activated the auto-navigator with drift control

and searched for a middle-of-the-road music channel serving more salutary driving fare. Requests were rejected, and the cabin was subjected to the raw, sneering strains of "Let Me Be Your Carpool Corporal" by the Three Marketeers. The Pidge auspiciously reached the Illinois community of Geneva on the northern border of Batavia and swiftly left it behind. The occasional stranded vehicle required expenditure of "power shift" and "power lift" avoidance thrusters, while roadside debris lent a few speed bumps to a ride otherwise distinguished by the manufacturer's touted "magic carpet smoothness."

An ebb and flow of whispers and giggles passed between Mercowitz and Tohnyin as the backseat palaver staggered through ever-dwindling spurts. "I have an anger management disability that requires an accommodation under the new A.D.A. mandate," Winterhalter submitted. "I have about as much control over my temper as a windmill does over the wind."

The landscape turned overwhelmingly bucolic as the celebrity consulted his Qilroy for real-time satellite imagery of a state armory at Camp Douglas. "So it sits up at the top of the U.S. map like a sore thumb," he snapped a taciturn spell. "What's it like – this Wisconsin?"

"Imagine a more frigid Illinois," Mercowitz explained. "Although don't deploy your blizzard gear just yet."

"It'll probably fit you, Ahab," Tohnyin speculated, "like a vanilla slushy at a monastery party." She eyed Jerry. "Wisconsin is in fact subject to a significant interannual climatic variability, but overall it's become positively tepid, hasn't it?"

"Perhaps to a certain extent." The Parallacts associate placed a cautionary hand on Tess's shoulder. "Culturally, however, Illinois and Wisconsin couldn't be farther apart. The tradition of stiff anti-intellectualism that predominates and hamstrings middle America is nowhere more robust than in Wisconsin. Think of it as Iowa with three major cities: Green Bay, which is something out of Alabama; Madison, which is something out of California; and Milwaukee, which is something out of 19th century north central Europe." He peered into the backseat. "If one of you offset-officers wanders into trouble, consider taking refuge in the student ghetto of the University in Madison, where you could easily pass as local trade. And if you should be challenged in the disposition of a shibboleth to spell 'Waunakee,' strive to avoid falling out with *J-u-a-n a-q-u-i.* Still with us, I.B.?"

Winterhalter wheezed and interrupted the game of "Bear Bait" on his Jatakar to reference serviceable information. "'Isthmus oasis' was sprung in the Shalom Op background." He skimmed and smirked. "Swosh shantytown. Says there's a glut of blues clubs in the area. Let's see, here's: CryptOn State; Club Crazylegs; Uncle Bucky's." He jammed a hard elbow into the celebrity's ribs. "We can lay odds old Ahab's going to be finding a reason to shuffle off in that direction sooner than later."

"That reminds me, night crawler." Tohnyin reached back and blindly pinched the celebrity. "Pass me the key to your Shalom treatment so I can familiarize myself with it while I drive."

The celebrity jutted his jaw and patted his flustered hands over his full complement of suit pockets. Winterhalter leaned closer in lusty anticipation of extreme personal humiliation. "I suppose," the celebrity engaged the reagent, "Bucky will actually prove to be your uncle, too."

"Not my uncle, pwigtinnus, my godfather." I.B. scratched beneath his chin, depressed his tongue with two fingers and flipped a string of saliva.

The celebrity wiped his neck and reached beneath his seat for the briefcase. "I thought I had it, Tess, but I guess not." He set the briefcase on his lap. "Anyway, I.B. has sourcerer in hand. Badger him."

"He was only given the concept." An uncommon thread of rancor permeated her voice. "I need to access the high-res scenario models. And I'd like to analyze your review of the background checks the feds conducted while Shalom was engaged in contractual work for ARPA and DARPA. I trust you did review that body of documents."

"Enough to recognize how deeply he resented any intrusion into his private life." The celebrity struggled with the lock on his briefcase. "He made a point of sabotaging all such efforts."

"Those efforts promise to be ripe with low-hanging clues." Tess flipped up her goggles. "You're an awful liar, Ahab."

"He's an awful everything," Winterhalter suggested.

Tohnyin emitted a long, exasperated sigh. "He's degenerated into an extraordinarily egotistical and insecure company hack." She turned away and clutched Mercowitz's hand. "When your star quality blinds you with the belief that it eclipses the objective you're supposed to be pursuing, you end up scorching everything that should be flourishing by your residual light. He *is* the great *gas-bag*."

Jerry puffed up his cheeks and nodded vigorously. "An insidious cynosure operative is a sure sign of an invidious operation."

The celebrity patted his pipeline curl. "Come clean, d'Urberville, your forked tongue boasts infinitely no fewer stretch marks than mine."

Tohnyin nibbled Mercowitz's fingertips. "Ahab, you're an azygous muscle! No wonder Natty Phil is so concerned about you." She released Jerry's hand and snapped her goggles back over her eyes.

The celebrity leveled an accusatory finger at the reagent in an attempt to obfuscate the trickle of classified information into uncleared ears. "Has Handsome Dan indicated to you in any way that he's worried about me?"

I.B. snickered. "I dunno, dudsicle, he's authorized your bobbing-head effigy as the standard target model on the shooting range. He's also ordered your sorry-ass mug to deface the label of all Bureau jars and vats of slayerous pathogens and plague-evil potions. I'd take that to mean he's partial to you." He rubbed his thighs. "Say, Madame Transportess, what's the polite company way of indicating I need to piss?"

"There should be a golden jug beneath your seat," Tess disclosed.

"I offloaded it at the hotel while I was waiting for you two hinky-kinks," Winterhalter countered. "It stunk!"

Tohnyin fixed the reagent with a scowl. "You mean you loaded it while you waited for us, and you neglected to bring it back on board."

I.B. produced a bottle of clear liquid. "However you want it put to you, I have the urge to stream again." He guzzled the contents of the bottle.

"My intel indicates that on the marksmanship range in California, you guys are instructed to shoot first and draw targets around your projectile holes later." Mercowitz smiled archly. "Is this the same guy: this Handsome Phil and Natty Dan?"

"They're conjoined twins." The celebrity failed again to open the briefcase. "And they're better looking than any other pair of brothers you've ever seen!"

"Any two sets of brothers put together," Jerry charitably upped the ante.

"I get it he's gone ahead with my name-dropping tip?" Winterhalter's countenance crystallized as a sneer. "This duo of rucked-out cuchu sacks don't favor the ziggly-Q scallopini scar the Big Sir has on his temple," he advised Mercowitz, "so they pinchcock him with this 'Handsome' shit. They don't care to recognize that he took that gouge for the public trust, so it's a mark of distinction, a true beauty mark."

Tohnyin turned to face the reagent, her eyes wide and pouty as glimpsed through the reflection of the cockpit LED courtesy lights in her goggles. "You know that 'Handsome' is a derivation spun from 'Hands-On,' for his staunch refusal to separate himself from the front line with standard administrative middlegrounders." She patted I.B.'s hand. "And 'Natty' like 'Handsome' is not a term of ridicule but an agency appellation of respect! He revels in these titles of endearment and wears them like decorations, doesn't he, Ahab?" She pulled I.B.'s hand to her lips. "You are addressing him with an honorific in the vein of, 'The mood surgery may have blunted your imagination and short-term memory and neutralized all but the most primitive of your emotions, but you still have your good looks, and we love you all the more for it.'" She tenderly kissed his knuckles. "I must admit I'm immoderately moved you'd be sensitive to that concern." She smiled demurely and kissed his hand again. "Aren't you, Ahab?" She turned and refocused on the causeway.

The celebrity puckered and grabbed Winterhalter's hand. "We're fond of Natty Phil to a fault." The reagent ripped his hand free. "Some to San Andreas of a fault, and those of us who've welcomed him inside the sovereignty of our homes and pants are especially well-acquainted with his overriding benevolent nature." The celebrity preserved his durable smile as Tohnyin and Mercowitz snapped their heads around. "That's code for deduction that a man who's been stripped of his personality and has yet been able to shake so much action must have some aesthetic gift working for him." He turned to I.B. "But I'm not implying I'm using code there the way your uncle does so he doesn't actually have to go to code."

The Pigeon veered off the edge of the highway and descended abruptly toward a thick stand of conifers. Tohnyin flipped her goggles to her hairline. "Let's take a relief stop!" The craft bounced and skimmed a short distance over a gravel road and came to rest in a glade.

Mercowitz reached beneath his seat and inflated a covered golden bucket with a bell-funnel attachment. "The rental package appears to include an equal-op reserve relief vessel."

"I will not be that crude." Tess's imperious eyes settled on the celebrity. "Ahab, you're the closest thing here to another woman." The cockpit bubble lock popped. "You accompany me for support."

"I can stand to go in a pair!" Winterhalter thrust the bubble wide-open with his head.

Tohnyin bristled. "Develop some personal discipline and wait till we return!"

The celebrity detached the dome light and vaulted out of the craft. He helped Tess descend the wing and touch down on soggy ground.

"Try not to crinkle your pea jackets," Mercowitz cautioned.

The celebrity escorted Tohnyin through a short expanse of blooming reed stalks and sedges until the gref was out of earshot. The aroma reminded him of the safe house. "Spot a red-footed busy-booby tailing us on the road?" he presumed.

Tess snatched the dome light. "You're wearing the *full* Studio pad ensemble?"

He smiled affirmatively. "I wear it to church."

She hopped in front of him and favored his groin with a ferocious knee. "You puff adder," she snarled, "are you just trying to ruin this operation or the whole Bureau?" She feinted with her left knee and addressed his lower right cheek with a savage slap. "What the hell are you telling those guys?"

He stepped back and rubbed his face. "No one advised me there's a new secret handshake."

"You're giving up agency protocol!" She jammed her hands in her pockets and circled him.

He turned with her. "You mean that bit about Ledbetter faking code? What about you shrilly broadcasting that I wear body armor and then carelessly blurting out Natty Phil's new name?"

Her eyes proclaimed him a pinhead. "You stuffed cloakbag of guts, don't ever call me careless! I serve a specially prepared platter of truth and lies." She poked him in the chest protector so hard she cracked either a nail or a knuckle. "By giving away the sub-obvious, I build credibility. Even were I to concede I tendered something unpurposeful or miscalculated, both of those stud-menaces are panting for me so hard they don't hear a word I utter unless some trail-grooming trouba-dour makes a big annotated stink about it and shags them back onto the subject!"

He reclaimed the dome light and gestured to an imaginary slate. "Look, San Francisco treat, the Kerckhoffs principle stip-ulates that the security of a system rests not on the algorithm but on the key."

"In this case, king of the Kerckhoffs, the key and the algo-rithm are the same!" She pummeled his chest protector with a sustained double-fisted staccato vehemence. "Lose this bloated baggage, you junior parade float. Not only is it enough of a fashion heresy to hold us out of a moderately posh night club, but I'm about *total* victory, and that entails looking good get-ting it."

He rocked forward slightly with fists on hips. "I don't know how many of Jerry Mercowitz's cohorts we can expect to run into tonight but I expect we'll be colliding with some velocity, and at least one of us needs to be up to the impact."

She pointed her toe at his groin and connected with a loop kick, the force of the blow absorbed by his protective cup but still sufficient to double him over. "Is that the impact you're guarding against?" She grabbed his collar and returned him to an erect position.

He winced and nodded. "Point taken."

"The point," she snarled, "is that the lab informed me you submitted a sample of my DNA with the request that they match it to Dan Aldred's to establish whether there's a famil-ial connection. I can't count the number of levels on which I'm offended."

He coughed. "What kind of man, moreover, what kind of spy would I be if I didn't check-"

"A double shot of both." She stepped back. "The disgusting experiment was aborted, so you can exercise your morbid voyeurism elsewhere."

"I already have." He readjusted his pants and posture. "I sent samples to two other independent labs as well, so I'm positive you're not I.B.'s half-cousin, despite the myriad behavioral parallels that might be discerned by someone more astute than myself."

The daggers in Tohnyin's eyes cut to the bone. "With all due respect to my foggy memories of my father, Ahab, I am assuredly not the product of my mother's affair with a prep school student, even if P.L. as a teenage boy was already the Handsome man."

"As limiting as it sounds, 'Big Sir on Campus' might've been a title of endearment with few boundaries." The celebrity smiled complaisantly. "I'm sorry I had your genes evaluated, but it did establish that you have an inside source at the lab passing you classified information."

Tess patted the celebrity gently. "Closer to home, Ahab, how clandestine can you be when you're built like an RV?" She slickly unbuttoned his jacket and shirt. "How do you get close enough to anyone to peel away their conflicting agenda when you're hidebound by insular superstructure?" She removed his jacket and shirt. "You know you'd be doing the rest of us a major disservice by subjecting us to increased performance pressure and greater potential risk." Her nimble fingers removed his layered protective exo-cage strong-suit with the spider-silk coating and tossed it to the turf. "All right, let's authenticate our cover and get back before they report us missing." She placed a heavy hand on his arm and spun him around. "A little privacy, swami?" She shed her trench coat.

The celebrity rescued his strong-suit and took six giant steps to the other side of a Scotch pine. "Tess, are you certain Mercowitz isn't an angler stringing us along on behalf of Parallacts to procure Shalom for the highest bidding interest, be that Wisconsin or even Illinois intelligence, if not a consor-"

"No one gets the drop on you, Ahab." She unzipped. "But I have it from reliable sources that the Illinois Intelligence Agency is a ragtag farce of a force like Nevada's. What little revenue they're allotted has to go through too long a receiving line to leave anything to fund significant projects."

He gazed in the direction of the Pigeon. "What reliable sources: Jerry, I.B., Jason Padata?"

She emitted an aggravated groan. "Ahab, I need sound cover before I can start." She hurled a stone in his direction. "Stop pissing and start urinating."

He took another step. "What role were you cast in this operation, Tess?" Jacket folded over his forearm, he clipped the light to the breast pocket. "Did Ledbetter send you up here as critic?" Cup in hand and pants hanging around his ankles, he began his cascade.

Over their confluence she finally proclaimed, "Celebrity."

He felt as though he'd stepped on the teeth of a rake and received the handle between the eyes. He became acutely aware of the way the lively breeze fanned the pungent country odors, and he shifted his foot in an unsuccessful attempt to keep his pants and Lord Clarksdales from being splashed. "Aldred, ah, Ledbetter has to serve me with formal notice to pull that rug out from under me."

"Check the hip pocket of your jacket," she replied, "and feel the burn."

The celebrity hastily concluded his discharge. He replaced his cup and restored the original arrangement of his outer garments. He retrieved his strong-suit and reached into the hip pocket of his jacket. He produced the scytale that Tohnyin had planted. Undoubtedly recording the moment with her goggles cam, Tess arrived at his side squaring away her trench coat. "Strictly," she cooed, "co-celebrity." She snatched the light from his breast pocket. "And along with the recast, I left you a little visual aid you might find useful in a night-club setting." Inside the hollow rod he discovered a vial containing a contact lens with nano-diodes around the edge that would superimpose a red-eye effect on anyone looking directly at him. "Back to work, Ophiuchus." She grabbed his arm and launched into a double-time strut.

Winterhalter waited outside the Passenger Pigeon. Tohnyin outpaced the celebrity, and the reagent took a welcoming step toward her. "What the fuck took so long? Did you have to keep fighting him off?"

She supinated her palms in a gesture of resignation and hopped onto the gref wing. "He got an idea of what's not his business about my biology."

I.B. fixed the celebrity with a smirk no less sanctimonious than it was salacious. "How twisted and noxious a candle you are."

Tess scrambled into her seat. "Open the trunk," the celebrity called, "so I can stow my armor."

"The trunk is full; you'll have to sit with it." Tohnyin smiled coyly at Mercowitz. "Would we be pleased with what was whispered about us while we were gone?"

Jerry put the finishing flourishes on his fingernails with a Swiss army file. "Just a moment, I'm polishing my no-compete claws." He interlocked fingers with Tess. "In your absence, I.B. and I both decided to change our names. From now on, I'm going to be Jetsky Omerta Spetsnaz, and what's yours, Stog?"

"Mashdonk," the reagent roared. "Stog Mashdonk!"

"We speculated that your director's name change might've stemmed from a leader-boarding incident at a state-sponsored golf tournament." Jerry panted furiously. "Handsome Dan and his caddies would've set upon another player at a water hazard and demanded the name of a ringleader of interest. When the victim finally broke and gave him 'Philander Ledbetter,' he took it and kept it."

"I bugged your beacon right before you left." Winterhalter pointed at the dome light and snickered. "We heard every scrap of smack you bushmeat cannibals put out with your zippers flapping." He redirected his finger toward Mercowitz. "He insisted we not let on, but I couldn't be that sneaky."

The Parallacts associate flashed a perky smile at Tohnyin and turned to the celebrity. "Did you clod-hopping California co-conspirators manage to pass some outside information via a cryptic message in urine?"

The reagent snorted. "Whose urine, and whose handwriting?" He tugged on the brass hoop ring adorning his fly and reached into his fuchsia leather pants.

"Step away from the vehicle, juggernaut!" The celebrity flopped into the backseat of the Passenger Pigeon atop his strong-suit.

Tess rubbed Jerry's shoulder. "Must you punish me for the treachery of my badinage, m'lord?" She edged closer, and I.B. unstopped a flash flood against the right rear quarterpanel of the Pidge. "Does not my humiliation stay thy fulmination, or will you dip into your font of invective and ream me a new one?" She kissed his neck, snapped her goggles over her irritated eyes and glared outside the cockpit. "Turn it around, huh, Mr. Wizard?"

Winterhalter began whirling and a torrent lashed the gref with each rotation. Mercowitz rubbed Tohnyin's neck. "I take you now as always *cum grano salis*." He kissed her. "You are deep in my debt, Contessa, but I trust we'll find a more profound fealty to forge."

The reagent climbed into the craft and pulled up his hoop ring after he seated himself. His eyes darted between the adjacent strong-suit and the celebrity. "Oobops, this your new squench?" He elbowed the armor into the celebrity.

Tohnyin started the Passenger Pigeon engine, and the gref leveled itself on a cushion of air. The take-no-prisoners electric-harp-fueled plinking of "Warmed Over Death" by Gaspar X probed the cabin, and the vehicle haltingly resumed its journey. The celebrity had 72 hours to decipher and acknowledge the formal alert of the scytale. On some abstruse level, cooperating with Tess pleased him, but if she had indeed been elevated to co-celebrity, he would be dependent on her to garner a positive reference for reinstatement in the Bureau. And she was probably employing her drive time contriving designs to oust him from the mission. "How much farther is Wisconsin?" he grumbled.

Mercowitz studied the celebrity with annoyance. "We infiltrated the state shortly before you weenies had to pit."

Tohnyin threw her head back. "That's one mean perspicacity you've honed, Ahab."

"No, dodo!" Winterhalter thumped the celebrity in the ribs. "We ain't in California anymore."

"Why would anyone who could live anywhere he wants choose to live in Wisconsin?" Tess wondered.

"No tollway culture to speak of?" Jerry assumed a posture of judicial condescension. "Illinois envies that."

Tohnyin guided the Pidge onto the westbound Highway 50 causeway. "I guess nothing does crush the spirit of living in a free country quite like receiving a Notice of Toll Evasion."

"It's an uneasy schism," the celebrity surmised, "reflected in the official state slogans of their respective license plates. Wisconsin is *The Last Refuge of Scoundrels* whereas Illinois is *Worth Practically the Price of Admission*."

Mercowitz turned again to face the backseat. "Wisconsin used to designate itself as *America's Dairyland* until you big Golden Pacific splashes-in-the-pan ousted them from the headcheese pedestal." He smirked with mock censure. "Is that tag line referenced on California plates now?"

"It says *Get a Whiff of My Big Dairy Air!*" Winterhalter snorted. "All the Ill-annoying plates have *Land of Lincoln Worbley*?"

"Illinois vanity plates read *The Graveyard of Empires*." Jerry faced the front. "Wisconsin bears the scars of the last ice age perhaps more than any other state in the union. Although as you move beyond the capital, you reach the driftless area that the current round of glacial impact snubbed." He peeked over his shoulder at I.B. and grinned archly. "The hilly manglement might be enough to give an infamously crusty, upwardly mobile cliff-dweller a hint of his own Western state of homeliness."

The celebrity snickered at the swither pasted across the reagent's features. "Jerry, are you suggesting that our I.B. is a trauma-headed throwback to the first tribe of hominids with the wheel to come highballing around the butte and discover the crumple zone?"

Tohnyin and Mercowitz provided a chorus of titters. Winterhalter flipped open his pinkie blade. "Oobops, you ain't all there, in so many ways." He leaned forward and sneered. "I'd prefer it, Spaznuts, if you never lump me lookswise with this grungion." He feinted a stab jab at the celebrity. "He looks like he rolled off Old Ugly Mountaintop and hit every sharp ledge on the way down. He has the face only a blind drunk woman could love."

"Now who's being a bit hard on Ahab?" Tess protested. "He has the scuffed scruffiness that some women desire."

"You can add that line to your resume, Bela," Jerry chuckled.

"If you desire some sad sack who strikes the appearance he works summers unfouling moving boat propellers," I.B. persisted. "Madelyn's friends who came over while we were putting up with him at the safe house thought he was 'fantastically goofy-looking.'"

The celebrity emitted an irked sigh. "Self-mutilators can be such a tough crowd to please." Winterhalter sliced open the back of Tohnyin's seat upholstery.

Mercowitz turned warily and faced the backseat. "Ahab, you strike me as a fairly amiable chap for an oppression-minded storm trooper. Are you sure you harbor enough hate to perpetrate crimes against the peace and security of the state of Wisconsin?"

The celebrity smiled complaisantly. "'Hate' is a word I prefer to reserve for people I encountered in high school. We don't hate the people of Wisconsin. We're responding to a climate threat that they pose."

The reagent scoffed. "He thinks he's such a professional tough shit. Right after we met up at Axel's, he picked a fight with some other mother's son at the bar and got beat down before I could shed my chair." He hissed at the celebrity. "Knocked flat. I meant to mention that prostrate becomes you."

"In the time it took to flee the scene, you recognized how self-effacing it would be to leave your whipped butter complexion in the care of your whipped butter combat skills." The celebrity failed again to open the briefcase. "That's using your fast-twitch grey matter."

"I cut my teeth on the mean streets of Sacramento, beach-flea!" I.B. chomped the air and retracted his pinkie blade.

"Intriguing." Jerry rubbed his chin. "As teenagers, you both considered yourselves outsiders?"

"She got you testing her crack up there, Mercy-croaks-bed-pan-breath?" Winterhalter projected an image of an ass-eyed adolescent from his Jatakar to the dashboard screen. The youth with the conceited grin wore a cream blazer and orange signal flag neckerchief tie. "Catch a blast of my yearbook gallery pics," he verified his image's identity. "No one with this pyro-packing chi-edged glister could be an outcast, mister!"

Mercowitz nodded. "You look like you think you did your classmates a favor by showing up to have your picture taken."

"It *is* distracting." Tohnyin distorted the photo.

The reagent dropped a heavy hand on the back of Tess's seat. "When I'd prowl the halls, girls would literally poke their heads out of the classrooms to get a fuller glimpse." He removed his image. "Sure, there's a few people I'd still love to slap and shove just to show there's no hard feelings, but on the whole, I recollect the time fondly."

"But not so much for you, Ahab?" Jerry challenged.

"Go ahead, salty pillow." I.B. snorted with irritation. "Fill in a few of your blank spaces."

The celebrity rubbed his neck. "In high school," he recalled, "I pretended to be in the drama club and got kicked off the football team."

"What got you kicked off the team?" Mercowitz prodded. "Did you only give 109 percent?"

"Gene thrusters!" Winterhalter pinched the celebrity's biceps. "He flunked his reality check."

The celebrity took the opportunity to ignore the reagent. "More like 111 percent because it was an incident of overzealousness. I was the third-string quarterback, so in practice I ran the scout team, which mimicked our upcoming opponent to give the defense a strategic preview."

The Parallacts associate shook his finger. "They kept you on the sidelines because you were so adept at stealing the other team's signals."

"The coaches took a cue from the cheerleaders," Tohnyin speculated. "Nada chants with them."

"That's vintage Oobops," the reagent cackled. "He'd be stronger and faster than anyone else there, and he can only make third-string."

"The son of the coach's best friend was second-string." The celebrity grimaced. "I thought the scout team was being utilized a little too much as tackling dummies one day, so I threw the best block of my life into our star linebacker and took his knee along with me, effectively ending his storied career. It couldn't be adequately repaired."

"So what," Tess sympathized, "you're still trying to purge your guilt over it?"

"It was a squeaky-clean hit, and that guy was the class asshole," the celebrity confirmed.

"What was drama club about?" Mercowitz rubbed his hands together. "Acting better than everyone else?"

"The theater became my battering ram." The celebrity tapped an inspired rhythm on the side of the briefcase. "It rekindled the fire lit when I was conscripted to play the lead in my second-grade-class adaptation of Milton's *Paradise Lost*."

"The lead?" Jerry pointed with both forefingers. "Cast that kid straight into hell and call him Amalek!"

"The stage name, sir, would be Lucifer!" Tess howled. "Some kids' natural aptitude is too conspicuous to waste." She favored the celebrity with a fond glance. "They probably gauged yours after your mother harped too hard on what a bright, little angel you were and they had to pry you off the wall with your head spinning and your pants smoking!"

The celebrity exhibited a tormented smile. "Years later, I spotted my teacher in a supermarket parking lot and thanked her properly for my immersion. I said, 'Remember me, Mrs. Phrompraky? I'm Lucifer.' And I punched her in the face and snatched her Qilroy."

Tohnyin turned completely around. "Even you're not that depraved, prince of dark ops."

The celebrity evacuated his deadpan. "One thing I don't exaggerate is the disappointment I felt my senior year of high school at being denied the lead in the class play. We staged an adaptation of Nabokov's *Lolita*, and in keeping with the third-string stamp in which they typecast me, I wound up as the understudy's understudy."

"That must've been more squeaky than clean," the Parallacts associate quipped.

"Why, you schoolyard letch!" Winterhalter punched the celebrity in the shoulder. "I reported on that rumpusorama for English class, and it got me more frustrated each time I pored over it. Humpster Humpster, right?"

The celebrity buried his head in his hands. "In one annotated sense."

The reagent patted the celebrity on the pipeline curl. "That English teacher once got so zerked with our class she gave us composition homework of personalized suicide notes. Nobody I know of found sufficient pangs to use theirs though."

"A stark miscarriage of potential," Jerry postulated. "Unless you're hopelessly myopic, I.B., you'll tuck that intellectual property away and retain custody of it with white knuckles."

Winterhalter slapped his hand on Mercowitz's shoulder. "I can load it up for you on the screen now, chigger-digger."

"No, please!" Tohnyin snapped.

The asymmetric curl of Jerry's lips suggested a fault line. "So it was your natural passion for the theater of the absurd, Ahab, that you pursued to college as an aspiring spirit gum warrior, and once there, you found your heart lay with the public service mission musical."

"I've always relished wading through hazardous material where the protagonist is under pressure to maintain his sense of duty," the celebrity explained, "because that indicates he *has* a sense of duty. It's the tension between a particular form and function that makes each new production a worthy effort, or not."

"Drop the drone on drama, Ahab." Tess glanced over her shoulder. "We should be utilizing this opportunity to evaluate Charlton Shalom, not to assess how you've cultivated artistic germs with your theatrical instrument."

I.B. emitted a horselaugh. "We could guess, bud, you've always been weird and dull."

The celebrity leaned forward. "The modern pessimist plays that Tess eats up where bestial appetites prevail are generally written by a class of elitist atheist teacups who'd be the first ones trampled if the conditions of anarchy that they pretend to embrace actually emerged."

"I'd advise you to criticize something you understand," Tohnyin countered, "but I'm too polite to tell you to just shut up."

"Set the tableau with me stooped on a sweaty gazebo wearing a wife-beater undershirt," the celebrity directed. "*Spydahs*," he transitioned to a heavy drawl, "up the post crawl some of them *spydahs*, them red, long-legged spydahs, the type that toss about incessantly till they've drained the bodily juices from their prospective suitahs."

"I can't imagine it playing in Peoria, Fortinbras." Mercowitz eyed the celebrity with an earnest cordiality. "But there's nothing wrong with a little staged elusion and falsehood in the interest of uplifting contemporary civic and cultural standards, is there? Exactly when did you exchange subtext for pretext and stagecraft for statecraft?"

The celebrity shrugged. "When I found myself uninspired, off-kilter, distracted, indifferent, listless, gloomy, grim, cranky, and I felt I could really use the sort of security net offered by steady state employment." He rapped the briefcase and passed it to Winterhalter. "Open this can of worms."

Tohnyin sighed heavily. "What really spelled the end of Ahab the Thespian was appreciation that the old Roman nobility considered all performers dreck and their assorted claques dreckees."

"So *saad* for *Iuyy* have deh perrrfect name for heem to change hees to," Jerry indirectly assailed the celebrity through a thick Middle Eastern accent. "'Ahmebad Akhtar.'"

"One thing the Romans would take a very sunny view of was a talented engineer," the celebrity offered. "What can you reveal about the nature of the relationship between the inscrutable Charlton Shalom and the ill-fated Lincoln Worbley?"

The Parallacts associate devoted several moments to silent reflection. "They both seemed to relish telling the establishments of their respectable professional environments to go pound sand. Link was smooth, more open and less brackish; I suspect he lent Chuckles some social moxie."

"Oobops, even your dildos are limp." I.B. opened and closed and opened the briefcase and laid it on the celebrity's lap.

"What's the idiopath packing in there?" Tess demanded.

"A survival belt with a suicide watch," Winterhalter gibed, "or verse vica."

"Keep your options open." Mercowitz produced a cigarette. "This rollicking road we're following is the route up which they hauled the ship we're going to board. They disassembled the littoral combat ship in Lake Michigan, transported the modules on Highway 50 and reassembled a cruise ship in Geneva Lake. Worbley was the overland wagon master, and I consider that marvel every bit as impressive as his polar shield or his desalination plant and water pipeline network."

A flourish of beeps sounded. The speed of the Passenger Pigeon diminished, its wings and tails neatly folded into pike position and its belly-pan rollers contacted the pavement. "Here's the town and here's the deal," Jerry asserted. "We can park free at Big Foot Beach Park and be conveyed to the ship on the valet shuttle, a strategy which would belabor my dear longstanding commitment to executive privilege." He flipped switches on the auto-navigator control panel. "To manage that, we'll turn south on Lake Shore Drive."

The reagent snorted disdainfully. "If we're not driving this motor hammock over the rolling whitecaps and grinding it into the P.T. boat's gunwales, fluke-face, I must question what the point of drifting up in it was at all."

The Pidge passed several blocks of shops in terrestrial mode and negotiated a left turn ahead of oncoming traffic. "The reason to streamline our trip with the gref, road-rash," Mercowitz advised, "is to vouchsafe ourselves an obscene performance bonus in the reduction of travel time allotted to enjoy each other's company, not unlike paying negative interest."

Winterhalter elbowed the strong-suit into the celebrity. "He really thinks you're a jerk, jocko." The celebrity donned his steel-blue confetti-splash necktie and secured the briefcase beneath his seat.

The Passenger Pigeon stiffly negotiated the curving road. The sound system blasted "Rage Therapy" by the patriotic metal band Jacket Racket. The gref turned into a driveway and stopped. "Destination reached," the auto-navigator stated.

A dimly lit gate four meters high stood about twenty meters ahead, and to both sides of it extended countless spans of chain-link fence. A blue-and-orange *Big Foot Beach Park* sign hung modestly on the gate.

"I'll let you pilot us in," Tohnyin engaged Mercowitz.

"Nonsense." Jerry placed his arm around Tess. "Let's earn the steering committee chair her wings. Boost the Pidge back to surface-scratcher stature and ease her forward."

The gref extended its wings and tails. It sputtered and rose on a cushion of air. Tohnyin positioned the vehicle in a radical California tilt and guided it slowly toward the gate. Mercowitz elevated his Qilroy and exchanged radio signals with the gate control box. The craft gained speed and approached the gate. "It's not opening!" Tess protested.

"It'll open!" Jerry insisted. "Drift a little right!"

"Power thruster!" the celebrity shrieked in Tohnyin's ear. "Leap it!"

The Passenger Pigeon swung right, dipped left and fired bursts of hypergolic propellant to take altitude. The craft spun and climbed, scraping metal. Its maneuver left it suspended nose-down perpendicular to the ground with the tail undercarriage caught on the top of the gate. "Evasive action!" the auto-navigator directed. The side air bags deployed, the engine stalled, and the gref became enveloped in a hissing blue haze. The gate opened.

The tangle of bodies found the celebrity sprawled between the front seats suffocating between Tohnyin's ankles and pinned in place by Winterhalter. He spread Tess's feet apart. "Back off, I.B.!"

"Oobops, deconstruct!" Tohnyin commanded.

"What the hell!" The reagent shifted his weight slightly. "We're snagged on the gate!"

"And that, fellow test dummies," Jerry offered weakly, "is gate crashing."

"A helicopter would've disintegrated." Tohnyin ran her

fingers gingerly over Mercowitz's face. "We're lucky we're still intact, but, Jerry, you're hurt."

"Quite all right really," the Parallacts associate chuckled. "Albins an iota or nose-ota more in the red than in the pink."

"Climb off me, sprinkler-head!" the celebrity reiterated. "I can barely breathe!"

"Your padding has me gridlocked, Gandalf." I.B. pitched and rolled in place for a minute, digging an elbow into the celebrity's scapula before pulling himself aside and anchoring himself behind Jerry's seat. "Power leap!" he mocked.

The gate stalled halfway open. The celebrity climbed onto the back of Tohnyin's seat. He groped beneath air bag skins as he expelled a series of coughs. Tess restarted the engine. The gate vibrated. The canopy popped open. The front of the craft lifted slightly but the tail undercarriage remained attached to the gate. "Full throttle!" Jerry exhorted. The front of the craft lifted and shook but returned to its suspended state.

"Don't power boost!" Winterhalter bellowed. "You'll power dump us down on our goddamn necks!"

"Bumbershoot might have it right for once." Mercowitz groaned and rubbed his face. "We need to call a truck with a winch – or a crane."

Tohnyin killed the engine. "Ahab, fetch the first-aid kit from my vanity case in the trunk." The celebrity rose unsteadily and pushed the canopy wide-open. Tess stuck a tissue beneath Jerry's nose. "You can remove the center panel of the back seat and get into the trunk without going outside!"

The celebrity placed the dome light between his teeth, bent forward and searched for the backseat passage. "I believe I got spanked by the air bag," the Parallacts associate admitted.

"I got gashed, too," the reagent announced. "It don't hurt much but I'm bleeding."

"That's Jerry's blood, rough-rider." Tohnyin grunted. "You and Ahab have heads of concrete." The celebrity removed the seat panel and plunged into the congested trunk. "What's taking so long, Ahab?" Tess called. "You're looking for a little, red toolbox inside the oval vanity case."

The celebrity withdrew the vanity case from the trunk, removed the first-aid kit and flipped it into Winterhalter's lap. "Good work, ass-wipe," I.B. allowed. "Anyone who says you're completely useless doesn't have all the facts." He handed the kit to Tess.

A car drove through the gate opening. The celebrity lunged from the cabin and caught ahold of tie-wire near the top of the gate. He climbed to the top rail and straddled it as he inspected the junction of gref and gate. The right-side flair-foil tail mount of the Passenger Pigeon had displaced a wire section, and the tail assembly sat wedged between a tension wire and the top rail. There appeared to be no chance that the craft could propel itself off the gate. Even if the frame of the vehicle could be pried loose, the nose would probably sustain significant damage when it dropped to the pavement.

Mercowitz mounted the back of Tohnyin's seat. "Squire, prepare to require repair?" He held a cotton wad beneath his nose, and a small bandage adorned his chin. "Tess, call for roadside assistance."

"Wait!" The celebrity moved along the top rail and evaluated the structure of the gate. "There has to be an inconspicuous way we can dislodge it ourselves!"

Jerry stretched his neck. "We'll all turn our heads, Ahab, while you slip into your leotards and cape so you can lift the Pidge off the gate." He snickered sardonically. "I'm surprised the engine even started again without the craft's safety features being reset."

"The gate is inside of the fence." The celebrity spotlighted a gate post. "If we can just detach the gate and push it from the top, it should fall to put the Pidge down over it on its belly-pan rollers. We can inflate its bottom air bags so it has a soft landing."

Tohnyin groaned. "Ahab, haven't you done enough damage already?"

Two cars sped through the gate opening. The Parallacts associate clutched his head. "Oobops, try to forget for a moment that you work for the government. Why go to a lot of needless trouble that may unwell end with you getting someone massacred? Let's leave this unwieldy job to some skilled professionals, have the ship's valets take us out to the *Janesy* and bury our troubles at lake." He moved clumsily to abandon his perch, extended his hand to Tess and tumbled into the cockpit.

"We apologize, Jerry, for not warning you beforehand that Tess's support skills are on par with her driving." The celebrity descended the outside of the gate to cabin level. "The gate is supported by its top and bottom rollers. If we can just loosen the wraparound bolts that affix them to the fence posts, we can liberate the gate enough to flip it on its side." He smiled complaisantly. "There wouldn't be a toolbox holding *tools* in the trunk, would there? Maybe one with a rescue saw or even an automatic adjustable high-impact wrench?"

"What do you know about tools?" Winterhalter rose, removed the seat panel and rummaged around in the trunk. "If Uncle Dan finds out we got stuck up here, we'll look like a bunch of goddamn numpts!"

"Look for a Milwaukee brand tool," Tohnyin recommended. "Use their own materiel against them."

Mercowitz leaned out of the cockpit and shook his head. "You people were born with a mission to punish, weren't you?"

Winterhalter produced a long-handled tool and waved it vigorously. "Power bolt-cutter!"

The celebrity moved beside the craft. "Come to this side, I.B., and pass it to me."

"I'll take care of this!" The reagent mounted the back of the Parallacts associate's seat. "Get out of my way, dookie!" Another car passed by the gate, and the celebrity climbed back to the top. I.B. lunged from the cabin to the gate. He lost a foothold and recovered. He started downward. He withdrew the tool handle from his pants and lost his grip. He regained a hold on the gate wire but the bolt-cutter plummeted to the pavement. "Fuck you, Oobops!"

Winterhalter scrambled to the pavement and retrieved the bolt-cutter. Another vehicle passed through the gate opening. The reagent employed the long-handled tool at the three posts annexed to gate rollers. "I *castratoed* six hex-heads, Bejuka Joe," he breathlessly reported. "You work it for a while!" He launched the bolt-cutter overhead, and the celebrity stretched from the top of the gate to grab a handle.

The dual tail assembly of the Pidge sat slightly askew and the right-side rear quarterpanel displayed a crease and a crumple. The celebrity cut wire away from the rear of the vehicle. "Tess, can you manually deploy the bottom air bags?" he directed.

"Anything to grease your squeaky wheel." Tohnyin pressed buttons and provided the cushions.

The celebrity severed the six wraparound bolts anchoring the top gate rollers. He shifted and jerked his weight in an attempt to coax the gate to the ground. It slipped and tilted slightly. He discarded the bolt-cutter and moved to the upper corner of the gate. He held the adjacent fence wire, planted his feet against the top rail of the gate and pushed. "I.B.!" he demanded. "Climb up on the other side, shake and ram and try to push the gate down!"

"In these pants, barricada?" Winterhalter scoffed. "Plus I'm not wearing the shoes for it!"

"Tess, you join him!" the celebrity ordered. "Jerry, you come up under me and increase the power load on this side!"

Amid a consensus of consternation and complaint, the quartet occupied the fence, applied concurrent pressure and forced the gate to the ground. The Pidge landed softly on its air bags and bounced on the gate. The troupe hopped back inside the cabin. Mercowitz reset the safety features and piloted the crippled gref to a convenient parking spot. "I believe we've come to convince each other in principle, Jerry," the celebrity submitted, "that no effort and sacrifice are too great in the interest of obtaining free parking." The foursome locked the vehicle and walked a short, quaint path to the embarkation point for the shuttle boat to the Geneva Lake *Janesy* cruise ship.

> *She's a piss poor minder,*
> *She's a sidewinder in a dress;*
> *She's a fine fault finder,*
> *She's an organ grinder name of Bess.*

> *She's a white hot poker,*
> *She's a Bram Stoker villainess;*
> *She's a heartbreak broker,*
> *She's a broadside choker – that's our Bess.*

> *But when a long, fast train*
> *Macked Mama in the hard, cold rain,*
> *No one but Bess*
> *Came out to help me tidy up the mess.*

> *She's a mean streak talker,*
> *She's a looserope walker sans finesse;*
> *She's a rhubarb stalker,*
> *She's an outline chalker, call her Bess.*

4TH MOVEMENT

Inbound. 1845 CST Tuesday 28 March.

"A thousand pardons there, also-rans!" The celebrity apologized over I.B. Winterhalter's expletives after the reagent cut across the sundeck running track and was clipped by a couple of joggers. "He's two schnapps short of his lake legs."

"No, it's their fault!" Jerry Mercowitz barked after the striders. "Watch your drift, you skimmer pukes, or we'll drop you in your own wake!" The pair promptly stopped and turned. The taller one, a lean man with Korean features and mildly disheveled hair, sauntered back toward them. Jerry extended an exuberant fist. "MacArthur, where've you been hiding yourself lately?" The fist evolved into an open hand.

The Korean man flashed a wide grin and shook hands with Mercowitz. "Do I know you?"

Jerry guffawed lustily and offered a sweeping introductory gesture. "Marty, these are three nonquals harnessed to the California state government corps with dink diplomatic jobs. Tess, boys, this is Mr. Park from the Chicago Department of Zoning Obstruction."

Park clasped Tohnyin's hands and nodded in the direction of the celebrity and reagent. "Ah, California, a verdant hillside's worst nightmare. If the brushfire and the mudslide don't get you, the infill development will. Tess, is it?" He pointed at the other jogger, clad in a black-and-white floral print hoodie, who remained several steps down the track. "This is Bud, an international consultant to the Chicago Department of Sustainability." Bud exhibited a tight-lipped smile and turned to answer the call of cardiovascular fitness.

"Marty is a flamboyant fellow," Mercowitz announced, placing a heavy hand on Park's shoulder as he watched Bud trot beneath the outer disc of the revolving Stomach Club restaurant. "He has more degrees than an obtuse angle but he's no worthless wonk. He has a Ringtail Lemur."

"Thank you, testimonial-breath." Park appeared slightly chagrined. "Some more cynical than I suggest that you bought it for me."

"It's one unholy glide," Mercowitz trumpeted. "If I could afford one like it, I'd have a better one." Jerry and MacArthur sauntered down the track several meters and chatted privately. The wavy reversed question-mark smudge that the parking lot gate had left on Jerry's jacket back appeared more prominent. When Bud had lapped them a second time, Park waved and trotted after him.

"Pair of turds," Winterhalter grumbled further about his indelicate introduction. "Elbows-out, line-jumping trolls."

The Parallacts associate pursed his lips. "Let's gather in formation and try to maintain ourselves as a tight working mob."

Winterhalter shivered and folded his arms across his chest. "I better get fed fucking fast."

Tohnyin took Mercowitz's arm. The celebrity grabbed Tess's unoccupied hand. "You needn't cling to him tighter than his executive tan, love." Tess shook free of the celebrity's grasp.

Jerry led the way toward the spinning sailor's hat dome of iridescent white over the tinted wraparound limousine window. "Let me take the opportunity to acknowledge what you've probably suspected." His features hardened with an unnerving earnestness. "I'm a trustee of the CIA." He recouped his impish smile. "The Culinary Institute of America. And that should translate to the Stomach Club favoring us with immediate seating."

The troupe reached the back of the bottleneck at the conic entrance beneath the restaurant. Tohnyin pointed at a man and woman in matching checkerboard suits ahead of them. "Is that garb considered stylish?"

"Club regulars." Mercowitz nodded. "It's considered Wisconsinish."

The celebrity squeezed Tohnyin's unoccupied arm. "Let's jump them."

Tess was quick on the scowl. "Why?"

The celebrity met steel with steel. "To prove we're kingmakers."

Tohnyin busily buffed Jerry's jacket back to remove the dyslexic question-mark smudge as the party of four wangled their way through a crush of mutually determined prospective diners. Ultimately, the VIP CIA creds of the Parallacts associate proved to lack sufficient clout for anything but a slot on the waiting list. "It's crazy for a weekday," Jerry complained as he led his company down to the dedicated lounge on the main deck to await word of table availability. "This pad isn't some epicurean epicenter."

The Mercowitz party settled into a tightly wedged corner table of the Slop Chest, a smoky bistro with a modest dance platform and a hologram jukebox. Bastardz R Us Daykare were performing their rendition of "Profligate Girl". A display case of various nautical knots decorated one wall, and intelligent fans labored furiously overhead to vacuum impurities from the air. Tess removed her trench coat to reveal a scarlet sequined cocktail dress worn off one shoulder. "Just another non-existent super-yacht," Jerry explained the acronymic significance of the ship name as an epilog to his running chronicle of a visionary entrepreneur who'd transformed an obsolete U.S. navy littoral combat ship into a floating nightclub and had successfully lobbied for the right to host an off-shore non-Indian casino.

"What's everyone drinking? I have the unsettling suspicion I'm surrounded by a coven that worships at a hill shrine to the conquered grape."

"Wine isn't what it used to be," the celebrity lamented. "Although we might consider as an adequate opener a Napa Cabernet Sauvignon of a trophy teenage vintage poured with some backbone in a wide bowl."

"We'll buy you your own bottle," Winterhalter scoffed, "so you can take it into the toilet and set yourself up with a really adequate bouquet-sniffing bowl."

"Bubbly California red is still where it's at," Tohnyin advised Mercowitz. "But let's all start out with the identical drink and proceed from there. You select it, Jerry; you're host by default."

Mercowitz clasped Tohnyin's hand. "In the Midwest, we're generally straight and to the point and die-hards for hardy grain alcohol." He squinted at the celebrity. "But as some of us seem to have been born to go against the grain, why don't we tempt ourselves with a more cosmopolitan potable like an unsophisticated, unspiced rail rum?" A middle-aged, dark-haired cocktail waitress appeared almost on cue. "Let's pick a theme for the evening and drink to it." He gestured subtly to Tess. "A hurricane for the lady, and himicanes for the gentle-men. What'll you have, I.B.?"

Winterhalter grunted. "Most likely your Old Jericho sec-retary of stale ass, whiskey sourpuss, cuz you're damn straight there's nothin' gentle about me."

Mercowitz effected the universal gesture of one entertain-ing a severe headache. "As my grandma the grammarian used to say, 'Never make a mad man angry.' Hurricanes all around, please." The waitress departed, and Jerry fixed his gaze on Tess. "To continue with the local color I was spreading on the sun-deck, most of the palaces on the northeastern shore were built in the late 19th century as single-family summer homes. You have to believe that both spouses worked." He paused as she chuckled. "The Wrigley family was a pillar of the campaign to create a Gold Coast up here, and their main estate Green Gables once exhausted almost a kilometer and a half of shoreline. Further legend has it that one year Mr. Wrigley gave his wife the mansion as her birthday present; the next year he gave her a green sweater."

"The name 'Wrigley' suggests a bait baron," Tohnyin quipped.

Mercowitz laughed. "I know the Wrigley specter still haunts California, too, with a shipload of namesake parks and points of philanthropy capped by the family monument on Catalina island." He turned to the celebrity. "The last thing you'd expect to have staying power like that is chewing gum, hmm?"

The celebrity nodded deferentially. "Old Man Wrigley's favorite expression was 'By gum!'"

Tohnyin groaned. "Ahab, the source of a remark that corny begs to be tossed overboard!" Her mien betrayed the desire to pursue some offbeat subterfuge. "If you could swim, we'd ask I.B. to accommodate you."

"That's a bit over the top." The Parallacts associate's darting eyes returned to the celebrity. "You can't swim, nature buoy? I had the impression you were a regular big yipper of the wet and wild."

"He's one bitchin' weapons-grade surfin' mother," Winterhalter affirmed. "Once off Lighthouse Point, he had a near-life experience."

The celebrity forced the gracious grin of a retired Russian roulette champion. "The thrill of surfing is pushed to its neuron-jangling crest when you can't swim. You taunt mortality."

A protracted horn blast seemed to shake the rivets and welds of the *Janesy*. Winterhalter sniffed ostentatiously, fanned the air and leveled a wry look at the celebrity. "Did you take the opportunity to jam in F-flat with that horn blow, perfect-pitch bitch?"

The celebrity channeled his animosity into a cocked eyebrow. "Background noise is your forte, tail-gunner." He studied an electronic poster on the wall that promoted the cranberry pie-eating contest of the upcoming weekend by depicting stick men devouring *tangy crannibal pies* until they attained *girdle-popping* girth.

"Cranberry growing is growing scarcer around here." Mercowitz detached the magneto lock fanny pack field purse from his hip strip, produced two auto-light cigarettes and dispensed one to Winterhalter. "Anyone else?" He returned the purse to his hip. "It's drifting north to Canada, where it's still cool enough to put a good blush on the berries."

The waitress arrived with the hurricanes. Tess smiled politely and took a hard gulp of her cocktail. I.B. tested his drink and held a grimace until the waitress departed. His disenchanted eyes settled on Jerry. "Are we going to get around to ordering our dinner now, spirit guide?"

"Electronic ordering is considered gauche." Jerry savored his hurricane. "Try that and they might ask you to disembark. The Stomach Club is an area of the ship where patron sourcerers must remain disabled, and patron communication remains an in-person proposition."

Scarlett O'Hara, a funky jazz band featuring a flugelhorn and a flutterboard, pumped out a bluesy rendition of J.S. Bach's "Ode To Joy". A couple of svelte, scantily clad blonde women gyrated across the dance platform. "Why don't you ask Tess for a dance?" the celebrity encouraged the reagent.

Winterhalter blew a smoke ring into the celebrity's face. "How about cuz I don't freakin' dance, ditwhistle?"

"Come on," the celebrity persisted, "let some lively jive swing you in harmony with the waves." He pointed at the sinuous blondes. "Play the eye of the storm, the ham of the sandwich, the base of the siege-works, maintaining strict west-coast frame, of course." The reagent skewered him with a glower. "Tess, ask I.B. to dance."

"You heard the cholla," she snapped. "Anyway, you and he are supposed to be together. It would balance the load if you two locked hands and rocked out as one."

"You might appreciate that Jerry and I have personal business to conclude," the celebrity grumbled, "proprietary business."

"Funny business." Winterhalter plucked the cherry garnish out of Tohnyin's glass. "Wanna feel like you'd never lost this?" He perched it between his puckered lips. The celebrity filliped the garnish out of the reagent's mouth. I.B. flung his cigarette into the celebrity's collar. "What's your issue, half-staff? That rhinestones are the primo jewels in your jockstrap?"

The celebrity clutched his glass. "It's a true mystery how you make it through the day without getting your cork popped every fifteen minutes, gewgaw. Learn to think outside the crotch."

One of the dancing blondes adjusted her top provocatively, and Mercowitz patted Tohnyin's wrist. "Contessa, take I.B. and fetch us all plates of hors d'oeuvres from the snack table, will you, please?" He pointed to a spot beside the bar.

Tess smiled at the celebrity. "Don't let your champagne-wit run dry, poetaster." She turned to the reagent. "Come on, watch-stander, you've been the one articulating hunger pangs." She strolled toward the dance platform, and I.B. indolently followed.

Two men in business suits passed the table. "Don't talk about Governor Buegher that way," one admonished his companion. "I've met him."

"Quite an impressive canoe, isn't it?" Mercowitz cooed. "You practically need to be reminded you're shipboard." Tohnyin walked around the dance platform and Winterhalter ricocheted between the vertiginous blondes.

The celebrity nodded and swept his hands beneath the edge of the table. "There's no telling when you might need to be reminded why you bothered to be shipboard."

Jerry chuckled. "I enjoy coming up to Wisconsin to partake of culinary delights dispossessed south of the border like licorice-studded, braised veal sweetbreads and terrines of duck foie gras drizzled with honey vinegar and decorated with candied pears or smothered in brandy and tobacco smoke." He took a long drag on his cigarette. "The casino is what initially juiced the *Janesy* after the high court decreed that Native American land rights couldn't extend into waters, and even though the Real Deal has now largely nixed the impact of that decision, the camp following has been established, and this trendy little sanctuary continues to thrive. It's where all the goblins gather." He took another puff, raised his glass and leaned closer. "Plus as Tess anticipated, when your table conversation goes stale, it's nice to be able to get up, go out on deck and inhale some mist-kissed freshwater air."

"Mist-kissed saltwater air is generally considered more salubrious because it's more consistent with the pH level of the human body." The celebrity smiled complaisantly. "I still think this modular tub is an outsized item on a little lake. It looks almost as top-heavy as Winterhalter's wanigan woman. And beyond that, most California cruise ships travel somewhere more exotic than in a small oval."

"This is the epitome of an appeal to the journey-oriented individual," Mercowitz snickered. "Geneva Lake is the second deepest body of water in Wisconsin, with an average depth of over ten metric fathoms. Legends abound of sea monsters and ghost ships. There've even been rumored sightings of the remains of murdered mobsters and a Russian nuclear attack submarine." The Parallacts associate savored another sip of his hurricane. "One of the reasons I so thoroughly enjoyed our rip rap on the way up, Ahab, is because I was able to peg you and Tess both as upwardly mobile battle-station placeholders." He surveyed the dancing blondes. "Tess is frighteningly attractive, isn't she? The woman is one gloriously embellished little sample of sensibility-crushing California muliebrity." He chortled.

"Penetrate the superficial supersymmetry of her exquisite face and extraordinary form, and you find substance, bearing and culture. She's a puzzle of contradiction and concinnity with a facile mind and an elan attitude. She's a hot Bodhisattva."

"She has the burden of beauty," the celebrity concurred. "A girl with a radical figure needs to be twice as smart to make it work for her rather than against her." He sampled his drink. "You'll never see Tess drinking expensive liquor and chewing cheap gum."

"Nothing purely physical could hold my tight focus." Jerry puffed on his cigarette. "Have you ever been privileged to witness her nude yoga routine? The way she can reconfigure those voluptuous roller-coaster curves from one position to another more impossibly seductive than the last is a fomental phenomenon to behold. The lass is one high priestess of tantra."

The celebrity clutched his glass. "If that's the same as a shrill princess of tantrums, I'm inclined to agree."

"She knows how to utilize every fiber of her being to elicit the illicit potential of a man's potency." The Parallacts associate unbuttoned his jacket. "She's a story that comes with a guaranteed happy nerve-ending. She might be the cautionary tail of a risky proposition, but after she was made, they broke the blow mold."

"With you and me it was the slime mold, eh?" The celebrity leaned closer. "It's a touchy subject, but if lust is an addiction, then a pretty girl is like a malady." He took a stout sip of his cocktail. "Now I'm not intimating that she's carrying the threat of an unintended piece dividend." He let an eyebrow spike. "I tease Tess about being a lady with a lot of priors, but her general medical records add no knocks to her psychiatric file." He smiled complaisantly. "She's simply a counter-proliferation specialist who collects powerful men like white velvet grabs dust and can inflict massive unrequited romantic damage."

Mercowitz folded his arms pensively. "She's vivacious, she's soft and spreadable as margarine, and she may be the world's first venomous herbivore." He puffed his cigarette. "I'm devoting serious alpha-waves to offering her a high leverage position in one of my organizations."

"Consigliere slash hostess, or hostess slash consigliere?" The celebrity glanced across the empty dance platform. "But before your new lieutenant comes marching back, let me cut to the reason I requested this private audience." He reduced his voice to a whisper. "Would you please explain, my cabal caballero, just what was with that little reception the good, gracious folks at Parallacts threw me when they threw me out?"

"You were there, weren't you, wapperjaw?" Jerry emptied the entire contents of his glass. "You can embroil yourszhelf in all szhortszh of collateral difficultieszh by not liszhtening closzhely." He extracted a cherry stem and wedge of orange rind and swallowed. "I inferred you were drawing me aside to warn me that playing your choice piece of classical sheet music was off-limits." He planed ice chunks between his teeth.

"I don't strategically classify her as untouchable." The celebrity raised his glass without drinking. "As I thought I demonstrated when we spoke last night, my personal feelings for her run about as flapjack-griddle deep as those I hold for I.B."

Mercowitz took a long drag on his cigarette. "Never lose track of the fact, my barrel-jumping hyper-hustler, that desire unsatisfied devours the desirer." He followed the re-emergence on the dance platform of Tohnyin and Winterhalter. "A preponderance of the general public keeps a lost cause on life support until it qualifies as a fool's errand. But you proved you have the ability to fail swiftly." Each hand balancing a plate of appetizers, Tess and I.B. paused to sway lyrically to the Max Frost revolution anthem "Shape Of Things To Come" as covered by the Constitution Singers. "Then you built further shareholder value by demonstrating that you have a long memory for those who've influenced you." He extinguished his smoke. "'Tis better to reign in Sacramento than to serve in Springfield, hmm?"

"He who can't appreciate political payback is lost." The celebrity noticed that the fashion slit in Tess's dress extended nearly to her hip.

"Of course," Jerry tittered, "the Parallacts board condemns any infraction in the identity theft family, and that message is what you as a routine offender were intended to take away from your scrimmage. You were granted an interview on the expectation that you were coming in to sell California classified information, and some of us grew awfully disappointed when it became apparent that your purpose was instead deleterious. Nevertheless, you strike me as a tricepsatops who can be counted on to responsibly radio the fire station and fire the radio station." Tess and I.B. set plates loaded with chicken wings, cheese balls and asparagus tips in front of the celebrity and Jerry. "Uncoded, that means you're tough enough to handle an emergency and keep it from going public."

"The pressure-point guy." Tohnyin brushed provocatively against Mercowitz and reseated herself. "Still talking gritty manly man stuff to prepare Ahab to survive in the real world?"

"Your name might've surfaced once or twice," the celebrity reported, "but it was inserted in an uncommonly favorable light."

"No venison sticks?" Jerry sorted his hors d'oeuvres. "One thing I must apologize for, Ahab, is your clothes. You've indubitably deduced that the board aims to delouse anyone who appears before it."

"He has lice, too?" Winterhalter leaned back far enough to challenge his balance on his stool. "You cooter, you ushed an infestation into my house!"

"Don't be pediculous," the Parallacts associate chuckled. "We had an inspector check his clothes and personal effects at the same time a masseuse examined his body for surveillance devices, but there was an accidental oil spill that ruined his suit, and poor Tiff the soft touch had to take the fall for the flub. Her avenue of redress for his despoilment was to persuade him to slip into a ghastly burlesque tux."

"Was it as offensive as what he's wearing now?" Tess crunched a celery heart.

"Ahab the Drama Queen loved the extra costume change." I.B. fingered chicken wings with both hands. "His shriveled soul still struts the planks of the stage."

"It was no less fashionable than a hospice gown." Mercowitz turned to Winterhalter. "What do *you* believe in, I.B.?"

The reagent sneered. "Likely about the same top-spin as you, skulk-cap: consuming as much of the world as time permits, making whatever don't amp me my own personal piss-pipe."

"He subscribes to a stark maximalist aesthetic." The celebrity found the buttered morels a particularly appealing delicacy.

Winterhalter redirected his attitude to the celebrity. "Eat those funk-chunks on the water, porthole-licker, and you'll sure as shit see them again." He snickered. "You'll gork yourself!"

"Can an old Navy man detect a hardtack military background?" Mercowitz vetted Winterhalter.

"Can you tell by the military earrings?" the celebrity wondered.

Jerry pointed a long asparagus tip at I.B. "What branch? Marines? Coast Guard?"

"Let's flatter the flag!" The reagent ripped a bite from a chicken wing and saluted sharply. "My high school guidance dick broke my balls to not join the Navy. He convinced me the guys I'd be shipping out with would be the ones I'd have to compete with for jobs and mounts when I got back, so I'd have way more organic reasons for wasting them than any rice-huskers or diaper-snipers I'd bump bows with overseas."

Mercowitz devoured a cheese ball. "They promote the military experience today as a trophy fishing excursion, where you get to strain for a thrill while your enemy has to strain for his life. You're entrusted with rigorous tasks that allow you to prove if not improve yourself, but their campaigns like those of most government service projects seem to leave society with consequences the exact opposite of their intent."

"I never met my high school guidance counselor," Tess reflected. "He was never in his office. He was rumored to have a problem with alcohol."

"It looks like at least three of four of us have a problem with alcohol," Jerry referenced the ratio of empty glasses on the table. "Waitresses tend to vanish around here never to be heard from again. Ahab, can we delegate you the vital assignment of harassing the bunker tenders until they deign to fire off another round for us?" He popped another cheese ball into his mouth. "I'd presume you can enlist I.B. to provide backup."

Winterhalter sprang to his feet. "Count me out, big bamboozle. I got to go drop off a hot, steamin' delivery in the male room." He started toward the back of the Slop Chest. "Fetch me a true hard toddy!"

"I need some top-shelf vodka." Mercowitz accented his grin with jaguar eyes. "I'll have a pink cloud, heavy on the spirits – they know how I like it."

Tohnyin ran her index finger over the rim of her glass. "If you'd be kind enough to portray a polydactyl, please bring me a classic Vin Mariani."

The celebrity grabbed his hurricane and started toward the throng at the near end of the bar. "A pink cloud is the concoction favored by our mutual friend," he heard Jerry tantalize Tess before he sauntered beyond earshot.

The celebrity strode the length of the worn wooden bar searching for an opening through which he might attract the attention of a sympathetic hospitality worker with a strong command of mixology. He stopped and impotently sipped the last drops of his hurricane behind a large woman seated at the far end of the bar. He backtracked the length of the bar. Tohnyin and Mercowitz chatted lustily, and he considered returning to the table under the pretense of having forgotten the name of Jerry's drink. A man toward the end of the bar sat attired in a white seersucker zoot suit with candy red pinstripes identical to his own. The celebrity drifted back alongside other patrons and discovered a gap which allowed him to touch the quartz-particle bar top by leaning over the shoulder of a stocky man in a green windowpane tattersall tunic. "You wouldn't know the difference between a largemouth and a rock," the tattersall man assured the dimpled man in a red plaid shirt seated beside him.

"You *are* a largemouth," came the reply.

"You are a rock," the tattersall tunic man settled the issue. He blindly cast his arms in the air and jerked backward, driving the celebrity two steps from the bar. The celebrity hoped the man found his next fishhook in a crannibal pie. He paced a few more steps and exchanged uncomfortable smiles with the man in the pinstriped seersucker zoot suit. He reached the end of the bar and produced the vial that Tohnyin had given him. He blindly inserted the reverse-scrutiny contact lens that could identify anyone looking askance at him. He spun crisply and locked eyes with the attentive man in the zoot suit.

"Nice duds," the celebrity offered.

"Get lost." The seersucker candy-striper abandoned his stool.

The celebrity raised his empty glass. "You're indiscernibly kind." He claimed the vacated space and attempted to attract a bartender with waves and whistles.

"You alone?" A lean individual with blond hair, pale grey eyes and mildly protruding ears flashed a toothy smile. He wore a crystal mirror-chain shoulder piece and collar harness over a black canvas vest featuring *GLAD* in silver letters.

"I'm here with my spongiostress." The celebrity leveled his thumb over his shoulder in the general direction of Tess.

"I noticed you with her before, but it didn't look like you were together." The *GLAD* man leaned closer. "If you don't mind me saying so, you look like you could sure use some discipline."

The celebrity nodded. "That's my business." He considered whether the recruitment attempt on the launch pad might be professional instead of personal. "I could use something along that line; I'm a chaplain."

"Well, I'm Alec, I'm a designated driver and I'm the toast of hell." The *GLAD* man raised his stained glass and sipped his soft drink. "What stripe of chaplain?"

"Conservative Christian." An idle bartender suddenly appeared, and the celebrity lunged to place his order, which included a reference to Mercowitz and a Mexican firing squad tequila cocktail for himself. Still confounded by the emergence of a potential pitfall or windfall, he turned back to Alec and extended his hand. "I'm Dante. Nice to meet you."

"Are you a tall drink of holy water, Dante, or do you put the 'fun' in fundamentalism?" Alec grasped the celebrity's hand and shook it. "I'm a devout nonbeliever. I don't even believe in global warming. But I'm fluent in classic Greek and Aramaic. Like a sample?"

The celebrity smiled complaisantly. "All right, how in ancient Aramaic would you say, 'The Coriolis force acts on the rotation of the planet to bend Northern Hemisphere winds in a clockwise direction away from high pressure zones'?"

Alec took a swig of his soft drink. "*Miesseh meshuneh.*" He rotated his forefinger in a clockwise direction around his ear.

The celebrity turned to find two men in open bomber jackets and ruffled silk shirts occupying the stools he and I.B. had vacated conversing with Tohnyin and Mercowitz. He checked the progress of his cocktail order. "Drink brandy whenever you're hungry," he advised Alec, "it's not just a diet but a spiritual exercise. And it's great straight."

"You're preaching to the anti-choir," the *GLAD* man asserted. "I'm a researcher in the field of French mathematics. We work hard to factor out fancy curves and then we go out and work harder to celebrate being single, seeing double and sleeping triple."

The celebrity craned his neck to maintain hard surveillance on Tohnyin's table. "You're obviously packing serious erudition; are you politically savvy?"

"You mean like Robespierre?" The *GLAD* man sighed. "You mean like Roman illuminati?" He opened his vest to expose his bare chest. "One of the main problems with our society, Dante, is that so few people suspect what side they really represent."

"Amen, brother." The celebrity wondered whatever happened to Winterhalter. "Constantine did Christianity a greater disservice than Diocletian. When the movement received a legal endorsement, hacks and charlatans of all ilks obtained a license to put it on and wear it for whatever selfish, nefarious purpose might serve them." Tess tilted her head and played with her double-hoop earring, perhaps defensively. "Every time some loon, some control-freak or some huckster comes out waving the banner of religion, my faith erodes."

"I'm not sure what that's supposed to signify," the *GLAD* man scoffed. "But I'm intrigued by a guilty good fellow who's quick on his knees and comfortable taking dictation there."

"That sounds like *Rules for Radicals*." As the bartender delivered four finished cocktails on a flimsy paper tray, the celebrity concluded that the *GLAD* man was working a purely personal angle. "I believe we're having separate conversations, Alinsky." He presented payment and cradled his drinks.

"Moving forward, you'll address me as 'Smackers,'" the *GLAD* man instructed. "You'll only offer your opinion when asked, and I'll only correct you once. We're going to commandeer some privacy."

"Sorry, I have domestic trouble to escalate." The celebrity executed a quarter turn from the bar.

"You can't leave now." Smackers swept his hand over his

chest, abs and crotch. "I haven't dismissed you. Do you need to be reprimanded publicly?"

"If I come back, Smackers, you'll know I thirst for it." The celebrity left the *GLAD* man to watch the fellowship he'd tried to establish rise to the top of his glass and pop. The interlopers no longer occupied the corner table, and the reagent had returned. The celebrity marched briskly back to his party and set down the tray with minor spillage.

"Zowie, Howie!" Winterhalter snatched his hard toddy. "It's our hero after the fact, the late Ahab Oobops!"

"We're pleased you resisted the temptation to overextend yourself playing rescue missionary, Oscar." Tohnyin sipped her Vin Mariani.

"Is your timing really as perfect as your pitch, hide-rographer?" Mercowitz lifted his pink cloud to his lips. "Or did you get lost navigating the vagaries of the troughs and ridges along the watering hole?" He produced a personal swizzle stick from his fanny pack field purse and tested his drink.

"Through limited visibility, Mercator, I held a steady fix on your position." The celebrity glanced over his shoulder to ensure that Smackers hadn't followed him. "Who were those flyboys? Did they cross the line of propriety?"

Tess rolled her eyes. "Those hardline gentlemen sought to sweep me off my feet, don't-gooder, because they believe that when you're a nice girl, you should be interested in performing charity work. Jerry spoke to them crossly as I.B. approached, and they took off."

"I trusted you could keep from getting carried away." The celebrity reseated himself. "If you'd sent me a body language distress signal, Tess, I'd have jumped at the invitation."

Jerry shook his head. "Or you might've gotten the wrong idea, Oobops, and that would be even worse." He sipped his cocktail. "Worse as this. What is this? Did you drop my name when you ordered?" He pointed at the celebrity's drink. "What's that supposed to be?"

"A Mexican firing squad." The celebrity savored a sip. "Remind me to treat you to one later."

The reagent slammed his mug on the table, releasing a wave of pulpy liquid. "This is no toddy! Whatever this sickly, chalky glob of cream they stuck you with is, Jercules, it sure as spoor comes with enriched ick factor." He slid his mug to the celebrity. "You're going back to the bar and you're going to exchange this cot-wash for a real toddy so the hard-working taxpayers of California get their money's worth on their investment." He eyed Jerry. "His notion of what makes the potion is what funky fruity powder goes into it."

"Balanced cocktails should flaunt and not conceal the tastes of their base spirits, as well as those of the ones who consume them." Mercowitz winked at Tess. "How's your Vin, sweetness?" He snuck another nip of his pink cloud. "Oobops, you were curating a curiosity before about Wisconsin, so here's a stat that might capture your attention: Wisconsin is first in the nation for number of arrests in proportion to the population."

The celebrity raised his Mexican firing squad. "While Wisconsin masses enjoy the secure, weatherproof confines of a jail cell, more Californians live out of their cars than do the denizens of any other state." He smiled with resignation. "That probably helps explain why we scrap like cultured scorpions on an electrified grid for the privilege of a parking place."

"We understand that Wisconsin is a great law-and-order tax hell on a Great Lake and the ones in office aren't often the ones in power." Tohnyin swept her fingers through her hair. "But the inner circle of initiates that constitutes Wisconsin's crony-island pales in comparison to the weighty, well-oiled machine that runs Illinois. Jerry, what are the peculiar intricacies of the political relationship between the two states?"

The Parallacts associate appeared to study Tess with an amused wariness. "All day long up here the authorities play non-stop commercial-free musical scandals, and each time the next one is exposed, their pols and pundits wag their hands and wring their heads and say, 'This is the sort of rampant structural corruption that distinguishes Illinois – we shudder to think it could happen here.'"

The celebrity shrugged. "We take that tone of moral superiority toward our neighbors, too."

Tess raised her glass. "*Vive l'eminence grise.*"

Mercowitz consumed his last morsel. "Humanity has always bonded over food and drink, with an epideictic emphasis on the intoxicating class of the latter." He rose. "Having already copped to being with the CIA, allow me to also acknowledge my ties to the NRA." He grabbed his pink cloud. "I speak, of course, of the National Restaurant Association. And as such, it is with Richter-scale chagrin that on this occasion, unable to procure personal dining space in a timely manner on a weeknight, I do hereby announce my intent to make a personal motion to the manager of the Stomach Club encouraging him to reassess the process of his reservation queue in a game-changing manner." He swallowed a swig of his cocktail. "Why don't you see if you can upgrade your drinks; I'll be back in a few."

"Spare a security stick, Scup?" Winterhalter extended an open hand. Mercowitz provided a toxin-detector swizzle stick plus a cigarette, exchanged affectionate glances with Tohnyin and strode out of the lounge with his pink cloud.

"Get this while you're up, dramshoppers." The reagent fidgeted with the cigarette tip. "I wound up following that Buddy, the chancre-shanker who clipped me up on the running track, into the men's head. Inside, there's three stalls: the one he took and two that have the doors leaning back over their ejector seats with 'Out of Order' signs hung on them."

"But that didn't stop you." The celebrity turned to Tess. "I trust that you and Jerry had a productive parley." He pointed to a table beside the dance platform that a young couple had just vacated. "Let's move there for a crisis summit." He plied his fingers against the underside of the table.

"You're concerned that he bugged us?" Tohnyin snickered. "I'm tired of deceiving him. We should be working to install Jerry as a stauncher ally, and you can rest assured I'll be pleased to relay any factoids that are bandied about here."

"Buddy's pants drop to his ankles, and he plunks himself down on the working shitter." I.B. replaced his cigarette tip before the phosphorus ignited. "So I'm pacing and pacing, and he starts to yak in some planet Najagogga alien tongue, I hear Jatakar tones, and he keeps on yakking, so I pound on the door."

"By process of elimination, why didn't you just head farther out to the next facility?" The celebrity rose. "Leave the pocket litter that Jerry gave you, and let's switch tables."

"Bud needs to know he can't hoard when resources are scarce." Winterhalter tapped the swizzle stick with rhythmic asymmetry. "I pound some more, and he still ignores me."

"Was it a code brown?" Tess smiled whimsically. "I predict you accused *Bud* of being out of *ordure*."

"I spy a bucket in one of the decommissioned stalls and fill it with hot water." The reagent gestured for the celebrity to return his toddy. "I yell 'Fire! Fire!' and heave the bucket into Buddy's stall!" He cackled convulsively. "And I'm out of there to take my business upstairs! I left him as irrigated as he was irritated!"

The celebrity leaned forward and deposited the toddy in front of Winterhalter. "Slick stall tactics." He turned to Tohnyin resigned to the idea that there would be no change of venue. "Before you make any snap career decisions, found-object, make certain you pay special attention to Jerry's menu selection at dinner." He splashed his fingers through rings of moisture on the table. "Now let's pool what intel we have on 'our mutual friend,' what we're up against and what we intend to do about it."

"You mean pool what intel I have?" Tess sighed. "Let's pause this team unity break, Ahab, to evaluate our loopy division of labor, where I do all the legwork and you grab all the credit."

"Last Sunday night Madelyn and me volunteered to take the housekeeping pressure off old Ahak by making us all pizza." Winterhalter slapped the celebrity in the shoulder. "We scattered our toenail clippings over his third, and he never had a clue they weren't some cheese slivers!"

"I switched slices with Madelyn while you were fondling her," the celebrity revised history slightly. "And the base ingredients I used when I made you guys that cotton candy were clothes-dryer lint and dust I gathered from behind the fridge." He turned to Tohnyin. "It's the age of specialization. You're light on your back, and you should always do the dirty work." He raised his glass. "On that quarter note, Torquemama, is there any operational progress to mark?"

Tess sneered. "Jerry has a connection to the chief of security of this ship, and I've enlisted him to produce recent surveillance video. They're both positive they can ID Shalom when they spot him."

"What's that going to do for us?" The celebrity took a hard swig of his Mexican firing squad.

"What that's going to give us, caudad-brain, is a clear picture of who we're pursuing as well as an opportunity to establish any associations with other persons of interest plus a frequency pattern that might help us predict when we can next expect to find his silhouette intermingled among the other night-stalkers who float this endless carousel of carousal." Tohnyin fixed her eyes on Winterhalter. "It would probably behoove one of us to plan on remaining aboard for a few weeks."

The reagent shook his head and stirred his toddy. "I've been fighting the feeling to fucking puke since we left land."

"Keep down the good fight." The celebrity considered

the prospect of returning to the safe house. "I'd be willing to accept argonaut duty, at least on a limited engagement basis."

"Thank you, Mother Courage." Tess sipped her Vin Mariani. "You may have to pay most of your shipboard expenses out of your own pocket, but it'll be worth it. This place is crawling with potential enemies. I've recognized at least two persons with a definite Anti-Alyce affiliation. They could be WIO officers."

The reagent blankly stopped stirring his toddy. "Exactly what the hell's WIO again?"

"Please tell me you're joking." Tohnyin gasped as the celebrity shrugged and shook his head. "WIO is Wisconsin's intel arm, their counterpoint to us, ostensibly run under the auspices of the Wisconsin State Historical Society and popularly known as the Small Engine."

"It has an impressive reputation for proficiency," the celebrity expounded, "especially for such a small economic market."

Tess nodded. "It's a formidable creep outfit. It doesn't have a record that Natty Phil would kill to equal, but if he could, he'd definitely lie, steal and cheat more to come closer."

"Lie, cheat and steal me some more wings." The reagent shoved his empty plate into the celebrity's face. "You're served for ferry duty this round, spice-cadet."

The celebrity snatched the plate. "Sorry, wurst-works, my nails have already been clipped."

"Plant your feet in the present, ragweeds." Tohnyin gaveled her goblet on the table. "I.B., I'm incredulous that you could've completed the Mission without hearing of WIO's two most notorious officers: Paige Eiffel is the bloodstained double-agent who did incalculable damage to CIB while on our payroll; and Superintendent Llewellyn Morse, the 'Super,' is an impassioned reformer, a transsexual-"

"Which direction?" Winterhalter wondered.

"There seems to be some discrepancy about that." Tess tossed the celebrity a deferential glance for clarification.

"That's a dedicated professional." The celebrity stirred his cocktail. "Somehow a name change pales in comparison." He slid the empty hors d'oeuvres plate at I.B. "Eiffel's dossier reads like a skaldic siege saga. Obtain it. Don't fall into a freebooting culture that counts on others to provide your essential research, least-wassail, and you might not end up eating an I.E.D."

Tohnyin rose and donned her trench coat. "I just received a message from Jerry that he's having difficulty convincing the security honcho to deliver all of the access we requested, so I'm going to try to inspire additional motivation for cooperation."

The celebrity clicked his tongue. "Add a few curves to the pitch count? I'd leave the wrap behind."

"I'm taking it in lieu of a purse." She removed a high-output LED halo hat from a pocket, unfolded the glowing spiked disc and crowned herself with it. "As soon as our full viewing privileges are secured, I'll summon you plastic straw men, and I'm guessing we'll surround the dinner table soon thereafter." The core of her face obscured by the glare of the halo hat, she tossed back the final gulp of her Vin Mariani. "My drink was a shade green, Ahab, but I liked it." She nibbled on a coca leaf. "Feel free to buy me another." She smiled and strutted out of the lounge.

"She can't dance for shit, but she has a swanky sway to her walk," Winterhalter observed. "What kind of precious princess is she trying to make out as with that headgear?"

"*Sexcelsior!*" The celebrity extended his cocktail overhead. "Statue of libido."

"You have a little urge going for her, don't you?" The reagent leered. "Your taste is probably far enough up your ass you think she's as hot a model as Madelyn."

The celebrity suppressed the urge to pump handstands of hilarity. "Tess is a sultry study in scintillation." He sipped more firing squad. "A man could raise a child with her as easily as a glass."

I.B. snickered. "She has a kind of lovely face. You do realize she's doing that old fart, don't you?"

The celebrity winced mightily. "She's playing him."

"Yeah, good thing she fucks like an old pro." The reagent emitted a sardonic chuckle. "Exactly what stake does Jetsky Spetsnaz have in our Shalom shell game anyway?"

"I'd classify Jerry as a protean entity with an economic edge." The celebrity finished his cocktail. "He probably fits the idea these outlandish inlanders have of a fixer. If he's present in any destructive capacity, it's to influence us to expend time, effort and capital resources chasing what he or WIO has determined is a no-value target. On the other hand, if he believes Shalom's stock is grossly undervalued, he might think he can hit whoever will pay the most with an outrageous finder's fee."

"So he's basically nothing but V.C.?" Winterhalter snatched his toddy, curled his lip and set down the mug without imbibing. "Or maybe, Ajab, *El-Eatist* will let us lead him to this whale-class blowhard, and then with a good-natured dig, he'll shish his kebab out." The reagent leapt to his feet and waved. "There's that damned stealth waitress!" He snapped his fingers. "Hey! Hey, Sub-Rosa!" She ignored him, and he scurried after her.

The celebrity continually glanced toward the bar. He lost track of Winterhalter, but when the crowd fanned into a loose spread formation, he caught glimpses of Smackers. The reverse-scrutiny lens revealed that Smackers was looking back. He held eye contact for a moment too long, and he feared he'd extended encouragement to the *GLAD* man for a further test of resolve. Mercowitz's tall Korean acquaintance passed the table, and the celebrity could hardly contain his enthusiasm. "Jogger-ninja! Seoul man!" He struggled to recall the crat's name. "I'm sorry, it's not Kim-"

"Marty Park," the man amiably offered over his shoulder. He turned and approached the table. "Where's Tess?"

"She's helping Jerry hustle a restaurant booth." The celebrity invited Park to occupy a stool.

"It's unusually busy." Park remained standing. "What specific dink jobs in California state government do you and Tess hold?"

The celebrity snickered self-consciously. "Jerry just likes to joke that everyone in California works for the state."

Park nodded. "His is a fascination with fascism."

The celebrity stirred the contents of his empty glass. "Actually, Tess and I do have jobs rather unique to the Coast. She's a divorce planner and I'm a death coach."

Park eyed the celebrity skeptically. "You're a contract killer and she's a social contract killer."

The celebrity patted his pipeline curl. "We actually polish environmental impact statements for the sorts of projects in which Jerry embroils himself. I gather you're pretty familiar with Jerry? With his engineering background?"

"Like boxcars." Park smiled slyly. "I know Jerry well enough to never believe anything he says."

The celebrity clicked his tongue. "It's troubling that someone so accomplished so freely pampers the impulse to exaggerate, even if the awards he's won are primarily for agility."

Park shuffled toward the wall. "You'll have to advise me on what projects he's involved with these days. It was my understanding that he's been exclusively focused on headhunting. His is the firm crutch of crutch firms."

The celebrity gestured to the stool that Tohnyin had occupied. "He indicated on the trip up that he's moved beyond local shadow-cabinet carpentry, and he now underwrites a business incubator that specializes in capitalizing on the ramifications of climate events. He's invested in adaptive global salvage, like the Coast solar desalination array and other unfinished business of the late Link Worbley."

"Are they going to try to shoot that stretch of water pipeline through Arizona like Worbley proposed?" Park settled into the stool against the wall.

"Tess questioned him about that," the celebrity prospected, "because we give Worbley major credit for the light footprint the pipeline has in the Valley, but Jerry's tentacles are apparently cramped around the polar shield. He alluded to an enhancement they have that's going to radically upgrade its effectiveness." He paused. "Have you heard what's in the works on that?"

"Mercowitz tends to magnify." Park popped to his feet. "I think Parallacts keeps him around mainly for his ability to break up a bored meeting. Here comes your nauseous superior, and I have to get back." Winterhalter approached the table carrying a tall pink-orange drink. "Nice to see you again, although I wish you could've been Tess. Give her my unflagging affirmative energy." He nodded to the reagent and walked away.

"The pleasure was all mine." Winterhalter straddled his stool. "What's down with Moon Tzu? He have a trunk full of rhino horns to unload?" He brandished his cocktail. "This is a citrus slut." He savored a swig. "You ought to plant your foam-blowing kiss-missers around one of these, Wanda. Beta-bear at the bar bought it for me."

A call from Mercowitz registered on the celebrity's Qilroy. "Ahab, I can't reach Tess direct. Let me speak with her, please."

"She's not with you?" The celebrity felt a kernel of panic sprout in the pit of his stomach.

"Cut the straight-man shtick, Oobops." The Parallacts associate jammed a cigarette into the corner of his mouth. "I'm on the verge of doing you people a mega-favor. I try to do one of those each year, and I decided for once to get it over with early."

"She said she got a message to join you in strategic discussions with the head of ship security." The celebrity staggered to his feet. "I'm calling her and not getting an-"

"I haven't had contact with her since I left you." Mercowitz's smile appeared alarmingly brittle.

"Tess is fucking missing?" Winterhalter slurped his citrus slut.

"She got taken or she's taken us." The celebrity flattened his pipeline curl pressing his hand against the top of his head. "How do you even begin to search a ship?"

Mercowitz sighed. "The gangway would be the immediate high-value point in securing the perimeter, wouldn't it, roustabout? Begin with Winterhalter flanking you, and end with you flanking him." He shook his head. "I'll tell you, Oobops, I'd be beside myself if Tess wasn't beside me." His Qilroy cam pivoted, framing Tohnyin's head, and he nickered raucously.

"Once more, Ahab, I'm inspired by your sweeping confidence." Tess lifted the shadow veil of her halo hat and exhibited a frustrated smile. "It borders on the tragic that you're shlumpf enough to fall for such an obvious gag." The reagent cackled and took another swig of his cocktail.

The celebrity exhaled deeply and nodded. "Always pleased to provide friendly fodder for the select co-chairs of the hoax committee." A smoke ring drifted past Tohnyin's face. "I trust, puff-piece, that the occasion of this communique is notification that we're finally restaurant bound?"

"The fact is, stemwinder, Tess and I are at the moment on our way to formalize our dinner reservation, so here's the situation." Jerry dominated the camera frame. "You're to meet the head of ship security, one Curly, right now at the Coat Of Arms, the VIP lounge up on the promenade. You'll be shown to the grey room, where two terminals have been loaded with libraries of assorted recent video surveillance that you can select to compare and contrast with the image of Charlton Shalom that Tess and I captured and posted."

"We couldn't believe it!" Tess cooed ecstatically. "We're as positive as the pope that it's him, and we acquired him in less than three minutes of search time!"

"There's also a real-time surveillance feed from a couple of points of interest in the casino, just to provide you with the opportunity to match prizes for the ultimate double jackpot." The Parallacts associate jabbed his cigarette at the cam. "Expect to be swaddled in video there for about half an hour. It'll probably remind you of your vaunted days under center, Ahab, in the shadow of your own goalpost. We'll call you when we're butter to roll."

"I need to eat first before I get a fucking headache!" The reagent snarled at the corner speaker, which blasted PartisAnn's jazzy "Rapsody On A Theme Of Rockmaninoff".

"You'll utilize your time researching video records!" The camera reframed Tohnyin. "We were precluded from downloading the image, so you're going to burn it into your brain in case Shalom happens to be the next guy you come up against in a public restroom. Ahab, you're responsible for his cooperation. Let's not lose sight of the prime reason we're here! After dinner, we'll come back and all log some more hard-core observation time."

"Curly at the Coat Of Arms," the celebrity verified. "Why don't you meet us there, Tess?"

"Within the context of me as a contact, Oobops, you should be able to stand on your own." Mercowitz twirled his cigarette. "Augment your emoluments with the amenities of the VIP lounge. In the meantime, Ms. Tohnyin has an indoctrination bridge to cross and black-tie entrée to betray." He broadened his grin. "See you two frackers in a bit." He terminated the connection.

The celebrity stared at his blank Qilroy screen. "I believe Old Faithless has presented us with a religious riddle: How many pinheads can dance in the palm of an investment angel? The working answer would appear to be: At least three."

The celebrity and Winterhalter proceeded to the shady, understated nook that contained the Coat Of Arms in an aft recess on the promenade deck. The head of ship security Curly proved to be "Carol Lee," a stalwart slab of an African-American woman with cream-colored hair who required that sourcerers be disabled and offered a ten-thousand-dollar "acception" for ship surveillance viewing privileges. The celebrity registered an obstinate civil protest in an attempt to negotiate a reasonable dollar amount, but Carol Lee explained, "The lounge price includes all gratuities. Are you paying or leaving?"

"Madam Security" ushered the celebrity and the reagent into what appeared to be a family room of mid-20th century America with atomic style retro modern chic furniture. "The grey room of the lunar lounge." The two observation terminals were situated on opposite sides of the area. Carol Lee provided brief tutorials on how to navigate the system so any surveillance point on the ship could be monitored in real-time and any video history in the library could be accessed. "On the left," she observed, "you have a live feed from the Heart O' Gold casino and on the right you have the image your handler selected of that famous buffo – Shaboom?" She didn't indicate any interest in the purpose of the review. "If you two thumpers don't need any more drinks, directions or distractions, I'll leave you to your sightseeing. I'll be back to check on your progress." She sauntered to the door and locked it behind her.

The celebrity scrutinized his quarry. He manipulated the still shot of Shalom into a medium close-up. Resolution wasn't at a premium, but the maestro of the polar shroud appeared gaunt, rumpled and frail. His lips formed a subtle, cryptic smile, but his sunken eyes were framed by darkened sockets. He wore his hair in a Janus cut, pasted onto the left side of his forehead and teased in cottony white wisps off his right temple. The celebrity zoomed out. The grand slam scientist wore a light blue T-shirt, grey vest and tan jeans, all of which seemed to stretch and strain to fit.

Winterhalter's hunger moans gradually ceased. He removed his shoes and seemingly grew riveted to the assignment. The celebrity scanned recent video logs and found Shalom at the

Gold Bar area of the casino. He utilized the biometrics con-
formation function for verification. The sky-tossing topologist
appeared attached to two other men, both of whom looked too
soft and casual to represent professional muscle or government
armor. A humorous remark from the companion with bulging
eyes induced Shalom's shoulders to shake. Sound was garbled,
but no laughter could be discerned attending the convulsions.
No inherent urgency to gamble manifested itself; the Nobel
laureate walked away holding his arms angled away from his
body like a cheerleader forming a human "A."

The celebrity perused logs with various clock and calendar
relationships in the interest of assembling a regular pattern of
Shalom appearances aboard ship. His tempered pessimism was
rewarded with a possible hit in the Slop Chest. A man who
couldn't be confirmed as Charlton sat locked in a neighborly
embrace with an exotic, young dark-haired woman. Perhaps
she was a former student or admirer in the process of forging
an iconic bond. The close companions rose and strolled out
of the lounge, and the celebrity verified the target's identity
by gait analysis. He wondered if Shalom's elusive CIB dossier
might be littered with pulchritudinous sisters-in-arms.

The celebrity reviewed video to the point of exhaustion.
When the wall clock read *23:30*, he staggered to his feet. "Over
three hours of this sequestration! We should've set a time limit
on our watch because we're apparently seen as shiftless!" He
received no response from the reagent. He marched across the
room and slapped the back of I.B.'s chair. "Report, pilliwinks!"

Winterhalter's eyes popped open and he sat erect. "I was
not napping, wetsleeves, fuck you very much! I project that
with a bit more momentum, I'll be able to hack into the ship's
control center!"

The celebrity grimaced. "That sounds like a tremendous
way to wear out the seat of your pants, pal-mal, but precisely
how does it promote our objective?"

Winterhalter sneered. "We convince these Sconnies we

can shut down their playpens, and they'll crunk to any request we make." He rose and stretched. "We just demand they hand over our charge-at-large Charlton and we can shit-can this creeping and slinking around!"

The celebrity snickered with festering aggravation. "Why don't we release an all-out media blitz? Let's issue a Charlton Alert and offer a reward! Or maybe the idea is to conduct our investigation quietly lest our extreme fascination incite these sons of lethargy to stash him or smoke him if they got him or deploy considerably more resources to finding him themselves if they don't. Jerry's task is obviously not only to monitor our position behind the scenes but to ascertain its orientation."

I.B. scoffed. "How is it Jerry Macro-Wise knows dope about us that we don't know about him?"

"Trading equities with Tess hasn't hurt." The celebrity scrutinized the reagent's screen. "We need to be more invested in alternative influence-peddlers to stay up to speed with the progress she's made." He thrummed the back of the chair. "Have you logged any Shalom sightings?"

"So many I've lost track." I.B. reseated himself. "He seems to be aboard this spittoon boat every Saturday night with some hot, young thing."

"A babe with dark hair, prominent cheekbones and an aquiline nose," the celebrity submitted.

Winterhalter hissed. "There's different ones, but mostly it's a blonde, a real pageant warrior type." He rubbed his neck. "She looks freshly familiar; I may have met her through Mad."

A hard, heavy knock rattled the door to the grey room. The door opened, and a strapping young man with apple cheeks wearing a burnt orange tuxedo entered pushing a cart packed with clattering covered silver pots and bottle-sporting ice buckets. "Good evening, video voyeurgers, my name is Burl, assistant to Carol Lee." He saluted. "As a gesture of diplomatic courtesy and professional appreciation, your conductress sends you roasty coasters some of the finest feastin' from our bitch'n kitchen."

"*Kibble!!!*" Winterhalter leapt to his feet and approached the cart.

"Jerry Mercowitz is the source of this spread?" the celebrity inferred.

"Who?" Burl wiped his forehead. "These are leftovers from a private party Carol Lee thought you might be able to use, so she sent them over. She hates to see good food wasted."

Winterhalter patted Burl on the belly. "It'd be a feed-bag sacrilege." He snatched a buffet plate and started overturning covers. "Praise be Carol Lee!" He loaded his plate with shrimp and his cheeks with meatballs.

The celebrity gestured toward Burl. "Let's wait for our gracious emissary to fix his own plate first."

Burl patted his e-badge. "Thank you for the kind offer, but I'm not permitted to fraternize on duty." He presented a bottle of Viognier to the reagent, who responded with an emphatic grunt. "You can afford to take a little break and enjoy." Burl silently removed the cork. The celebrity dismissed the assortment of savory aromas and returned to his terminal. Burl squinted with irritation. "You have two hours yet available on the room, so there's still time to work up an appetite."

"Don't mind him." I.B. reached past Burl for a spoon. "He's a shallow-witted, feeble-willed petute who tries to compensate by always putting on a show like he's more committed than everyone else, like he's always in HEET."

Burl smirked. "I figured there's a reason why he flips people off with his pinkie." He scratched his head. "But he thinks he's in heat?"

"Hostile Environment Endurance Training." The reagent ladled chili into a cut-glass boat. "A program the company we work for puts us through before it puts us in the field, and which Haboob can't seem to let go of."

"Could you fix him with dehorning paste?" Burl giggled.

"One last item, creepy peepies – we got a reading from here earlier that would indicate sourcerer activity." He eyed the celebrity pejoratively. "Maybe from force of habit you temporarily forgot, but if it happens again, we'll have to crush the resistance by confiscating your vitals, and you'll be asked to leave the club."

"Uh, we'd have to refuse." Winterhalter swallowed and gestured to the celebrity. "He has galloping O.C.D. to do whatever he's ordered not to." Burl chortled incredulously and left the grey room. The reagent shoveled shrimp into his mouth. "Got to be something here that you find appealing enough to chow down on, Bopalooza." He uncovered the crumb cake. "You're not retracted with terror that they poisoned it, are you?"

"If they poisoned the napkins, John of Salisbury, they went to a lot of trouble for nothing." The celebrity resumed his video survey. "I don't like the idea of not being able to wait out Tess and Jerry."

"Everything is a competition with you!" The reagent transferred crumb cake to his plate. "That's high on the list of reasons why you're so pathetic and disgusting."

The celebrity nodded. "I.B., the top item on your bucket list is to beat someone – anyone – at something – anything." The live feed from the Gold Bar area of the casino on the left panel of his screen grabbed his attention. He leapt to his feet. "Hey, come here and look at this!" The reagent grabbed a bottle of cherry Chardonnay and sauntered to the celebrity's side. A familiar halo hat over bare right shoulder conversed with Mercowitz over drinks. The Parallacts associate looked directly into the overhead security cam and flashed a wide, defiant grin. "What are those loose tacks doing there?"

The celebrity headed for the door. "Come on, backlash! They seem to have us sucking up an integrity vacuum."

"You go, Hugo." Winterhalter headed back to the food

cart. "I'm sort of in the middle of things here: dinner, a cyber-attack, the 20th century."

The celebrity paused at the door. "After Tess's decree that not another precious moment be squandered outside this holding room, don't you feel the need to demand an explanation?"

"I'm vacating the op." The reagent took another plate and probed the cisco. "You've lost command. You want to strafe the foemantic couple and pinch their heads off, you step right out and get to it." He speared another meatball. "When you were away from the table before, they called you a 'light load' and a 'pain in the bug-out bag.' You'd be better served, Baba ghanoush, to stick around and learn not to fear your food."

"Ib, you have a gift for irrelevance and futility." The celebrity slammed the door behind him.

"Suck my bulge!" Winterhalter shouted through the crescent porthole.

Outbound. 0020 CST Wednesday 29 March.

"Where timing is the ticket, you're holding a failure to yield." A second dinner invitation to the Stomach Club from Jerry Mercowitz at 2100 hours blinked gratuitously from the top of the celebrity's Qilroy message queue. Weaving through ship patrons in a long-striding society-tempo dash to the main deck, he considered with no little vexation how acutely aware the Parallacts associate had to be that the Coat Of Arms held its occupants incommunicado. The tourist flow density increased in proximity to the Heart O' Gold casino. The celebrity approached the Gold Bar from the rear and immediately located Mercowitz's dyslexic question mark and Tess Tohnyin's halo hat. Tess stood facing the bar gesticulating. The combination of gold-coin pixie holographs circulating through the pulsating black light over the bar and the garish amber glaze of her halo hat lent a burnt sienna cast to her hair. Perhaps it was an odd psychological manifestation, but her butt appeared a size and a half bigger as well. Jerry, by contrast, straddled his highchair regally.

The celebrity emerged from his wave of pressed flesh. "If sports aren't basically about personal humiliation," Mercowitz asserted, "I guess I miss the point." He sighted the celebrity without change in deportment.

The slit in Tohnyin's dress exposed the edge of her black lace panties, which she'd evidently found cause to change since she'd exited the Slop Chest wearing a turquoise undergarment. "In the thick of things, tingle-puss?" The celebrity smacked her in the posterior with a controlled fury.

"I formally beg your pardon?" The woman in the scarlet sequined dress rubbing her glutes wasn't Tess. She stood a bit shorter and her chestnut hair had a gentle wave. She had a narrow aquiline nose which probably appeared longer in the shadow of the headgear, a wide mouth with full, pouty lips and a strong chin. She appeared to be his age, perhaps a few years older, although if he were pressured to guess he'd find a slightly less measured way to phrase the appraisal.

The celebrity cringed. "I'm so sorry, I mistook you-"

"Que sarong so wrong, Kidon," Mercowitz scolded. "The fashion industry mantra that the clothes make the woman tain't quite right." He set his unsavory purple concoction on the bar but didn't release it. "Where the hell have you been hiding out? If you weren't rude enough to ignore your invitations, you could've had dinner with the glam crew who steer the ship for the captain."

"Could've had?" The celebrity growled. "I passed on grey room service. You know they insist that Qilroys go dark up there. Why didn't you summon-"

"For once in your life, you walking anti-authority streak, you actually abided by some regulatory claptrap?" Jerry rolled his eyes. "You imbecile." He slurped his drink noisily. "I slipped the security advisor a generous five-hundred-dollar inducement to arrange your viewing privileges." The Parallacts associate snickered. "I got the sense that she's a striker, a real sucker player. Did she try to trip the tipping point with you as well? How many more shekels did she shake out of you?"

"Nothing close to what you paid." The celebrity pointed to the woman. "Club uniform?"

"This was Tess's dress." The woman effervescently raised her arms as if to present herself for inspection. "Didn't you catch our joust?" She gestured to the jumbo long-stemmed crystal goblet with a Jacuzzi-size bowl that stood in the center of the horseshoe bar. "In the tradition of Camelot, to the victor went horse and armor – with a pinch of skin tossed in to the mix, a little hide on the side."

"She now owns the Pidge," Jerry chortled. "So how are you getting home? Ahab, this is Iris, an attorney. Iris, this is Ahab, an imbecile."

The woman extended her sleek, manicured hand. She had captivating dark eyes, pronounced cheekbones, a deeply dimpled, mischievous smile, a firm grip and a striking familiarity. She wore silver ankh earrings. "How's imbecile pay these days?" Her fingertips were extraordinarily long, and he suspected that she was a second-wave bioneer in the eager league of neo-trend-setters undergoing genetic enhancement of their extremities for cosmetic advantage. "I'd expect overcrowding in the field to exert downward pressure on wages."

The celebrity smiled complaisantly. "There's always room at the top for a natural." He spied Tess's double-hoop earrings on the bar. "When Jerry started out, he couldn't spell 'IQ' if you spotted him the 'I.'" He shifted his gaze to Mercowitz. "Where is *tovarich* Tess?"

"The body of the dearly dismantled Tess is beneath the burning blade of the ship's scrimshaw carver," Iris tooted, "enduring the final flourishes of my proud personal emblem as it's brattooed into her broken, little butt." She pressed her tongue into her lower row of lustrous, rail-straight teeth. "That was our side bet."

"Whack the panic attack, Jack." Mercowitz oscillated an index finger between his lips. "The Contessa is getting a brat-too at the boutique, where I laid out for a new lime-green pant suit to cover her shame and soothe her injury once she's charred and tinctured."

"Haughty, swan-necked girl, she couldn't believe I got the best of her." Iris slipped easily into the role of the virago with a fresh kill. "I returned her trench coat because it's frump wrap and it was full of her vomit, but it was euphoric stripping her down. If you're hers as well, you can appreciate that." She stroked the celebrity's wrist. "I enjoyed cutting deep into her psyche and removing some self-esteem."

"Iris is a sharp cheddar." Jerry enjoyed another sip of his cocktail. "As we speak, she's pursuing her third post-grad degree: a soc psych Ph.D."

"Care to test my prowess as a student of the human condition?" Iris offered the celebrity a nearly empty basket of nuts and dabbed at the corner of his mouth with a crumpled bar napkin. "Let's see how accurately I can describe the dynamic of the personal connection between you and your embedded yes-woman." Her smile appeared less mischievous and more malicious. "I'll bet Tess continually tells you how smart and talented you are even as she bends over backward to make you feel stupid and worthless."

The celebrity nodded pliantly. "Except for the part where she tells me how smart and talented I am, that's pretty much how we coalesce." He cast an implicative glance at Mercowitz. "Were you able to extrapolate that with minimal leading from our expert witness?"

The Parallacts associate snatched the basket of nuts from the celebrity. "I might've mentioned that Tess is your personal trainer and she resents having to clean your cage." He raised his right hand. "But honest, Ahab, I cagily suppressed the inside intel that you're virtuoso players in the California state legislature band. Does that pass muster coverage-wise?"

"A musical band?" Iris chuckled. "Why does the legislature have a band?"

"Music brings people together," the celebrity improvised. "Political parties can have bitter arguments on the issues, but people in government will always be in strategic agreement that in the end they want to be treated to a good time. We march in and throw them the party to end all parties."

Iris snatched a Qilroy core and the pair of double-hoop earrings off the bar and placed them in the celebrity's hands. "I don't want Tess's noisy accessories. You can graciously return them to her." She took her colorless drink in one hand and pulled the celebrity by the arm onto her empty barstool beside Jerry. "Relax and expand. What instrument do you play?"

"I'm a sawyer." The celebrity clicked his tongue. "I grew up playing the uilleann bagpipes, but one night my dad over-reacted and hacked them to pieces with a rough-cut hand saw. While he was still panting, I picked up the saw and became musically proficient with *it*. My dad later apologized by buying me a theremin, but the genie was out of the bottle and a sawyer was on the stage. I've toyed with a host of other instruments since, but I've never found one, including the banjo, as existentially empowering."

"Lord love the philosopher-minstrel," Mercowitz scoffed. "In the symphony of life, Ahab is a brassy sour note. In college, he was a drum major, snared as a sidekick by the campus bully, steadily rolled and soundly beaten."

"And it was an all-girl military school to boot," the celebrity attempted to allay churning tensions.

"Then properly, you're a philosopher-menstrual," Jerry gibed.

"Guys, dispense with the needle exchange program?" Iris sipped her drink. "So what part of California are you from?"

"El Centro," he lied upon a vague survival instinct.

"El Centro?" she tittered. "That's not a place; it's just a

name. It's like saying you're from Leftoverville or Plasticburg, California."

"Legend has it that Ahab is a by-product of Suction City, a brat born on the edge of Fallout Canyon beneath the Spunky Mountains in Pole Vault, California." Mercowitz raised his glass without imbibing.

The celebrity hoisted an imaginary drink in return. "And here's tossing the Chicago salute with a California blush back at Jerry, who hails from Cut Corners, Illinois, downstate and downwind from Soothurst, industrial base of his current residence outside Over Barrington in the gated community of High Hand Park." He patted his pipeline curl as Iris laughed. "How do you know about El Centro?" He rose and gestured that she should claim his barstool.

Iris brushed her fingertips lightly over his forearm and hip. "Please sit." She tapped the shoulder of the man on the next barstool. "Sir, could you and your friends please shift down a stool so I can sit beside my colleague?" The three men in question grumbled, conferred and chivalrously obliged. A look of grateful condescension flickered across Iris's face as she rejoined the ranks of the sedentary in synch with the celebrity. "We rode through El Centro on a bus tour I took of the most destitute, wretched areas of the country." She grinned. "We started in the back-streets of the most extreme Jersey inner cities, we experienced the bad side of Hazard, Kentucky, the most depressed patches of back bayou swampland, and we finished in makeshift settlements of the great Slab of the California desert, along with the region around the Salton Sink."

"That's a vacation?" The celebrity caught a peripheral glimpse of an approaching bistrosta in puffed white blouse and silk navy kerchief.

"It was two college credits in sociology." Iris's mien hovered somewhere between sly and cynical.

"Let me perfect that for you, sir." The bistrosta sunk

some organic matter into Mercowitz's glass and wiped away the overflow.

"There was probably more academic merit in my trip than in Tess's senior thesis." Iris pressed her tongue into her lower row of teeth. "Her diploma must've come gift-wrapped."

"She told you tales out of school?" The celebrity hoped his overriding concern didn't register in his voice. "I wonder what's keeping her."

"What, or who?" Iris puckered her lips and leaned into him. "How has she always found the time to strike intimate ties with so many men? She must have a lot of grit. I imagine she lives on a street with a name like Lotus Lane." She squeezed his biceps. "Care to view the replay of her electro-demolition?"

"Tess's residence is in the Signal Hill area of Long Beach," Jerry interjected, "aiya, Ahab?"

The celebrity felt as if he'd been body-slammed awake. "Electro-"

"What's your pleasure, sir?" the bistrosta accosted him.

"Bring the quivering gelatin-mold of a man a Molotov." Mercowitz reached across the celebrity and pinched Iris's exposed thigh. "Take heed of what this lady advises. She's an irregular conflict expert. She's resolute, a perfectionist and a winner, and she's one of the country's leading Wisconsinologists."

The celebrity surveyed the F-117 Nighthawk nose wreckage display protruding through the ceiling across the main aisle from the bar. "Such a credential could suggest she's a sympathizer."

The Parallacts associate sighed. "It should suggest she's a mapparatchik. She's a cultured pearl, a self-possessed woman of the world and a helluva nice person." He stroked her shoulder. "She'd drive us home, but she lives in Madison. If nothing else, we'll rent a limo."

"She's a pearl all right." The celebrity lightly patted Iris's unexposed knee. "Her optimism bias is precious. It would've been a mean feat to play Tess for the Pidge because the Pidge isn't Tess's to lose."

"Not anymore it isn't." Iris narrowed her eyes and flashed an intrepid, clenched-jaw smile. "It was a sound transaction that I guarantee would withstand any legal challenge." She pointed to the jumbo crystal goblet behind the bar as two shirtless contestants sporting protective eyewear entered it from the top of a ladder. "The interesting money changes hands here." The slighter, brown contestant worked to gain a solid foothold in the viscous, bile-green liquid which filled the base of the bowl. The fleshier blond contestant scratched his crotch. "I enjoy betting against the combatant who I evaluate as the bigger pig."

"Speaking of such enhanced sizzle-pants boat-swine," Jerry bantered, "I wonder where oh where I.B. might be?"

"We split," the celebrity reported. "He's still lapping up low theater in the grey-"

"That's the perfect place for him." Mercowitz smiled archly. "Anywhere elsewhere."

A man with puffed grey hair clad in iridescent vertical stripes scaled the ladder toting a yellow hand cannon. "D.J. the master bartender officiates the events," Iris explained. "He's a super notary."

The bistrosta presented the celebrity with a blazing torch topped with a jagged mound of cadmium-red cream which supported a pair of yellow licorice twists fashioned like hand tools. A horn blared and the lights over the bar dimmed. A red spotlight illuminated the jumbo goblet. D.J. barked an introduction of the combatants and proffered gaming codes with the rapidity of a master auctioneer.

"What do you say, small-swell shredder?" Mercowitz engaged the celebrity. "Are you a player, or what?"

The celebrity cupped his hands within the chromosphere of his Molotov. "Dabbling in a game of chance I've never seen played promises a payoff no less robust than hanging ten at the end of a rope, but I have a fire to fight."

The Parallacts associate shook his head. "Let it burn itself out, dunce." The celebrity sat frozen and the cocktail continued flaming.

"Wagering complete!" D.J. handed the weapon to the slighter combatant Farnoosh. A hush gripped the vicinity of the Gold Bar as the players took turns tasing each other with increasing voltage. Ultimately, Farnoosh suffered a spastic fit. He dropped and slid through the slimy green mash at the bottom of the bowl. Spectator reaction seemed divided between enervated exultation and delighted disappointment. The blond man Bob Burcholz raised his arms in triumph.

"Yes, sirreee, Bob!" Jerry applauded. "Branch manager who they'll soon be leaving in charge of the entire plant."

"Damn." Iris shook her fist at the slighter man. "Enjoy a long night of hallucinations and vomiting, reality-sport loser!"

Buoyed by a billow of relief, the celebrity leaned into Iris. "That's how you stunned Tess?"

"Darts are a kiddie joust." Iris took a swig of her cocktail. "Tess and I competed in the house specialty game of full-contact shock-value dinging. You press a wand that delivers electroshocks of increasing intensity into poignant areas of your opponent's body." Farnoosh continued writhing in the slime, and D.J. lowered himself by rope sling and extracted him to a smattering of boos. "Tess and I put our money where our mouths are, which drove our side bet on who could swallow it farthest without suffering a gag reflex." She snickered. "That wouldn't be the last time she'd vomit from our contest, and I bested her by ten centimeters."

"A foudroyant lunch launch." Mercowitz shook his head. "I couldn't believe she'd lose such a sumptuous meal so easily. I hope it's not her regular behavior."

Iris produced her purse and removed the Passenger Pigeon operation kit. "How would you love the chance to win your glide back?" She waved the kit under the celebrity's nose and rubbed her hand over his pipeline curl. "In fact, Tess has a weird body – her clothing doesn't fit well – so you can win that back, too. I'll let you peel her dress off me right up there in the goblet like I did to her – if you win." She chuckled. "You can field-strip a weapon, can't you, foot soldier?"

"I'm certain you'd best me by the full length of the wand." The celebrity smiled deferentially. "But the point is moot because my code of professional conduct debars me from engaging in any game of chance or skill for material gain."

Jerry leaned into the celebrity. "These games are all fixed, so they don't technically qualify as gambling."

"No, they're not, you spoilsport!" Iris playfully punched the Parallacts associate in the shoulder and grabbed the celebrity by the collar. "You'd have as much chance to win as I would, maybe more because of your imposing physicality." She puckered her lips. "There are far less taxing, more stimulating house games for people of quality, and if it's forbidden, that should just add another level of allure."

"It didn't deter Tess." Mercowitz placed his index finger over his lips.

"Where's my Qilroy?" Farnoosh emerged from behind the bar. "I want my goddamn Qilroy!"

Iris smirked. "He sounds like Tess, albeit a little less profane, a slightly classier competitor."

The flame of the Molotov suddenly rose. The celebrity extinguished it with a clap of the hands and disgorged a cross-section of red cream across Iris's chest and lap. "Oh, I'm so sorry!"

"Yes, you are, buggy-whip." Mercowitz dabbed at the cream splotches on the satin sequined dress with a lipstick-stained handkerchief. "Would the gentleman like the drink transferred to a shockproof baby bottle? For future reference, the flame always flares right before it burns out."

Iris coolly surveyed her damages. "Now you have to lock nerves with me on the crystal stage or pay for the dry-cleaning."

"And for the rented limo." Jerry wiped a dollop from Iris's neck with his finger and tasted it. "I'll guarantee your hard-working taxpayers are spared the expense of your trip back if you put some skin in the game."

The celebrity eyed Iris squarely. "Did I by chance spot you in recent ship surveillance video in the company of an elderly gentleman with wild hair-"

"Jerry told me you're out to locate C.S." She placed her head against his, crushing a portion of the halo. "I've entertained him and ascertained a bit about his social routines. If you'll do me the honor of facing me as my worthy adversary in fishbowl theater, I'll share."

"That's the pitch that broke Tohnyin's resistance." Mercowitz slapped a heavy hand on the celebrity's shoulder. "Man up, Oobops. You operate from a chronic siege mentality anyway."

The celebrity felt his defenses soften beneath the pressure of his curiosity. "Say I was sucker enough to join you in close quarters combat." Iris rubbed her nose against his cheek. "The prime question to pinball is what you'd have me contribute to your personal treasury in the event of my unlikely upset." He tapped his side vents. "Not my suit?"

"Please," the attorney scoffed. "I'm not familiar with any charity outlets for good-humor scalawags." She placed her hand on his knee and squeezed hard. "You don't have the reek of affluence, so I wouldn't seek booty of intrinsic material worth. I'd just take your body."

The celebrity laughed self-consciously and took a hearty swig of his cocktail. "Alive, dead or something in between?"

Her fingers savored his pectorals. "Should you fail to prevail, Angstelino, your left nipple will be replaced by a permanent lead stud burned with a code pledging your full organ resale rights to me upon your death." She smiled sweetly. "Slightly dangerous, but a bargain. Want to play?"

"Those stakes offend me on every conceivable level." The celebrity dabbed at wet areas on the bar with a charred napkin. "And even under terms of the Real Deal, something that ghoulish can't be strictly legal."

"It's absolutely legal." She started unbuttoning his shirt. "The transaction just needs to be notarized and witnessed." She stretched his ear lobe between her teeth.

The celebrity wiped his upper lip. "I'd be haunted by the concern that I might annul the bet by outliving you." He wondered how long courtesy dictated that he pretend to consider such a ridiculous notion. "On top of that, I recently intercepted a report that predicts the staggering rate of advance in organ genesis will render the organ transfer industry defunct within ten years everywhere except a few third-world regions."

"I travel a lot." She massaged his chest and abdomen. "And I wouldn't correlate being a close confrere of Tess with a long life-expectancy."

The celebrity cackled. "I wouldn't deny such a self-evident truth. Would *you*, Jerry?"

"Rise above your leaky, sinking station and make the sacrifice for the state, oceansider." The Parallacts associate sipped his cocktail. "Better yet, propose a joust where the advantage might be yours, like T-ball, which is a glorified staring contest." He produced a cigarette and popped the tip. "Who do we know whose basic job requirement presumes the ability to maintain a highball eyeball?"

"I'm up for T-ball!" Iris summoned D.J. "It measures one's fortitude. It's a healthy exercise in the conquest of self. It's a fun kissing game." She usurped the taser cannon from the master bartender and ordered the crystal stage to be primed for T-ball.

"About the only thing we're missing here is the sound of me consenting to this exercise in lunacy." The celebrity reached into the nut basket and scraped the empty bottom.

"*Cojone* problem, honey?" Iris pointed the cannon at the

celebrity's groin. "You're not afraid of showing up Tess if you win here?"

"There's some commotion about their commission." Mercowitz emitted a smoke ring. "I have another shiny trinket of intel about our charmer Charlton that I neglected to slip to Tess that I'll let slide to you, Ahab, if you play along."

The celebrity turned over the empty basket. "You seem awfully eager to see battle joined, Jerry."

The Parallacts associate patted the celebrity on the head. "Music depreciation aside, I detect a decided decency deficiency in your lax California upbringing, Oobops, and I'd risk the rent to see the rough edges tumbled off you."

"T-ball is fundamentally a face-to-face raw stare," Iris explained. "D.J. will hold a PVC T-pipe between us, and we'll each insert our tongue. A soft loss occurs if you accumulate twelve points. You're charged one point for a blink; two points for a tic or a tear; and three if you push, pull or jerk the pipe. Losing your tooth-hold on the pipe is instant disqualification." She swept her tongue over her teeth. "Periodically, D.J. drops little poppers like tangy tansy mustard pellets – they promote head-banging – or lachrymators into the pipe to enliven the game. Each player tries to work the popper with his tongue into his opponent's mouth."

"The poppers make the game compelling." Mercowitz nudged the celebrity. "See D.J. dipping his gloved hand inside the terrarium?" The bartender rapped on a glass display under black light. "The poppers he'll drop into the pipe might include slightly noxious mushroom chunks or nearly incubated spider eggs."

The celebrity stood to get a better look. "So D.J.'s the referee, the official scorer, the pit boss?"

"You look like a nerd standing." Iris pinched the celebrity's butt, and he reseated himself. "Dusty is not an adjudicator, only a proctor." She sipped her drink. "Scoring isn't arbitrary; the cameras record it. You'll be looking directly into my face but in the periphery over my shoulders will be sensors that'll calculate our scorecards."

The celebrity sipped his cocktail. "I'd risk some serious blood and treasure for a solid lead on Shalom, but these stakes stink." He clicked his tongue. "Replacement organs are a bit trickier to come by than a replacement ride."

Iris stirred her cocktail. "Here's a Charlton party sampler; you judge whether it has nutritional value." She savored a protracted sip. "When our bad, old boy of interest started threatening the old continent, and his children placed him in a succession of retreats, he finally found the road to recovery couched in Hollywood fare of the World War II era. When you finally corner him, old-movie talking points may be the key to worming your way into his confidence."

The celebrity's eyes darted from Iris to Jerry and back. "So they took perhaps the greatest scientific mind in history and turned him into the world's foremost authority on Judy Garland."

Mercowitz launched himself to his feet. "What's crazy is Ahab happens to be a self-styled expert on all golden ages of popular culture."

The celebrity patted his pipeline curl. "You give me too much credit, Mr. Hughes."

The Parallacts associate massaged the celebrity's neck. "Well, it's impossible to underestimate you, isn't it, wrecking ball?" He emitted a smoke scud. "I have the urge to experience wet porcelain." He jammed his cigarette between two of the celebrity's fingers. "Guard this till I return, will you?" He wandered into the crowd beyond the bar.

The celebrity offered Iris the cigarette. "Jerry's a great guy for someone delivered rectally, isn't he?"

Iris reached across the man beside her and provided an ashtray. "Here's another hook that may land you your tuna. In his advanced age, C.S. has become a steadfast advocate of the creature comfort, and there's no combo that he craves more than a great soak, a great stroke and a great smoke. There's an all-night spa and resort in Wisconsin Dells called Hootenanny's that counts him as a habitue. He's likened the bleak, deserted atmosphere of the Turkish bath midweek midnight to interdimensional space travel."

Dustin Justin approached. "If you've never been a player before, you need to understand that we consider these contests serious business." The master bartender reiterated official game rules for the house specialty joust of T-ball. The celebrity detected the scent of astringent fireball capsules on D.J.'s hands. He clutched his glass.

Iris nudged the celebrity. "Is your mood right yet to greenlight this project, balalaika-bender?"

"Has the nerve yet been struck to return me to my senses?" He took a hard swig of his cocktail. "I might be coaxed to risk a brattoo in the butt like Tess, but I'll not be tagged as a walking organ tree-"

"Agreed." Iris pumped the celebrity's hand and recalled Dustin Justin. "Tess and I should've competed stripped to our undies to protect the dress, and I suggest you and I take that ordinary care not to tempt fabric mutilation." D.J. returned, and Iris rubbed the celebrity's pipeline curl. "He's decided to commit."

Dusty presented a contract of competition. "Failure to comply with terms of the agreement may result in forfeiture of entry fee and entitle the victorious party to seek and recover civil penalties." The celebrity declined to leave a thumbprint, but he provided enough account information to send the master bartender away satisfied that the event had been authorized.

The celebrity shook his head. "The last vehicle before the Pidge on which Tess had any claim of ownership got wrapped around a light post like a feathered boa."

"You don't talk about yourself much, do you?" Iris removed the halo hat and flashed a furtive smile. "I'd like to know all about you. Do you do more than dodge blame for a living?" She placed her hand on his shoulder. "Won't you tell me?"

The celebrity clutched his Molotov. "That sort of seems like a waste when we could be talking about you."

"That sounds almost genuine." She sipped her drink. "I believe we're both jockeying to get a head start on our head games." She smiled suggestively. "Let's play a trick on Tess. I have a spice powder that could be added into her food that will make her body break out in severe acne. She thinks she's such a siren, let her scream like one all the way to the O.C. run-not-walk-in dermatology clinic."

He nodded. "That's a nasty little scheme for such a self-possessed woman of the world, isn't it?"

"In fact, it's not my style." The attorney pointed the taser cannon at the celebrity's forehead and placed it on the bar. "I poison minds, not bodies." She rubbed her hand over his chest. "The body is sacred."

D.J. extended his forefinger and pinkie toward the celebrity and Iris. The attorney sprang to her feet. "Mr. Oobops, we're on!"

"You're certain you wouldn't like to reconsider?" The celebrity rose slowly to let acceptance of the cockamamie dope-slap of a campaign he'd commissioned metastasize.

"Find the itch to scratch, Ahab?" Mercowitz reappeared.

The celebrity followed Iris around the end of the bar to a closet beside a liquor cabinet. "This is the change room." She opened the door, activating a bare incandescent bulb. "I'll go first." She shut the door behind her and emerged a minute later wearing a scanty black bra and matching lace panties. She smiled provocatively and stepped aside. "To keep it even, I'll let you keep any two articles of clothing. Might I recommend your socks?"

The celebrity marched into the change room and slammed the door behind him. He held an irritated eye on Tohnyin's dress hanging beside the mirror as he removed his suit coat, shoes and pants. "A movie buff," he muttered, "a spa hound." He eyed Iris's pointed-toe stiletto-heel shoes as he removed his tie and shirt. He wondered if she maintained a permanent cabin on board which currently stored the clothing in which she'd begun the evening. He heard the event horn sound. He consulted the mirror, primped his hair and observed how foolish he looked in his shorts and socks. He pulled off his socks and fired them at Iris's shoes.

Overcoming a modicum of difficulty opening the change room door, the celebrity reappeared ready for battle. Iris awaited him beside D.J. at the base of the jumbo goblet. Upon his approach, she climbed the ladder and swung her legs over the brim of the bowl to cheers and whistles. He embraced the consensus calls of disparagement that accompanied his walk to the goblet with a bobbing-head sneer. He saluted Dusty and received no response. The slick metal rungs of the ladder punished his feet. He entered the bowl, and the master bartender scrambled up the ladder toting a stick with a tee-fixture head.

The celebrity dropped into the viscous pea soup which filled the base of the bowl. It stung his feet and shins. Iris's features blazed with pugnacious anticipation as he nearly lost his footing. "You'll regret it for a few days if you fall in," she advised. "Delectable urticant." She unclasped her bra and spread the cups to shoulder width, greatly escalating and coarsening the approbative clamor that had greeted her. "Would you like to make this even more interesting and go *au naturel*?"

"Remove my shorts?" The celebrity found her crude attempt to intensify his agitation amusing. "It's only the middle of the week."

Iris accepted his insistence on skivvy support with a twisted-arm tolerance. "You really *are* an imbecile." She reclasped her bra to a smattering of objections and rolled her tongue behind her upper row of teeth, exposing a substantial canker.

Dustin Justin directed the combatants to their respective

game places on the crystal stage. Iris slapped her hands on her knees and crouched slightly. The celebrity mimicked her so their faces were separated by about two decimeters. She edged closer. She peered straight into his eyes, her tender face grazing his and her supple lips ready to receive him. She stooped a bit lower. "Omigod, this is close." She smiled cloyingly. "Rushmore called – George wants his nose back."

"There's a reason why they called you." He peeked over her shoulder. "Expect another call from the Sphinx."

D.J. extended his PVC pipe and suspended the tee-fixture between the combatants' mouths. He recited a litany of gambling parameters. His high muzzle velocity made the temptation to shove him over backward almost overwhelming. Both the celebrity and Iris took nearly half of the tee-fixture in their mouths, clenched it between their teeth and inserted their tongues. "Wagering complete!" the master bartender screeched.

Cameras dropped, timing started and the audiovisual scorecard indicated that the celebrity trailed 0-1. He blinked and fell behind 0-2. Iris blinked, shifted her weight indelicately, blinked again, suffered a tic, blinked again and found herself down 2-8. Then no one blinked for eight solid minutes. Her eyes bulged, glistened and finally glowed like coals in the glare of the klieg lights. His eyes burned with increasing intensity and his nose started running. She shed a tear, blinks were exchanged, and he led 7-11. The intermittent poppers that D.J. blew down the pipe generally had the consistency of marshmallows. The celebrity and Iris compressed most of them between their tongues until they burst, releasing bitter flavors and inducing sensations of nausea. Finally, the celebrity recognized the jojoba wax coating of an astringent capsule and lost another two points crinkling his nose with intensity in an effort to release the toxic fireball. Iris exhibited the expression of one embroiled in a death struggle on a window ledge.

Something pinched the celebrity's tongue, and he could

no longer locate the astringent capsule. He wondered whether Iris had swallowed it because her gaze became glassy and she retracted her tongue. Another popper arrived, and her tongue poked his again. She manipulated her tongue beneath his and squashed the charge sublingually. A burning sensation permeated his scalp and destabilized his perception. A point of light appeared to reside directly beside his face before he recognized it as negative space with a distant source of illumination. The burning sensation flowed through his body. Colors flashed brilliantly, then returned darker than normal. D.J. stoked the pipe with another popper. Something slid across the celebrity's papillae and squeezed the tip of his tongue. He experienced light sensitivity and became disoriented. Something constricted his tongue, and he pulled back. He bucked instantly to override the move, slipped, lost his tooth-hold and plunged headlong into the soup at the base of the bowl.

Klieg-blind, the celebrity thrashed in the goblet pool before staggering to his feet. The jeers from the Gold Bar area seemed more reserved than he would've expected. Iris sat perched on the brim of the bowl. "The fog of war lifting, Ahab?" He felt an imbecilic grin spread across his twitching lips. She removed any doubt as to whether she would comport herself graciously in victory by sticking out her tongue. The astounding length of the organ was overshadowed by the extraordinary undulations into which she warped it. "We salute another fallen hero." She curled and contorted her tongue tip.

He shuddered like a flounder on the tart end of a harpoon. He coughed and spit slime, brine and perhaps a bit of blood. "That's the bump." He pointed impotently. "You have a secret weapon."

"Are you implying that I cheated?" She flexed her right biceps and calf. "You used your upper body strength; I used my designer tongue. Would you like to employ the intelligence you've gained and engage again?" She held her mouth wide open. "How skilled are you at holding your breath? Say we arrange an underwater extended free-dive booby-trap deactivation contest?"

The celebrity sighed. "Not unless you have additional information on my weathered target."

Iris glared. "Now you're insinuating I'm withholding something?" She swung her right leg out of the bowl and paused at the top of the ladder. "I'm a woman of my word." She eyed him haughtily as she climbed down.

He pulled himself over the brim of the bowl and surveyed the bar-belt body electric. Voting blocks of obscene gestures popped up like umbrellas in a downpour. He located Mercowitz standing beside Winterhalter. "Damn," he vented, "Rissy is a slippery strain of bad kitty, isn't she? An assiduous ballbreaker of a grimalkin!"

"Oobops sweating and swearing," Jerry lamented. "Oh the humanity, oh the humility, oh the humidity."

"Gurgle, slurp, snuffle, honk," the reagent echoed. "Hide your head while we issue you a tissue or two, flopcorn." He snorted. "At least she's an edgy shaft-jammer."

"Under any circumcision, to gamble is to grumble." Mercowitz raised a cloudy amber-colored drink. "You may hold entitlement to the gripe that you were gypped, tear-monger, but you wasn't robbed, so shake it off and live to wet yourself another day."

"You guys are two prime cuts of humanity, too." The celebrity traded the goblet for the ladder and dizzily descended to the floor.

The master bartender provided a pink towel. "You have ninety days to comply with terms-"

"Don't mess with me, hoss." The celebrity snatched the towel and twisted it around his body as he headed to the change room.

"Turd," he was toasted by an unknown gaming patron. "You're hard as slop, you mild-ass musclebound wuss!"

He unsuccessfully attempted to turn the dressing room

door handle twice. "Don't have a wargasm, Mukhabarat," Iris's voice scolded. "I'm about finished." She opened the door and stepped out clad once more in Tess's scarlet cocktail dress. "I prefer to make a man fall for me in the romantic sense and then leave him emotionally devastated, but in your case that could take well into the weekend." She eyed him squarely for a moment and departed.

"Iris," he called after her, "your dimples are perfect, you have perfect legs, a perfect waste." He shut the door quietly behind him. He removed his shorts, wrung them out and slipped back into them. He finished drying himself and sat trancelike on the bench for several minutes. He finally repopulated his suit, emerged from the change room and sought the company of his uneasy coalition.

Mercowitz, Winterhalter and Iris formed a tight three-smokestack unit. Jerry received the celebrity with a sweeping arm gesture. "The historical debris fields of American night-life are littered with fools such as this." A canny grin crossed his lips. "Your key takeaway from the inferiorating events of this evening, shogun, should be that government digests its citizens-"

"Dig his friggin' fried eyes!" I.B. waved his finger. "They're bloody stoplight red!" The celebrity rubbed his sore eyes and examined his hands. The reagent cackled. "You're such a sapling, Oobops!"

The celebrity hailed the master bartender. "J.D., or D.J., pour my inside advisor a snifter of your best house pesticide, will you?"

Iris directed a subtle head gesture toward Winterhalter. "I take it you hold a toothless job that's choked you down whole, too?"

"It spits," I.B. retorted.

Mercowitz displayed his Qilroy. "While you were gumming and mugging in your low-slung stance onstage with Iris, lickety-split, I received the opening measure of another original score that you can send up your fretboard."

Tohnyin's image appeared on the Parallacts associate's sourcerer screen, and he replayed the communique. "Jerry, I'm disembarking to pursue an urgent lead in Madison. I believe I have a line on a strategic *ohmage*. Tell Ahab to hang tight – I'll link back up with him later."

The celebrity gazed at the Qilroy incredulously. "Why wouldn't she just leave *me* the message?"

"She has histrionic personality disorder." Iris sipped a white drink. "She requires constant social validation to satisfy and support her natural self-congratulatory tendencies."

Mercowitz nodded. "She should've taken more of the guest work out of the arrival of a rival." He poked the celebrity in the shoulder. "Her idea was most likely that I rescue you from the friendly confines of the grey room."

The celebrity winced and eyed the reagent. "I'm pleased that *you* were finally able to pry yourself free from that exile. Run out of spread or stomach space?"

Winterhalter snorted. "My hactivism didn't dead-end, Dudedrops." He snatched a tall, layered cocktail of multi-colored levels punctuated with lime slices. "My porn scareware snare should hatch and take down a clod klatch of these kicka-poos, though for the ten G's you laid on the imperial guards, they should've opened you a chute through the Great Firewall of China."

Mercowitz gasped. "How much in dumb money did you donate?"

"You're a regular stealth barnacle, I.B." The celebrity winced. "Curly scalped me."

Iris tittered. "Tell me, I.B., does Ahab generally do well with the ladies?"

Winterhalter stared blankly. "He holds his own."

The attorney soft-shoed around the celebrity and slapped

his butt with no little ferocity. "Will you prove to be enough of a man to honor your debt?"

The celebrity emitted an indignant breath. "I'll honor it right now, sinsemilla tips." He spanked himself with an energy equal to hers. "I believe on my way here I passed the chop-shop where they perform the mandated desecration. You can all come along if you like and watch the gorefest."

The reagent smirked. "We wouldn't miss it, Captain Tug Noodle."

"I would." Iris crinkled her nose. "The sickening smell of distended, burning flesh, those harsh, glistening blades drawing all that blood – it's too grisly to witness. I'll resend the Head my personal emblem, just like I did for Tess." She pressed her tongue into her lower row of teeth. "Come back and show me when it's in."

"Vasovagal reflex here, too." Jerry draped his arm around Iris. "And how could I leave a stunner who can simultaneously beat the snot out of you two recipes for ruin and retain her femininity?"

I.B. emitted a sardonic chuckle. "We know you have more wrinkles to show her than the original fan dancer, Irving."

The celebrity grabbed Winterhalter by the arm and steered him toward the casino exit. "Let's get this moon mission behind us." The duo negotiated bottlenecks of pedestrian traffic and reached the pink light and adequate ventilation of the corridor. "You know what I was thinking in the change room?"

"You might find some old coins on the floor?" I.B. kept pace with the celebrity.

"Tess's egression is more than a little suspicious," the celebrity persevered. "And now Jerry presents her message in a manner to defuse any skepticism about its authenticity. I need to interview people who might've seen Tess at the boutique." He checked his Qilroy for mixed messages. "I'm very concerned."

"You're always up a fig tree about her, mistletoe," the

reagent scoffed. "Why don't you fix her up with a harness and a leash?"

"She could stand to be less of a publicity slut." The celebrity decided to rally Winterhalter's camaraderie around a platform of shared resentment. "Jerry the old clotheshorse-trader certainly seems to have seamlessly swapped fondle-pots to make Iris, as he might say, 'the bedeficiary of his mounting frustration,' hasn't he?"

"Her dark-side appeal is what urged *you* into the punch bowl with her, isn't it, slum-dog?" I.B. lobbed his cigarette butt in the general vicinity of a receptacle.

The celebrity tried unsuccessfully to reach Tohnyin. "I engaged Iris in civil combat in exchange for a tip on the whereabouts of 110328A/404. I probed and vetted, and I'm convinced of her veracity."

"Yeah, now you have a degree in forensic interviewing, too." Winterhalter stopped at the aft elevator. "So what's the lead? Where's Shellac?"

The celebrity dragged the reagent to the stairway. "I've ascertained that our super-chilled stargazer favors a 24-hour spa called Hootenanny's in the tony town of Wisconsin Dells. I predict one of us is going to set up a long-term observation post there."

Winterhalter fingered his Jatakar. "Hell, this ozone-sparing tuchis is living off-grid like some hermit crab? We should be able to find him by following the bouncing marbles."

The celebrity and the reagent reached the promenade deck. The celebrity slowed his gait and groaned as the Swelled Head boutique appeared on the left. "You're the most disturbed oomphus of all, ass-burger," I.B. submitted. "Why even bother with this sorry foray for self-mutilation? If it was me, I'd respectfully instruct those elite all-night nurples to go suck a weed-whacker with deadly force."

The celebrity inhaled and exhaled a substantial chunk of the atmosphere. "Sometimes you go along to get along, go ahead to get ahead. I've put too many state tax dollars in play to back out." He strutted into the boutique. "Is this the charhouse?" He slapped his butt. "I need a brattoo."

Seated at her desk surrounded by glittery showcase shelves teeming with handbags, shoes and sunglasses, the receptionist possessed a sweet face beneath her bushy ginger hair and heavy eyeliner. She wore a low-cut pink top, which revealed a chest brattoo of thin, blue flames. "Lucky for you, the skin artist is available." She eyed him circumspectly. "Is the brat the child of a casino wager?"

"I'm relieved that's obvious." The celebrity displayed a picture of Tohnyin on his Qilroy. "We're also looking for a woman who should've gotten the identical brattoo. Was she just here?"

The receptionist smiled apologetically and raised her hands. "I just arrived on duty." The image of an eye graced each of her palms. "If it's really important, you can ask the artist." She checked her incoming orders. "The brattoo is in care of Iris Ingersoll?" A garish personal emblem in the form of a blood-red palmprint with teardrop finger points appeared on the desktop. The name *Ingersoll* in Old English script ran along the main lifeline, and each of the four finger points held a letter to spell *I-S-I-S*. In thumb position resided an indigo scarab.

A touch form appeared on the desktop, and the receptionist directed the celebrity to authorize a fee payment of up to four thousand dollars, then complete and retain a copy of the application. He submitted his personal information with a cushion of factual elasticity that listed his occupation as "personal revenge service options specialist" for employer "Brash Brush Last Ditch Debt Elimination LLC." The receptionist administered a toxicity test and disappeared through the door beside the shoe case. She wore a short skirt and had chalk-white legs.

"Step-sister spinster," I.B. snickered. "She's leggy like a tomato vine with insufficient sunlight."

The celebrity pressed his fists into his hips. "As a further inducement to spur me into the glass ring, Mercowitz promised me more vital intel on our anti-luminary, and he never delivered."

The receptionist poked her head out the door. "Mr. Oobops, Benji is ready for you."

The celebrity and the reagent entered a tiled room partitioned by a cubicle barrier wall. Muffled voices and strains of "Whipping Boy" by Cover Girl lilted softly in the background. The receptionist presented a thick-haired, olive-skinned man in light blue scrubs seated at a counter tapping the surface with a steel-wool brush and studying the *Ingerso!!* emblem on a monitor. The man swiveled, sniffled and shook I.B.'s hand. "Ahab, is it?" Dense, grey-flecked stubble surrounded a subdued, weary-eyed smile. "I'm Ugarmesh, your body modification practitioner." An amethyst pendant dangled from his gold chain necklace. "You call me Benji."

"I'm Ahab." The celebrity kicked himself forward and brandished Tohnyin's image. "You must've just given this woman the same brattoo I'm about to get, didn't you?" The receptionist slinked out the door.

Benji scrutinized the photo and brushed past the reagent to reach an autoclave on the counter. "I really couldn't say."

"Her name is Tess." The celebrity smiled complaisantly. "The problem is we're supposed to have matching posterior brattoos, and I want to confirm it."

Benji removed two trays of instruments from the autoclave. "Sorry, I don't know."

Winterhalter scoffed. "What kind of a ho-tard would you have to be to not know?"

Benji hissed. "Maybe if you show me a picture of her ass." He stacked his trays and snatched a set of patterns from the printer. "If she's your friend, why don't you ask *her*?"

"I'd hate to postpone my ritual degradation." The celebrity anxiously thrummed the counter. "But imagine my chagrin, skinflint, should I discover that Tess never actually preceded me to this freaks' abattoir."

Benji sneezed. "As a Wisconsin-licensed body modification practitioner, I'm required by law to maintain strict guidelines on client confidentiality. Even under the Real Deal." He carted his preferred articles of articulation toward the back corner of the room. "If you want the brattoo now, come along!"

The celebrity and the reagent followed. The body modification practitioner pointed at I.B. "Are we going to let your flack observe?" The celebrity nodded, and Benji pulled the curtain halfway around the work station.

The celebrity continued pumping Benji for information as he removed his coat and shirt, climbed onto the cot belly-down and dropped his pants and shorts below his knees. He transferred a crisp thousand-dollar sweetener into an off-shore account, and the body modification practitioner verified that he'd just roasted Tohnyin's rump with the familiar *I-S-I-S* brattoo.

Benji grabbed a cup, took a sip and coughed several times. "I can slip you a mild narcotic-"

"We don't need no stinkin' painkiller!" the reagent snarled.

Benji switched on the spotlight attached to an accordion boom and positioned it over the cot. He donned a bonnet, gauze mask, aviator safety glasses and latex gloves. He arranged red towels over the red sheets so only the celebrity's head and buttocks remained exposed.

"Nothin' left but the shine on the A-Train's caboose," I.B. chuckled.

"Draping them dehumanizes them," Benji explained. "I can usually render a better professional result if I only see the meatspace, and it can also provide me with hygiene relief."

Winterhalter bumped the tray table. "Are you calling this street-heart a funk-wad, scrape-goat?"

"Nothing personal, *bharwas*." Benji lightly slapped the celebrity's buttocks and steamrolled them with a juicy sponge.

The celebrity produced his Qilroy. "A casual business harangue won't distract you, will it, lancer?"

"I stay on my game." Benji applied light razor pressure, and the celebrity called Mercowitz. "Tell Tess, tell Mom — you're really going through with it!"

"Ahab, you lovably loopy carless cutlass," Jerry answered, "Iris is disappointed you left without asking about her drink. It's an absinthe-based cocktail which she heartily recommends for you called death-in-the-afternoon. It seems a bit late to be sucking on such a concoction, but it's always afternoon somewhere beyond California, and absinthe makes the heart grow fonder, hmm?"

"I'm calling from beneath the capable hands of the Swelled Head's one-man demolition crew." The celebrity felt a duller, heavier pressure traverse his right buttock as he switched the call to speaker. "Because it occurs to me that you pledged to divulge further significant information on our mutual friend if I took up the goblet, and you never divulged-"

"You're not into insider trading, Oobops." The Parallacts associate extinguished his cigarette. "If you were, you'd realize the profit principle is being violated by what you suggest. I offered to pass you raw intel in order to motivate you to do battle, but you waded in anyway, so that voided the offer. If you've learned nothing from me, it should be that the top leaves no margin for genuine generosity."

The celebrity winced mightily. "Jerry, you're as genuine as a five-legged snake. This time make it an adder!"

"You never miss the beat to cheat, do you, Jerry-Rig?" I.B. contributed. "You're a gear-grinding, waste-laying power slug!"

"Down dander, granola-chompers, don't cannonball off the deep end with delusions of adequacy." Mercowitz raised an empty glass. "I'll still share – I just require that you pursue me to the concessions stand for a chaser." His features grew stern. "Iris has advised me of a foul wind gust headed up from the sunny Southwest carrying an opprobrious militant element with the means and intent to disrupt carbon output in the Midwest on multiple fronts from cyber-terrorism to physical infrastructure upheaval. It all adds up to seedy Surfdom USA. Until you deny it, Ahab, I have to believe it's you. And when you deny it, then I'll be sure it's you."

The celebrity signaled Benji to momentarily suspend activity. "Not only is that reasoning circular, the political shtick of providing false alarms and invented menaces is ridiculously archaic."

"It's a square circle then." Mercowitz recovered his smile. "Oobops, I wanted you to face-off against Ms. Ingersoll so you could explore your extreme vulnerability. As I commenced commenting before you and your stief of chaff stuffed me, a soldier is a balls-to-the-wall pawn whereas a spy is a value-judgement-capable bishop. Consider your motivation for disregarding whether your organization's objectives are worth placing yourself in a ticklish position."

"Easy, Procrustes." The celebrity struggled with the distraction of Benji repositioning his pelvis. "If I've learned anything from you, Jerry, it's to never judge a man by the color of his cocktail, but I must confess the main lesson being distilled in me now is to never trust a man who wears long sleeves in warm weather."

"From D.J. with love." Mercowitz displayed a tall, red drink crammed with garnishes. "Here for what it's worth, my poor blubber-room slobgollion, is your lode to pant for. The Janesy Club infrequently sponsors verbal sparring matches called flytings, a salute to a sport designed in the courts of Scottish nobility in medieval times and practiced by skalds, sometimes preceding armed combat or even precipitating it. Lincoln Worbley liked to be a rubbernecker at these spectacles and claimed to have turned on our mutual friend to them. Worbley reported that he would witness pure elation etched on the face of our missing math myth for the duration of the function." He savored his cocktail. "You know 'Good Time

Charlton' had the rep for rarely turning out socially, but he's said to have found a good flyting irresistible, particularly when it carried the salty aftertaste of a strong political undertow."

"You mean like battle rap?" Winterhalter challenged.

Jerry grimaced. "I'm not altogether familiar, but the flyting would seem to be a little more purpose-driven and a little less juvenile, silly and intellectually lazy. It weds the agility of wit with the power of perspicacity. It's a value index vanity fair." He smiled with stout aplomb. "In their finest concatenations, the encounters unfold with a veritable heroic purity. The combatants exchange barbs, claims and countercharges until facades fall by the wayside, realities are deliberated and points of vulnerability become exposed. The supreme volley virtually has a will of its own and inflicts its injury on whomever its process selects and to whatever degree its thrust deems justified."

The celebrity propped his head on his elbow and pushed Benji away. "When is the next of these flytings scheduled?"

"I checked the proprietary Janesy Club calendar and didn't find one." Mercowitz conducted a brief, muffled side conversation. "They're rare, but they tend to bubble up quickly. Listen, my fussy, refocused refuseniks, Isis – yes, that's her real name — is talking about burning the Tess dress, so I have to go. But we look forward to seeing the solid impression this fluid situation has made on you, Oobops, and hope that your personal development can be a lesson to us all." He terminated the connection.

The celebrity eyed Winterhalter. "What do you make of that rigmarole, lunch-pail mandarin?"

I.B. scoffed. "You're circling the drain, hammerhead. Nobody can lean in to fish you out."

"Sorry for the delay, doodles," the celebrity apologized to Benji. "Please soldier on."

The body modification practitioner roughly redoubled his efforts. He sniffled harshly as he pressed, pinched and poked.

The reagent tickled his Jatakar. "Where are you natural to, snot-machine?"

"Janesville." Benji jammed a towel into the celebrity's mouth. "Here on a J-1 student visa from Sri Lanka." He snorted, withdrew a small bucket from beneath the sink and spit into it. "Can't get over this cold. He need restraints?"

"Hell, yeah, butt-munch!" Winterhalter roared. The celebrity vetoed the idea with a violent headshake.

Benji tapped a door beneath the instrument table and donned heavy gloves. He opened the door and released a heat wave. He tossed a damp towel over the celebrity's head. "Take three deep breaths and brace." On the second breath, the body modification practitioner pressed what felt like red hot talons into the celebrity's right buttock, occasioning a full-body tremor. "There's your preliminary strike." He snickered. "A shadow impression, a shallow burn." The celebrity shed his head towel.

Winterhalter snorted. "While we waited after your drubbing for you to stop spazzing in the dressing room, squatto, psycho-diva mentioned how she challenged you to an underwater bomb deactivation contest. After checking *my* ass to make sure I hadn't laughed it off, I informed her not only can you not swim but you can't change the battery in your air quality alarm by yourself much less dink with an explosive device!"

"Those alarms can be tricky." Benji sliced into the celebrity's flesh with a compact hand tool that squealed like a power sander. "How are you doing, tough-duff?" He stroked and gouged with a special mechanical vigor. "*Ahhchhh!!*" he wailed.

The celebrity disgorged the mouth towel and twisted around. "What did you do, Buonarroti?"

"Lie flat!" Benji backhanded the celebrity's shoulder. "If you can't stay still, we'll use restraints, or you'll goo up the piece!" He staggered in a circle. The celebrity rolled back onto his stomach. The body modification practitioner sneezed. "I'm sorry, Bobo." He began tapping his heel against the floor rhythmically. "I stepped on your brain-trust's foot and rolled my ankle." He pushed the reagent aside. "Back off, jabroni." He limped to the table and exchanged his electric blade for a scalpel and sponge.

Winterhalter hissed. "Gotta watch where I'm going, Kemosabe."

Benji flipped another damp towel over the celebrity's head. "Take three deep breaths and brace." On the first breath, the body modification practitioner pressed the pattern deep into the celebrity's skin and seared it for several seconds. "We've moved in beneath the nerves, so this shouldn't bite so lustily as before." The celebrity experienced another full-body tremor. Benji scraped and gouged some more. Enveloped by the smell of burned flesh, the celebrity tried to cope with his throbbing agony by focusing on strategy to force Shalom into the open. The Latin jazz stylings of NicNak Contra Band with "Handiwork For A Rampage" filled the room.

"Yechhh!" Winterhalter exclaimed. "Look at all that blood!"

"He's finished; he's through." Benji squirted fluid on the celebrity's butt and wiped it around. "My process is designed to maximize scarification and at the same time minimize the time it takes to heal. Patents are pending." He removed the celebrity's head towel, and the scent of burnt rosemary became overwhelming. The body modification practitioner slapped a cold gel pack onto the brattoo. "Hold this here for fifteen minutes, Boshintang," he directed the reagent. "Gentle like a butterfly so the ammonium nitrate doesn't rip his ass apart." He and I.B. shrieked in unison.

The celebrity struggled to contain the fluttering in his chest. "Now what, nawab?" He looked over his shoulder and was startled to find a person with the face of a barn owl standing between I.B. and Benji.

The newcomer shook with laughter and turned around. He wore a black turtleneck, and he was stocky and shorter than Benji. He'd had the hair on the back of his head dyed in a close-up illustration of an owl face. The front side of his head featured bright eyes, a boyish smile and an ample shock of platinum blond hair bordered by a black streak. "Eureka!"

"You reek worse!" Winterhalter replaced the cold gel pack on the celebrity's butt.

Benji snorted. "Is this the 'mutual friend' you're seeking that you spoke of on your business call?"

"That'd suit me, jocks." The owl man placed a supportive hand on the reagent's shoulder and leaned toward the celebrity. "You must be the California spies the boat is buzzing about, aren't you?" Before the celebrity could explain the blush on his nose as a by-product of a hearty snowboarding season in the Upper Peninsula, the owl man persevered, "It's obvious, isn't it? Your look, the way you carry yourselves, your nihilistic bent."

The reagent slapped the back of the celebrity's head. "You're a regular walking *HOLLYWOOD* sign, marked man!"

The owl man leaned closer. "I heard your ruckus on the *awther* side of the partition while gettin' the emergency hair-rinse and *wondered* over to investigate." He extended his hand, and the celebrity shook it. "Name's Noyce, Guy Noyce from Western Australia, producer of musical theater currently assembling an ostensibly all-female cast searching for a pair of ringers not afraid to walk on the wild side and turn up in the middle of the madness." Benji coughed with increasing frequency as he collected his instruments. "We're trending toward a substantial payday. Are you both performers?"

Winterhalter sprang to attention. "Where do we apply?"

"We don't, bottom-feeder." The celebrity watched Guy furtively train his Jatakar on I.B. "Please don't capture our images." He leveled a mildly threatening glare. "The nature of our business makes it vital that we maintain low visibility."

Noyce snatched the Jatakar from atop his head. "Objectionable shots deleted."

"Now who's crying about privacy, *Haalparuwa*?" Benji pulled the curtain wide open as he gathered towels.

"The musical roles are no more demanding than they are demeaning." Guy smiled disarmingly. "But if I can't interest you in helping revive alternative burlesque, maybe I can interest you in helping revive alternative justice." He returned his sourcerer to his scalp. "You blokes are experts in dirty tricks, and I'm in need of a dazzler. You must be familiar with Giselle Engelhart, aren't you?"

"She was just nominated for a film award, wasn't she?" The celebrity vaguely linked the name with the entertainment industry. "*Chinatown*, I believe?"

"She's unparalleled as an actress, yobbos – see her play the courtroom – and she looks the part perfectly with those big, sad doe eyes." Noyce widened his eyes with his fingers. "She's the Aussie poster girl for sexually charged teenage tragedy who was abducted in separate incidents three times."

"No shit, mite?" Winterhalter flashed four fingers. "You want us to make it a foursome?"

"We want to put poetic justice in the form of a good psychological mauling." Noyce relieved Winterhalter as holder of the cold gel pack. "Giselle was first grabbed at age fifteen by her counselor. Turned out he was having more trouble at home than her. He steadfastly insisted that the girl had facilitated the incident with an adult sophistication, but that's beside the point. Giselle and her family learned to settle their personal differences by billing everyone else for them. They sued everyone remotely involved including purveyors of media coverage and made out handsomely."

"How we doing, teacup?" Benji returned.

"My mouth has the taste of mothballs," the celebrity reported.

"Hmm, I wouldn't think that has anything to do with the brattoo." The body modification practitioner removed the cold gel pack, admired his rendering and replaced the pack. "Good tincture. Good charnage. Few more minutes." He limped away again.

"I can't believe Giselle doesn't register." Noyce gently repositioned the cold gel pack. "The coverage in Stralia was massive, as no one is more aware than me, because I was a prime contributor for *The Excavator* on the series of photos accompanying accounts of the search and its aftermath."

"Toss me my shirt, will you?" the celebrity directed Winterhalter.

Noyce shuffled around the cot, plucked the celebrity's shirt off the floor and handed it to the reagent. "So six months after her return," Guy persevered, "poor Giselle succumbs to another invitation to escape her repressive father and is picked up by a trucker." The photo-opportunist recounted how the trucker finally deposited the girl at a luxury hotel in Melbourne, where a techno-age ad industry convention was in full swing. When the convention ended, Giselle left with an ad guru named Cadugan. "They remain at large for eight months, and when Giselle is serendipitously rescued, Miles Cadugan corroborates the trucker's tale that Giselle had repeatedly resisted being released."

I.B. flung the shirt over the celebrity's head. "Cadugan, Cadoggin, a crease across the noggin."

"This time the Engelhart lawsuits targeted the tabs for invasion of privacy, in particular *The Excavator*, where Cadugan confessed first finding photos of precious Giselle and becoming addicted to sensationalized depictions of her initial inveiglement." Noyce's face appeared flushed with contempt. "As a result of the final judgement, *The Ex* failed and the enterprise was liquidated."

The celebrity struggled into his shirt and sent the cold gel pack to the floor. Winterhalter fanned the air over the celebrity's butt. "You're so bad-ass now, Norvis, you could part the futtocks."

"Who's your caddie?" Noyce retrieved the cold gel pack

and slapped it onto the celebrity's brattoo. "But just when Giselle thought it was safe to step back in the billabong, she was dragged under again." Guy related the deeds of the Denlingers: Kent, the husband who abducted Giselle after viewing her provocative image in the tabloids; and Muriel, the enabling realtor wife who stashed the demanding girl in vacant upscale properties that she controlled. "Kent claimed he was so affected by how forlorn Giselle looked in a photo I placed in *Dinkidi Fair* that he suffered an episode of acute nympholepsy. *Dinkidi Fair* afterward referred to Muriel as the 'dirt bag realtor.'" The photo-opportunist rubbed his brow. "So the Denlingers followed the Engelhart injury-mining operation in suing the tab, and in the end the court placed such an onerous burden on *Dinkidi Fair* that it was forced to fold, too." He folded his arms defensively. "Winsome village trampoline Giselle just turned 21, and she's come across the pond to Hollywood to serve as technical advisor and play a cameo in another film about her amazing life. I imagine you tall poppies can find a proper way to throw a good scare into her and hold her up to a bit of public ridicule."

"We won't be party to molesting some girl, Guy." The celebrity hiked up his shorts and gingerly swung his legs over the side of the cot. "And I emphatically urge you to reconsider your urge to sponsor any sort of such sordid business." He sprang to his feet, raised his pants and endured a significant twinge. "Let's not become dirt bags ourselves."

"Ordinarily, I'd agree with you, but we deserve the last word!" Noyce clutched his head. "The Engelhart family has fabricated a cottage industry off its own victimization, and all they had to do to accomplish it was ruin scores of other people's livelihoods. They're the lowest, most reprehensible band of shakedown artists, and they require a reckoning!"

Winterhalter smirked. "You'd really be something less than a dirt bag if you remained focused on the purpose of the act while you were doing the molesting, Ahab." He turned to

Noyce. "Nothing amiss about devoting your passion to tagging a fabulous sheila-devil for the common cause, oye, mite?"

"I overheard the receptionist tell the hair designer that you're a revenge services specialist," Guy revealed. "Surely your scruples are accustomed to accommodating a bit of moral relativism."

"If these people view their daughter's virtue as a commodity, then I agree they're dancing the limbo." The celebrity tested the pain level of lateral movement. "But visiting the sins of the family on the child is a cynical, misdirected proposition with an objective that is by definition unsatisfactory."

"That means don't hold your whistle for our help, wagstattle." Winterhalter slapped Noyce on the back. "Our two-fisted chaplain has decided he needs to keep his hook-eyed hypocrite nose clean. He might want to run for pope someday."

The celebrity endured a stiff twinge. "If I were pope, Ib, I'd confirm you as the second person in the history of the Catholic Church to be irrevocably consigned to eternal damnation while still living." He exhibited Tohnyin's photo on his Qilroy. "She might be the third. Guy, you didn't by chance notice this woman around the boutique, did you? Perhaps in a lime green pant suit?"

"She was likely rubbing her ass." Winterhalter patted his buttocks.

The photo-opportunist stepped forward and studied the picture. "While I was up front tarrying with a hot towel, a similar sheila in pale green did appear. Rather racked with pain, she was escorted by a square-jawed, mustachioed battler, right?" His lips formed a confident smile. "That's her. She bought a tin of Copioids before they left."

"You're certain?" The celebrity scrambled Tess's photo. "Had you ever seen her cohort before? Did they give any indication of where they're headed?"

Noyce ran his hands through his hair. "Toward the capital? A resort? I can't honestly recall-"

"Already covered up, *passa*?" Benji reappeared. "Drop, display your seat of power and we'll review." He clutched a large mirror and offered the celebrity a smaller one.

"I don't want to wear out my brand spankin' new insignia with premature overanalysis." The celebrity endured a stabbing pain. "We have to leave, so I'll inspect it when the inflammation subsides."

Benji shrugged. "Look after it yourself, Dalits. Let it breathe openly for a few days. A sweat lodge or mineral springs may provide compelling relief but don't overindulge because it can leech out colors. The receptionist will give you a Kare Kit on your way out and she can handle a *baksheesh*."

"Hootenanny's!" Winterhalter whooped. "Your destiny calls your carved jack-o-lantern ass to an extended stay at the spa!"

"You're speaking of Hootenanny's in Wisconsin Dells?" Noyce queried. "I'd resolved to add that to my itinerary – maybe as early as tomorrow."

"The Wisconsin prairie is a long ricochet from the Outback." The celebrity donned his seersucker suit coat and jammed his tie in the pocket. "How is it you're familiar, Guy?"

Noyce chuckled. "Well, it's water-world-renowned, isn't it, with its communal co-ed Beaver Isle nude area."

"What?" The reagent turned eagerly from the photo-opportunist to the celebrity. "What the fuwhyfor we clinging to this barge, Ooclops?"

"Are you suggesting you're inclined to investigate immediately?" Noyce checked his Jatakar. "I don't guess I'd mind flying you up. I've a rented Ianto, a Sparrow."

"That's a generous offer, Guy, but we're not in the position to accept such favors." The celebrity started toward the exit. "We're stuck on site."

Winterhalter snapped a leather restraint into the celebrity's buttocks. "You're always such a whipped weinie, Mabel."

An aftershock of pain buckled the celebrity's knees. "Widdo boy scared to wet go da tub widdout Boss Tess say-so?"

The photo-opportunist held the celebrity's forearm to steady him. "I'd be chuffed to have some company on the trip up." He smiled intently. "We can make the rest of the night of it."

The celebrity bounced the tip of his forefinger off the center of the reagent's forehead. "The next time you take the slightest cheap shot at me, tallow-head, expect to be put squarely in your place, which is to say body-slammed into the nearest dumpster!"

"Yes, honey." Winterhalter wiggled his tongue. "Stay aboard and romance your wound." He gestured to Noyce. "Osmodias and me will head out to Hootenanny's and set up shop for surveillance."

The celebrity eyed the photo-opportunist. "Would you recognize Tess's companion if you encountered him again?" He gritted his teeth. "Can you have us back before breakfast?"

"Hope springs." Noyce sauntered toward the door. The celebrity and the reagent exchanged malignant glances and followed. At the front of the Swelled Head, the receptionist rose to bid Guy a perky farewell, and he purchased a tin of Copioids. She perfunctorily handed the celebrity his body modification Kare Kit and returned to the woman who awaited resumption of her nail treatment.

The celebrity struggled to keep pace with Winterhalter and Noyce as they strode across the promenade deck. Walking was painful but preferable to standing, and he dreaded the prospect of assuming a seated position. He left Tohnyin a message chiding her for not updating the team on her whereabouts. He finally reached the gangway and joined the reagent and photo-opportunist in waiting for the shuttle boat. "How's it healing, mate?" Guy broke the seal on his Copioids and extended the tin.

The celebrity declined the candied meds. "Pain is my advisor, not my commissar."

I.B. leered. "How are you going to expose your refinished hump to Psycho-Isis, pookie?"

The celebrity moaned. "Benji can send her my cold gel impression." He perused his Kare Kit tips, and Guy again offered the Copioids. The celebrity reached toward the tin but retracted his hand.

I wonder what you're thinking,
You're wailing in my ear.
The puddle grows a pond becomes a sea.
You're really saying nothing,
Just using lots of words.
Are you the bucket case or is it me?

I copy what you're feeling,
You're spuming down my neck.
A hurricane to darken my foul mood.
Your restlessness is painted
In jagged broad-brush strokes.
The attitude lays anchor on my nerves.

The lemonade we're brewing
Is gutter-watered down.
The sour aftertaste of ruin persists.
The riper fruits were higher;
We couldn't shake them loose.
Our discontent transcends each galling sip.

5TH MOVEMENT

Inbound. 0300 CST Wednesday 29 March.

"I got no stomach for playing it safe, wingman!" I.B. Winterhalter pounded his point into Guy Noyce's headrest as the photo-opportunist piloted his sun-emblemed Sparrow volantor through the Flyway 51 air vector to exotic Wisconsin Dells. The soundbars pinballed the asymmetrical accentuation of Stravinsky's *Rite of Spring* throughout the well-insulated hooded cabin, and the celebrity sat in back at a delicate angle on his cramped corner of the lightly padded thwart, hugging the luggage pile that partitioned him from the reagent. "You don't pogo to honcho by going mozo. I've smelled blood, and I liked it!"

"Oobops!" Noyce called. "Notice the way the night sky has suddenly lit up?"

The celebrity rotated gingerly to peer out the small window. "Lightning? UFO?" Tohnyin's precariously perched vanity case tumbled over his shoulder. "Gamma ray burst? I don't see anything."

"Right, that's the bright-line beltway of the capital city." Guy rubbed his brow. "It's passed now."

Winterhalter's gloating face appeared in the shoe-box-size gap atop the luggage pile. "Spiv, you don't look so good, even for you."

The celebrity strained to maintain distance from the

luggage without intensifying the burning and itching of the *Ingeroll* brattoo. "I've been fitter," he affirmed.

"Still no fadey for blisty stingy?" I.B. snickered. "What a freagkhhing pansy-ass! I minted both of my honey buns in tandem. Didn't blink, didn't shrink, didn't fluster me a frit."

"What is it exactly that you have raised back there?" the celebrity wondered. "A spare pair of nipples?"

"*Assterisks!*" Guy cackled and clutched the side of his head.

"My apple sections," the reagent snipped, "are more than vainy veneer, broncobusters. They're symbols of my personal struggle, statements of control by choice, my tribal yin-yang pome *etoiles.*"

"That sounds a bit busy," the photo-opportunist commented.

Winterhalter fed a sleeve of Evans's blazer through the luggage pile gap. "You want to sit on this again, trash-o-tron?"

The celebrity slapped the fabric. "No, it makes it worse." Working on the premise that personal property in the Passenger Pigeon wasn't part of Isis's bet bargain, the spa squad had detoured to the gref in the Big Foot parking lot for the purpose of reclaiming accouterments. The celebrity had wedged his forearm into the opening beneath the canopy created by the brush with the gate, opened the cockpit and retrieved his briefcase. He'd further extracted Evans's blazer as well as Tohnyin's garment bag with the hidden Velcro pocket and expandable trolley along with her matching diplomatic strongbox and golden-ratio oval vanity case. Tess's ocean-foam-blue triad all carried the CIB logo and had been indelicately added to the top of the Sparrow's back seat luggage pile. "Let her beg for her bags!" he'd remarked.

"Another ripping item about a brattoo we did for *Dinkidi Fair*," Noyce contributed. "Married couple name of Pettigrew, I recall. The wife Bambi resented her mate Conner for being unfaithful and squandering their money, the usual toss. But one day she decided to forgive him unconditionally if only he'd take her back in his cheating arms, and to celebrate their fresh go, she got him to consent to mutual brattoos of interlocked hearts embroidered into their pubic mounds."

"Did *Dinkidi Fair* whack out mostly that order of crud?" I.B. slapped the back of Guy's seat. "Cuz if that's all the fiber you got in your frosted flake, kookaburra, it's no wonder your rag folded under."

The celebrity invoked the categorical imperative to smooth international relations before anyone lost their good humor or ride. "The paparazzi serve a valuable purpose. By capturing the world's most beautiful people off-guard when they look like something fit to be stacked at the curb and hauled away, they offer hope to everyone else."

"Even for you, punchline-face?" Winterhalter jabbed a window scraper through the luggage pile gap and clipped the celebrity in the chin. "Only the grossest, obscenest prefab pay dirt is worthwhile."

The celebrity drove the scraper handle back into the reagent's shoulder and commandeered the instrument. "You should've heard this goosebump," he advised Noyce, "before our company's finishing course polished and refined his act."

"To finish off the Pettigrews," Guy huffed, "Conner was apparently unable to piss away quite enough of the family fortune because long-suffering Bambi still had sufficient funds to commission the brattoo artist to use contaminated tools and dyes on her triple-dipping spouse." The owl man cited the case history of rare, complementary social infections that Conner subsequently contracted. "The scunge wound up marred and trimmed to a crotch rot of the first degree, rendered physically unfit to rise to the occasion for further adultery or give so much as a command solo performance. Checkmate: Pettigrew Wound Profile." A painful clinical photo sequence of a man's cropped and scarred pudenda filled the dashboard screen. "The private hell of hells."

Winterhalter jarred the luggage pile. "You know, Bops,

you ought to suck on your own similarity. Say your Isis is a WIO working girl, and she paid off Bengigi or tampered with his irons and inks, so your brattoo got smacked with some subtle poison. You could be slowly dying here as we speak." He pressed his face into the gap, his features blazing with relish. "You might want to haul your ass to some hospital and get checked out."

The celebrity smiled tartly. "Maybe it's a radioactive poison, so I'm infecting you two buzzards as well."

Winterhalter slapped Noyce on top of the head. "Kluge us in, down-underbelly. What's the sickest, most radical, block-shocking shit you ever slung for public consumption? Like did you ever dip your bailiwick into the ritual torture and rape bag, some snappy South Seas brain-eating wotfoal, or such?"

"My half-brother's a hermaphrodite," the celebrity suggested.

Noyce blinked and squinted into the distance, apparently scouring the stuffed coffers of his memory for a suitably lurid journalistic nugget. "Well, there once was a lad north of Perth-"

"Who had length but just pencil-thick girth," I.B. gibed.

"Who was voted most outrageous kid in his high school class – the supreme subcultural honor at the institution." Noyce engaged Winterhalter with a wry smile. "As it most likely was at yours." The photo-opportunist floated a tabloid tease about the progression of Larry, a displaced, "disinvolved student," who landed at a college of visual arts and developed a fanatical fascination with the artist Vincent Van Gogh and the local sportscaster Twyla Rutledge. "When Twyla gushes and coos on camera about an exhibit featuring old Vinnie coming across, Larry is satisfied his lucky stars have lined him up with his soul mate, and he sends her effervescent notices of amatory regard backed by sunflower poetry, hand-dipped chocolates and aura-altering powders and lotions. Twyla ignores his overtures without so much as a polite rejection, but she does come out shortly thereafter with the startling public revelation that she's a lesbian. A local club in Perth – it was Dream Snatchers – has been offering a huge monetary prize for the most outrageous legal act, and in a decisive fit of molly-aided inspiration, Larry dismembers himself and sends Twyla the product as the ultimate token of his unshakable devotion. But can you believe it? Even as Larry lay in the hospital receiving emergency gender reassignment, Twyla recants her declaration, reaffirming her staunch heterosexuality." The mechanical twang of automation artist Cross Hairs singing "Are You Lonesome To-Night?" permeated the cabin.

"Don't you think you mixed that cocktail a bit strong, Guy?" The celebrity shifted his weight uncomfortably. "I presume the sportscaster was vying for the club prize, too?"

"The proof is in the archives, Oobops!" Noyce clutched his head. "Checkmate: Scared Straight. Research it yourself!" An article entitled "Scared Straight!" appeared on the dashboard screen. "As far as Rutledge goes, she wasn't about any prize; she was a professional and naturally all about ratings."

"Tough stuff," Winterhalter grudgingly surrendered high praise. "Larry earned the prize."

"He did, but *she* never collected, because the prize was a fake!" The owl man snickered. "She sued the club but apparently came up empty on the whinge because the club crapped out delinquent, rolled over bankrupt. Now that's outrageous!"

The reagent fumed. "I would've demolished that club, loaded the rubble into a cargo copter and dumped it all onto Twyla's TV station while she was on the air!"

"How unladylike." The celebrity tried sitting on his hands. "Gender-bending just keeps on burgeoning into deeper sub-genres, doesn't it?"

"Does sexual variance perplex you, Oobops?" Guy snapped his head around petulantly.

The celebrity shrugged. "Seeing girls dance together without forming a line does give me some heebie-jeebies and whim-whams." He pressed his shoulder into the side of the cabin. "I was raised to view any homosexual act that isn't limited to fabulous-looking women as unsavory."

"He's got a terminal case of the Sundays," Winterhalter interpreted. "The Bops can't flap his chops as company chap by being all rainbows and mountaintops; he has to get up the prigs and peeves to obsess over order and décor and shit all put in its proper drawer." He snorted. "That about bust you to the core, brimstone-breath?"

The celebrity experienced a pain spike. "That sounds about like the joyful noise inmate I.B. will be making ten years from now when he's accruing frequent rider kilos on the Trans-Identity Shuttle Bus between Pelican Bay and Chowchilla."

A guttural sound emanated from beyond the luggage pile. "It'll be a far shorter ride for you, Cup-Half-Empty."

The celebrity leaned into the luggage pile as the owl man cackled. "On the topic of communal co-ed bathhouse breaks, Toodyay Today, are we close to the remote termite hill at our journey's end?"

"Yeah, where the hell is this stinkin' waterhole?" Winterhalter jarred the luggage pile.

Guy turned with a smirk. "How did I wind up with a bashin' backbench of shonky rat-bags with hard-ons to heckle the driver?" He sighed. "I predict this crotch-of-heartland-America state treasure has enough to offer that neither of you will be able to easily leave. It's quirky with applied mad science all over. They're taking advantage of the warming trend to develop deciduous trees genetically engineered to hold spectacular colors. And the Dells boasts more per capita golf holes than any other census district in the Midwest. It's a celebration of shape-shifting and metamorphosis in the environ-"

A close craft warning yipped. "Want to pay more attention to piloting, puffball," Winterhalter snapped, "before you shift our shittin' shape to a crash-and-burn crater?"

Noyce adjusted the Sparrow's course, and the celebrity

leaned forward. "We understand the Midwest is cultivating more and more crops traditionally exclusive to the sunny South."

"You're better rooted than I in what amber waves of planterworts and dieselchokes they're putting in," Noyce reasoned, "but I must register my dismay over how poised to pounce on Lady Opportunity you Napa-siders were when France's climate went bodgy, and now that these other regions are turned out with a whiff of the Mediterranean seasoning to wrest hold of your growing edge, you're madder than a cut snake about it."

The celebrity nodded. "How long did you prowl the Valley to have caught such a strong bouquet of the native vibe?"

Guy scratched his head. "I haven't been in your neck since the new year began with me chasing rumors of soldiers selling a used armored personnel carrier to the philanthropic arm of a think tank."

"That's an intriguing stratum of elbows to rub." The celebrity offered a wry smile. "You must've found some booming side niche if you can afford the Gore Tax to operate this lanto."

"You make everything sound so shady, Oobops." The photo-opportunist giggled. "The nether realm of classified salvage serves my inquisitive ailment more than my need to suck at the teet of filthy lucre." He again turned his back to the windshield. "The Dells, for instance, makes proper use of a sort of decommissioned amphibious hell-raiser for a joy ride down the road and river. And I'm following a bonza thread about a group at a camp for disadvantaged youths just up the road that has reconditioned the twisted shell of an antique Blackbird spy plane into a fully functional fighter jet. Word from the source blog-stormer is the junior skunk works is looking to celebrate the completion of their first flight by cooking a pizza on the steaming hot skin of the aircraft."

"We save time and energy while we're driving in California by fastening slices of bread to the roof racks of our cars to make toast," the celebrity exaggerated slightly. "If we're spotted by the state authorities, we score double negative carbon points, right, I.B.?"

"I'd take I.B. for a bloody bloke who likes to cram jumbo marshmallows on his enhanced aerial regardless." The photo-opportunist faced forward.

"You'd take it we have the connections to line your arse up a buyer for some tricked out, preowned military metal?" Winterhalter prospected with the velvet charm of a clanging radiator.

Noyce banked the Sparrow roughly. "You professional phonies consider my veracity suspect? Do I come across as some sort of threat? What are *you* up to?" He took the craft into a precipitous dive.

"Please pardon Ib's interest," the celebrity labored to buff the breach. "He was the careers correspondent and gossip columnist on his high school newspaper." He set himself to lunge for the yoke. "Gonna give us some air, Guy?"

"Don't distract me!" Noyce flipped switches, endowed the windshield with an infrared view and scrutinized his instrument panel. The road gear of the Sparrow thumped hard twice and held pavement. The windows descended, and the photo-opportunist turned to face the reagent. "You want to know how I blazed into the glitter biz?"

"I want you to close the fucking windows!" I.B. decried the cool, methane-smacked night air filling the cabin.

"My struggle to reach the stars started when I served as Pilot Officer, flying a desk in the Royal Australian Air Force." Guy closed the windows. "Squadron Leader Rex Riddell, a robust man with a rich, thick-throated voice, occupied the corner office. He'd leave his door ajar, sit on the phone all day and fill our work area with his booming horselaugh." The celebrity determined that the Sparrow sat on a desolate country road. "So the logistics staff conspired to execute a hovering gag. The instant Rex let out with his har-har-hars, we'd all join in and hoot-hoot-hoot our fool arses off. The trick was to be full-on quick and make it sound sincere, so he couldn't suspect the logs pukes were mocking him. It wasn't long, of course, before Riddell became vexed by the chorus and endeavored to get to the bottom of the peculiarity. Naturally, he came to the conclusion that his office was bugged, and for some hazy reason he pinned me as the master insect. So as not to confound old Rex's expectations, I ultimately did place him under personal surveillance. And I parlayed these skills I developed in the military to fine advantage first as a freelancer and then as a staffer for tabloids that could appreciate a good fist: *The Excavator* and then *Dinkidi Fair*."

The celebrity clicked his tongue. "And now you've come back full boomerang to freelancing?"

Noyce snapped his fingers. "Would one of you be kind enough to hold up your sourcerer and accept my geo-stream? I'd like you to admire the new mag I've begun propping pix for."

"Send it back, swags," Winterhalter instructed. "Oobops will take it in quarantine and sift it for mal-content." He eyed the celebrity. "You can do that without my support, right, supergrader?"

The celebrity charily activated his Qilroy receiver and authorized transfer protocol. When Noyce's stream arrived and scanned clean, he opened the file to find a video sequence of a shirtless, muscular young man chopping wood. The intro to *Strewth* magazine also touted intense coverage of the Latin Dance World Championships in Havana as it pummeled the luggage pile with the heroic power of a paso doble rhythm. "Perhaps not lowest of the motley common denominators between dance and wrestling," the celebrity observed, "is the seemingly inexhaustible supply of champions?"

"What the hell is that music?" I.B. protested. "More classical blast like Rimshot-Kalashnikov?"

"It's not important." Guy shook his head. "What is important is we're just down the road from the spa." He guided the

Sparrow over the hard bumps of a narrow backroad and into a driveway. "I hope you'll each share the *Strewth* sample among your friends and associates and you'll all subscribe."

"That could net how many through you, Ahab," the reagent probed, "one for Tohnyin?"

The Sparrow proceeded around a large carton of a building with pueblo flourishes and parked on a dimly lit blacktop. Noyce grabbed a ditty bag and led the spa squad through the mammoth dark chocolate oak double doors of the main entrance. A rustic foyer with a stone floor and benches of colossal scale situated around a cylindrical counter four meters high welcomed them. The counter girdled a blazing chemical torch. A leather strap festooned with sleigh bells extended from the skylight ceiling to the floor. A bold red sign at the top of the counter read *Ring For Service*. Guy shook the strap, strafing the air with a critical mass of sense-numbing metallic chirps.

The head and shoulders of a giant blue-eyed woman sporting a tower of blonde beehive curls rose over the counter as the torch faded and vanished. "Good evening!" the hologram fluted. "Welcome to Hootenanny's Frontier Chalet Spa. My name is Mishy. How may I be of service?"

"G'day, Mishy!" Guy shouted. "Landing *partay* of three! We'd like to ride your slide and settle into the communal bath for a bit."

"Very good, sir." Mishy wore a green sash. "If you'll please present billing information, agree to abide by the house rules and sign a safety waiver, we'll set you up and get you going. There are no image recorders on the premises outside the screening booth."

"*Mishy?*" the reagent scoffed. "Sounds like what you get when you smash your ice cream cone on your shirt."

"Shut up," the photo-opportunist counseled, "I think that's ethnic. Anyway, it's an intelligent hologram; she'll come back and let you have it."

"Sheyitt!" Winterhalter rubbed a spot on his chest. "I got this big rocky-road mishy on my clean white shirt!"

"My full name is Melisha Piddleman," the hologram declared. "Tell me yours. You lairds from out of state?"

"*Raweeyt*," I.B. adopted a triple-thick Australian accent, "a leedle sath cross the paund." The reagent suspended his weight on the bell strap, swung awkwardly and bumped the celebrity. "This one's real name is Dag Dudevitch." He flipped the strap at the owl man. "Spin the head of this guy and you'll see why the wallaroos of Handblowedbong know him as Noah Count."

"An upper-cruster." Mishy emitted a coarse, hearty laugh. "What d'ya dingoes do for a living?"

"Great work," Guy grumbled, "you yarras have made her chatty. *We're really here*," he raised his voice, "because this is the one well in the territory where a team of super spies from California who need a straddling nanny to remind us of home governance can grab ourselves a hoot of a sitter!"

"Obviously." The celebrity forced hefty guffaws, and the hologram imitated him. "We're actually landscape architects on our way to a puzzles conference. Are you familiar with the 4-D Storm Aftermath series of jigsaws?"

"I believe my grandson has a mess of those," Mishy remarked. "But funny you mention spies because we harbor a Confederate spy in the neighborhood. Supposed to be buried within the Dells city limits somewhere. Now, where is she?"

"*She?*" Winterhalter exclaimed. "I told Tess not to wear blue tonight."

"Aw, I'm sure she'll turn up," Noyce allayed concern about both women.

"Very good, I'll turn you loose in the facilities, fellows, as soon as you register." The hologram directed the spa squad to a flashing green screening booth on the west side of the foyer. On the wall inside hung a portrait of an elderly man in a glengarry named *WALLACE*. His eyes served as scanners, and the bottom of the gilded frame provided instructions. Guy and

I.B. each completed the requisite transaction by text. Wallace accepted the celebrity's billing information but rejected the rest of his input four times, citing an "encryption exception," and instructed him to hold for interactive video. An image of Mishy was overlaid on Wallace. "You must sign a waiver certifying you have no personal condition which might make us dangerous for you or you dangerous to us." She presented an extensive medical checklist worthy of a nosy waiting-room nurse.

"Aren't you getting a little intimate?" the celebrity challenged.

"Are you inshinerating we look like we have to pay for shex?" the reagent proved that the booth was far from soundproof.

"Extraordinary gents sometimes arrive here expecting the spa to be something it's not," Mishy explained. "It's an adult establishment, but it's not that adult." She paused. "Why, *have* you paid for it?"

Guy barged into the booth. "Without exception, one way or another."

I.B. clamped his hand on the celebrity's shoulder. "He's paid for it, but he still didn't get any."

Mishy's raucous laughter overpowered booth acoustics. "At least you got stiffed one way or another, huh?"

The celebrity reluctantly pressed his palm over Mishy's and completed his transaction. Her eyes gleamed. "Bear in mind: no intoxicants of any sort allowed in the soup, and no sex of any sort and no surveillance or active recording devices allowed anywhere on the premises." She whooped. "Savor the spa experience!" The Wallace portrait was restored.

"Chatty," Noyce repeated.

The owl man led the celebrity and the reagent out of the foyer and through a damp, narrow passageway to a cramped locker room. Crafted with cedar-crate elegance and illuminated chiefly by LED boundary spotters and the glow of artificial logs in a caged pit, the alpine-scented accommodation featured a column of shiny metal poles running parallel to a wooden bench and wall lockers. Guy pressed a large button beside the door, and the locker room lurched. "Please deactivate electronic devices," an androgynous voice directed. "Boarding complete?" The door closed, and the compartment started moving. "Good-looking load!"

The photo-opportunist shook his fist. "Here goes a fighting man's outfit!" He opened a locker and inventoried the contents. "Thongs for wimps, and towels for the rest of us."

"A barrel sits at the base of each locker," the androgynous voice continued. "E-nitial the tag, key a combination you can recall, and pack everything that's not actually you inside. Upon arrival at the top, flush them down the tube and retrieve them in the bathhouse locker below."

The celebrity advanced to a pole halfway between Noyce and the front of the compartment. He clung to it for support as the lift car swayed on its sluggish, twisting climb. "You seem to have a regular's handle on the routine, Guy."

Noyce beamed with satisfaction. "At the start of your last autumn, the Dells hosted another international folk-dance exposition that I'd hoped to attend. An affiliated bull-roarer of mine did come up and gave me a bird's-eye review of this stronghold."

"Does your squench Giselle dance?" Winterhalter split the distance between the celebrity and the photo-opportunist. "Cuz when you're looking to arrange a public humiliation, the dance floor holds a shitload of potential." He opened a locker, unzipped and unbuttoned with an instant-gratification urgency and thrust his pants and undershorts to his ankles.

"Quite right." Noyce extracted the barrel from his locker. "If you could entice her to perform an ornery set of prisiadkas, and we could secretly capture the spectacle, we'd be well on our way off square one to settling our score." He separated his turtleneck from his furry torso. "We seem to be citizens of the only two half-cultured sovereign corners of the globe that generally view dance as an opportunity to abnegate rather than accentuate one's manliness."

"At the top of the hill," the androgynous voice persevered, "riders will populate air-cushioned bubble orbs called snow-balls. A cannon fires each snowball into the sky, and when the orb returns to earth, it bounds, caroms and glances around the features of the hillside course before it ultimately rolls down a ramp and ends up making a big splash in the warm, sparkling water of the pool."

Noyce removed his tan, low-cut boots. "The zone I come from not even the women are stoked by dance." A thin vapor enveloped the compartment. The photo-opportunist extolled the virtues of recreational dance and attempted to demonstrate points with the reagent. By the time the spa squad stood naked with possessions stowed in barrels, Guy and the celebrity had become engaged in a heated debate about modern perfor-mance dance, particularly paso doble vis-a-vis bullfighting as a legitimate cultural expression. "Life is presented as a blood sport, a duel of flirtations. This is the verve, the rich tradition, the essence of the bullfight."

In the thickening, sultry haze, Winterhalter screeched and flapped his elbows like a bat. "I can't help but recall," the celebrity asserted, "the disgust my Mexican great-grandmother expressed for the corrida in her living memoir, although I believe trouble with surrounding spectators over the obliga-tion to remain in her seat exacerbated the consternation."

"It's dodgy, Oobops, to demonize a dance." Seated on the bench, Guy held a towel on his hip.

"Frontier air must agree with me!" The reagent emerged through the ripples of vapor, pumping his knees like a deranged cyclist, his huge uncircumcised penis flopping wildly. "I feel the adrenaline surge, invigorated, even more virile than usual!" He turned and repeated his bouncy swagger to the front of the compartment.

Noyce positioned his towel more strategically. "Ahab faces Moby Dick," he giggled.

"You could've used him in the Royal Air Force." The celebrity experienced a pain surge. "When he runs naked, it rotates 360 degrees like a propeller."

"I feel your obsession, potoroo," the owl man cackled. "Consider all the exertion you likely put out to maintain your muscle mass to compensate, and the green aura you're oozing demonstrates it's still not enough." He raised his arm to detain the returning reagent. "Don't mean to cross your private line, mate, but since you practically slapped me in the bugle on your last swing past, could I ask a frank morph question? It's my understanding there's a chronic dull ache in the anatomy-"

"I got no morph, Manfred!" Winterhalter faced Noyce squarely. "No implant! This is all me, all natural, all night!"

"I meant no offense, hangman." The photo-opportunist nodded toward the celebrity. "He just intimated it was prehensile."

"What the hell would he know about it?" The reagent crowded closer. "The only thing Oobops has ever grown is frustrated. My mount says his gherkin is the reason he's always so negative and obnoxious. Her pet name for him is Stump the Expert."

"Madelyn," the celebrity scoffed. "Not the brightest blip on your sonar screen. She has the hips to field a torpedo."

I.B. pounded his buttocks. "Yeah, I am a torpedo!"

"You're self-propelled and self-destructive." The celebrity gestured toward Guy. "How crazy would Mad be about him? She might decide his hirsute hide suits her better than your precocious prod."

The reagent leered at the celebrity. "*You* need a morph, glad-hander!"

The photo-opportunist grinned. "As we're wont to say in the theater, there are no small parts, raweeyt?" He dabbed at the sweat on his chest. "When we've all arrived safe and sound down in the common pool area, Oobops, won't you please stop dragging our conversation onto the sleaze track?"

The lift car slowed and swayed to a stop, and a stuffy lethargy attended the compartment. Noyce began bobbing in the fog. "Better beef up on BTUs, battlers, because it's going to be a cold start to the trip down." The celebrity exchanged socially maladaptive squints with Winterhalter. "We could, of course, assuage that hardship through the popular will to all go together. Two squeeze nicely into the double bubble, but it'd be ripper to try to cram three!"

"Climate change recognizes no boundaries, and we're always prepared to confront it." The celebrity delicately seated himself on the edge of the bench. "We won't risk being diverted from our diplomatic agenda to heavily indoctrinate my fanny-bright in mineral salts." He flung his towel at the reagent. "Solidarity, rebarbative-breath."

"Take some solidarity upside the skull, your assholiness!" Winterhalter turned to Noyce. "You must regularly get the jones to get back to the Oz homeland, don't you, Bizbrain?"

Guy sighed. "Strangely enough, what an old sand-groper may miss most is the national treasury of wildlife." He fidgeted uncomfortably. "The birds and mammals of America remind me of the insects and arachnids of Stralia."

A series of soft bells sounded, and Noyce popped to his feet. "Lounge tough long enough then, cabana kahunas? Bring your laundry barrels up to the drop-off, and let's get ready to tumble!" He wrapped his towel around his waist, tipped his barrel onto its side and kicked it ahead of him to the front wall. The celebrity and the reagent secured their barrels and followed.

Guy pressed a large button at the front of the locker compartment. "Boarding procedure for slide activated," the androgynous voice announced. The lift car swayed, moved laterally and dropped a short distance. A door opened, and a chilly breeze whipped through the sauna. The owl man ventured onto the loading platform, where the top of a large transparent orb protruded through a round opening in the floor. He placed his barrel inside a white pedestal and flushed it away.

The androgynous voice imparted instructions. Noyce released his towel and propelled himself feetfirst into the opening at the top of the orb. When only his head and arms remained unenveloped, he saluted inelegantly. "See ya yobbos in the boiler room!" He nestled in his snowball. The lift car rose and moved laterally. A whop sounded, and the owl man's snowball hurtled into the air.

The lift car settled over a fresh orb. Winterhalter flushed his barrel and penetrated the clear snowball headfirst. "What's the chance," the celebrity wondered, "the 'boiler room' is what Aussies call hell?" The lift car rose and moved laterally. Another whop sounded, and I.B.'s orb headed skyward.

The celebrity flushed his barrel. The androgynous voice advised caution. After a delay of several minutes, the lift car returned to ready position. The celebrity discarded his towel and attempted to enter the orb without scraping his brattoo. He found himself standing like a prize vermin specimen in a box trap on the slippery inner surface of a double-walled polyurethane bubble. Golfball-size perforations populated both walls, which were separated by airbags. One could only distinguish general forms through the double-membrane in the soft light, but he thought he discerned a chalet a short distance away. He wrapped himself in the double-belt that hung from the top of the orb and connected the tips in accordance with the accompanying instructive diagram. LED lights in the orb were deactivated, as the lift car hissed and moved away.

The snowball shot a short distance into the air. For a moment, the celebrity experienced the sensation of floating. In the next breath, a furious gust of wind seemed to capture the orb and dash it to the ground. The snowball bounced and tumbled off the side of the hill, rolled and came to rest at the base of a stand of conifers. For a few minutes, the celebrity lay dazed and uncertain whether his orb had followed a course designed to be part of the amusement ride experience. When it became apparent that he was only going to grow colder in his present predicament, he pressed the emergency button at the top of the double-belt. The microphone lit. "A man lost his ride on the slide and needs to be picked up!" he reported. For several minutes, he waited in vain for a response. "Hey! Piste-bashers, come on!" he repeated his call for wayside assistance. "A naked man is stranded up on the trail!" For several more minutes, his signal elicited no noise.

The celebrity fought his way out of his harness and emerged from his shell. He started climbing down the hill. He clawed for better holds and continually slammed his forearms and knees into the rough ice as he struggled to dig his fingers and toes into snow. He reached the trail border of truck tires, which were braced by packed powder. He hopped from tire to tire, coughing with exhaustion in the raw air. A flash emerging from the stand of evergreens caught his attention, and he staggered to his feet as another snowball started down the ramp. He instinctively lunged for the orb as it whisked past, sending himself sliding over course moguls on his belly and hip. The distance by which he trailed the snowball increased exponentially, and he ultimately slid to a stop on the final jump. The steamy translucent bathhouse double doors closed ahead of him. He surmounted the icy ridge on all fours and banged his head against the doors. He stood, slipped and fell, stood and fell again. He struggled to his feet and searched for a means of manually prying the doors open from out-side. Finding none, he pounded on the doors vehemently. He slipped and fell again. The doors remained closed. He stood and waited twenty minutes for another snowball but no such vehicle arrived. He considered heaving a truck tire or large ice chunk through the translucent glass but opted instead to seek an alternate means of entry. Finesse separated the master operatives from the master pretenders.

Outbound. 0530 CST Wednesday 29 March.

"No agitator can accuse you of having a *tankless* job, bubbles." Immersed in a tub of tepid healing mineral salt crystals beneath red LED lights in the therapeutic arm of Hootenanny's Frontier bathhouse, the celebrity stood on command. "But you should know what it's like to court the hearts and minds of the locals with token capital infusions which pay tribute to their native cultural heritage and get betrayed for your trouble."

Therapist Phouvieng conducted the celebrity through the fourth and final stage of his superficial burn-and-laceration treatment by spraying cold water up and down his back. "You're raving pretty wildly again, Mr. Oobops."

"Now that's not Noyce, is it?" Monitoring activity in the natural-spring-fed pool plex below through a tinted window, the celebrity thought he spotted Guy Noyce clinging to an electric-blue frying pan flotation pad at the near end of the men's section but realized he was mistaken.

"I'm sorry." Phouvieng had previously disclosed that in her spare time she capered as a medical student at the University of Wisconsin. "Please squat again." In response to his more pertinacious inquiries, she'd identified the dominant active ingredient in the thick liquid that blanketed his body as finely milled peat moss and was confident it was scientifically proven to be effective. In a related vein, she'd claimed that she wasn't aware of any science luminaries who patronized the spa, although she had recently spotted one of her chemistry professors in the bistro on the hill.

The celebrity sank back into the tank. He examined the cuts on his hands and elbows. "The fact is I didn't really sustain all of these nicks and scrapes in a wheel-of-cheese chase." His ordeal to escape from the snowball course had left him with an overall body sting, but his feet probably hurt more than any other part. He'd been unable to exploit any port of re-entry until he'd walked halfway around the building and returned through the main entrance. He'd ducked through the foyer, popped into a lift car to grab a towel and thong and followed the passageway signage to the third-floor therapy center. A prickly itch had displaced his raw brattoo pain.

"Your seasonal affective disorder should be getting better, isn't it?" Phouvieng directed a warm, gentle water stream over the celebrity's neck and shoulders, redoubling his wasted wooziness. "Will you stand for this?"

The celebrity staggered to his feet and wiped his eyes. "There's our punky flunky!" He positively identified I.B. Winterhalter fronting an angular woman in the centrally located mixed-gender cool pool. "That chick's a good head taller than him!" The celebrity was suddenly seized with recognition anxiety. She wore her hair short and darker now, but the grallatorial girlfriend had the familiar mannerisms of treacherous WIO double agent Paige Eiffel. He couldn't be certain from such a distance. "Where's the nearest stairs?" he demanded. "I need to get right down to the pool!"

"Mr. Oobops, why?" Phouvieng grabbed him by the hand. "You want to complete your circuit, and then you need another twenty minutes in the quiet room to rest and recover. One of the key ingredients in station four is *madashaunda*, and if you leave now, you're going to be subject to nausea, vomiting and extreme dizziness, maybe even a nosebleed!"

"I need to send his apple cheeks up here immediately so you can purge his toxic masculinity!" He surveyed his surroundings. Phouvieng sighed with disgust, handed him his thong and looked away.

On feet that had been rendered as tender as the average debutante's, the celebrity scissored past the four therapy tubs and scampered to the exit. He reached the unilluminated quiet room and tripped over a chair. His tumble triggered the motion sensor, and the light flickered. He struggled to his feet, fully activating the light. The room seemed split into separate dimensions, each spinning inside and outside of the other. He spilled out of the quiet room and into the corridor. He took about five minutes to locate the stairs and carefully descend them. He took another five minutes to find the door to the men's section of the pool plex. He barged through it and stumbled to the edge of the pool. He found himself adjacent to an open clamshell flotation pad inside of which Noyce happened to be lounging. Racked by a pounding headache and severe joint pain, he clutched his abdomen.

"Oobops, come a gutser?" Guy maneuvered his clamshell closer. "Where've you been tarrying?"

"Why did you wander off again like you're demented?" Winterhalter emerged from behind Noyce on a green whale flotation device. "Anyhow, Ayab, thanks for the prunes." He displayed his wrinkled fingers.

"Where's long-shanks?" The celebrity surveyed the empty cool pool and points surrounding it. "The cathedral-ceiling headbanger you were withstanding center stage?"

"Long fucking gone." I.B. snickered. "Avablanche was leaving when I held her up. Wade out there yourself and see how frigid that pit is! Only a goddamn idiot or somebody waiting for one would hang around."

"The co-ed cool pool is known about as a bit of a harsh awakening." The photo-opportunist flashed a wry smile. "I.B. suggests you fancy the leggy ladies, Ahab?"

"Just the legates." The celebrity eyed the reagent intently. "What personal information did you collect? Do you have any idea of where she is now?"

Winterhalter vacated his whale pad. "She'd douse your spark before you could spit out your intro, Horatio. She gave me the twice-over and said, 'Nice suit.'" He slapped his soft lower belly in the waist-deep water. "She gets off on 'a real man with a real midway.'" He shrugged. "Maybe she's up in the grog-hall on the hill."

The celebrity sighed. "My bubble orb got blown off course,

and I had to clamber back into the building. Thank you for your concern."

"We reported you to the lifeguard, beach-head," the reagent snarled.

"We told him an old tramp was left behind," Guy attested. "I said, 'Arrange a search-and-rescue mission, Danger Dan!' He said he'd check with the top of the hill and they'd send down. Then he got shirty with us for shaking his ladder. He insisted they'd handle the situation on the course."

"I'm not strictly authorized to prowl along this section of the waterworks." Phouvieng knelt beside the celebrity and deposited his robe, slippers and towel on the cement. "There are no drinks allowed in the pool area either." She handed him a paper cup containing a hot beverage. "Sit back, Mr. Oobops, and replenish your depleted fluids by drinking this naturopathic painkiller. It's blue lotus tea. It'll make you fit to rejoin the general bathhouse population."

Winterhalter splashed gregariously. "Yeah, Ahab, you're not someone like Tess who can look sexy puking in the pool."

Phouvieng rose. "If anyone challenges you, tell them I granted you special permission." She left hastily as he sipped his tea.

I.B. leered. "We're relieved you haven't been denying yourself any basic comforts, dip-thong."

The celebrity set his cup on the lip of the cement and propelled himself into the pool. "This thong *is* eating into my brattoo wound." He advanced to deeper water, clenched the cup between his teeth and gingerly removed his thong.

Guy pointed over the celebrity's shoulder. "Aren't you the popular one, Oobops?" A tanned, muscular figure in official lifeguard plaid trunks approached along the edge of the pool carrying a bullhorn. "That's the slide attendant, isn't it? What's he doing over on this side?"

"Maybe they rotate posts to keep it surreal." Winterhalter pivoted.

"Excuse me, you three!" the lifeguard shouted. "*Hey, you three jokers!*" the voice blared through the bullhorn. "Don't walk away from me!" The reagent and the owl man turned to face him. "Be advised that the pool plex becomes 'clothing mandatory' in a half hour!" The celebrity redeployed his thong around his chin and wrapped his towel around his head. "I thought I spied a cup!" He pointed at the celebrity. "Do you have a drink, hotshot? You know that's not allowed in the pool area!"

"Don't go hard on Ahab, mate!" Noyce interceded. "He's the cobber that got tossed from your slideball and nearly wound up a sitzmark on your ice course!"

The celebrity pulled the thong away from his mouth. "My aqua therapist gave me medicinal dispensation!" He raised his tea and took a swig.

The lifeguard glared. "I'm telling you to get rid of it or get out of here! Our bistro is up on the hill if you want to drink!" He leaned forward and shook his finger. "If you're strapped in properly at the start of the ride and you don't rock the orb, malfunctions like that don't occur!"

Guy scoffed. "Go 'ave a sit on your board, ya wowser!"

"What?" The lifeguard dropped his bullhorn. "I'll assume you troublemakers are too obtuse to know any better! If you were from this country, I'd have you ejected from the spa!" He regained his bullhorn. "If you're still standing naked with a drink like a stiff when I come around again, I'll change my mind and take action!" He swaggered away.

"No rebuttal, Ahab?" Guy giggled. "You'd let that hoon ream you out for being an ignorant alien?"

I.B. tugged on the celebrity's thong. "You can't expect this acorn to match wits with some sword gourd who'll devote his summer to relieving slews of 14-year-old bimbos of their virginity."

The celebrity flipped a handful of water at the reagent. "From now on, you can assume that everything I say to you goes double for him." Slurping tea, he led the spa squad to deeper water. A hefty blonde woman squatting poolside on the thick dividing line between the men's and women's sections summoned them to the edge.

"Come on, slapstick." Noyce patted the celebrity on the shoulder. "Let's take our plight to her majesty in the flesh." The photo-opportunist led the defection to the blonde woman. "G'day again, Mishy. We'd like to validate a rule waiver."

Mishy eyed the celebrity. "Phouvieng advised me that you're legal, sir." Clad in a low-cut black body suit, she had buttocks that would've been proportional for her hologram and a cute face with virtually no double chin. "You really shouldn't have the drink in the water though. If you could finish it up, I'll take your cup, and all will be content with the world."

The celebrity savored a minty sip. "Your turnout seems a little light tonight." He surveyed the sparsely populated pool plex. "Is the unseasonably warmer weather cutting into your business?"

"It's trending colder." Mishy grimaced. "Two years ago we set a record for snow manufacture."

"Here's to challenging nature!" The celebrity toasted her and took another sip. "It's been bruited about that a colony of science and technology bigwigs, the veritable sons of Prometheus and blood brothers of Lincoln McGuay-O'Toole Worbley, favor your gracious wild-heart-of-America retreat."

"Making artificial snow's nothing." Mishy appeared to sense with some irritation that she'd missed the thrust of the celebrity's comment. "We're pleased to entertain all kinds here." She looked askance at Winterhalter and endured a facial tic. "You foreign blokes don't blink at combing the soup in the raw, do you? I studied art for a stint, did a lot of figure-sketching, so I can appreciate the human form, but an open mind can be a hard sell in the staid, conventional Midwest, so we're considering abolishing the pool nudity."

"Are you a transplant?" the reagent challenged.

Mishy assumed a kneeling position. "Ever heard of a tiny, rail-splittin' stockade town up north named Spooner? Shortly after I was born, I became a prop and my father became mayor. After that, he got a variety of other government appointments, so we moved a lot and I grew up in obscurer places."

"Keep your sandals ahead of the scandals," Guy tittered. "Interesting that you mention props, because I have to wonder if a house yowie attack is part of the flash-bang spa slide package." He slapped the celebrity on the back. "This bludger and I both about lost control of our balls, meself due to a collision with an uncouth and irregular sub-human lifeform."

Mishy rose and stepped back. "You hit a beast? We have a flock of Scottish black-faced sheep that keep the hill grass mowed in summer." She emitted an invective sigh. "That big, old ram Tarmac keeps straying off, and we'd be more than offended if some untoward thing happened to him."

Noyce rubbed his head. "The night bites with your g's in the breeze."

"Turkish delight!" Mishy leveled her Qilroy at a small drone hovering overhead and dumped a shower of crushed ice onto a reveler on the other side of the men's section. "You knockabouts originally claimed that you drifted up this way from a convention hoping to fit in a little hunting, didn't you?" She waved to her ice cap victim and snickered mirthlessly. "What's your prime pleasure: Mallard? Bluebill? Wood duck?"

"It's a tungsten duck," the reagent asserted.

The celebrity slurped his last drop of tea. "As true sportsmen, we don't shoot at anything that can't shoot back at us." He crumpled his cup and tossed it poolside.

Mishy snorted. "Well, if you homeless romantics decide to cast anything to the wind more dangerous than your farts, I can put you on to a gentleman with a hunting preserve a little farther north. He'll fix you up with white elk and white buffalo, not susceptible to DNR regs because they're clones.

With the Real Deal now, he doesn't need to burden himself so much with discretionary exceptions."

The celebrity winced. "How can we obtain a discretionary exception to hunt him?"

Mishy expelled a coarse, hearty laugh. "What are you really? Some animal rights wacko?"

"Of course not," Guy snapped. "He lacks the focus to be a specific sort."

"If you can keep a secret, Mishy, we're thinking even bigger than you." The celebrity smiled complaisantly. "We're set to launch a particle application whose potential value to society could be almost beyond description – it concerns expansion of cloud surface area reflectivity – and with the endorsement of a famous physicist folk-hero or any of his hand-picked aides-de-camp known to pitch their tents on this patch of ice, we could attract all the seed money we'll ever need." He lowered his voice to a stage whisper. "And it strikes me that making this connection could be to our mutual benefit, because promoting your soak-method healing process as a sideline might be a bonus coup for our broad scientific enterprise."

"Why should we cut you in on our miracle healing process, windsock?" Mishy rocked and retrieved the discarded tea cup. "You'll find the place to make contacts at this country club is up in the bistro. Ask my husband Graham if he can be of service." She sauntered onto the women's side of the pool plex.

"Slick." Winterhalter thumbed his nose at the celebrity. "In one greasy, gooey mouthful, you exposed our position and revealed our strategy; you thoroughly mangled our chances."

"Turkish delight!" A crushed ice deluge pummeled the celebrity's head. Mishy waved archly.

"Chances of what?" Noyce inquired. "Hijinks with Mishy?"

"Of surprising the world with a peaceable kingdom." The celebrity removed the towel from his head and purged ice. "I suggest that we scramble up to the bar and get in on the networking action our lodestar proprietress hints we might encounter there." He climbed out of the pool and donned the robe and slippers that Phouvieng had issued. Guy followed immediately and guided the spa squad into the cramped, sticky locker room, where three forlorn barrels bobbed in a trough that divided the lockers from the showers.

"The system is not designed to work this way." Noyce reclaimed his barrel. "They should route to a receptacle locker and the e-nitials display in the label." The members of the spa squad all found their belongings soaked. An astringent fireball capsule in the celebrity's pocket had degenerated into a gelatinous stain. The owl man's Copioids, however, survived. Each man staged a cursory exsiccation, homesteaded a new locker and hung his clothes to dry. The troupe returned to the lift car depot attired exclusively in robes, sourcerers and slippers.

A more subdued atmosphere accompanied the second trek to the top. The air remained dry and the conversation turned dark, as Noyce and Winterhalter discussed whether humankind had lost the ability to experience pleasure. The celebrity considered whether Guy's "not yeti" orb incident might've entailed more than a collision with a sheep. Could WIO have been made aware of the presence of unregistered agents?

"Again as to Giselle," the photo-opportunist divagated, chasing the focus of the celebrity and the reagent into their respective Qilroy and Jatakar, "the fall of my industry would necessarily threaten yours, in the challenge to privacy restrictions."

The lift car reached the top of the hill, and the spa squad disembarked through the gate on the leading edge of the loading platform. The trio entered the rustic chalet gloriously illuminated by the backdrop of the rising sun. The dim, eerie barroom inside featured large oak picnic tables painted in condominium project pastels lining the walls and a checkerboard of circular tables featuring tartan tablecloths occupying most of the floor space. Five patrons sat in two clusters among the tables. Nobody looked like a WIO agent or famously reclusive quark master. A neon sign over the empty antique bar advertised *Lautenschlager*, and a bagpipe lullaby that sounded hauntingly like "Mrs. Lily Christie" flowed through a carousel of invisible speakers. Behind the bar lurked a scrawny man with a goatee and a long, stringy bonnet of brown-grey hair. He wore a dayglo green apron featuring an active heart monitor line and no shirt underneath. He kept his lips puckered in a manner which camouflaged whether he was amused, irritated or insane.

Noyce reached the bar first. "Leg up on the evening, innkeep. Three monster tankards of usquebaugh, if you please, and canvass my mates to see if they'll be drinking."

"Take us to your liter!" Apparently in the grip of a similarly voracious thirst, Winterhalter pounded on the bar. "And bring out your floozies!"

The bartender groaned, produced a rag and began wiping the rail. "Please excuse us, sir," the celebrity strained to raise the timber of the badinage, "our manners are a little frazzled. In honor of Sir Walter Scott, I'll have a Rob Roy." He plunked himself on a stool and rebounded to his feet with a stabbing brattoo reminder. "Wait, I've reconsidered!" He pointed to the *Lautenschlager* sign. "That's a beer brand, right?"

The bartender twisted his glassy countenance into a sneer. "Do you think it would be a frikkin' Mexican vodka?"

The celebrity clicked his tongue. "No doubt Trotsky's favorite off an endorsement by Maximilian. If it's your powerhouse top-seller, fill each of our flasks with a medium-size side sampler. Also, down in the pool, we were headed up by our regional facilitator Mishy to seek Graham. Is he around?"

The bartender flipped his rag over his shoulder. "I'm Graham, but I'm not serving you French film rejects. Get some decent clothes on, damnit!"

"Our duds got dunked by your defective barrel transport system," Guy protested.

"Then buy new ones." Graham pointed to a clothing kiosk in the corner of the room that appeared to feature traditional Scottish costumes. "Cuz management ain't responsible."

"Oobops?" Noyce's demeanor lit up like Graham's apron. "You've been keen to find a way to compensate me for flying you ballsy blokes up here?"

"We've got *them* outvested." Winterhalter pointed to the casual businessman with his bare feet propped beside the hookah on his red tartan tablecloth.

Graham leaned forward, a nimbus of stale perspiration supplanting the fruity tobacco aroma of the bistro. "Yeah, but I don't *despise* them."

"The pub got a name, governor?" The celebrity hoped his grin conveyed enough sincere affability to promote a truce. "What do you call this little watering hole out in the Styx?"

"Brig-A-Dune?" Guy guessed. "The Firth of Fifth?"

"Scotland Barn Yard," I.B. suggested.

Graham deflated his cheeks in tetchy short bursts. "This is an Irish bar, you mutton-heads! You can get-"

"Get yourselves some new garb, guys!" The celebrity pointed to the kiosk. "Pick out something formal; I'm footing the bill." Noyce dashed to the wardrobe racks. "Now that I trust we've purchased a little good will, Graham, would you be kind enough to provide us with a wine list? Or might you have something a spot fancier like Margaret Mead?"

"I'll have a Bloody Mary," Winterhalter announced. "And none of this tomato juice filler. Make it the genuine article, Barnabas."

Graham pointed toward the exit. "You want a shot of wine, get it from the vending machine beside the door where you came in. It dispenses chewy gin bars, too. 'Be a man and try one.'"

"I believe we'd really all rather just try a Lautenschlager." The celebrity smiled complaisantly. "Did you verify, Mishkin, it's a malt beverage?"

"Craft sour ale." Graham sighed. "Three Schlags?" He dilatorily rinsed three pewter tappit-hens and carried them to the end of the bar. He began filling the hens with Lautenschlager and confirmed the celebrity's credit.

"What do you hear of the combatess?" The reagent emitted an exasperated breath as a prelude to the chore of qualification. "Tess! Remember Tess Tohnyin?"

The celebrity explored his Qilroy for hidden missed messages. "It's amazing gracelessness for her not to share her current whereabouts."

I.B. watched Guy paw material in the kiosk. "Call the P.C. and have her pissin' somatag tracked."

"If she doesn't contact me soon, I'll report some troupe discombobulation." The celebrity resisted the urge to scratch his brattoo.

Graham returned sliding the three loaded tappit-hens along the bar, the lid knob of each vessel garnished with a pink-fleshed apple wedge. "Have a drop apiece and hop on the dress train, will you?"

"I admire your direct sales putsch," the celebrity advised the bartender. "You have a mentality fit for Santa Monica Beach concessions." He took an initial sip. Lautenschlager presented the palate with a distinctively vibrant flavor and left a disturbingly bitter aftertaste.

"Ahhh!" Winterhalter completed a series of gulps. "Shades of flipping rotten crab apples in the blender with pickle juice." He sucked his garnish.

"Pomes don't get as dense with the warmer weather," Graham growled, "and the product suffers in quality." He joined Guy in the kiosk and escorted him out of view.

The reagent raised the owl man's hen along with his own. "I'm going to bitch at the cracker that he underfilled this one." He began guzzling ale from both vessels in his custody. Graham resurfaced in the rear of the barroom wiping tables. I.B. supinated Guy's hen and headed for Graham.

The celebrity chewed his garnish. He gently patted his brattoo and focused on the jiggy pipe music lilting through the bistro. He engaged the underperforming directional mic application of his Qilroy and attempted to capture the gist of the exchange between the bartender and the reagent. He obtained chunks of the conversation between the casual businessmen at the center table. "Chip and Flip have pestered us to have shark meat," the barefoot man in the striped shirt related, "so we relent and serve these shark-burgers."

The celebrity attempted to adjust the mic range-finder without success. "I understand it reeks of urine if it's not prepared just right," the man in the open lavender shirt offered.

The cordiality of Lautenschlager improved with each successive swig. I.B. followed Graham to the end of the bar and accepted a cigar. He lit his smoke and jawed with the bartender, lingering after both tappit-hens were refilled. The celebrity attempted to monitor the parley but received no intelligible signal, so he returned to the casual businessmen's chatter. "Flip has the audacity to say, 'What did you do: cook them under your armpits?' I say, 'No, but I did boil my shorts to start the soup.'"

A tap on the shoulder heralded the appearance of the photo-opportunist in a buckskin suit. Guy raised his arms and pirouetted. "There's some grouse lounge wear to be had, Oobops." He straddled a stool and exhibited moccasins festooned with sparkling red bison. The celebrity summoned Winterhalter with a determined wave. "Until I spied this number, I was having a time deciding. At two thousand U.S. dollars, this is a deal."

"It's a great deal." The celebrity swallowed a throatful of Lautenschlager. "A great deal more than we can justify to the accounts payable department. Unless, of course, we report the money was funneled to Graham to supply a resistance force on the condition that he be furnished sanctuary in California afterward, pursuant to the idea that we'll apprehend him when he arrives and recoup the sum when he jumps bail."

Guy nodded. "The headdress doubles the price, and I don't want to look greedy."

"That Graham is a honey-battered crumb-crust!" Winterhalter set Noyce's tappit-hen on the bar in front of him. "Everything ends with 'Mishy wants this' or 'My wife wouldn't like that.'" He puffed hard to keep his cigar lit. "I asked him why his roundhouse squeeze is such a grouch lady. I say, 'Does the brutess stuff her bra with shrapnel, mill-dude?'"

"Mishy," Guy snorted. "I wonder if her father the former mayor of Spooner is a centaur." He slurped sour ale. "She's a bite short of a bit."

"My father the stoner mayor of Spooner is a major mother forker!" I.B. cackled. "D'ya know what Indian maiden name Mishy took to boost her through her rebellious teens? Thunder Packer!"

"Buffalo Gal!" The owl man clanked tankards with the reagent, drawing a crossfire of glares from the bartender and the businessmen.

Winterhalter felt the forearm fringes of Noyce's rugged, new garment. "Keepin' it Cochisey, huh?" He coughed and dribbled a stream of sour ale. "I'm going to pick up something mack, daddy." He strolled to the clothing kiosk.

Noyce became preoccupied with his Jatakar. The celebrity drank sour ale and monitored more of the casual businessmen's conversation. "Flip says to Chip, 'Did you know that Dad designs rockets?' And Chip says, 'Of course. What did you think Dad does?' And Flip says, 'I didn't know.' So Chip says, 'Flip, you're in the sixth grade; didn't anyone ever ask what your dad does for a living?' Flip says, 'Sure, lots of times.' Chip says, 'Well, what did you tell them?' And Flip says, 'I told them I didn't know.'"

"What's got you so gripped?" Guy inquired.

The celebrity seized the camaraderie-building moment. "The guilty pleasure of eavesdropping on the hookah-smoking guns at the table behind us."

The owl man leveled his thumb over his shoulder. "You can hear those two?"

The celebrity turned and sneaked a peak. "The barefoot suit has a kid named Flip who's a real youth sleuth, a veritable charged particle beam of a boy."

"Dry glass." Noyce coaxed home a few final drops of Lautenschlager. "Still your shout, Oobops?"

The celebrity automatically signaled for another round but found no available server. "Hey! Graham?" He tapped his tankard on the bar. "Where are you, Graham? We sense your presence!"

"Graham!" Guy bellowed. "*Grahaaam!!!*"

"Shut up!" one of the casual businessmen admonished.

Graham emerged from the kiosk. "What is it, spud-suckers, you're empty?" He ambled behind the bar.

"Two more Schlags, please." The celebrity set the tappithens of Noyce and Winterhalter on their sides and spun them. Graham snatched the vessels and slid them to the end of the bar.

"I thirst for justice, Ahab." Guy watched Graham fill his tankard with Lautenschlager. "The only quencher can be a decisive vengeance against the little iron maiden who leveled a legitimate industry. And I invite you to portray the turret of the lead tank."

A rude yank separated the celebrity from his earbud. He found Winterhalter flanking him in a kilt and sash of yellow tartan with red stripe and black blocking over a high-collared ghillie shirt. "I have glam gams," the reagent submitted, "and I'm ready to share them with the world."

"They are flauntables." The photo-opportunist scrutinized the spectacle. "An inheritance gift from your mum?"

The celebrity nodded. "It was the least he could expect from the lady who originally named him 'Who-The-Hell-Knows Jr.'"

"That's the MacLeod tartan." Graham returned with the

next round. "Their motto is: 'Hold fast for I shine not burn.' It's popular with some frugal heavy-hitters on both coasts. It's nicknamed the Spartan tartan."

I.B. swatted the celebrity in the lower back. "Wend your way to wardrobe and corkscrew your butch booty into a new putting outfit, Dimrock of Snidesburgh." He gulped some sour ale. "Take extra care because miniature golf is your personal trademark game of destiny."

"I do have something on the rack that promises to match your unique sartorial requirements." Graham grinned ravenously. "I'll join you directly." He handed Winterhalter a fresh cigar.

The celebrity took a hefty swig of Lautenschlager. He ventured into the kiosk and stood among the array of tartans. He examined a green kilt with red and yellow stripe and blue blocking. Graham arrived and shook his head. "A lot of rubes gravitate to that one, but you can do better than to wear a tablecloth." The bartender grabbed a kilt and sash outfit of white silk tartan with yellow stripe and green blocking. "This is the Arisaid tartan." He pressed it against the celebrity's waist. "This is the fabric traditionally worn by men of prestige in Scottish society, heroes who distinguished themselves on the battlefield or in more modern times the athletic field. It's a signature of those rising fast and seeking status in the world, those unafraid to live!"

"There's a vaguely unfamiliar aspect to the pattern." The celebrity caressed the price tag. "I know what it is," he prospected, "there's a famous photo of a group of prominent American scientists wearing these. No, it's actually a group of Nobel laureate physicists. I recall Charlton Shalom was one. Any chance they picked up their festive garb here? Shalom has been notoriously camera-shy. Was he photographed here?"

Graham squinted. "Shalloon?" He shrugged and pointed to the men's room. "Use the can as a fitting room. Your other mule-tool stood out here stark naked."

"This is unappealing." The celebrity turned up his nose at the Arisaid tartan. "I just don't like the look of it." He wandered down the rack. "Appropriately perhaps, your Native American merchandise appears expensive in relation to your cheaper Scotch stuff." He produced a green tartan with white stripe and blue blocking. It commanded a more reasonable ransom than any of the others he'd handled. "What's the lore on this, Graham?"

"Abercrombie tartan." Graham shadowed the celebrity. "Motto: 'He seeks high deeds.' The crest is a bird with its wings spread."

"By gum, let's call it a keeper." The celebrity smiled complaisantly.

Graham curled his lip menacingly. "You'll look like a schoolgirl without a shitload of proper accessories." He ushered the celebrity to the end of the aisle and began piling items in his arms. "Ghillie shirt, two wool breechcloths, wide black belt and matching sporran, brogues, two pairs of white knee socks with swale-green tartan flashes-"

"I've no use for these in my condition." The celebrity returned the breechcloths and proceeded to a stall in the men's room. He exchanged his robe for the Abercrombie tartan costume, glimpsed his new Highland Pete look in the mirror and re-emerged.

Graham brandished two diced glengarry bonnets a step outside the door. "The bonnet is the most important element of the costume after your kilt, and it should always be worn military style as tight around the brow as you can stand it." He slapped one of the caps into the celebrity's hands. "The kilt is supposed to hang just below the knee. Yours fits as perfect as if it was tailored." He fluffed the flannel sash selvage. "But the sash should be worn over your right shoulder. Over your left is national socialist." Raucous shouts emanated from the bar area. "Now what do your pipsqueaks want?" He marched toward the bar.

The celebrity returned inside the men's room. He removed the bodkin pins from the envelope inside the glengarry and anchored the bonnet to his head at a stylish angle. He switched the sash to his right shoulder. He assessed his appearance in the mirror and allowed that he cut a fine figure of a color guard. Beyond that, the kilt wore comfortably, and his brattoo pain had diminished. He opened the door and heard sounds of a scuffle. He rushed to the bar and found Graham expertly positioned between the opposing factions of the casual businessmen and the spa squad.

"What's that supposed to mean?" the stubble-free barefoot man in the wrinkled striped shirt interrogated Winterhalter. "Are you saying my son's stupid?"

"A good little soldier doesn't question the program," I.B. snarled. "It's a parent's field of wet dreams."

"If analytical types are wearisome," Noyce contributed, "how much more so when they're kids."

"Nice dress." The slightly larger, dark-haired, stubble-faced man in the open lavender shirt fixed his eyes on the celebrity. "It'll take more than three of you."

"None of that," Graham snapped.

"Here's how perverted your reality is," wrinkled stripes advised the cigar-chomping reagent. "Your moronic Tournament of Roses Parade was on New Year's Day, and Flip asked, 'What's the purpose of a parade?' How many 12-year-olds are reflective enough to pose a question that sophisticated?"

Winterhalter shook his cigar for emphasis. "Since you've gone to the trouble to work yourself into a lather over it, frostneck, we'll make the effort to be impressed!"

"Get that thing out of my face!" Wrinkled stripes turned to the celebrity. "Who the hell are you supposed to be?"

"Nothing more to discuss here!" Graham spun wrinkled stripes away from the bar. "Let's call it a morning." I.B. flicked the cigar past them.

Wrinkled stripes smoothed his hair and straightened his

shirt. "Wisconsin leads the nation in out-of-state garbage received for landfill disposal. That must explain how they got in, hmm, Graham?" He started for the exit in lockstep with the bartender and bumped shoulders with the celebrity.

"I trust you explained to little Flip," the celebrity called over his shoulder, "that the human clutter take time out for pomp and circumstance to divert their attention from the reality that they'll ultimately get sick and die."

Still in Graham's grasp, wrinkled stripes whirled, charged and lunged at the celebrity. "You son of a whore!" The celebrity repelled the attack with a forearm shiver. Wrinkled stripes threw a right hook that clipped the celebrity on the chin. The celebrity shoved the barefoot man and the clinging bartender onto a table, flipping it over along with its two chairs. Open lavender shirt faked a right jab, and the celebrity caught his wrist. Winterhalter and Noyce bumped him. Open lavender cocked his left fist behind his ear, and two hands grabbed it.

"That's it!" Mishy draped herself around open lavender's neck. "You're done!"

Graham returned to his feet and oscillated his forefinger between wrinkled stripes and open lavender. "You two crap-magnets leave the premises now!"

Wrinkled stripes staggered to his feet and pointed at the celebrity. "This douche wished my boy dead, Graham!" He rolled his neck. "How can anyone be such a complete piece of shit?"

The celebrity released open lavender's wrist and received a token push. Open lavender assayed his partner. "You okay, Coop?"

"He slammed my head pretty good." Wrinkled stripes patted his occipital bone. "I don't know. I'll see my doctor."

"You have their personal information, Graham?" Open lavender brandished his Qilroy. "I recorded the entire incident. You can expect to be contacted by our attorneys!"

"Good frikkin' night!" Graham decreed with an irascible

finality. Wrinkled stripes and open lavender slinked out of the bistro, pausing to flash threatening looks and collect the former's shoes.

"Graham, you ninnyhammer!" Mishy slapped her husband. "You couldn't keep five customers pacified? You couldn't maintain order if you were here by yourself!"

Graham pointed at the celebrity. "I had them set to disperse until this twit showed up, and it all mushroomed!" He slapped an adjacent table top. "Now you can sit nicely and wait for the sheriff. See if your smart mouths can keep you out of the clink." He limped back to the bar and retrieved his Qilroy.

"Is there a dent in a tappit-hen that we can cover?" The celebrity evaluated potential escape routes. "Playing patty-cake with the P.D. won't profit anyone. I strongly entreat you to revoke their invite."

"Too late, dumbbells." Graham puckered his lips.

"Cancel it!" Mishy flipped the chairs onto their legs. "If you purchase one Hootenanny's couples' deluxe season pass and consign your awesome overnight package to us, we'll pardon your mischief."

"Don't anticipate my largesse soon." Winterhalter chugged Lautenschlager. "We're going to be busy sweeping downstate for Charlton Shalom."

The celebrity allowed his bill to be inflated with the prescribed pork, including a two-percent Wisconsin environmental preservation tax. He led the spa squad outside to the transportation terminal abutting the chalet, and the trio caught a lift car and headed down the hill. Descrying blood on his pole, the celebrity realized that his chin was cut. "How did your scrum with those two scum-blossoms start?"

Noyce turned and straddled the bench. "I advised I.B. you'd been earwigging the Flip lip, so he and I started doing it. And we got caught." He popped a Copioid. "Everyone notice that Graham got aroused when Mishy was humiliating him?"

"His pubes standing on end?" Winterhalter rose. "Oobops is the one trained to observe that sort of shmut."

"Any idea of who those prick-heads are?" The celebrity experienced a moderate brattoo twinge. "At least one claimed to be involved with rocket design."

"They were discussing I.C.B.M.s when we mic'd them up." The owl man offered an affected smile. "Incontinental bowel movements."

"Graham told us they're defense contractors," I.B. submitted. "Safety engineers. Missile inspectors with dead-end jobs in nuclear weapons." He and Guy laughed raucously. "They were talking ring shells, roundels and crackling rosettes."

Noyce rubbed his chin. "So one might fairly suppose that you're 'aving a go at beating the bushes for Charlton Shalom, the old Nobel laureate scientist."

"Ib was just name-dropping an exit strategy." The celebrity gently banged his head against the pole. "We're still pounding the luke-cool trail for our playpal Tess." He shifted the subterfuge. "And any mission that degenerates into finger-fighting the local citizenry, even those who provide direct succor to the other side, is by definition a failure."

"What other side?" Noyce challenged. "Are our sparring mates likely to be waiting at the bottom of the hill to ambush us?"

The celebrity experienced a painful brattoo itch. "Hard-charging lawyered-up snow-bunnies named Coop pose little street threat, although we'll let I.B. pass through every door in front of us."

The lift car reached the bathhouse depot, and the photo-opportunist led the celebrity and the reagent to the locker room. The troupe gathered yesterday's damp clothes into plastic bags and strode into the cool, breezy morning. Puffy cumulus clouds filled the sky, and the celebrity's wary eyes probed the parking lot for movement. "We want to get airborne as quickly as possible, Guy, before Graham reconsiders recommending us to the local Stasi."

"Mishy wouldn't let him do that," the owl man asserted. "When they co-sign a document, I'm sure she requires that he express his name totally in lower case letters below hers."

"Her rectum wrecked him." The reagent reached the Sparrow first. "She recognized I was man enough to accommodate her in the pool, so I knew she'd have our back to have us back."

The spa squad boarded the volantor without incident, and Noyce executed an unauthorized liftoff before they'd left the spa premises. "I'm circling southwest outside the ambit of the converging flyway grids," Guy announced. "Let out a squeal if you spy any obstructions like windmills or high voltage lines, won't you? We'll re-enter the grid legally off this Devil's Lake checkpoint." He shimmied in his seat and rubbed buckskin. "I love the feel of this raiment against my skin. It'll be splendiferous to dance in, as should your tartan tweedies."

The celebrity surveyed his Abercrombie tartan and laughed. "I never expected to touch a suit this expensive, much less own it."

Winterhalter emitted an irritated snort. "Shit, Ahab, that magic dream suit you slipped over the junior princess road warrior down banana way must've cost a peck and a nut more than anything gimpy Graham ever gouged his grubby hooks into."

"What's I.B. referencing?" The photo-opportunist turned to face the celebrity. "He mentioned you were slumming in the poor, parched Nicaragua realm of Latin America." The gusto with which he spoke sprayed spittle. "What's bloody bubbling over in that part of the world?"

The celebrity smiled complaisantly. "I was sent there to fan a little dry diplomacy." He sent the reagent an urgent message: "Operation Foxhound is classified, Brother Doorkeeper! What's your source?"

The reagent returned a vulgar text and pressed his face

into the luggage lacuna. "I pimped Tohnyin into opening her fur vault, and once I shined my line in that mine, I learned about the hoodoo you were dropping on that pair of deuces you tailed to San Juan del Serpent."

"*Lady in back*," Noyce crooned, "*the only shade that won't betray you is black!*" He devoted some attention to the control panel. "You drongos keeping secrets back there?" The sound system pumped a 4/4 bagpipe march through the cabin.

"Endless summer; endless surveillance." The celebrity could scarcely contain his indignation. "She couldn't have divulged that information!" He suppressed the urge to bury I.B. beneath the luggage pile. "You have nothing but some vague, disjointed factoids and innuendo."

"You gave her crude you weren't supposed to spill, didn't you, hush-gush?" Winterhalter smirked. "Women don't burn *me*."

"Is high school where you both learned to hold females in such low regard?" Guy wondered.

"It's where we learned to hold everyone in low regard," the celebrity confided.

"Bops really believes I can't hack his ass?" The reagent slapped the owl man's headrest. "Two homegrown freshwater sharks named Skowron and Castells legally looted our state treasury and retired beyond the storm of controversy they stirred up to the coast of Nicaragua, where they now receive their obscene luxury pension payouts. Disgraced former Governor Zlatko requested a state *vigilancio* to track them down and clamp a tooth-hold of constant harassment on their collective tuchises to demonstrate they couldn't outrun the shadow of natural justice. Skowron's daughter was a preppy track star before Ahab left her in a steamin' heap."

Noyce gaped at the celebrity. "And you had the hide to deliver an earbashing about how misdirected my collateral retaliation might be?"

"I.B.'s account doesn't capture the context of the campaign." Trapped, the celebrity opted to salvage the situation by providing a filtered version of Operation Foxhound. "The pair of Nebelwerfers he mentioned bamboozled a cadre of our distinguished state legislators to support a 'well-crafted fiscally neutral budget-saving' maneuver that shuffled state government employee entitlement funds to the benefit of select government officials, including the two prime architects themselves. The taxpayers were left with an unsustainable debt, and a message begged to be sent. The 17-year-old steeplechaser profited from the patriarch's malfeasance, tooling around in her classic Hummer, wearing designer clothes and savoring the sublime life courtesy of California state revenue. In my professional judgement, she was mature enough to be held accountable after the fact."

Winterhalter chortled. "Everybody found out just how mature, shock-jock."

Guy banked the Sparrow hard left. "Precisely how in your capacity as official walking pox, Oobops, did you clobber the girl?"

"It was a basic wardrobe malfunction trick." The celebrity felt a muted brattoo pain and leaned to the side. "I became privy to a superacid that's activated by moisture. When spandex or a similar active wear fabric pretreated with this chemical absorbs an elevated level of perspiration, the material disintegrates almost instantly." He snapped his fingers. "I was able to substitute an identical garment coated with this superacid for Bonnie's – that her name? – two-piece running suit, and I did so right before a major meet." He leaned forward. "So to set the international stage, the occasion found me seated amid a fair crowd on a muggy day to catch the coming out party I'd planned, and she ran and jumped and ran some more, and nothing happened. I was about to conclude that the product was grossly overrated when I realized that the runaway heiress had no shorts."

I.B. jolted the luggage pile. "Damnit, I need to piss!"

"Bonnie remained unaware that she was bottomless," the celebrity continued, "and made her move to vie for the lead. Some of the spectators noticed the omission and raised a commotion. When her top disintegrated in the space of a few meters, she caught on. She reflexively raised her hands to try and save it but the fibers blew right through her fingers. She hugged herself and kept running. Then she stopped and turned, perhaps to go back and collect what was left of her top, and she collided with another chaser, knocking them both-"

An alarm yipped and red lights flooded the cabin. "Collision avoidance!" Noyce pounced on the yoke. The Sparrow sustained an impact, which rocked its body and cracked the windshield. The owl man banked the craft hard right and struggled to regain control.

"Did we hit a goddamn tower?" Winterhalter screeched.

"I can't believe that!" Guy labored with the instrument cluster. "It seemed like a roof strike! It could have been some balloon or kite!"

A flickering object that initially appeared to be a gargantuan moth flashed directly in front of the Sparrow. It proved to be two people on an open aircraft with side-mounted paddle-wheel rotating wings. Noyce slammed the volantor into a downward pitch and radical yaw, throwing the luggage pile and the celebrity onto the reagent. "Identify, shit-for-brains!" Guy transmitted. "Are you trying to cremate us all? Who are you?" He silenced the collision avoidance alarm. The ensuing radio silence overpowered the background bagpipe march.

"That's a cyclocopter, a crotch rocket bike!" The celebrity attempted to restore the structural integrity of the luggage pile. "That's a naked woman at the tail! *It's Tess!* Stay on them!"

"Are you that sensually deprived?" Noyce took the Sparrow into a climb and veered away from the hostile craft. "We're going to gain separation from their lethal influence and alert the authorities!"

"That may *be* the authorities!" The celebrity clutched his

head. "They have Tess tied on! We have to try to force them down gently!"

Noyce turned to glare at the celebrity. "You'll make a cute threesome when you bail out and land in her lap, galah!"

"Why did you ever join the Royal Air Force, cavalier?" The celebrity leaned over the front seat. "To learn how to take flight from trouble faster?"

Winterhalter hissed. "Zero hero's never really been in the Royal fucking Air Force, have you, buzz-bomb?"

A streak of light split the sky and rattled the Sparrow. "That was an RPG!" Guy shrieked. "A rocket fired from the ground!" The collision warning yipped again. "It's those beastro bastards! Why'd you two have to be such vicious bitches to them?"

"Unidentified aircraft, acknowledge." Free-flight ADS air traffic control issued the Sparrow an ultimatum: "Identify, report your position and state your emergency."

"Don't respond!" The celebrity extracted his briefcase from beneath the seat. "The safest thing now is to use the airbike as a shield!"

Winterhalter pounded Noyce's headrest. "Yeah, ya bloody wombat, stay glued to his ass! Run it up his tailpipe! Ram him and wreck him!"

"Ram him and ruin us!" Noyce banked the Sparrow left and closed the gap with the hostile craft. "I've no weapons aboard! Smash a nacelle, and we'll whirl about down to a final thud!"

"The objective is to ruin no one!" The celebrity thrummed the long, curving titanium beak of his California Thrasher kite. "He just needs incentive to land, like if his fuel tank got punctured."

"One of our fuel tanks is about empty," the photo-opportunist submitted. "I could try dumping the fumes on them. It might trick him into believing he has a leak."

The celebrity strained to view the cyclocopter. "That might not yield the best outcome should they have a rough landing."

Tohnyin's head appeared bent back at a radical angle. "Aw, hell!" He coded his Qilroy for kite control. "Flank him, Guy, so I can take our cheapest shot. Secure all that flutters and lower my window."

"We're approaching a water body," Noyce announced. "Devil's Lake."

"Is that a problem, Fosdick?" Winterhalter challenged.

"For her, if we force them down, and she's pinned to the vehicle frame." Guy lowered the celebrity's window, and a vortex whipped through the cabin, dislodging I.B.'s glengarry.

The Sparrow cruised slightly behind and parallel to the airbike at a distance of about 20 meters. The celebrity poked his head into the pummeling wind and made eye contact with the gagged Tohnyin. He hoped she understood his hand jive that she should protect her face and neck. His ear aching and eyes watering, he retreated into the tortoise shell of the cabin. "Guy, hold us level at 30 degrees ahead and above them!" The owl man repositioned the volantor and lifted the nose to the desired altitude. "I don't know how turbulence is going to affect this shot, and that sky cycle is yawing like a gnat!"

The reagent scoffed. "Not that you need anything like an excuse in advance, flubbard!"

The celebrity extended his head and arms out the window. He measured and aligned the kite with the cyclocopter fuel tank. The bike pilot produced a handgun as he veered north, following the lake shoreline. He suddenly dipped and reversed his course south. The Sparrow performed a similar maneuver, and Tohnyin's vanity case tumbled against the celebrity's back. Squinting against the morning sun, the celebrity launched the kite. The scythe-like bill of the California Thrasher pierced the bike pilot's thigh and stuck there. The cyclocopter rolled violently, and the pilot lost his firearm. He ripped the head of the kite out of his leg and flung it away. He poked behind him as if to loosen Tess's bindings. "Spray him, Guy!"

"Don't get the tanks mixed up!" Winterhalter pleaded. "Is

your toy spent, razor-bill, or can you curtain-call it back for another crack?"

"I nailed the pilot!" The celebrity attempted to retrieve his kite without success. "He should be hemorrhaging the most high-value kind of fluid!"

Noyce closed the window with a thump and an expletive. The Sparrow cut in front of the airbike, clawed for altitude and dumped fuel. The pilot raised his helmet visor and wiped his face. He began convulsing, and Tess tenaciously kept her chin tucked into her clavicle. Free-flight air traffic control issued another ultimatum.

The cyclocopter descended in a funnel of tightening arcs drifting southeast over the lake, and the volantor rolled to match the pattern. Noyce cast a sideways glance at the celebrity. "Ahab, you're quite sure we want to risk another rocket in the teeth diving here?"

I.B. grunted. "Land this cannonball before my bladder's left with permanent stretch marks, cackbold!"

The cyclocopter accelerated out of its dizzy descent, soared beyond a grove of fir trees on the lake's eastern shore and landed halfway up a panoramic bluff. It climbed to a point below another cluster of trees near the top and seemed to slide to a momentum impasse. The craft stood poised on its rear terrestrial wheel for a protracted instant before toppling onto its side and tumbling a short distance down the bluff. The volantor achieved a softer landing at the top of the bluff. The celebrity burst out of the craft first. Briefcase in hand, he scrambled down the steep top ridge and raced over sharp-edged rocks through a patch of budding maples and oaks in time to view the bike pilot reach cover behind a large rock and pair of sickly pines ten meters below the smoother terrain of his landing site. The airbiker fired an errant shot in the celebrity's direction.

The celebrity retreated to the line of trees near the top of the bluff without drawing another shot. Noyce arrived out of breath. "Wonderful, Oobops, he's got a side arm."

"It sounds like small caliber." The celebrity watched Tess squirm against the cyclocopter frame in the rocky dirt. "Winterhalter having kilt trouble?"

"I won't repeat this order!" the bike pilot shouted. "The three of you walk into the open with hands empty and raised over your heads! Advance to the sky cycle and drop to your knees!" He grunted. "Otherwise, Tess's pretty head gets filled with bullet points!"

"Who are you?" the celebrity demanded. "What's your interest-"

"My name is Dennis," the pilot proclaimed, "and that's all you need to know!"

"That's true, isn't it?" Guy remarked. "There's something different about blokes named 'Dennis.' One minute a Dennis is your happy, little vegemite and the next he's snapping at your throat."

The celebrity extended his Qilroy antenna. "So we keep this sport pinned down for a few days and wait for him to mellow out?" He attempted unsuccessfully to establish linkage with his kite. "Time isn't your ally, Dennis! You're bleeding pretty freely by now, and you need to get that wound fixed!"

"You think time is on your side, snowflake?" Dennis coughed. "The authorities will be here to dispatch you any moment!"

"You wouldn't have called the police!" The celebrity experienced a brattoo pain spike. "You'd trade that piece you're holding for an automatic ten-year prison sentence!"

"It ain't about the cops, kelp-herder!" Dennis seemed to favor a low crouch. "The authorities are my ground crew, the ones who should've turned you into a steaming cinder back there and will be charging over the ridge right behind you!"

"Forget roadside assistance, coprolite!" The celebrity abandoned hope of retrieving his kite. "Your position deteriorates with every heartbeat! If you're too weak to walk away, come out in the open, toss your gun, fall on your face and stretch your arms out!"

"I'd like to press my carbon footprint between your shoulder blades, too!" Dennis guffawed. "I'm doing better than your sky-clad weather witch! Since we stripped her of her security clearance, she's suffered a lot of exposure! My method stresses tactiles over optics, but did Tess start out last night with blue nipples?"

Noyce planted an anxious hand on the celebrity's shoulder. "Tess isn't one of those people with naturally orangish nipples, is she? Because that's not what you want either."

"Guy, what the hell are you talking about?" The celebrity watched Tohnyin cease struggling against her restraints.

The photo-opportunist crunched a Copioid. "I'd like to propose a trade agreement. Put your miracle disintegrating fabric in my sticky hands and I'll fix you up with a vast scoutocracy of scrutineers who'll enable you to locate the most obscure individual. For example, if you *were* interested in shining the spotlight on Nobel laureate Charlton Shalom, your prospect of gaining easy access to him in the next few days is fail-safe."

"We're keeping a tight focus on Tess's situation at the moment." The celebrity grappled with the increasing weight of the urge to act. "Dennis, we just called the sheriff, so you better clear out!"

"Everything about you is a big bluff, blue-fang!" Dennis howled. "You keep inverting your triage; you better take care of your sentimental favorite first!"

"Where are you thumbsuckers?" I.B.'s voice emanated from a point approximately twenty meters up the tree line perimeter.

"Don't stick your nose beyond the tree line!" the celebrity shouted. "We have a standoff with the gunman!"

Winterhalter hustled beyond the tree line carrying a small

blue box. "Where the fuck *are* you, Oobops?" The sound of a shot and a cry echoed through the area. "Uh, ha ha – I'm hit!"

The celebrity charged beyond the tree line. Extending his briefcase as a shield, he headed toward the trembling reagent, who staggered back behind a fir tree. The celebrity glimpsed Dennis beside his rock. He chased around the nearest tree to reach I.B. without drawing another shot.

Winterhalter crumpled to a knee. He held a CIB SFX package. "I'm wounded." He emitted a chuckle of incredulity. A bloody hole punctuated the right shoulder of his white ghillie shirt.

"Why can't you take direction?" The celebrity inspected the injury. "You don't needlessly jeopardize your life until I tell you."

"You got no weapons!" Dennis bellowed. "Come out slow, hands up and prostrate yourselves at the sky cycle! My crew's a minute up the trail, and we can medevac your wounded people out!"

Noyce arrived. "Time to capitulate, mate?"

"To a wounded earth poacher with a one-shot peashooter?" The celebrity sneered. "If we can't get at him to squash him directly, could you set the Sparrow down on the bluff between him and Tess?"

The owl man grimaced. "It's not a chopper, stingo!" He pointed at the reagent. "And it only takes one shot."

"I hacked Tess's luggage." Winterhalter opened his box and produced a California Least Tern kite in its original wrapper. "At least she has *something* that's never been used." He shoved the package into the celebrity's hands. "Analate that nodule!"

The celebrity removed the gadget's wrapper and unfurled the band from the leg. "She told me she'd never carry one of these."

Guy patted I.B.'s shoulder wound. "The shirt's ruined. Strawberry mishy, eh?" He eyed the celebrity. "How long can he wait for medical treatment?"

"I can't leave Tess." The celebrity tapped the band for protocol values and formally introduced the device to his Qilroy kite control app. "If my next combo doesn't knock out this pistol-whip, will you convey I.B. to the hospital without me?"

"Ever delighted to swap favors," Noyce reiterated.

"So you just happen to have a solid lead on Charlton Shalom?" The celebrity activated his new kite. "That's awfully convenient intel." The eyes of the Least Tern flashed red and glowed. "At the Mission, where we trained, they taught us that coincidence is a mythological beast."

"You're again saying I don't pass your smell test?" The photo-opportunist paused as the celebrity successfully launched the small kite and set it in an elliptical overhead orbit. "Allow me to slap a free sample of good faith on the bargaining table. I have it on well-situated authority that old Uncle Charlton is scheduled to make a surprise public appearance this Saturday night in Las Vegas!"

"This little marvel can emit a scraping whistle that'll stretch our enemy's brain and stomach till they've switched places." The celebrity kept an eye on the kite as he advanced to the tree line. "Worse than any contemporary pop glop."

Winterhalter pushed ahead and pointed. "He's getting away, pud-wax!"

His helmet again adorning his head, Dennis lifted the cyclocopter onto its wheels. He swung his leg over the seat of the vehicle, but Tohnyin had worked a leg loose and delivered a prohibitive kick to his crotch. Dennis elbowed her in the shoulder and slammed his forearm against her chest. He dropped the airbike and staggered to the side. He backpedaled and fell on the seat of his jump suit. He withdrew his firearm from his right boot and pointed it at Tess. The celebrity dealt a Least Tern strike that tore the gun from Dennis's grasp and placed the kite in a screeching overhead orbit. The Tern was smaller and slower than the Thrasher but more maneuverable.

"Many happy returns, Dennis!" The celebrity administered a light kite strike to Dennis's shoulder. "This spitfire has a drop-acid function to brighten up your day!" He wished that the kite package actually included the incendiary accessory.

Dennis scrambled to his feet and retrieved his handgun. He fired an errant shot at the kite and reloaded the Derringer-type weapon. The celebrity guided the kite in another dive at the firearm but missed. Dennis extracted a tactical knife from his left boot. He pivoted, looked upward and advanced. Displacing rocks and following a zigzag, hitch-gaited quest for footholds, the airbiker charged up the top portion of the bluff toward his standing adversaries. The kite struck his helmet, and he flipped up his visor. "I want your raven maven to see you all chopped and ventilated like the birds in your shittin' wind farms before I peel her like an onion!" He flipped down his visor and brandished his clip-point-tipped knife as he continued his arduous ascent.

"Fall back to the Sparrow!" The celebrity attempted to harass Dennis with light kite strikes. "Guy, take I.B. to the hospital! I'll stay behind for lawn darts!"

"Aren't you suddenly the man!" the reagent snarled.

"Scramble!" The celebrity shoved Winterhalter toward the top of the bluff. Guy slapped I.B. on the butt and hurried past him toward the top. The reagent followed at a deliberate pace. The celebrity retrieved his briefcase, retreated behind the tree line and collected a pair of baseball-size rocks. As he placed the Least Tern in a higher, faster orbit, he heard the Sparrow engines roar.

The celebrity guided the Least Tern in a precipitous dive at the side of Dennis's neck when the sky cyclist reached the tree line. The strike missed and the kite bounced on the rocks. Dennis fired wide of the celebrity's position. The celebrity hurled a rock that tree branches blocked.

Dennis emerged on the ascendant side of the tree line reloading his weapon. With his visor raised, he held the knife in his mouth. Broad swaths of the upper regions of his navy-blue jump-suit pants appeared to be discolored with blood, and he moved with a limp. The Sparrow engines continued humming as the celebrity retreated along the tree line, and he wondered why the volantor didn't take off. "Dennis, all parties have donated blood to the cause to prove we're sincere! Can't we come to some understanding before someone's broadsides do permanent damage?"

Dennis crouched amid a cluster of pine branches. "Spew all the details of your current state initiative to combat climate change, or your cheerful detachment will cost Tess her head, too!"

"I wish I had something to spew!" The celebrity re-established linkage with the Least Tern and guided it through the trees. "But can't we at least agree that's what civilization is – controlling the environment, not being controlled by it!"

Dennis fired a shot past the celebrity's shoulder. "We rather like the new order. We're not interested in freezing our nuts off up here so you can have better tannins in your grapes!"

"Think of your own cranberries!" The celebrity tugged nervously at his kilt. "Your trout! What about your pome ale? Plus warmer weather brings out more vile, noxious lifeforms, and that's just among humans!" The Least Tern transmitted a prime POV shot of Dennis reloading.

"You'd be the occupier, Aldo; I'm just a civil engineer!" Dennis lowered his visor, rose and started farther up the bluff.

Winterhalter reappeared at the top of the ridge smoking a cigarette. "Get back!" the celebrity shouted, stumbling out of the trees waving his briefcase. Dennis whirled and fired a shot into the briefcase. The Least Tern swooped and buried its bill in Dennis's lower back. The civil engineer dropped his weapons and collapsed to his knees.

I.B. pounded his cigarette into his shoulder wound. "Like a hood for your execution, clit-head?"

Dennis pounced on his handgun and shot I.B. in the abdomen. Blood spattering, the reagent moaned and staggered back out of sight. The celebrity charged Dennis. The engineer turned, pointing his firearm and reaching into his pocket. The gun clicked harmlessly as the celebrity reached it. The celebrity batted the weapon out of Dennis's hand with his briefcase and knocked the helmet off his head in the return swing. Dennis blocked the next head blow with his forearm, knocking the briefcase out of the celebrity's hand. He kicked the celebrity's feet from beneath him, rolled onto his side and grabbed his knife. The celebrity dived on top of the airbiker and fought to pin him on his back. Dennis introduced a serious knee to the celebrity's protected groin and sliced his hand and forearm. The celebrity rained blows on the engineer's ear as he rolled over him, twisted his wrist and forced him to release the knife. He batted the weapon away, and both men regained their feet. Dennis made an unsuccessful attempt to reclaim the knife, and the celebrity heard the Sparrow lift off as he took the engineer to the ground again. The grappling tangle of enmity that ensued rolled both men down the bluff as far as the sky cycle. The wrestling match ended when the celebrity landed a solid forearm smash to the gasping engineer's jaw and flung him twenty meters farther down the bluff.

Dennis staggered to his feet and tossed a rock wildly. The celebrity hurled a rock that struck Dennis in the head. The celebrity hobbled to Tohnyin and collapsed breathlessly beside her. "Tess," he mustered, "how bad are you hurt?" She emitted a gurgle that sounded more defiant than deflated. He rose and surveyed the nether region of the bluff. He couldn't locate Dennis. "Go rot at the bottom of this glacier hole, you knuckle-scraping slough skeeve!" He moved to a position behind Tess. He removed the ragged, grey briefs that served as her outer gag. She opened her mouth wide, and he grabbed the moldy white sock swaddling her tongue.

Tess coughed. "Aw, Ahab," she rasped. "Avert your eyes for a second." She coughed and spit. Her eyes followed the trickle of blood from his forearm to her shoulder. "I need a shower."

"Winterhalter will need more than that." The celebrity tore his left sleeve loose and rewrapped it around his forearm and hand. "He collected two bullets."

"He's shot?" Tohnyin winced. "He'll recover, won't he?"

"I pray that he made it to the hospital." The celebrity rose. "Yell like hell if Dennis comes back." Racked with dread that he'd find the wounded Winterhalter sprawled on the ground gasping for a final breath, the celebrity scrambled to the top of the bluff. All that remained of the reagent were blood stains and a cigarette butt. Tohnyin's three luggage pieces, including her open survival kit, were left at the site. So was his own plastic bag of wet clothes. He snatched the survival kit, retrieved his briefcase and Dennis's tactical knife and returned to Tess.

The celebrity produced the survival kit water bottle and squirted the contents into Tohnyin's mouth. "A guy we met on the *Janesy* flew I.B. out for medical treatment." The celebrity cleaned and closed his wounds with derma-bind and secured his bandage with the lace from his ghillie shirt. "The torso shot he took looked pretty bad." He began unfastening the cords that pinned Tess's arms against the wing-supporting Aerographite backrest. "He wasn't even strong enough to give me some nice parting gibes."

Tohnyin took a deep breath. "What you did out here, Ahab, was practically valorous." She turned her head toward his. "There's a heavy scent of beer on your breath. If you spent the night guzzling courage, it was well worth the effort."

He hopped to his feet and leaned over her as he struggled against the intricate network of knots. "How did you end up in such fine company?"

"All in a night's work." She sighed sardonically. "Why does a glengarry sit atop your pointy head?"

"A space-age hairpin." He experienced a heightened level of brattoo discomfort. "Frankly, I'm amazed it's still there. However, aviatrix, I believe your bound-naked condition entitles me to conduct the first round of examinations."

"Are you deliberately prolonging this?" Her demeanor grew poutier. "Dennis attempted to summon support at least twice, so you might want to channel your inner alacrity before we attract a hostile audience."

He smiled complaisantly. "Did Dennis discover what a project you are to work with?"

She stared at the ground stoically. "Why don't you use his knife?"

"On myself?" Scrapes and bruises marred her shoulders, but most surface points exhibited fairly healthy coloration. "I'm concerned that the rusty, serrated edge might have a more profound effect on your sensitive skin than on these stubborn cords." He gained some slack. "You'll be pleased to learn that your complete three-piece luggage set awaits you at the top of the bluff."

She raised her eyebrows. "How?"

"How indeed?" He freed two cord ends and carefully extricated her. He lifted the cyclocopter and helped her to her feet. Standing behind her, he completed the task of untying her hands. She winced and flexed her wrists and fingers. "What hurts most?" He removed his sash and passed it over her shoulder. "Your brattoo?" A large padded bandage covered her right buttock.

Draping herself with the sash, she turned to face him. "And how did you become aware of that?"

"Your little red cocktail dress told me." He lifted the seat of his kilt and whirled. "I guess *your* slash-and-burn exhausted Benji's supply of fancy bandages."

She recoiled with empathy. "A scourge named Iris?"

"Call me catnip and her beside me herbicide." The celebrity clicked his tongue. "She proved to be a little more than the executive lickspittle I expected, too." He lifted the cumbersome airbike back onto its wheels and stowed his briefcase. He began dragging the futuristic vehicle to the top of the bluff.

Tess kicked the sky cycle. "I tried to mangle the wings to

make sure he couldn't come back and take me up in the air again. Why don't we *use* gravity and ride it *down* the bluff?"

"Maybe the low road leads back to Dennis?" The celebrity resumed dragging the cyclocopter upward. "We're 83 percent of the way to the top. Join me in crunching a little more gravel, gather every souvenir of combat and let's get free and clear of this pit." Tohnyin pushed furiously, halting briefly to retrieve Dennis's gun. The celebrity maneuvered the cycle within two meters of the rim.

An urgent message arrived on his Qilroy and arrested their progress. "There may be an update on I.B.'s status." He waved and released the airbike fork. He received notification from the Q.C. that he'd been named in a workplace harassment action brought by Radmilla Eisenstadt and was instructed to return to the Santa Monica P.C. within 72 hours to be deposed on the matter under the auspices of D.C.I. P.T. Ledbetter.

Tess stood with arms akimbo. "Well, cliff-hanger?"

"Personal foolishness." The celebrity shook his head. "People like to show their appreciation to those of us who lay everything on the line."

She adjusted the sash. "I wasn't aware that you have a personal life."

"That's because I'm a savvy spy." He practically lugged the craft the rest of the way to the top on his hip. He surveyed the area and observed no human traffic. Tohnyin retreated a short distance with her luggage and returned in a smart beige blouse, tangerine suede slacks and slingbacks. He bundled their mutual gear into a touring tailpack, and he and Tess mounted the cyclocopter. "I hope you operate this monster the same way as a regular bike." He surveyed the puzzle of the instrument panel. "And I hope I can remember what that is."

He located the ignition switch beneath the seat. He pressed the starter button, eased out the clutch and applied the throttle. The airbike popped an inadvertent wheelie and edged forward. He couldn't force the front wheel back to the ground, and the craft started overland on one wheel. It hit a rut, lost its balance and tumbled into a ditch. "Aw, Ahab," Tess moaned, "are you really drunk, or are you that much of a natural putz?"

The celebrity and Tohnyin found the secret to ride on two wheels and crept through the Devil's Doorway section of the park, pausing periodically along the trail to scout for potential enemy combatants. They maintained radio silence and stealthily exited Devil's Lake State Park, heading east on a circuitous country road before doubling back to ensure that they weren't being followed. They avoided an approaching convoy of military trucks by taking cover behind a stand of roadside oaks. When the caravan had passed, the crypto-crats cleaned Dennis's firearm and knife and discarded the weapons in a Wisconsin Recycles receptacle. Stopping only once for fuel, they reached Highway 12 by mid-afternoon and cruised south toward the locality of Prairie du Sac in search of lodging.

Need of a clue fast; tune in the newscast.
Doll more than cute in her power suit.
Ice sculpture steady; hope diamond ready,
Fine lines she packaged 'xclusive to me.

Indulge my cravings; withdraw my savings,
Cut to fine clothes, long-stemmed rose and car.
Curious nature; seduced by danger,
Investigative lead happening.

Want to meet the broadcast girl,
Need to know the broadcast girl,
Die to hold the broadcast girl,
Born to love the broadcast girl.

Park with indifference; studio entrance,
Prompt on the hood says, "This Is Your Life."
Limo door open; step in, I'm hopin',
Drive you downtown and make you my wife.

6TH MOVEMENT

Inbound. 0730 CST Thursday 30 March.

"Need a consciousness-raising, wasteoid?" A firm slap in the face awoke the celebrity to the irritating glare of the sun. He sat bolt upright on the asphalt motel mattress and shielded his eyes as he massaged his brow. He still wore his Abercrombie tartan kilt and diced glengarry bonnet. Unique Agent Tess Tohnyin stood over him. "Time to roll out those lying baby hazels, slugabed, before the maid comes in and embalms you."

The celebrity's temples pounded out a battle hymn, his parched throat harbored a chalky grout and his stomach made him feel like the winner of a clay-eating contest. He returned her affection with a salty cordiality. "How would you like some caustic soda in your bath oil beads?"

She flipped the lapels of her bay-teal terry cloth short robe with the gold CIB logo. "I've already undergone my ritual purification; I just took a cyber-shower with Natty Phil." Her voice became a cheese puff. "The old boy was immoderately passionate this morning. Did you know that he keeps a compact refrigeration tank over his tub to chill his shower water?"

The celebrity rubbed his face. "How does a man with a lobotomy get immoderately passionate?"

She scowled. "How does a man with blurred vision see the eye doctor?" Her mouth redefined itself as a mischievous smirk. "You know what Phil likes to do in the shower?"

He felt his eyes open wide for the first time since he and Tohnyin had hit their respective beds upon arriving at the motel. "For the love of Catalina, Tess, please don't tell me!"

She displayed a legion of teeth and bent forward so their noses practically touched. "He roars like a lion." She emitted a roar. "He does it continually, and with his booming bathroom echo chamber, it sounds frighteningly authentic."

"Super," he groaned, "today's already been a vast improvement over yesterday, a veritable epiphany."

"Listen, you uraeus sausage, after the events of yesterday morning, I took it upon myself to persuade P.L. that you're a top-notch cloak-and-dagger man, and there's no reason why you should've been terminated. I told him that he ought to return you to active standard duty at once before the rest of the intelligence community brands him the horse's ass that those of us who know and love him know he is. I was so diplomatic I practically ran out of euphemisms."

"You did that, Tess?" The celebrity was struck by the possibility that his termination had been some test of allegiance, psychological experiment or agency misdirection play. It may even have been an elaborate practical joke orchestrated by Ledbetter to advertise his reconditioned ability to orchestrate practical jokes. If that proved to be the case, the celebrity resolved to attain jocular retribution by entering Natty Phil's complete psychiatric file into the public domain. "What did he say?"

Tohnyin smiled shyly. "When I broached the subject, his viceregal pre-eminence was obstinate and unwilling to listen. However, I have been known to possess considerable powers of persuasion, so I pursued the matter." She flipped the lapels of her bathrobe. "By the end of the shower, he was listening intently – antenna up, feathers ruffled, bristling. He told me to shut up." She snickered incredulously. "Just when it seemed like he might threaten to fire *me* if I mentioned one more word about you, that's exactly what he threatened to do. I wish I could tell you I told him he was arguing with success and using a wrecking ball to do it, further that I dug in and pointed out that his dominant hemisphere is below the belt, but then he might have huffed and puffed his way through another heavy-handed hatchet dance and cut my legs out from under me, and we'd be looking at a double debacle."

The celebrity surveyed her sleek legs. "I'm not ready yet to classify my debarment as a debacle, but the Big Sir does seem bent on bettering the Bureau by bludgeoning me, doesn't he? Combine that with our significant breakthrough deficiency to this point, and as pal Jerry might say, I'm making a bleak statement for reinstatement." She probed a thigh bruise, and he averted his gaze. "How are your, ah, appendages, your digits, faring with frost effects?"

She flashed a wan smile, hooked her heel over her shoulder and deigned to wiggle her fingers and toes. "All my goods are great."

He withdrew his bodkin and removed his glengarry. "The Big Sir's seat of reason does seem to abide below the belt, doesn't it? What did he say about our cost of doing business at Devil's Lake?"

She sat down on her bed. "I told him I'd have you furnish details after you woke up."

He swung his legs over the side of his bed and staggered to his feet. "So he doesn't know WIO engaged us, or that I.B. got hit?"

"I alluded to it, but in my zeal to vouch for you, the thrust of the discourse swiftly digressed from setbacks." She reclined on her elbows. "I informed P.L. you degraded considerable resistance elements and restored regional stability. He'll be waiting for your call the instant he sets foot in his office."

"Why hasn't Guy called?" The celebrity surveyed his surroundings. "His device captured my number." He snatched his possessions from the highly figured mahogany veneer night stand and activated his Qilroy. "I hope that's why." He discovered a series of garbled voice messages and instant disconnects. He repaired to the bathroom with his Kare Kit for a little more than an hour. When he emerged, he'd reclaimed his pants but still hadn't heard from the vagarious Aussie, so he placed another call to the reagent's Jatakar. Dressed in a grey pointelle tank top with rib-exposing fashion tear and clinging jeans, Tess sat at the escritoire composing her fustian. A connection captured the image of Guy eating a potpie framed by a misty vista of waterlilies, an intrepid escalation of the Monet schematic on the wall behind him. "Guy!" the celebrity practically shouted. "Guy, what's happening?"

Noyce clutched his head. "Aren't you getting my messages, Oobops? I've been leaving cords on your Qillie. It's possible I'm not doing it right. Yankee doodle high-tech, for all its ballyhoo these days, doesn't exactly knock the queen's bloomers off, does it? Anyhow, I'm over here in a hamlet called Baraboo with your lad at the Corner Hospital & Bait Shop. The autonav had a bit of a go finding her; it's a wing of the Stuttering Cockatoo Trading Post. They tape a lucky penny to the foot of every gurney, so it looks like a cutting-edge operation."

The celebrity felt his dread turn to skepticism. "Baraboo? It sounds like a nude beach in Queensland. Are you playing the didjeridoofus, sport?"

Guy chuckled. "Superbly." He wiped his mouth. "I *am* in the borough of Baraboo, but their medical facility is actually four-star, and I'm pleased to report your boy is doing, if not A-Okay, at worst C-Okay."

"He's going to *be* okay?" the celebrity betrayed an urgent need for a straight answer.

"Righto, he's going to be I.B." Noyce smirked. "He's recuperating from surgery. The medical team took out the two slugs and his spleen."

"His spleen?" The celebrity eyed Tohnyin. "They had to remove I.B.'s spleen. Tess, come here." He scissored beside her and guided her head into camera range. "Guy, here's Tess. She seems no worse for wear." He patted a minor sickle-shaped laceration on the side of her face.

"Hellooo, love," Noyce intoned, as the celebrity shuffled away from Tohnyin and linked his Qilroy with the wide-screen wall TV. "*The day finds you looking much peachier!!!*" The excruciating volume rattled a framed picture of a paddle-plying whitewater warrior off the night stand, and the celebrity pounced to manually reduce the sound as Tess clutched her ears.

She unpursed her lips. "Thank you, Guy, we appreciate your allegiance. I.B. is expected to recover, isn't he?"

"Fully. The medics assure me a spleen is a luxury organ, much like, Oobops, what a harmonica is to a garage band. A perfectly normal life is a cinch without one." Guy munched some crust. "I.B.'s past critical and steadily improving. They've moved him into his own room. He has passing episodes of lucidity and tries to hit on the nurse."

"He's intact." Tohnyin expelled a relieved breath. "His prime sympathetic reflex works."

The celebrity felt unburdened as well. "Wait until his full faculties start whirring and he finds himself in acute caregiving camp unencumbered by pants."

Noyce howled. "He'll be expecting them to take a number to give him a sponge!"

The celebrity stared solemnly into the eye of the camera. "Have the cops questioned you?"

"An Officer Osterseitzer came and had a yack with me." Guy slurped his soft drink. "I didn't favor the hoot he had at my barn owl, and I presumed your agency doesn't care to answer to local law enforcement anyway, so I put the strain of the Strine on our relations, waltzing him a bit about the Ocker track dishing the dinki di in the lingo. 'Strike me lucky, Jack, am Oi the dobber, here's a jing and a prang and me Oi'm spit-tin' the dummy and sinkin' the boot in the dust full on, where Oi cobbled bloody I.B. staggering to delirious reviews just down the road from the back of beyond!' The walloper wagged skeptical about the incident, thanked me weakly and marched off, I think, confounded on whether I'd come the raw prawn with him. But I don't care to get embroiled in any study in scarlet here myself. A bloke can get into nearly as much trouble talking to the cops as to the media."

"Smashing serve." Tess rose approbatively and turned to the celebrity. "Winterhalter needs to be coached on how to handle the local heat."

"I believe he'd be better left to his own devices." The celebrity rubbed his chin. "He's such a natural shademeister he won't be believed no matter what he says, and being granted some quality downtime in an asylum might be just the watershed event his life needs."

"I can't tell when you're joking anymore." Tess glowered. "Can you?"

"Of course, if you want to hand the blue heelers the dinkum later on about what sort of good fist you were making wayfaring the Never Never, there's nothing to prevent you." Noyce collected his plastic utensils.

"Smashing Strine-along," the celebrity concurred. "We need to keep the impeccable California brand concealed, and we can't afford to end up on any Threat and Local Observation Notices. What's more, we can't allow the undertow of the skirmish on the lake to drag us off course." He eyed Tess. "We'll reimburse Dennis and derail the WIO bullet train ourselves once we achieve our primary objective."

"I knew you'd be panting to give I.B.'s woman the good guts on him, so now you've got the ridgie didge unabridged." Guy smiled and repositioned the Jatakar. "I'm heading out of this hospitable hashery to see I.B. once more before I apply to have my Sparrow released. I'm sending you the articles of navigation as we speak."

"One last blast, Guy," Tohnyin pleaded. "Do you have any idea of what tragic magic Ahab was gobbling to have woke so much more delusional than usual? He's prattling some frothy scuttlebuttery to the effect that you have a hot pursuit angle on Charlton Shalom, the Nobel laureate scientist. You supposedly have a wicked tip that Shalom'll be surfacing in Las Vegas no less than this Saturday night to receive a Golden Choice award?"

"People's Globe," Noyce verified. "That's the fair dinkum from my desert bureau colleague Binko. It was supposed to be a surprise, but Shalom's son Tycho dropped a clanger on the appearance after the event organizers reneged on their guarantee that Charlton was a lock to collect the lifetime achievement award. Binko's practice is lousy out there, so he's counting on getting in some good head shots." He sucked the last few drops of his beverage. "Speaking of what you can count on, Oobops, I felt bad leaving you with your unit snagged in the thunderbox yesterday, but I didn't expect you'd generally have much trouble coming unstuck. Another item though, if you'd give me a contact name and address for your organization should my lanto renter's agreement not cover the night's damages, I'd be only too right with it."

"I'll do better than that, Guy." The celebrity couldn't squelch an infusion of ambassadorial mawkishness. "I was in a diamond-press of a bind, and your cooperation contributed tremendously to its favorable resolution. I'll petition the governor to favor you with a commendatory medal of merit as a token of our gratitude."

"I've always had a soft spot for the fluffy stuff." Guy's tongue peppered the pie tub, and he attempted to tear away a bite only to discover that the green container wasn't the edible type.

The celebrity smiled complaisantly. "The medal would entitle you to a fabulous carb-cred cachet like immunity from carpool restrictions and the privilege of carrying a concealed sublethal-duty weapon. Naturally, it would also include a pre-approved application for honorary California citizenship."

"Glad to be handy, but if you really want to thank me, Oobops, help me with my personal project." He populated the pie tub with his used utensils as he wobbled his mandible. "I am committed to it, I am consumed by it, and one way or another, I will complete it." He crumpled his spent napkin. "Be a benison and 'av a go, mate! Whad'ya say?"

The celebrity patted his abdominal muscles. "I'll think about it, Guy. May the day wear good on you." He terminated the connection.

Tess eyed him quizzically. "What did you do there? You let him snap the book shut on Shalom before we fully siphoned the reservoir." She tapped his wrist. "And what was that wrapped package he wanted to drop in your lap at the end?"

The celebrity snickered at the predicament. "He wants me to help him with his girl problems." He paused to let her raise and lower her eyebrows. "There's this teen queen he blames for suing his former employer out of business, and he desires technical assistance in exacting some good-hearted, clean-handed payback."

Her eyes became twin trebuchets. "You'll unkindly inform him it's his hard-assed misfortune *that* prize doesn't come with the commendation." She managed to harden her features further. "You have just enough decency not to lend an extremity, don't you, Savonarola?"

"Just barely." The celebrity drew a protracted breath. "He certainly makes me feel guilty about doing the right thing."

She delivered a crisp slap of encouragement to his shoulder. "The right thing to do now is talk to the D.C.I." She displayed local conditions on the TV screen. "Look, we're at 8:58 barbarian time, so your name's already been bouncing off the tempest shield of his anechoic office walls for three minutes."

The celebrity stretched and performed a superset of calisthenics to gather his nerve before facing the widescreen squarely. "I'll keep this on panorama so you can participate, Tess."

"No, I'll give you some privacy. I'm going to finish getting dressed." She plucked her strongbox suitcase off her bed, grabbed her slingbacks and took her slight limp into the bathroom.

The celebrity left his Qilroy linked with the TV. He called the Subdirectorate of World Free Visions & Operations, entered the priority code and reached Radmilla. "The D.C.I. is anticipating my call. This is Ahab Oobops."

"Who?" Radmilla sighed heavily.

"Oobops," the celebrity hissed. "Put your katabatic pipes to good use and blast me through to P.L. before I refer you to the Mission for more scratch-post training."

"Can you spell the last name?" she snipped.

"Not with equanimity. Link me to Ledbetter like now, Rad, you hellebore ruderal."

Radmilla remained silent for several seconds. "I understand that Mr. Ledbetter is no longer expecting your call. He was thrown as he adjusted his chair and he's preoccupied with the accident. Please reconsider whether the substance of your intended exchange would be worth the director's professional time."

The celebrity felt his brattoo pain spike. "What's your inside story, Raddy? Do you resist any sensibility above that necessary to numbly bumble through the day? Did your board-certified bug doctor leave town with your jar of better hormones?"

"I am compelled to wonder, Mr. Oobops," Radmilla asserted, an uncommon tremor permeating her voice, "if you are capable of emitting anything beyond the lonely cry of a cornered con man."

The celebrity attempted to smile through his fury. "Your esteemed slug-driving dictator has been blustering for a much greater give-and-take in our organization, and if you don't connect me to him immediately, I'm going to give you a titanic opportunity to take some jumbo blame!"

"Don't slice and dice my words, Oobops!" The voice was Ledbetter's. "I'm on the line to witness in real-time the habitual picaresque abuse you seem dedicated to heaping on these poor secretaries. If it doesn't stop, I will authorize them to hold you down, insert a fire hose nozzle in your mouth and turn the water on full blast."

"P.L.," the celebrity appealed, "E.A.S.E. give me your direct number!"

"Oobops," Radmilla cooed, "you macerating raisin, get a job in a whinery." Her smirking image dissolved and was replaced by that of Natty Phil.

"You know I can't imperil office integrity with special favors." The director pressed his thumb and forefinger against his brow. "So *Oobops* with a 'U,' is it, or is that an 'O,' like an Irish name?"

"Aye, Ulsterman," the celebrity grumbled. "Although it could always be I'm playin' a grand, ol' Sinn Feiner trick."

"Indefatigably." Ledbetter produced his ice pick. "Oobops, where in hell are you: some posh bed and breakfast?"

"It's more like a dour divan and dinner, you frill-seeking vibrometer." The celebrity began pacing. "We're in some fleabag French honeymoon chateau south of the holy city of Wisconsin Dells: *Le Motel Droit Du Seigneur*, or such. Didn't Tohnyin tell you?"

Natty Phil cleared his sinuses. "French names all sound like Fruit of the Loom with a mouthful of Novocain." He mussitated. "Do you like Italian food, Oobops?"

The celebrity felt an eyebrow spike. "Ah, yes, most."

"Heychh," the director scoffed, "I don't even like Italians." He bared his teeth. "You're Italian, aren't you?"

"Now that you mention it once more, I'm mainly Scots-Irish, but Tess has a bit of the 'It' in her-"

"Then I profoundly apologize for that misaggression." The

D.C.I.'s expression became sullen. "We had our Operation Crescent Wrench victory party at Spatula's La Dolce Vita last night. Would you care to explain to me how an Italian restaurant can botch spaghetti?"

"You should've ordered it with the sauce." The celebrity smiled complaisantly. "The culinary arts can be a lot trickier than they appear."

Ledbetter hiccuped. "Let's not drift off the subject on a raft of excuses." He traced his temporal scar with the ice pick. "Ahab, what are the two things that can be lost but never stolen?"

"An ancient civilization and the personal treasury of life's base, natural pleasures? You're not alluding to a shoulder and a spleen, are you?"

Ledbetter sneered. "Must your rhetorical template always be so damned abstract? For life's journey, one need pack but two entities: his dignity and his honor, matching accouterments which can only be forfeited with his benighted consent. Brief me off the record if you will on the disturbing beats of early yesterday morning."

The celebrity fidgeted with the room master control. "Should you ever abandon the Bureau, P.L., you could direct a mean funeral, but I digress. Let me begin by reassuring you that we didn't lose anyone and we gained a valuable toy and some key information. Did Tess tell you we have a tip, albeit a slightly flighty, aleatory one, on the projected whereabouts of Charlton Shalom?"

"Don't double-deal yourself a losing hand playing non-full disclosure." Natty Phil glared. The celebrity spun his troupe's lack of traction from the time it left Hootenanny's until he and Tess reached their motel as gain by elimination. The D.C.I. impatiently traced his temporal scar with the ice pick throughout the report. "It's a shame," he finally commented, "the case has defied a cyber-active inroad. Winterhalter's ability to damage and destroy cyber-estate could've become the stuff of legend." He mussitated. "I want the fustian filed in my cache 24 hours from now, and I want your perfumed butt back in this office 79 hours after that waiting for me when I return from a savory, sauce-embellished power lunch so you can be deposed on Radmilla's complaint and then we can discuss the progress of the operation in all its radiant warts with one of our key strategists."

"You'll have it all, P.L.," the celebrity promised, "spiced with enough pulp and puissance to satisfy the most ravenous of intelligence oversight committees."

Ledbetter stretched his collar. "How solid is the chemistry you're developing with Unique Agent Tohnyin, Oobops?" He patted his hair. "Is she available for recognition, or is she back in the sack?"

"She's back in the bathroom," the celebrity answered dutifully.

"Have you thrust her into the throes of the drug culture?" The D.C.I. steepled his hands. "She doesn't need you to protect her. You wouldn't be the first to implicate Tess as a substance-abuse risk liable to land in a compromised position." Nostrils flared with anger, Tohnyin emerged from the umbra of the doorjamb slowly shaking her head.

The celebrity appraised Tess from head to toe and back again. "I find the idea of anyone fingering our office coquette as a usable user most untenable." He patted his triceps. "But while we pause here to electrify the moat, P.L., perhaps a re-examination of our operational places is in order. At the risk of being classified as a petty, anal turf worm, what's with Tess's celebrity billing?"

"That's a remarkably trenchant self-portrait, Ahab." Tess folded her arms. "I need to give you more credit for being so introspective."

"How is it, Oobops," Ledbetter inquired, "the instant your homemade sourdough biscuits are pulled out of the oven, you feel the need to vent the aroma throughout the neighborhood?

How did Winterhalter's female resource tolerate the unfortunate news of his casualty status?" The celebrity hesitated, and the director cleared his sinuses. "You have made notification to her and offered a token of gratitude conveying 'shock' and 'awww' on behalf of the Bureau, haven't you?"

The celebrity jammed his hands into his damp pockets. "I felt my call to you rated a slightly higher priority, Natty Phil, but now that you move me to weigh the touchy-feely factor, I'm haunted by the concern that extending my deep regrets to Winterhalter's comrade-in-arms might be hijacking Radmilla's thunderbolt. After all, what authoritative stamp could be put on miserable tidings to equal the distinctive bell toll of a call from Rad?"

Ledbetter bristled. "You're entrenched with his full-service asset, you're our agency-endorsed spiritual advisor, and you'll seize the commission to extend her the courtesy of a standard-issue pity party. I can't imagine how you hope to achieve reinstatement when you continue to miss the most elementary and loaded of opportunities to redeem yourself."

"On that running note," Tohnyin interjected, "what's our escape strategy from this red zone? Will you insert a F.E.S.T. team for an airlift, or will you instruct Raddy to arrange our extraction by land vehicle?"

"A vehicle?" The director snorted. "You're ordering a quick response force? Remind me by what means you arrived at the particular outpost oasis you're occupying."

"We rode the beastly WIO rocket bike that we captured." The celebrity smiled archly. "How few months ago were aeronautical experts assuring us that a preternatural winged street-fighter of this sort would never get off the ground? Tell me you don't get a supercharge, Natty Phil, imagining it suspended as a trophy in the P.C. karmamentarium."

"A consolation triumph." Ledbetter traced his temporal scar. "If you have ideas of flying it through the rarefied air over L.A., I hope it's a dirt bike." He delineated an arc and jammed the ice pick into his desktop. "Very well, ride your crotch-copter to Winterhalter's safe house, and arrange to have it transported from there by common carrier."

"I'm not getting back on that damned thing!" Tohnyin stood with arms defiantly akimbo.

"Is that a general off-road aversion, Tess?" The D.C.I. bared his teeth. "I concur that the acquisition seems egregiously convenient; you are to presume your ultralight hell-raiser is equipped with a booby-trap. Send back the coordinates of its present position for aerial counter-surveillance and abandon it. Accept the challenge of employing your survival training to secure alternative transportation by any means available and make your way back across the border to the safe house. From there with any luck, you can engage commercial air travel to Santa Monica that leaves you a Saturday night layover in fabulous Las Vegas, where you'll have the chance to debunk the hype your audacious Aussie gadfly is circulating regarding access to our target."

"We'll get to the bottom of the hokum," Tohnyin promised.

Ledbetter plucked his ice pick from the desktop. "I owe Director Hawk Fleming of Nevada Intelligence Bureau a favor for choreographing our W.M.D. response seminar, so he is to be advised of your extraterritorial operations. Please distinguish the Studio in meeting all of your obligations." He terminated the connection.

"Don't be had getting Mad," the celebrity muttered. Before dread of the distasteful chore he'd been delegated could metastasize, he placed the advisory call to Madelyn. "*Piano Sonata Number 17 in D Minor,*" he recited, "*The Tempest.*" Madelyn appeared on the widescreen draped in her sheer moire wrap. Newly blonde, her frazzled strands stood poofed as if she'd let the Santa Ana winds style her hair. She still managed to radiate a peculiar neo-expressionist sensuality, although Tess gasped at the spectacle. "Hi, Mad, it's Ahab Oobops calling from behind the lines in the Wisconsin wonderland."

"What?" Madelyn dragged her fingers through her patchy tresses.

"I have a message about I.B." He rebuffed the impulse to shudder. "He's alive and, ah, not well, but on the mend-"

"Where the hell are you?" Her tone evinced a chafed concern, and her glare confirmed the desire to mutilate.

"The extreme environment of the Wisconsin wilderness." He shambled to the side. "I.B. is post, ah, postoperative, I trust resting comfortably. He's unavailable, but he's in stable condition."

Tess scowled. "You make it sound like he's being groomed for a horse race."

"Who the fuck is she?" Madelyn tousled the gilt chaos atop her head.

"I'm California Unique Agent Teretsara Tohnyin." Tess swatted the celebrity on the side of the head and displaced a quadrant of hair. "I apologize that Ahab didn't introduce us."

"Give me a chance, hmm?" The celebrity dispatched a loose backhand swipe into Tohnyin's raven mane and the transmission popped as she jarred the escritoire in her attempt to sidestep it. "We were embroiled in gunplay yesterday. I.B. hasn't been able to contact you-"

"You two woebegone-wits are trying to say what?" Madelyn demanded.

"I.B.'s in the hospital." Tohnyin edged in front of the celebrity. "He was struck by two rounds, but he's expected to make a full recovery." Agape, Madelyn slid her Kells knot Claddagh ring across her cheek and plucked a hair.

"Don't do that, Madelyn," the celebrity pleaded. "I.B. took a slug in the shoulder and another in the gut. They removed his spleen, but the elite organs are fine, and he should be able to cartwheel home to you in a couple of days."

She extracted two more hairs. "How did he get shot?"

"An enemy agent had her." He tapped Tohnyin lightly on the back of the neck. "We pursued and pinned them down. In the ensuing firefight, I.B. took a hit. I subdued the shooter, but not before I.B. put himself in jeopardy in his haste to rescue Tess and was shot again."

"It was really rather heroic," Tohnyin offered.

"Which one of you," Madelyn snarled, "was the senior mando-jammer responsible for looking out for him? I know – there's an ongoing investigation, so you can mosh on each other about it, and it ends up nobody's fault, right? What did you do, Oobops, use Ian as a human shield? Anyone else get shot? How is it neither of you is even scratched?"

"We all notched some stripes last night." The celebrity flashed his forearm and pointed to his chin.

"What are you showing me?" Madelyn squinted. "A Qilroy scratch? You sock puppet, you had that when you were here, didn't you?"

The celebrity pressed his forefinger against Tohnyin's chin and turned her head, exposing her full profile to the camera. He slid his finger upward to highlight the hook-shaped laceration beneath her cheekbone. "Our skirmish resulted in Tess taking this beauty-"

"Stupid, honey," Madelyn scoffed. "If you need to do that, you cut your arms or your legs, not your face, no matter how dissatisfied you are with it."

"She was strapped to the back of an extreme machine, a sky cycle, and the WIO gun-bunny piloting it grazed us, nearly ramming us head-on, but we finally grounded the winged-"

"What?" Madelyn's voice wavered. "You bangas were playing chicken?"

"Ahab," Tess scolded, "stay sensitive."

"Consider clearances?" The celebrity expelled an aggravated breath. "Winterhalter's going to give her the whole enchilada anyway. We might as well sprinkle a little grated truth on it."

"Oobops, what kind of issues must you have to keep hauling out this all-consuming food fetish?" The glare that

Madelyn exhibited indicated that venom was available to be harvested. "What if Ian can no longer work? Will you try to get yourself promoted to principal prick and boot us out of here?" Her hands became fists. "Take me to him! Get back here and take me to see Ian right now!"

"Listen, Mad, it's no more necessary than it is feasible for me to personally convey you, but I can-"

"Not feasible?" Madelyn screeched. "Show some human decency, Oobops! Do you know anything about that?" She dragged her ring through her sparse thatch, harshly extracting more hairs. "I helped you when you really needed it, you ungrateful, selfish suppository stick. How can you be such an asshole?" She started sobbing. "For shitsakes, you're supposed to be a public servant! What is the *matter* with you?"

"We'll send a car for you that'll take you right up to the front door of the hospital," Tohnyin volunteered.

Madelyn hiccuped. "Whoever you are, you ass-sucking bitch, stay out of this!"

"It'll be a limo," the celebrity enriched the idea, "a lanto limo. Everything's going to be fine!"

"Do you want me to have an episode?" Mad clutched her temples for a composure moment and plucked a hair. "I'm having a freakin' episode! You really reek, you blubbering beach-taco! You think you can buy me off, dis me, use me like you used Ian? It's not Ian who's sick, it's you! You're sick as all fucking hell, you rancid rash, you armpit lump, you stump-grinder, you fetid feta cheese puke stain!" She began flailing her fists and smacked herself. "I want someone else up to his miserable twat in this to come and get me and take me to see Ian! Now! Not later! Can your prune-pit short-order blackhead of a brain understand that? *Now!!*"

"I tell you no lie, Mad." The celebrity gesticulated earnestly with both hands. "At this moment, we have our Australian asset at the hospital hovering over I.B. like an outback angel.

If you genuinely feel it's necessary, I could ask him to abandon his sentry post and pick you up-"

"You better make something happen, you goddamn sour cream Monterey jack off!" A trickle of blood emanated from Madelyn's nose.

The celebrity nodded. "I trust I've succeeded in depleting your reserve of expletives, damsel blue. Compulsive cursing not only renders you something akin to classless, but when the time comes that you really have something to swear about, no one will pay attention."

"Don't yell at me!" Mad made an exuberant arm swipe. "I wish I could rake my nails across your face and scratch your eyes out! Save yourself the frustration of inviting him in if you've had children, lady, because he'll never muster the stretch to meet yours. It'll work like trying to screw the big cap on the little med bottle! Oobops, you're petty, you're puny, and you're pathetic!"

"And my little dog, too?" The celebrity smiled tartly. "Sit tight, and wait for the man from Oz to call with instructions." He terminated the connection.

Tess realigned her disheveled locks. "Ahab, you take that parley as license to generalize about women and I will slice you into bacon strips!"

"I wouldn't think of it." His lungs discharged a gale of relief. "She's all right for a jiggle-stunted whack-job with a burn-buffer brush-clip. We're just lucky she's no longer 'Maple Leaf Rag' cranky like she was when I was holed up with them."

Tess sneered and shook her finger at the celebrity's nose. "Comb your hair, flying monkey. Then call your Aussie shuttle driver and dispatch him to his maiden fare." She poked him in the chest. "Better yet, he can pick us up and drop us off about O'Hare on the way to fetch Madelyn, so it'll be a productive round trip."

The celebrity contacted Noyce again and learned that the battle-scarred Sparrow had passed police inspection and was currently in the care of a restoration mechanic. Guy was reluctant at first to accept the assignment of interstate trafficker, but after a bout of light cajoling and the hint of a gonzo bonus, he relented and agreed to a Saturday morning rendezvous.

The celebrity left the motel room to record the location coordinates of the cyclocopter. He contemplated how abruptly the photo-opportunist had blossomed into the most serviceable of assets, and his suspicion intensified that the Aussie was packing some surreptitious tie to WIO or another opprobrious revolutionary organization. He sauntered around the colonnade of pines that concealed the dumpster behind the motel where he'd embosked the rocket-bike, but the spot held no spoil. He scoured all points in the vicinity, but the vehicle had disappeared. He returned to the hotel room blank.

"Some needy person of entrepreneurial spirit must've chanced on our thundercloud-nuzzling hard-tail and made off with it," he reasoned. "We can only hope that they at least tripped over it first and it was broken beyond repair."

"Who steals my purse steals trash." Tohnyin's cheer in the face of collateral calamity was as troubling as it was underwhelming. "Plausible deniability is best not directed inward, Pollyanna."

The celebrity rubbed his face and sighed with resignation. "All right, wise-lass, for our next political sleight of hand, let's turn this bunkhouse bunker back into a vacant room before WIO seizes the opportunity to repossess *us*."

Guided by the best escape and evasion tactics that training at the Mission could provide, the celebrity and Tohnyin packed their bags and arranged for a semi-private ride with ties to the Alice network to take them northwest up Highway 12 for 50 kilometers to Wisconsin Dells. The crypto-crats then backtracked on foot and found fresh sanctuary at the First Resort, a hotel that catered to wild, screaming children and boasted a cavernous hot tub not inferior to Hootenanny's. Upon Tess's request, Pazzionette forwarded the Operation

Shalom treatment as part of the complete Charlton dossier, and the celebrity couple immersed themselves in the classified Wisconsin mystique beneath the glaze of filtered, chemically sanitized ultraviolet rays in the hotel Sun Spot luxury heliorama. "Charlton has claimed to cherish the air and dread the water," Tohnyin remarked, "but he refuses to fly and loves to sail."

"He enjoys watching people suffer pointlessly by their own volition," the celebrity noted. "That spans some unexceptional possibilities."

Outbound. 1450 PST Saturday 1 April.

"Are you aware, globe artichoke, that Wisconsin schoolchildren are taught the Great American Patriotic Martyr was pinko-inquo Joe McCarthy?" Unique Agent Tess Tohnyin seemed bent on provoking another gratuitous argument, even as the subsonic flight carrying them from Chicago began its approach to Las Vegas.

"Wisconsin," the celebrity decreed, "is the small Satan."

A wry smile flickered across Tohnyin's lips. "What kind of world-view does a system like that develop?"

"History isn't D.O.A., Tess." He crossed his arms. "It's a living, breathing entity, a slumbering beast, continually rolling over, uncomfortably shifting positions-"

"All right, gibbon, don't overplay the metaphor." She swept her hair back.

His lingering brattoo pain spiked. "The caption behind the statue of Honest Abe at the entrance to the University of Wisconsin law school states, *The greater the lie, the more likely it is to be believed.*"

She emitted a sardonic chuckle. "That axiom is inscribed on the facade of every top law school."

"But at least," he pleaded for a collegial bond, "it's on the more respectable ones in Latin. I was viewing state legislature highlights a few weeks ago, and the way they were bandying Joe McCarthy's name around in testimony before the House Committee on Un-Californian Activities, it was hard to tell whether they were commending or condemning him."

Tess scrutinized the flaked kunzite polish on her cracked nails. "Was that when they were comparing him to Governor Roache?"

"I don't recall." The celebrity smacked his lips. "You know names are my Achilles."

She regarded him with an irked incredulity. "Do you remember if it was the House of Commons or House of Lords?"

"It's been nearly a hundred years since the Great Martyr fell." She'd promoted herself to the top of his rapidly expanding list of concerns yesterday. They'd braved the 15-degree dip in Wisconsin Dells temperature to walk down the street and procure light lunch orders at a gastro boutique postmodern enough to sustain itself without the encumbering overhead of a sign. She'd seemed to sink into a vortex of melancholia which reflected the overcast sky, and he'd wondered aloud if her raw exposure to the elements at the mercy of WIO could've occasioned a malaise. She'd scoffed at the suggestion and pronounced herself in peak condition. But after finishing her maize dog, she'd begun pressing the base of her spine into light posts and conceded she needed a Kundalini Shakti session to counteract her compression. "Even prickly attitudes are changeable."

As the plane landed, the celebrity recalled the expedient morning pledge he'd made to Noyce in the Sparrow that he'd serve as leading actor and associate producer of the Giselle project. He wondered how he'd best skirt his commitment with dignity and honor.

Tohnyin limped slightly as she disembarked from the aircraft. "I suspect Radmilla ratted me out for not reporting pot use in the panic room." She looked as striking as ever in her yoga Capris and sage wraparound popcorn-stitch sweater that exposed her alabaster shoulders. "What's her issue with *you*?"

The celebrity hesitated. "Classic harassment."

Tess rolled her eyes. "Get the bubble-head some bubble-wrap." She bit into a crunchy quinoa zinger. "It's more important to you, Ahab, so I'm withdrawing any claim to on-site tactical command." She smiled purposefully. "Operation Shalom is your baby." She placed a tender hand on his shoulder and passed him her crumpled garbage. "You can take full credit for the fiasco. I'll inform Natty Phil when I see him."

No wallflower amid the concourse collage of monster electronic posters competing for the attention of inbound passengers at McCarran International XX Airport, Aladdins III proudly presented the *People's Globe Science Awards at 8 Tonite!!!* in the newly renovated Aladdin Green Zone Theater with regular act *Trick Turners Magic Corner returning Tomorrow!!* The celebrity fetched the luggage as Tohnyin retrieved the rental car, and they were soon cruising north on Las Vegas Boulevard. Boxed by heavy Saturday afternoon traffic, their Ford Escort moved slowly past the dazzling noble gas light fountains, which endured as gleaming vestiges of the transformation from an aquatic base in the days of the drought panic. "Whereas the original Aladdins stood midway up the strip, Aladdins III marks the living end, where the glitzy hotel signs become motel signs with missing letters and missing lights," the commercial guidance system displayed its folksy sense of humor. The rental car passed the Aladdins III and after doubling back found its way to the parking structure on the side.

The celebrity and Tohnyin checked in and proceeded to their adjoining rooms, where they took possession of formal wear for the evening's event which they'd ordered from the CIB Wardrobe Department. The celebrity's apparel fit perfectly, although his crisp, white shirt sported several tiny scorch holes and his jacket was vented by three parallel vertical tears and a pair of bullet holes. A progression of intensifying moans emanated from Tess's room, and when she allowed him to enter, he found her dressed to excess for prurient combat. "A little tight?" Her seafoam bandeau bra overflowed a turquoise crushed velvet body sleeve with zippers on both sides seemingly stuck halfway up their tracks. "That's a real side-splitter." The single spaghetti strap of the dress clung to the edge of her shoulder. "Size negative two?"

Tess flashed an irritated grin. "You know any 10-year-old anorexics in need of a cocktail dress?" She ran her fingers over the frayed edges of his customized tuxedo punctures. "You didn't just mutilate this yourself?"

"I didn't have time." He adjusted his bow tie.

Her mood brightened palpably. "Do you realize what this is?" She dashed her dress to the floor. "License to shop. We'll go downstairs or down the street and pick up new working garb." She cupped her hands over her breasts. "But we'll go solo, because shopping with a man is generally as delightful as spotting a scaly tail disappear behind an appliance."

Guy's correspondent Binko had ordered his snoop troops to eyeball lodging guest lists and transport passenger lists for any mention of Charlton Shalom. In the meantime, the celebrity patrolled the accessible spaces around Aladdins and the adjacent Stratosphere looking for a lucky encounter. As he wandered, he revisited the Shalom dossier with a vengeance. Information had run progressively dry in recent years, and the few items that existed appeared radically slanted to either denigrate or deify the ground-ozone-owning scientist. The more points strayed from scientific considerations, however, the more instructive he found them. "The Peace Prize is the Nobel equivalent of a participation trophy," Shalom had been quoted in his most recent offering. "The hyper-educated people are always more offended than astounded to learn how incomplete their data sets are." Charlton had been coaxed to participate in the online interview from Ra'anana, Israel shortly before being extended a diplomatic invitation to leave the country two years ago. Upon arriving back in New York City, he'd marveled that he could miss "this scrubland of America." Accompanying notes from CIB Lead Analyst Leland Montoone described Shalom as a "vain and waspish academic, a compulsive whiffling excursionist" who disdained all "constraints and responsibility." The celebrity expeditiously purchased a new dinner jacket at a bargain price in one of the shops of the retail gallery on the second floor of Aladdins.

Tohnyin reappeared shortly after 1900 hours wearing a turquoise crushed velvet dress of the same design that remained on the floor of her room except that it hugged her sinuous form like a double-coat of fair-weather paint. He entered her room, and she fixed her gaze on his new jacket. "It's deep purple," he volunteered with a subtle smile of satisfaction. "I got the taxpayers a deal on it in the notions department of the Dez's store downstairs. It's actually wild indigo, and if anyone notices, they'll just think the lights are playing tricks."

She grimaced. "In women's magazine parlance, hang close and it shouldn't matter because everyone's eyes will be glued to me." Her features softened. "Not that I value your fashion sense more than any of your other opinions, Ahab, but do you think I succeed aesthetically?"

"You're bound to melt a monocle or two." He couldn't conceal his appreciation for her raw beauty. "Arrestingly lust-worthy. You certainly didn't pick up that number anywhere plainclothes officers shop."

A sly smile graced her lips. "It came from an off-boulevard boutique called Casus Belli Couture Atelier, and I'm pleased it's worth the handsome sum we paid for it." She pushed him gently toward his room. "Go put on your finishing touches and be ready in ten."

Tohnyin emerged from her bathroom approximately thirty minutes later with the addition of pearl orbital earrings, a gold Mobius-strip bracelet and crystal stiletto heels. Her eye makeup had thickened and an inspirational fragrance enveloped her. She grabbed him by the arm and lent an aromatic draft down to the Aladdin Green Zone Theater, where they chased the tail of a slow-moving queue. She exuded confidence about making a solid connection with Shalom at the point of contact, or if not, the opportunity to ply him with enough tracking devices to provide his ongoing location.

The celebrity lowered his voice as others approached. "I wonder what wine is most appropriate for an extreme rendition."

Tohnyin emitted an exasperated sigh. "You stress too much."

A man tapped Tess on the shoulder. "Are you guys in line?"

"Rarely." Tohnyin towed the celebrity into the meat of the queue. "In gaps and pauses this afternoon, I verified that our mutual friend hasn't recently cracked the passenger list of any commercial carrier. As expected, it suggests he enjoys another layer of protection. I'll bet the home hermitage turns out to be a long astronomical unit from Wisconsin."

The celebrity and Tohnyin reached the theater entrance. The two choice VIP tickets that Noyce had vouchsafed them proved to be counterfeit, but the celebrity acquired a replacement pair from an attractive young couple in line behind them who radiated little disappointment about exchanging the awards show experience for a generous lump sum. The newly acquired seats were located on the aisle in the penultimate row of the FIP section situated directly behind and without access to the elegant round tables of the VIP section. Fairly Important Person positions featured folding trays and cup-holders.

Tohnyin produced her high-power-scope wi-vi opera glasses and directional mic. As the muddy sound of Low-Key Norse Force chanting their hit "Chill Factor" filled the theater, she searched the VIP section for distinguished elderly gentlemen of interest. The celebrity produced their golden envelope festooned with a double bow that held an invitation for Charlton Shalom to meet his "most passionate devotee" at the Aladdins casino bar Hocus Pocus after the awards show "so she can congratulate you in her own personal way." He marched to the front of the FIP section with the article in hand, and with no little difficulty bribed an usher in the VIP section to deliver the note to its intended recipient.

The celebrity returned to his seat. "He's dropped it off," Tess reported, "to another usher." She trained her opera glasses on a section of the theater behind them. "Wouldn't it be just like someone who loved to pretend he was invisible when he was a boy to be here up in the cheap seats relishing his obscurity?"

The celebrity kept his gaze fixed on the usher with the golden envelope as another Low-Key Norse Force offering "Smarter Martyr" rumbled through the theater speakers. "She's on the move," he alerted Tess.

"I have her." Tohnyin trained her wi-vi glasses on the VIP section. "She's bending over a man, engaging him, displaying the article and leaving it at his place." She employed the micro-zoom function. "That can't be our boy-" She pursed her lips. "He can't be fifty." The man who'd received the envelope sported a head of thick, dark curls, a mountain ogre beard and appeared fairly stocky. "The guy with the high forehead – all of the men at the table look vaguely familiar. I'll bet they're old colleagues." The man with the thick curls opened the envelope, read the card and glanced around nervously. "The Asian man could be fellow laureate Ving Zang." She pointed her Qilroy and took pictures of all four men at the table. "I'm going to match some face."

"Cover before striking." Low-Key Norse Force fell silent and the theater lights were extinguished. A quick synthesized staccato with gradually rising indefinite pitch pulsated through the speakers with the suggestion of something cooking. The stage roared to life with a chorus line of young women in lab coats and oversized goggles in a flash of brilliant light. Each wing of the stage sported a giant helix populated with ascending bubbles.

"Up and *atom*, you high-energy S.T.E.M. aficionados of every stripe, shape and orientation," an announcer screeched, "off your d-branes and out of your p-branes, for the science extravaganza of the year!" The chorus line kicked, twirled and shed their lab coats. "It's the *People's Globe Science Awards* from the newly renovated Aladdin Green Zone Theater at the Aladdins III in fabulous Las Vegas!" The popular co-hosts for the event, a stand-up funnyman and Hollywood heartthrob, were introduced and strode onstage arm in arm fortified by toothy smiles and swat-worthy waves. "Thank you, ladies and gentlemen," the funnyman wailed, "it's got to be a great program because who's ever had a bigger blast out in the desert than a house full of physicists?"

"I'm closing in on the man with the 29th-century forehead," Tess whispered through clenched teeth. "Gotcha!" She displayed the 97 percent biometric match. "It's Mikhail Razumovsky, the Russian astrophysicist who shared Shalom's second Nobel. They call him Mako." She worked her Qilroy. "I'm still winnowing candidates for Hairball. *You* could make yourself an asset, Ahab, by climbing into the cloud and searching for the Asian man. Wait!" She shook with excitement. "Wait for it. Our curlmeister *is* Shalom – Charlton's son Tycho Shalom, relatively undistinguished evolutionary psychologist on leave from UNLV." A sly smile flickered across her lips. "He was throwing us off with better bushcraft; this must be the first time since middle school he's appeared in public sans fusty glasses and scraggly sorcerer's apprentice goatee. He may be a considerable drop-and-roll from the pawpaw tree, but there's no intel to indicate he's formally estranged from disappointed old Dad – at least not to the same bitter extent as his sister Bebe the ex-conservator and power-of-attorney holder."

"Bring up her picture." The celebrity rubbed his chin. "If Senorita Shalom has a fluffy Santa Claus beard, too, we can conclude that Dad has always placed science above family."

"In the words of cosmologist Carl Sagan," the funnyman bantered, "me and the oak are made of the same stuff."

Tess patted the celebrity's knee. "Maybe we can match one of the women at Tycho's table to Charlton's companions on the *Janesy* surveillance logs."

More pomp and sonoluminescence attended the stage presentation. Tohnyin surveyed more of the audience. The celebrity tapped her opera glasses. "You'd really refuse to presume that father and son would be seated together if the former were here?"

Tess rolled her eyes. "Ahab, I'll never understand why everyone laughs when I tell them you're a genius."

The celebrity nodded. "Maybe because it took you so long to figure it out."

The awards show progressed through the compulsory "fun guy of fungi" and "primordial soup was cold when brought to his periodic table" riffs in scaling the hierarchy of scientific disciplines. Time seemed to expand as anticipation of the Lifetime Achievement Award mounted. Finally, the culminating presentation of the *People's Globe* science extravaganza pit the record-breaking three Nobel Prizes in physics of Charlton Shalom against Anselma Robbins, researcher on the behavior of unified groups and cohesive aligned structures, and Seth Boepple, designer of the human weight-reduction gene-editing shortcut that reprogrammed white fat to brown. A two-minute bio of each nominee was presented, and Shalom's retrospective neatly omitted the dustup over his disputed explanation of dark energy and subsequent kerfuffles with the mainstream science community. His research on electric fog was cited as the inspiration for "the locus of the concerted effort to combat the plague of climate instability in the form of the polar shroud."

Theater and home viewers were entrusted with the heady responsibility to vote with their consciences and Qilroys.

"You've taken care of this?" Tohnyin confirmed. "The rigging is tight, right?"

"Did I miss a signal? A code?" The celebrity arrested his irritation long enough to deploy a bot army capable of bolstering Shalom's chance of winning. "I don't like to tamper with the sacrosanct institution of the democratic process unless I have to."

Tess configured another block of votes to influence selection results. "It'd just be too easy to follow the Albert right to Charlton, hmm?"

The celebrity experienced a prevailing brattoo pang. He regretted that he hadn't populated the gold leaf of the invitation with more smart dust grains but he'd sought to minimize the risk that the recipient might realize the card was laced with miniaturized RFID transmitters or worse suspect the presence of some deleterious powder. "How's your signal, boffin-boggler?"

"Weak but steady." Tohnyin analyzed her Qilroy display. "Actually split off and broadcasting from two positions." She grabbed his hand and scrutinized it. "Aw, Ahab, are you full of dust?"

"Wow, do you guys believe in close races?" The funnyman referenced his enormous prop Qilroy. "The final vote totals are 33 percent to 33 percent to 34 percent."

"Our quality of life owes a substantial debt to each of the nominees," the heartthrob granted, "but by less than one percentage point, we proclaim the biggest debt is owed to *Charlton Shalom!!*"

"Charlton Shalom!" the funnyman echoed. "You are the winner of the *People's Globe* Science Lifetime Achievement Award!" The theater rumbled with a cacophonous fusion of cheers and boos. Seven out of eight people at the Shalom table leapt to their feet, danced jigs and pumped gestures of triumph. Tycho and Mako hustled to the stage.

"Accepting the Lifetime Achievement Award in Science

for Charlton Shalom," the announcer intoned, "is his son Tycho Shalom."

The younger Shalom received the Albert from the heart-throb and kissed her, Razumovsky and the statuette. "It was apparent to me from inside the incubator that Pop was no ordinary Senex iratus!" Tycho proceeded to deliver a tortuous encomium laced with obscure tangents such as "venturing out to purchase doughnuts for the study group only to return with deodorant." He concluded his remarks with the tease that he'd be dissecting his father's vanities with more rigor in his forthcoming biography: *The Highly Nontrivial Man*. He and Mako drew polite applause as they returned to their table.

"Has there been bread-crumb drift?" The celebrity accepted the opera glasses from Tess and located the golden envelope on the Shalom table. One of the women vigorously rubbed the Albert until the statuette exhibited its triboluminescent property with a lush green glow. "Glom onto that Albert, Tycho."

The co-hosts exchanged closing observations, and Tohnyin elbowed the celebrity in ribs that Winterhalter had previously tenderized. "Up and atom." She reclaimed the wi-vi glasses. "Remember, Ahab, to keep him from using the bathroom."

The celebrity rose. "I'll keep rubbing my hands on my pants until he imitates me."

Tess caressed the toe of the celebrity's balmoral oxford with her crystal stiletto. "If you drop the reins of visual containment, work your way down to Hocus Pocus unless I instruct you otherwise." She dragged her heel up his instep. "I'll stay with the signal movement, and we'll all meet up for the big crunch."

The celebrity felt his brattoo pain spike. "We'll code that as the head-on encore, eh, tokamak?"

The program ended abruptly, and the celebrity encountered a bottleneck as the pop canticle "Overeducated Lover" by Sweet Nothings rattled through the theater. He nimbly extricated himself from the crowd, darted down the narrow ramp and reached his destination outside the theater lobby, where he shambled to claim a pocket of space as he conducted a cursory survey of heads. He caught glimpses of Mako and Tycho accompanied by their cute redhead and blonde companions. The blonde carried the glowing green Albert.

"Denied access," Tess messaged. "Lost eyeball. Signal fragmented. Help?"

"Mark positive," the celebrity assured Tohnyin that he held a lock on the Shalom cell. "Repair to Hocus Pocus in anticipation of arrival." He positioned himself at the bench beside the escalator and lost track of his targets. "Stand-by." He surveyed the main floor below as pedestrian traffic on the second level dwindled to a trickle. "Mark negative," he disgustedly submitted. "In focus at Hocus Pocus?"

"Pick up, Ahab!" she responded. "How do you lose a mob in the middle of the floor?" She emitted an exasperated breath. "My signal is split but the strongest stream seems to be moving toward the southwest corner of the casino. Conduct a foot surveillance in that area and try to regain visual. And if you spot them, make sure you provide the wigs with a fat, fluffy cushion."

He hopped on the escalator. "Do not approach because they may be armed with smart weapons and dangerous?"

"In that case, I'd beg you to approach." She smiled tartly. "Contact me so we can apply standard agency approach protocol."

"You want to remind me what your idea of that is?" He assessed players at a bank of slots as he reached the main floor.

"We wait until they've settled somewhere, and you assault me in front of them." She cringed at the prospect. "Just rough me up enough so Tycho can rush to my defense and run you off. If necessary, I'll lose an earring in his drink so I can buy him another." She finished her cocktail. "I'm on the move." She terminated the connection.

"And what if they're geek or freak enough to have already retired to their hotel rooms?" The celebrity hustled to the perimeter of the casino and reached the High-Stakes Slots lounge. He combed the area without sighting any members of the Shalom delegation.

He strolled around the casino floor and received a message from Tohnyin: "Tess has left the building!" She switched to voice communication. "I'm next door at the Stratosphere," she reported. "The source of my signal is 250 meters directly above me. This building and its antennae might cause radical altitude D.O.P. but there couldn't be that much horizontal distortion." She smiled intently. "I received a wicked tip at Hocus Pocus that there's a pool party for *People's Globe* VIPs on the 25th floor and I'm headed up there now. It'll be easier for me to gain access if I'm unaccompanied, so I'll contact you when it's favorable for you to bump-and-grind this way. Remember, Ahab, just in case the good doctor should still be in your building, you are charged to grandstand down!"

"You close the distance." He extracted his earpiece and headed around the table games in the casino core. "They've probably already blown town." He glimpsed the back of an elongated head. He approached a craps table and positively identified the younger Shalom and Razumovsky sans tuxedo jackets evaluating particulars of the spectacle. He drifted to a Kredit Kiosk where he could maintain a peripheral view of the power couple, and he created a casino account. He camped at an adjacent Original Rat Pack slot and spun twice. The targets entered the craps game. A farewell Original Rat Pack spin scored a moderate return on the taxpayers' stake. He added the yield to his account as he watched Shalom fail to achieve his prescribed point. He took a deep breath and strolled to the spot at the craps table directly to Tycho's left. He ordered ten thousand dollars of chips and nodded to the evolutionary psychologist. "What do you think, Herr Professor, does God play dice with the universe?"

Razumovsky moved from Shalom's right side to a position between him and the celebrity. "I think you will show us."

The celebrity chuckled and matched Shalom's $100 pass bet. The shooter opened with a six. Tycho and the celebrity both laid the maximum triple-odds bet. "Nobel laureate Richard Feynman," the celebrity offered, "concluded that the odds bet in craps provides the house with less built-in advantage than any other." The shooter rolled eleven.

"A figure he calculated as .007," Tycho inferred, placing a $600 come bet including maximum odds. The shooter rolled a two and then a seven.

The celebrity moved to Shalom's right and matched him in extending the next shooter the courtesy of another $100 pass bet. "I was pleased to see you win the *People's Globe*." The shooter established her point at five.

Tycho curled his lips into a perfunctory smile and laid another $300 odds bet. "Couldn't compare to last year's show." The celebrity nodded cluelessly and matched the odds bet. The shooter rolled a six.

The celebrity laid a $500 come bet. "More suggestive music and dance, wasn't there, and the featured discoveries had more applications for mass destruction?" The shooter rolled an eight.

"Astrology and parapsychology were categories." Razumovsky stepped back to engage the celebrity as the shooter rolled a ten. "It was held in L.A."

"I'm eager to read your memoir." The celebrity watched the shooter roll an eight and snatched his $1,000 of chips from his come bet. "Intriguing title."

Shalom shook his head. "My seventh choice." The shooter rolled a six, and the evolutionary psychologist placed a $200 come bet with $600 odds.

"*The Man Who Cubed Infinity* was already taken by a recording artist," Mako interjected. The shooter rolled a three.

The celebrity smiled complaisantly. "And there were other titles besides?" The shooter rolled a seven.

Tycho exhaled heavily. "*Our Mesonic Temple*; *Toss the Double-D's Another Einstein-*"

The celebrity snickered. "What might the Double-D's be?"

"Ditch-diggers, among other things." Shalom guided the celebrity in winning two $100 pass bets as the next shooter rolled a pair of natural sevens before establishing a point of eight. Tycho added a $600 odds bet to his $200 pass bet.

The celebrity added a $300 odds bet to his $100 pass bet. "As a fellow scientist, you must be in a unique position to evaluate your father's professional exploits." The shooter rolled six.

Shalom cast an irritated sideways glance. "Zounds, buy the book!" He placed a $600 come bet with maximum odds. The celebrity wagered similarly with half the amount. The shooter rolled a twelve.

The celebrity smiled complaisantly. "I must admit I was disappointed not to see your father in person." The shooter rolled eleven. "I haven't heard of him in a while." The shooter rolled an eight to make his point.

"The organizers promised this year to present four nubile nymphs cloned from the DNA of classic film vamp Hedy Lamarr," Razumovsky offered. Shalom placed a pass bet of $500 while the celebrity settled for $100. The shooter rolled a four. "The ruse was almost enough to suck ol' Chutz out of the igloo." Tycho added an odds bet of $1,500 and a come bet with maximum odds of $600. The shooter rolled a seven.

"You still see him often, Dr. Mako?" The celebrity stepped around Tycho as the evolutionary psychologist placed a $200 pass bet. "He lives in Wisconsin, doesn't he?" The next shooter established his point as six.

Razumovsky shrugged. "We've had no direct contact in years." Tycho maximized his odds bet, and the shooter rolled a twelve. "Ask this one. He just took a job at the University of Wisconsin."

Shalom grimaced and placed a $750 come bet including maximum odds. "Pop as always is out of touch." The shooter rolled another twelve.

The celebrity patted Tycho on the shoulder. "A friend of mine swears she spotted Charlton at a spa in Wisconsin Dells." The evolutionary psychologist placed a $600 come bet including maximum odds. The shooter rolled a three and then a seven.

The celebrity stepped around Shalom and accepted the dice from the stickman. "The naturalist's son comes out." He laid a $500 pass bet. Tycho sneered and placed a $500 don't-pass bet. "A learned skeptic." He snatched and shook the dice. He rolled a hard eight. He and Shalom both padded their wagers with $1,500 odds bets. "Artesian wells beneath the Dells." He rolled a two. "I'll bet your father plays a musical instrument." He rolled another eight.

"Just bet," Shalom grumbled. He matched the celebrity's $600 pass bet with a don't-pass bet.

The celebrity rolled a seven. "As you may know, the Dells is notable as the site of the hottest surface temperature ever recorded in Wisconsin."

"All I know is I was winning before you arrived," Tycho whined. He countered the celebrity's $1,200 pass bet with a $200 don't-pass bet. The celebrity established his point at ten, and both players maximized their odds bets. The celebrity fired a hard eight and placed a $600 come bet. He rolled eleven.

"I resented my father," the celebrity attempted to re-establish diplomatic relations with Tycho, "for putting me through forced music lessons." He rolled a three. "But I learned to relish them about the time he could no longer stand listening to me." He rolled another hard eight.

"I copy that." Shalom placed $600 on the eight. "It must've been a wind instrument."

The celebrity rolled six and followed with ten. He placed a $4,000 pass bet and rolled a hard eight. He maximized his odds. Shalom was no longer betting. The celebrity rolled another hard eight. "What do you think, Herr Professor, are discrete mathematics of any value in a proposition bet?" He pushed $15,000 in chips toward the center of the table. "Service bet," he declared. "Another hard eight." He laid a $6,000 pass bet and eyed Tycho. "Good vibrations?"

Shalom placed a $4,000 horn bet. "Why don't you zip it and shoot, crapehanger?" The celebrity rolled another hard eight. The other players and dealers hooted and clapped.

"Shoot one more of those, mechanical man," Razumovsky remarked, "and they'll take you out back and shoot *you*."

The celebrity maximized his odds. "Just don't break my fingers so I can still play the horn."

"We don't appreciate that sort of humor at the table, Mashallah," the boxman admonished.

The celebrity rolled a two, eleven, ten, nine and four. Goaded by other players, he ordered a $20,000 service bet on another hard eight. Tycho placed a $2,000 field bet. The celebrity rolled a hard eight. He breathed deeply as he added $207,600 in winnings to his chip pile. He placed a $6,000 pass bet and opened with a two. "Hard two!" He evoked polite titters. He placed another $6,000 pass bet and rolled a four. He maximized his odds and rolled a seven.

"Hard landing, hot-hand?" Shalom smirked and collected $700 on his counter-wager with maximum odds. He selected a pair of dice. He laid a $1,000 pass bet. The celebrity placed a $1,000 don't-pass bet, and seven of eight other players followed his lead to bet against the evolutionary psychologist. Tycho rolled an eleven. The players jeered, and most repeated their respective bets as Shalom laid another $1,000 pass bet. He rolled a hard eight. He padded his wager with maximum odds as did the celebrity and most of the table. Tycho sneered and pushed his remaining $5,400 of chips toward the dealer. "Specialty bet," he declared. "Another hard eight."

"No, don't!" Razumovsky pressed his advisory capacity beyond logging rolls. "At least diversify."

Shalom redirected his wager to be evenly distributed among the *4*, *Six* and *10* boxes for place bets. He wound up and threw the dice off the table. He shot again and rolled a seven. "Aughhhh!" He waved his hands dismissively and pivoted.

"Stick it out, Herr Professor," the celebrity pleaded. "Prospects change."

Shalom extended his tongue. "Don't depress me." He started away from the table and nearly collided with Tohnyin.

"Congratulations on your *People's Globe* victory, Dr. Shalom," Tess cooed.

"No drink." Tycho rocked back and scanned Tess from head to toe like a long lost executive producer. "Excuse me." He brushed past her, and Mako followed.

"Look what's arisen from the alternative underground," the celebrity acknowledged Tohnyin. "How long have you been table scenery?"

"Outstanding situational awareness, Ahab." Tess advanced to the celebrity's side. "I arrived at the point where he likened your virtuosity to a toxic air contaminant." She surveyed the craps game as it progressed without the celebrity's participation. "I lost my signal in the Strat. Then you didn't respond." She sighed. "What beyond exactly what I requested that you not do did you do to chase Tycho off?"

"Scared money always shrinks." The celebrity thrummed his sprawl of chips.

She raised her eyebrows. "You know the Studio owns your winnings, faith-shaker, so don't get overly attached."

"You should still want to kiss my dice." He smiled aristocratically. "At the rate my luck is running, I can erase the state deficit in about another four hours."

"Salvaging the op is the priority." Tohnyin eyed her Qilroy. "I gained a solid lock on our mark when I bumped him."

She tugged on the celebrity's collar. "Let's go perform some damage control."

The celebrity credited out with a $351,660 profit. He trailed Tohnyin out of Aladdins III. She increased her pace, and he overtook her as she entered the Stratosphere. "Is one of Tycho's roundtable cuticles still lugging around his Albert?"

"I never found the pool party." Tohnyin squinted into her sourcerer. "Our original signal is still jumbled. Maybe she won it off him." Tess grimaced. "If either of these intellectual-legacy-poaching Shalom kids would've reproduced, I'm sure doting Granddad could be easily lured out to mid-grid."

Tohnyin led the celebrity across the Stratosphere casino floor. No persons of interest appeared in the vicinity of the craps tables. "I firmly believe he's above any more gambling," she asserted. "His signal is coming from an altitude of 262 meters." The duo reached the base of the tower and boarded the elevator. "My friend Fuzzy just came up here." Tess showed the security woman operating the elevator an altered photo of herself draped around Tycho. "You don't recall which floor you deposited him on, do you?"

"He would've been accompanied by a fellow with a head like a sports team mascot," the celebrity submitted.

"AirBar." The security agent seized the opportunity to be helpful. "All the way to the top."

Tohnyin shoved the celebrity out of the elevator. "I've decided to approach them alone. You hang back for a few moments. When you come up, dock yourself somewhere out of sight at the end of the bar behind a jumbo ice coffee." The doors closed, and she ascended.

"What's your angle going in?" he messaged her. "Grill Tycho on exactly how much Charlton detests ceremonies. Ask him if he theorizes his funeral would bring Pop out."

The elevator returned twenty minutes later. The celebrity boarded and nodded to the friendly security agent. "AirBar, please."

The elevator began its ascent. "Your gal pal seems pretty determined. She lit into the AirBar so fast she practically left a contrail."

The celebrity nodded. "Brunhilde's celerity through a tiny social ingress remains legendary."

The elevator reached the top floor, and the celebrity sauntered into the AirBar. He plunked himself onto the end barstool and ordered a snowshoe cocktail with ship-aged bourbon. "Reached air base," he messaged Tohnyin. "Await cue." His snowshoe arrived, and he stared into the shelves of liquor as he sipped it. He employed his Qilroy directional mic and acquired scratchy bits of Tess's conversation. He dedicated further research to Tycho's sister Bebe, a family law attorney who resided in Ra'anana, Israel. Given the name "Elealeh," she had originally been tabbed "Lala." As an expatriate, ex-patriarch and ex-pariah, Charlton was more than unlikely to carry a residual connection to the old homestead.

The celebrity attempted to open Tohnyin's Qilroy mic remotely. He finished his snowshoe and accepted the bartender's recommendation of an admiral cocktail. Six sips into the admiral, he heard what sounded vaguely like a cry of distress from across the barroom. He drained his glass with a robust gulp. He opened Tess's mic and heard her cry again. He darted around the end of the bar and found her emoting at the table of Shalom and Razumovsky. Tycho spotted him first. "You again!" He rose. "Are you following me, you wazzock?"

"He's stalking *me*!" Tohnyin leapt to her feet and flipped the celebrity to the floor. "He's my former manservant." Razumovsky stood and signaled a waitress. "No, please, he's harmless. He also used to be my cousin. He's just a pest." She leveled a finger of censure. "Ahab, take a cigarette break and smoke the pack." The celebrity staggered to his feet, and Mako shooed the approaching bartender.

"I can relate to the burden of a family nuisance." Shalom dropped back into his seat. "As I was saying, Pop always coveted dark-haired, bright-eyed beauties like Paulette Goddard and Hedy Lamarr." He returned his starry gaze to Tohnyin. "Tough, high-powered combinations of beauty and brains-"

"Joan Crawford is another from that era hot enough to drive any scientist mad," the celebrity attempted to run interference, "and *she* won an Oscar. You can't ignore *Mildred Pierce*." He clenched his fists at his sides, bent forward slightly and snarled imperiously at no one in particular, "I'd like to slap your face so hard your head spins a triple axel."

Tycho tittered derisively. "She really said that?"

"Uh, no, not in a film." The celebrity seated himself at the adjacent table.

"An epic documentary that you authorized about your father's life couldn't be ignored." Tess's method dissolved to fawning. "Although after what the Nobel committee put him through, it wouldn't surprise me if he generally detests awards."

Tycho groaned. "Pop's notoriously had as much trouble accepting praise as giving it." He shifted his weight uncomfortably. "According to him, I could never do anything right."

"'Never do anything *correctly*,'" the celebrity issued a grammar-police warning.

Shalom fixed the celebrity with a scowl. "I'll tell you what – is it 'Wahib'?" He removed a small cylindrical package from his hip pocket. "The Nevada Department of Cultural Affairs sent these, and I forgot I had them." He extracted three gold coins from the package. "There's a radiant redhead named Lisa who's flaunting our award." He turned to Razumovsky. "Lisa's wearing a green dress with lavender sparklies, right?" He redirected his attention to the celebrity and replaced the coins in their wrapper. "She's down on the third floor in the high-roller lounge." He flipped the roll to the celebrity. "Do me a favor and deliver these tokens to her there." He raised his index finger. "I'll message her to let you keep one for your trouble." A sly gleam flickered in his eyes. "Lisa can then let you fetch her and our Gina and our Albert up here when the tokens are spent."

"Keep your lucky streak going, Ahab," Tohnyin prodded.

The celebrity rose and bowed accommodatingly. "I trust you'll find Tess highly engaging, Herr Professor. She's always poised to claim her next club footman."

"His name is 'Ahab'?" Tycho remarked as the celebrity exited. "I called him 'Wahib.'" He snickered. "Whatever."

The celebrity returned to the elevator and boarded. "How's Brunhilde faring?" The supportive security woman suddenly seemed intrusive.

"It's the only thing to appease a looker," he briefed her. "For the megacephalic man, size is the only thing."

The celebrity disembarked on the second floor and proceeded from the tower to the hotel proper. He took the stairs to the third floor and entered the high-roller lounge. He spied the Albert on the center stool before a bank of slots. The statuette was flanked on each side by a stool holding a woman in a cocktail dress. He approached the one with red hair wearing a green gown with lavender sparkles. "Gina, I mean Lisa, I presume?"

"You're Ahad?" She forced a brilliant smile. "Here with our capital reserve?" She extended her hand and looked away. "Subtract your service fee."

"Taking a token would be exploitative." The celebrity smacked the roll into Lisa's palm, and she eyed him warily. She turned and handed the blonde in the yellow dress a token. "Have you known Tycho long?" Lisa responded with a silent ennui. Each woman loaded a token into her respective slot, pulled a lever and waited in vain for a payoff. "And you're Gina?" he vetted the blonde.

"And you're a talent scout?" Lisa countered impatiently. She turned to the blonde. "He's trying to figure out whether we're pros."

"Pros like me?" The celebrity felt an embarrassed grin

spread across his face. "I thought we might've connected at the last Geneva convention." She hissed. "Fossil-fuel addicts on Geneva Lake, Wisconsin?" She rolled her eyes. "Puff buffs on Mono Lake, California?"

The two women shared secrets over the statuette and rose simultaneously. "This may be your lucky day," the blonde advised him. "We're placing the Albert in your protective custody." She and Lisa strode to a bank of slots in the most distant corner of the lounge.

The celebrity plucked the statuette off the stool and meandered after them. He approached Lisa after she'd exhausted another token. "I had an impertinent exchange with Tycho at the craps table and I'd like to get him a room fixture as a peace offering. Could you suggest a piece that suits his décor?"

Lisa emitted an irritated sigh. "I've heard his man cave compared to a natural one." She walked away.

"You're so lifelike," he called after her. He decided to allow her more space and headed to a neutral corner. He set the statuette on the pale green fainting couch and amassed images of the two companions. He also enabled his Qilroy with forensic analysis apps and scanned fingerprints on the surface of the award although he had little reasonable expectation that they'd prove to be of value.

Lisa hit a modest jackpot. She and the blonde strutted to the colossal NASA-themed Shingslot To Saturn machine at the center of the lounge to reinvest the mini-bonanza. The celebrity grabbed the statuette and settled it in Lisa's lap. "Lavatory break." He smiled primly. "Mind Albert while you help the space program." He checked his Qilroy for a message from Tohnyin as he hustled to the nearest men's room. He relieved himself and headed around the corner to the sinks, where he found a familiar glower.

"Hey, you're Kim's – er, no, Park's colleague from the jogging track on the *Janesy*, aren't you?" The celebrity began washing his hands. "Running into you again here certainly is curious." The man's lip curled chinward but he remained silent. "I understand my underling water-bombed you. I apologize that he's such a walking depth charge." The man mumbled with agitation, removed his Jatakar and placed it in his pocket. "Your name is Bart, or no – Bud, isn't it?"

Bud snapped a vicious kick into the celebrity's hip, hopped and delivered a roundhouse kick to the lower abdomen with the pointed tip of the other foot. The celebrity caught the rancorous ankle. "Italian leather, oh, yes." Bud reached beneath his jacket, and the celebrity flipped soap. He lunged into his attacker, grabbed the concealed hand, absorbed a glancing punch to the side of the head and thrust an elbow to the chops. He slammed Bud's head into the countertop. He ripped open Bud's jacket and shirt and began frisking him. "Who are you?" He found no weapon but dashed the sourcerer to the floor. "Who sent you?" He turned Bud over and held his head in the sink. "What's your tie to WIO?"

Bud emitted a furious growl. "I'm from Bangladesh."

The celebrity waggled Bud's head to induce water flow. "Try harder." Bud squirmed out of the celebrity's grasp and threw an easily parried punch. The celebrity pummeled Bud's ribs and shoved his head back into the sink. "There's an existential truth in fighting, Big Bad Bud. At least that's what the girls tell me." He waggled Bud's head to induce more water flow. "What's your connection to WIO?"

Bud cursed and spit. "I'm from Bangladesh!"

The restroom door opened. The celebrity pulled Bud to an upright position. "You're all wet."

The newcomer peeked around the corner. Bud grabbed the celebrity's arm. "This man is a criminal! He is a terrorist! Hold him for the authorities!"

"*You* hold *this!*" The man retreated to the urinals.

Bud slipped out of the celebrity's grasp again, scrambled around the corner and out of the lavatory. The celebrity turned to retrieve Bud's Jatakar but felt a sharp pain in his side from the initial kicks of the skirmish. He exchanged glances with the urinating man. "Prices these days." Listing slightly, he staggered into a stall, closed the door behind him and leaned against it to recuperate. A noisy group of about eight entered the restroom. He found that he couldn't stoop without losing his balance. When everyone else had vacated the lavatory, he emerged from his stall. Bud's Jatakar had disappeared. The celebrity deduced that the inscrutable Bud had virtually invited him to confiscate his sourcerer for counter-tracking purposes, so it was best left with an unconcerned party. Discerning no further trace of the soggy-headed Bangladeshi blighter outside the restroom beyond a few scattered droplets of blood on the carpet, he waddled back to the high-roller lounge.

Lisa and the presumed Gina were gone with the Albert. The celebrity messaged Tohnyin a warning of his imminent return to the AirBar. "Don't stink up the show!" her return message instructed. "Meet me on the main floor near the craps tables." He duly tottered down the stairs and resisted the temptation to pad his windfall as he waited. Tess finally approached carrying the glowing People's Globe statuette. She waved it and placed it securely in his possession.

She snickered effervescently. "He didn't exactly draw me a treasure map, but he's going to arrange an exchange where we deliver the Albert to Charlton personally. An intermediary is going to provide us with particulars through the dark net."

"Salutes and plaudits, Unique Agent Tohnyin." He beamed through her stinging hip bump. "But why does one hand over a prestigious prize to complete strangers?" His residual brattoo discomfort screamed louder. "What did you have to leave him with the impression that you'd promised him?"

Tess hissed and started toward the exit. "He indicated that he wants to re-establish contact with his father, and he hopes this might break the ice. He said Charlton would derive no gratification from the award itself, but if he can tell him a green goddess is coming to present him with another one, he'll be amused and receptive." She played a recording of Tycho's voice on her Qilroy: "When Pop learns there's a trophy diva holding his trophy icon, he should dust off a place on his arm for you."

The celebrity rubbed his face. "Nobody's called me a trophy diva since I shaved my mustache."

"As a matter of fact, you look a little cockeyed." She stopped and assessed him from head to toe. "Did little, red-headed Lisa make life rough for you in the high-roller lounge? Were you able to work her for any viable intel?"

"You know what I like about redheads?" he observed. "They're said to feel pain more acutely than the rest of us."

Tohnyin expelled an irritated breath. "You didn't even ascertain the nature of her relationship to Tycho?"

"I made exploratory overtures." The celebrity followed Tess out of the Stratosphere. "She and her golden cohort are flesh-eating Fingal's cave women, I believe, shopping for something with a higher maintenance threshold." The crypto-crats hustled along the uncongested curb. "Did you score more?"

"I didn't pursue that line of questioning in the two minutes the two babes were in my presence because I presumed you had it covered, ash blond." She smiled provocatively. "What was I thinking?"

He dodged a parking car. "As famously as you and junior Shalom seem to have gotten on, you must've pumped plenty more from that well."

"He's as aggravating a raconteur as you are for the exact opposite reason." Tess patted the head of the statuette. "He obsesses and digresses on objects, details, tallies, until one's sensibilities go numb and number."

"He's the prodigy who can identify all the notes but can't hear the music," the celebrity offered.

"I don't know." She rubbed her brow. "That sounds more like you, too. Tycho spent a chunk of time itemizing war-era memorabilia owned by his family. He boasted that they had the only known hockey stick autographed by the Yankee Clipper, and in their den they used to display a mounted pair of Max Baer's boxing trunks before they were proved to be a fraud."

"They weren't really Baer's or they weren't really trunks?" He returned a courtesy nod to a passerby who emitted a congratulatory shout at the Albert.

Tess grimaced. "The worst part came when he launched into depictions of his icky animal experiments. He's immunized mice to rattlesnake venom and trying to condition them to fight back."

"That might explain his proclivity to roll a two at the craps table." The celebrity opened the door and followed Tohnyin into Aladdins III. "You don't think the sprig was trying to send us a warning?" He endured her prickly scowl. "You have to admit circumstances have fallen as if to set us up as a couple of the most naïve gobemouches in the annals of spydom." He rubbed his abdomen. "Would you like to hear some juicy details about my last bathroom break?"

"What are you suddenly," she carped, "Winterhalter's stand-in?" She repossessed the Albert. "What could Charlton be hiding from? When he accepted his gig with ARPA, the feds gave him a lifetime immunity from taxes. But there must be some economic angle."

"Insanity abhors a vacuum," he speculated.

"I've changed my mind about the op," she decided. "I'm all in."

Doh-sa-don't let's Red Square Dance;
Rock step, lock step, kick, drab pants;
Promenade and form a star;
Dragon's breath swing Ursa B'ar.

Hoe down, swing a sickle now;
Interlock arms, two-step plow;
Four-chain, eight-chain, handshake hold;
Two-faced lines to leave you cold.

Turn and trade and deal from right;
We can cross trail through all night;
Circulate that ocean wave;
Pinko's twinkles all the rave.

Naming names as folks pass by;
Call them out and make them cry;
Cultivate a blacklist field;
Maypole Mayday, that's the yield!

7TH MOVEMENT

Inbound. 0800 PST Monday 3 April.

"Man is a blind, witless, low-brow anthropocentric clod who inflicts lesions upon the Earth." As he shot his Duryea Statement through the crawl of terrestrial traffic from his North Hollywood digs, the celebrity mussitated the acerbic sentiment of late 20th-century city planner Ian McHarg. A tailgate bandit snatched the opportunity to pass on the right, and the celebrity hoped the car-length gained by the quotidian squish was worth the kernel of road rage he'd engendered. The heat of the day became manifest in his mood escalation, and he found his medius still twitching on the button that deployed the spike strip from beneath his rear bumper when he turned onto the newly created Venona Boulevard cross street approach to the CIB Santa Monica P.C. headquarters.

The chains on the double flagpoles mounted beyond the Checkpoint Chico security chutes clanged in the breeze as the Statement Exelectrix trimmed the stress of the slow-moving queue in full auto-navigator mode. His agitation supplanting the residual soreness from Bud's kicks, the celebrity leaned out his window and smiled boldly for the remote monitors in Sacramento. Temperamental motorists in the queue honked their horns. He cleared the checkpoint. "Out West we tolerate ideas," he controverted the commentary of a radio talk show host. "The Midwest only entertains beliefs."

The celebrity claimed his favorite corner space in the fortified underground parking structure beneath the O Building. Briefcase in hand, he strode the length of the O Building, validated his ID at the security cell entrance and arrived in the spacious four-story karmamentarium lobby. He held his gaze on the north wall and the perpetual encrypted rolling credits of those heroes who'd made a significant contribution to promoting the success of the organization and preserving California lifestyle quality as he rode the double-crossing spiral escalator to level four. He paused upon disembarking to overlook the containers of beneficial California vegetation which decorated the main floor of the karmamentarium. He noticed that the castor plants and bitter almond trees had drooping leaves and needed water.

As he proceeded through the clear Plexiglas skywalk tunnel to the U Building, he surveyed the victory sculpture garden vista which constituted the compact compound courtyard. The four life-size replica suncatcher Easter Island monoliths that bore an arresting resemblance to the 37th president of the United States peered out of their bamboo semi-enclosure with an eerie glow. Meditating employees were already walking the labyrinth within Boohenge confines, although this morning they shared the course of self-realization with a comedian trundling through on a Segway personal transporter.

The celebrity paused for another moment. The bronze statue of former Governor Arnold Schwarzenegger striking a double biceps pose at the center of the garden reminded him of the maxim attributed to journalist Murray Kempton inscribed on the pedestal: "The true heroes are those who die for causes they cannot quite take seriously." One of the labyrinth voyagers took refuge on an outer bamboo bench and plucked a couple of tissues out of the armrest dispenser.

The celebrity continued to the end of the tunnel, looking out toward Ocean Boulevard and the curtain of royal palms which shielded the front of the compound from the street.

He presented himself and his briefcase for supervised scanner inspection, passed without issue and headed toward the elevator bay. Two of the four notoriously defective lift cars had been temporarily removed from service for unresponsiveness. The golden elevator doors opened, and the two men waiting boarded. "Hold it!" His footsteps clomped across the hard grey-tiled floor. "Hold it, please!"

The shorter blond man in the tan pants and matching suspenders turned to face forward. He offered a frozen stare. The celebrity wedged his briefcase between the closing doors and achieved a momentary stalemate. He felt pressure forcing the briefcase out of the elevator and found himself performing an isometric exercise to hold it stationary. The elevator doors finally reopened, and the celebrity shoved the blond man back with his briefcase. He withdrew it with the snap of his wrist, and it popped open, depositing its contents on the floor. He watched his blood orange roll into the lobby, and he angrily thumped the *Emergency Stop* button.

The bearded man in the powder blue suit strode out of the elevator to the stairs. The blond man pushed buttons on the elevator control panel as the celebrity scrambled to gather his possessions and reassemble them in his briefcase.

"Twelve," the celebrity announced blithely.

The blond man sneered. "You're Ollwogs, the jism-head who ruined our lunch. You spewed ugly all over the commissary and nearly got us shot."

The celebrity smiled complaisantly. "Sorry it degenerated into a mess hall."

The elevator doors closed loosely. "That's all the apology you have? You *are* sorry, but the trouble is you don't believe it yet. We're still calculating our personal damages for you."

The elevator started its ascent. "Lucky it wasn't a veritable St. Paddy's Day massacre, hmm?" The celebrity closed and reopened his briefcase as the elevator stopped on level six. "I trust security will employ the review of their recklessness as a learning moment."

The suspendered man stood with arms akimbo. "So now it's a positive thing?" The elevator doors opened but no one waited to board. "My God, they were firing lethal ammo over our heads! There are those who were so upset they may never return to work!"

The doors closed again and the elevator resumed its ascent. "I am grateful the only innocents harmed were a few buckets of rice fries."

The elevator stopped on level seven, and the blond man waved his finger. "We should be able to depend on a safe environment in which to take our meals without having your personal slime trail smeared all over them!"

The elevator doors opened. "Proprietary conversation!" The celebrity prevented a man from entering by extending an officious stiff-arm. "Think stairs first, or catch the next one!"

"Yes, sir." The man backed away from the elevator. The celebrity and the blond man exchanged unblinking glares as the doors closed.

The elevator resumed its ascent. "If I leave you too emotionally disturbed to eat, pamper-pot, you won't have to buy lunch today, and we'll be square, right?" The celebrity snapped a suspender.

"Are you threatening me?" The suspendered man brandished his Qilroy cam. "You *touch* me again and you'll be in so much trouble you'll never claw your way out!" He sneered as the elevator stopped at level eleven. "By summer's end, I'll have completed my final degree and be well-positioned to fill the vacancy as senior compliance analyst." The doors opened but nobody waited to board. "My first order of business will be to pull the plug on whatever illicit, worthless project you're part of!"

"Ah, credentials, the billboards on the mural of life." The celebrity held his briefcase as a shield against the security cam.

"You get enough of them, you got wallpaper." The blond man strode to beat the closing doors, and the celebrity gave him an extra shove but retained a handful of suspenders.

The doors closed. "*You jerk-wad!!*" the aspiring senior compliance analyst screeched from the other side. "*Open up!! I want your badge number, your direct-*" The elevator resumed its ascent. The suspenders stretched, a bump ensued, and the celebrity arrived at level twelve holding suspenders.

The doors opened, and two women prepared to board. The celebrity draped the suspenders over the shoulder of the closest one as he brushed past her. "Tell the deprived clog waiting on level eleven," he called over his shoulder, "threats are the tools of desperate people." He proceeded through two clusters of cubicles to the newly installed security checkpoint outside the door to the Subdirectorate of World Free Visions & Operations. He passed the checkpoint, entered the department and weaved through the honeycomb of cubicles to the top echelon offices at the northwest corner of the building. He opened the door of the anteroom and headed up the center aisle to the three-headed secretariat.

"Kite-surfing on a wakeboard led to my being positively keelhauled on two or three occasions." Assistant Deputy Director for Operations Leland Montoone stood before Radmilla Eisenstadt's desk describing the diplomatic junket that he and his family had taken to Cornwall on the southwestern tip of Great Britain. Raddy tittered with delight. "They call it getting 'tea-bagged' – quite appropriate for a predicament in jolly ol' England, what?"

"Such a drag." The celebrity attempted without success to capture Radmilla's attention.

"My wide body was sturdy enough!" Montoone transfixed Rad with the series of living photos he submitted to her terminal monitor. "That's my son Coy on his rail doing back rolls and tootsie rolls and monkeys." It was a curious chronicle for a man who looked like he hadn't been exposed to the sun for the better part of a decade.

"Excuse me, Monty," the celebrity applied the moniker that the urbane Montoone despised even more than "M" to pierce the polysaccharide cocoon of obliviousness he'd erected. "Rad, if you could make yourself marginally useful and announce me-"

"Urgent matter; gotta go." Montoone pivoted with eyes riveted to his Qilroy, and the celebrity nimbly skipped aside to avoid a collision. Monty's duties included serving as the Studio overseer of counterintelligence, an exalted position he'd risen to as "the great profiler" among strategic analysts.

"Greetings from the abyss." The celebrity advanced to Radmilla's desk, set his briefcase lightly on the floor and placed his hands heavily on her desktop. "Like to hear how I danced across Disko Bay, Greenland?"

"Just a moment." Rad put her head down and dedicated herself to another administrative task for three long, tense minutes. Finally, she raised her head, slid her rose-colored Jatakar glasses three centimeters down her needle nose and peered over them. "Name and nature of your business?"

The celebrity expanded his Qilroy screen and displayed his official ID beside his plastic lapel badge and clearance tag. "The name is Montoone, Leland Montoone. Wait, let me change that to Ahab Oobops." She squinted at the Qilroy display as if to discern his hidden agenda, and he discharged a silent groan. "Oobops, like Montoone, with three O's."

"Mr. Ledbetter is expecting you, Oobops?" She surveyed him through mannequin eyes. "Because we have no record of you."

He snickered with irritation. "Rad, you entomophilous bagatelle, as much as I like to surprise people with good news, you know I'm here by special invitation of D.C.I. P.T. Ledbetter to review the progress of our external operations and internal aberrations at nine o'clock high. Do the state the monumental favor of hot-buttoning me in to the Big Sir before the next return of the glaciers, will you?"

"Amber, shoot him!" Radmilla eyed her undersecretary as she pointed at the celebrity. "I want an independent record of his confabulatory offenses as backup for my own video!" The red light blinked as she enhanced her eyewear-frame cyclops cam. "You're here to be debriefed again, Oobops?" She expelled an exasperated breath and ostensibly sent the director a message.

The celebrity patted his cheeks, fluffed his hair and waved at Amber. "Put Natty Phil on speaker so we can all profit from the wisdom of his counsel."

Raddy scowled. "Mr. Ledbetter will not be put on exhibit. Sir?" She raised both pinkies. "Ahab Oobops says he has an appointment." She paused. "Hostile, creating an ugly atmosphere of intimidation in the office, generally out of order like he's ready to start hyperventilating, a degree or two short of toxic meltdown. He indicates it's important, but it's Oobops."

The celebrity tugged on the collar of his muted yellow plaid clash action suit. "Let's extend each other the respect that two people in designer wear deserve, Rad."

"According to our records, sir," Radmilla fussed, "Oobops has not completed three requisite training refresher courses: Environment Health & Safety; Emergency Preparedness; and Standard Code of Conduct." She paused. "May I remind you that without documentation that he's recently processed this information, our insurer could maintain it's not liable for his damages, even if he's technically just a contractor." She paused. "Yes, of course, Mr. Ledbetter." She paused. "I'd be glad to."

Radmilla removed her glasses to better emphasize her smug propriety. "Mr. Oobops, I hardly know where to begin. Mr. Ledbetter is currently with someone else; he wasn't even available for Mr. Montoone." She placed her palms beneath her chin and leaned forward. "Another appointment after that supersedes yours as well, so the D.C.I. has issued a retraining order against you requiring you to complete the three review courses I will be messaging you links for now." She pointed over his shoulder. "Access them on a visitor's terminal. Navigation should be self-explanatory. Average time to complete the triplet is ninety minutes, and you are advised to co-utilize the interval as a cooling off period." She returned her glasses to her face. "You will notify me when you've finished, so I can verify it, and then you are to-" She paused. "Patiently wait."

The celebrity smiled through his umbrage. "The next time you pop over to your chiropractor, Rad, please inquire about the attitude adjustment." He withdrew to a visitor's terminal, logged into the training center and booked the three courses.

Raddy received another call, and her cozy voice cut through his concentration before he could complete the introduction to his first lesson. Midway through Environment Health & Safety as she jawed about work challenges and riffed on health issues, he rose and proceeded back to her desk. "Well, I thought she had uterine fibroids," she informed her prattle partner. "She was supposed to have an embolization." He flapped his fingers, and she waved a hand in the universal shooing gesture. "Just a moment." She muted her Jatakar. "Oobops, this doesn't concern you unless you have ovaries, so I suggest you keep grinding."

The celebrity nodded. "I don't have ovaries, but I plan to order a full histogram." Rad fixed him with the mother of all glares. "My course bids that I not continue until I produce a drug-test specimen for my administrator. Will you initial a cup and trust me to go fill it?" She moaned so robustly that both undersecretaries cackled. He parted his lips amorously. "I can't help but feel, Raddy, you smoothbore, escharotic cotquean, that your receptivity toward me grows with the escalating intensity of your grimace."

"I'll call you back." Radmilla terminated her connection and hissed. "Oobops, *are* you ill? Perhaps you really ought to consult your doctor."

"And your tailor," Pazzionette offered. "You need a trendier suit."

"He should visit whichever one can do a better job of sewing his mouth shut," Amber reasoned.

The celebrity leveled a glare at Amber. "I'm going to consult my horoscope, Radish, and if it doesn't warn me to remain wary of redheads, I'll order the decapitation of the astrologer."

"You're color-blind along with everything else?" Amber continued recording him. "I'm a strawberry blonde."

"Mr. Oobops, calm down," Radmilla warned. "I'm fresh out of Dixie Cups. I will contact you at the end of my midmorning break from the employee lounge in the west wing of the commissary. You can meet me there and provide a urine sample in the restroom-"

"Oobops!" Pazzionette interrupted. "Payroll calling! They missed you at your desk, and they're trying to track you down."

"Payroll?" The celebrity anticipated a break in his employment status. "Send it here; I'll take it!" He activated his Qilroy receiver and authorized transfer protocol. "Hello? Hello, payroll? Hello? Hello, treasure-crat, purse-holder?" He eyed Pazzionette perplexedly. "There's no one here!"

Her eyes proclaimed him a clod. "I sent it." She returned to her previous assignment, muttering syllables heavy with hard consonants.

Radmilla smirked at the appearance of his ineptitude. "Your pay, such as it is, can and will be withheld until you have fulfilled your retraining order, Oobops, so you would be wise to conquer the coursework at your earliest opportunity." Her mien grew pouty. "However, Mr. Ledbetter has just notified me that he will see you immediately."

The celebrity retrieved his briefcase and marched to the ion curtain. Rad unlocked the blue double-doors and suppressed their electrification. "Have a generous review." The celebrity touched the handle, and the heavy doors opened. "You can't imagine how tempting it was to del-" Her thrust was sequestered from earshot by the hum of re-electrification and the hiss of closure. He optimistically ambled past the door to Montoone's office and the unmarked door and entered the door still embossed with *Director of California Intelligence Danforth O. Aldred.*

"Don't flatter yourself," Director P.T. Ledbetter squawked into his secure golden leadership finger-phone, "you wouldn't believe what I understand." Natty Phil sported a vandyke, and he flexed his bare toes on the desktop. "I may not be a fellow practitioner, but common sense assures me you'll be unable to purge your impotence until you unburden yourself of whatever unresolved issue you're carrying around inside you." He motioned with his ice pick for the celebrity to park himself in the visitor's wingback curule on the near side of the desk. Unique Agent Tess Tohnyin sat in the one on the far side. "Surely, the woman's frustration is understandable as a function of the ignominious burden of her husband's inadequacy." Tohnyin kept busy with her Qilroy. "Don't you really think a wife should know when her husband is impotent?" Ledbetter bared his teeth. "Curtly inform her you're equal partners in a lost proposition." He paused stoically. "There are scores of those drugs on the market. Try another. They're perfecting concoctions in our lab that could fix you up like a rhinoceros." He hiccuped. "Beguiling diseases snap their bitter jaws incessantly, devitalizing and diminishing all affected persons, but can you really afford to trade on your hard-won trust and risk her gilded respect?" He paused. "Very well, might I suggest that you immerse yourself in the culture and feature a beret – perhaps a black touring cap? I am urgently needed at the office, Doctor. Good luck to you." The D.C.I. terminated the connection.

"Fade in, Ahab, you've become privy to a pet personal project of mine." Ledbetter removed his feet from his desk. "I've systematically persuaded my psychiatrist that he finds his wife repugnant and with a surreptitious side order of biochemical reinforcement have rendered him essentially impotent." Tess gazed at the celebrity blankly. "I am on the threshold of convincing him to conceal his condition from her behind a veneer of pseudo-homosexuality."

The celebrity nodded. "I take it he's wangled his way onto your enemies list, P.L.?"

"In fact, the man amuses me." Ledbetter patted his hair. "He's a prop psychiatrist. My hour shoots by like a rocket." He bared his teeth. "And much as you two, he's at my constant disposal."

The celebrity eyed Tohnyin, and she looked away. "Did Tess recommend the beard, P.L.?" He coughed. "I like it. You ought to shake your fist and call for the head of Czar Nicholas."

The D.C.I. traced his temporal scar with the ice pick and scrutinized the celebrity. Tohnyin sighed. "Our charismatic cacafuego is slaying us with crisp, cleverly-crafted quips," she explained.

Ledbetter leapt to his feet and jammed the ice pick into the desktop. "Immutably." He ripped the faux vandyke from his face to reveal a partial week's growth of genuine chin whiskers. He rubbed his chin vigorously.

"It must be that Winterhalter." The celebrity clicked his tongue. "Everyone associated with him ends up tearing their hair out."

Natty Phil's irritated eyes settled on the celebrity. "While federal law leaves me no liberty to disclose the medical condition of your reagent, a reasonable person might extrapolate from the pleased twinkle in my eye that neither his injuries nor the major surgery necessitated by them should prove insuperable to his long-term prognosis."

"The official office rumor," Tess reported, "is that bioneers are morphing him a new spleen as we speak."

"Indeed, Radmilla intermittently finds her desk bugged." Ledbetter looked askance at Tohnyin. "I.B. is set to undergo an experimental procedure invented by a personal associate of mine. When it succeeds, young Winterhalter's name will be uttered with the same reverence as such other originals as John Stapp, Lewis Washkanski and William Kemmler."

"Immortals all." The celebrity smiled complaisantly. "I hope at least young Winterhalter's new spleen appreciates the way the crew laid it on the line for him once he was wounded. When can I expect confirmation that the itinerant Australian with us will receive the commendation I recommended?"

"Winterhalter confirmed that the shooting incident occurred, Ahab, because he confronted an armed combatant who was threatening you." The D.C.I. snatched his ice pick. "When you prepare your fustians, some of your best work seems to get left on the cutting room floor. If Tess hadn't enumerated the killing you made at the Las Vegas craps table, I'd never have reckoned its magnitude." He cleared his sinuses. "But let's not cast ourselves off Broadway. What of Shalom?"

The celebrity endured a brattoo pang. "As Tess has probably hinted, we've reconfigured the target's happy trail and expect to meet with him soon."

The director pressed his thumb and forefinger against his brow. "The analysts studying your fustians have made a net assessment. Since the sustainability of the planet hangs in the balance, you two orbiters are to be given only another week to resolve this imbroglio. If at the end of that period we still lack Mr. Shalom, another unique agent will take command of our effort to capture his heart, mind and adjunct vitals. Presumably, our recent FBI transfer Rondo Bracey will succeed you."

"My apologies." Tohnyin rose. "I routed calls from all points but the lab to messager." She accepted a Qilroy call and paced away from the desk. "Oh no, tell me anything but that!"

The celebrity rubbed his neck. "She must've been waiting for a G.I.A. analysis of her spy ring."

Ledbetter reseated himself. "The people in Human Resources couldn't be more impressed with Bracey. He held eye contact with them until even Josh Gillitzer blinked. What marvelous confidence. What cold superconductivity."

"I guess that settles who you'll be staking at the company poker social, P.L." The celebrity smiled complaisantly. "He sounds like another of your nephews. Our state motto should be: Our favorite word is 'favoritism.'"

The D.C.I. stood and plunged his ice pick into the desktop with enough force to warp it. "Perhaps at some point, Oobops, you'll refrain from raising the shrill cry of nepotism long enough to entertain the notion that families often cultivate precisely those traits which predispose them to excel in a particular vocational environment, with this formula for success passed down through nurture and nature from generation to generation." He stretched his collar. "As it happens, my daughter is currently working undercover for an enterprise similar to ours in the Virgin Islands."

The celebrity nodded. "She's posing as a virgin?"

"Ahab!" Tohnyin returned to the desk in time to deliver an open-hand admonishment to the celebrity's head. "That works for *you*, doesn't it?" She raised her eyebrows. "P.L., I have to run over to the wet lab. One of the tests they ran in the process of examining Shalom's People's Globe Lifetime Achievement Award may have damaged it. They want my input prior to the restoration." She turned toward the door. "I'll catch you guys sometime."

The celebrity sprang to his feet. "If you're finished with me, P.L., I'll escort her."

"You remain strapped in." Ledbetter pointed the bent ice pick at the celebrity and skewered the air with the dexterity of a fencing champion. "I have summoned Unit Bracey, so he can question at least one of you on matters material to the op."

Tess scurried out of the office, and the celebrity reseated himself. "Maybe they'll end up crafting the Albert a new spleen, hmm?"

An agonizing silence ensued. "As we await Rondo's arrival,

I am reminded that you and I have personal business to address." The D.C.I. bared his teeth. "How much consideration have you devoted to how you will conduct your defense before the reinstatement tribunal? How will you answer charges that you can't stay on point, that you freelance wildly and don't play well with others?"

The celebrity extended his hands apologetically. "Natty Phil, does *Danforth O. Aldred* remain emblazoned on your office door as a lingering element of the great name change deception?"

"Let's stop pulling punches." Ledbetter patted his hair. "Ahab, have you ever struck a woman?"

The celebrity coughed. "Of course not, P.L., she might strike me back." His guilty recollection of the understated transvestite at the Parallacts Associates board meeting popped into his head. "I've never knowingly hit a miss."

Ledbetter reseated himself. "Have you ever considered how a longitudinal section of the female reproductive organs bears a striking resemblance to the fork and handlebars of a sports motorcycle? This shape similarity may explain the subliminal attraction women have to these vehicles." He deposited his shoes and socks on his desktop. "When you recently reviled Radmilla, did you uncork some crusty locker-room poke at her gender?"

"Did I crack an eggshell?" The celebrity thrummed his abdominal muscles. "It's a hoot that the secretaries want to get down and litigious. Before Rad places me in the crosshairs of a workplace discomfort complaint, she should consider the dirty laundry list of office procedural violations I can compile-"

"Oh, don't do that, Oobops." Ledbetter cleared his sinuses. "I'm already up to my axillae in grievances and disciplinary actions. The company arbitrator is paid by the hour and has earned more this year than anyone else in the organization." He placed his bare feet on the desktop. "Your punishment for your careless disregard of bylaw boundaries is the exhaustive denial you'll be required to complete. Lucky for you, I didn't rise to my position without earning several master's points in the deployment of sophisticated weaponry like intimidation and bribery. So you leave it to me to summarily scare and buy off Radmilla." He gestured to his feet. "Now would you be so kind as to do the honors?"

"Natty Phil, I'd rather re-letter your door." The celebrity picked up the faux vandyke and placed it on the director's desk.

"Straighten this." The D.C.I. extended the bent ice pick. "Don't be emboldened by Tohnyin's effrontery." He pulled the object back as the celebrity reached for it. "Heavy-hackers who play hardball with me tend to get drilled."

Unique Agent Rondo Bracey entered humming. A tall, immaculately cultivated man with short, brown hair, perfect posture and a graduate degree in communication, he strode to the wingback curule Tess had vacated and seated himself. "Good morning, P.L." He nodded perfunctorily to the celebrity. "What couldn't wait for the completion of my conference call?"

"We need to borrow a stick of spirit gum." The celebrity smiled complaisantly.

"The issue at hand is the survival of the planet as we know it." Ledbetter steepled his fingers. "You've reviewed most of the Operation Shalom fustians, Rondo, and you're here so Ahab can present a collateral workplace challenge."

Bracey squinted at the bent ice pick in the director's hand. "Is Oobops responsible for damaging that property?" He possessed a deep, resonant command voice and the thick, fresh aroma of spice cologne.

The celebrity tapped his heart. "Rondo, how did you know that spice is my favorite fragrance?"

The D.C.I. removed his feet from the desktop and slipped the ice pick into a drawer. "The loser of the challenge not only gets to reunite my feet with my footwear but must also serve at the discretion of the other for the next seven days in the execution of the op." He bared his teeth. "Ready for it, Rondo? Disregarding leadership indiscretions that allowed personnel to fall into enemy hands and sustain life-threatening gunshot wounds, Ahab defies you to cite one gross misstep or egregious omission in the investigation that he has conducted to locate Charlton Shalom."

"That's too easy." The former FBI negotiations specialist tapped his Qilroy. "He's committed two tactical errors so basic I'm ashamed to admit I work for the same agency." He smirked authoritatively. "First, by making direct contact with son Tycho our prime social network link, and shortly before that link is scheduled to relocate to the search hot spot I might add, Oobops has ceded the element of surprise." He pinned the celebrity in his oppressive gaze. "Deception is used, warhorse, so we don't drive a fugitive deeper into hiding. And then by enlisting a paparazzi network as lookouts, he's assured us we'll be deluged with a plague of bogus Shalom sightings."

The celebrity stiffened his neck. "Additional eyeballs in convenient places are more likely-"

"Will you conduct a séance?" Bracey emitted a low growl. "For the past ten days, the production team of your expeditionary force has presumably scoured all of the shallow holes and level peaks of your search zone for Shalom and has returned with empty hands. So either he's hopelessly deceased or you're hopelessly inept. Which is it?"

The celebrity experienced a brattoo pain spike. "Seriously, sinkholer, how does it make more tactical sense to do a devious dance around a mark when one can approach him directly?"

"One of Charlton's carrion-craving kids most likely engineered his demise!" Bracey expelled an irked breath. "The old man was precisely the kind of kook who'd present himself as a climate change denier just to upset the scientific community, so you can imagine what kind of miserable excuse for a father he must've been."

"The rampant filial disconnect of the age is astounding." Ledbetter pressed his thumb and forefinger against his brow. "It would be a relief to ascertain that such a heinous act didn't occur within California borders."

"Here's the fundamental strategic flaw at the crux of the operation." Rondo rose. "Charlton the man has no value. His ability to read clouds, to estimate what sulfate concentrations to release into the stratosphere at what points, does. Even though it would seem that the only person Shalom ever really enjoyed talking to was himself, his climate model projections must exist somewhere. His harshest critics might be unwitting sources of this information."

"A proxy solution?" The celebrity winced mightily. "Come on, begonia-wit, your chimerical theory that Shalom is dead is just a hedge against failure. If you can't find him, then he's beyond finding."

Bracey folded his arms. "Oobops, you ought to be cut loose right now, and if this Bureau had any gumption- "

"Let's not get so ahead of ourselves that we can't stay out of our own way." The D.C.I. bared his teeth. "The complaints and excuses that populate Oobops's fustians wear my patience mosquito-net thin as well, Rondo, but I'm curious to see evidence of the progress he claims they've made. So I'm declaring him the winner of the challenge and extending his and Tohnyin's command of the operation another seven days. I'll expect you to serve him in an advisory capacity for that period."

The former FBI agent scoffed. "Recall me in seven days when the smog has lifted, P.L., and there's an active role for me." He headed to the door and pivoted after he opened it. "You could use a boob job, Oobops. That's all you're qualified for." He slammed the door behind him.

The celebrity turned to Ledbetter. "That petty coattail-surfing scolex can't just walk out on you, can he, Natty Phil?"

"I wouldn't respect any high-level officer who didn't." The director slipped his feet into his socks. "Bracey goes for the jugular even after his victim is dead." He put on his shoes. "I'll re-enlist his full participation later." He rose. "One final piece of unpleasant stage business remains, Ahab. I will now conduct you to your restricted-area work station so you can remove the personal belongings from your desk. You may surrender your credentials and weapons to me there, and I'll then take the opportunity to officially escort you off the Studio campus." He patted the celebrity on the lower back. "Take me to your cubicle."

The celebrity patted his briefcase rhythmically and followed the D.C.I. through the door. "You mentioned Josh Gillitzer before, P.L. I'd been struggling to recall his name. When he hired me, he speculated that my background in musical theater would translate to a heightened proficiency in handling the nuances of proxemics and oculesics." He smiled sheepishly. "I think I'll use this working hiatus to perform some remedial name retention exercises."

Ledbetter remotely suppressed electrification of the ion curtain from his Qilroy. "If you've absorbed your object lesson too well, Ahab, present it as a strength at your reinstatement hearing." He gestured that the celebrity should precede him. "It's easier to accept the necessity to neutralize if you can consider a personage slightly less than an individual." The celebrity pulled open the door and stepped into the anteroom. "Failure to grasp a proper name is a prime indicator that you've achieved precisely that."

The only secretary at her desk, Pazzionette signaled the director. "Mr. Ledbetter, Radmilla is ready for Oobops in the west wing lounge of the commissary to administer his drug screen."

"Impeccable timing." Ledbetter cleared his sinuses. "Message Rad to wait for Ahab there. I'll send him down as soon as we empty his desk. She can facilitate the procedure and from there conduct his official walk of shame and oversee his dismissal from the Prosecution Complex premises."

Natty Phil ushered the celebrity out of the executive suite and through the subdirectorate cubicle maze. "Optimally, Ahab, there's a place for you." Honoring the secure site designation of the trash receptacles, the D.C.I. confiscated a set of empty boxes from an unattended cubicle. He also snatched a loose CIB-issue shoehorn. "A time and a place for you." The crypto-crats continued their slow charge until they were a few steps from the celebrity's work station. The director smoothed his suit and detoured around the corner. The celebrity followed him to Tohnyin's cubicle.

Tess sighed heavily at the sight of her visitors. She rose and lifted an object out of the large, crumpled shopping bag on her desk. With some difficulty, the celebrity recognized Shalom's Albert. The crystal dome around the statuette's head appeared rough and cloudy. The torso had been stretched into a twisted greyish mass, and scorch marks punctuated the hips. Both legs exhibited cracks and one of the feet had been crushed. "The techie team thought it might hold hidden powers," she fumed, "and they went watch-grinder on it."

The celebrity dropped his briefcase. "It looks like a metal monster's Turkish taffy." He felt the damages. "P.L., this is the token of lifetime achievement we're set to hand over to Shalom."

Ledbetter patted his hair. "Perhaps when you clean out your desk, Oobops, you'll find suitable substitute swag to offer him. Check the remoter recesses of your bottom drawers for the packet of golden CIB golf tees presented to you last summer."

"We have the ultimate replacement prize package right here." The celebrity tickled his Qilroy. "What does any theoretical physicist with a penchant for Hollywood memorabilia really want?" He exhibited his sourcerer screen featuring scantily clad Hedy Lamarr in *White Cargo*. "A time machine." He held Tohnyin's head beside his Tondelayo image. "We take this kid down to wardrobe for a wig of wild curls and some bangles and scarves, and we leave the station traveling into the mists of yesteryear."

The D.C.I. compared the faces of Tohnyin and Lamarr. "A close friend of mine at the golf course is a cosmetic surgeon. The man can perform veritable magic with a sand wedge." He squinted. "He'll turn Tess's eyes blue, laser-plane the bridge of her nose and add a micron of fullness to her lips."

"Maybe it's time for Ahab to man up to the occasion." Tohnyin shook free of the celebrity's grasp. "He looked pretty appealing in his kilt, and I'm told the she-wolf who was such a pain in the ass at the floating nightclub in Wisconsin admired his chest."

"Unit Bracey suggested that his pecs need work." The director thumped the celebrity in the chest. "But you say a woman has wormed her way beneath Ahab's armor-plated skivvies?"

"His backside bears proof that he was receptive to her advances." Tess raised her eyebrows. "Of course, something about her wasn't aboveboard besides her fashionably morphed chin, cheekbones, fingers and tongue."

"Ah, woman, that beguiling font of mystery." A rapt glaze crept into Ledbetter's eyes, and his deportment grew debonair. "Ardent urges to scale the pinnacle of unencumbered desire dangled inexorably in the close space between them, sultry invisible currents there to be tasted and felt. She was at once unnerving and pacifying, the strength and hunger of a full-blooded woman and the disarming bright-eyed smile of a young girl. To cherish her, to love her, to merely behold her was to live. And as life pleaded to be defined within the bounds of the invigorating fervor which she inspired, not even unmitigated self-sacrifice could be considered too great a cost for the safeguard of his ecstasy." Tess pressed against Natty Phil as if to field a culminating kiss, but he merely took a deep breath and hiccuped. "My golf partner the doctor would take copious chin planings from Oobops and from them build an enormous snub nose." He stretched his collar. "Nobody of an opposing interest would expect this sort of revision. Ahab could walk among anyone virtually incognito." The director became nearly excited. "Oobops, will you submit to it?"

The celebrity rubbed his chin. "If Operation Shalom falls to Unit Bracey, let's delegate the honor of this opportunity to him."

"The computer lab indicates that they have a hazy lead on a dark link from Tycho to Charlton." Tohnyin rebagged the mangled Albert and deposited it on her visitor's chair. "But as my big sister would advise, let's secure our invite to the dance before we worry about what to wear."

"Start worrying about what you're going to wear to Carson City later today." Natty Phil cleared his sinuses. "You are to report to Bob Hope at 1600 hours, Tess. A delegation from the capital currently in L.A. is flying over on a fact-finding mission, and you're one of several local-area functionaries who will join them."

The celebrity smiled complaisantly. "Do they expect to find whether 20 black is actually a heavier number than 7 red?"

The D.C.I. pressed his thumb and forefinger against his brow. "Director of Nevada Intelligence Hawk Fleming wishes to vet you on what was ascertained in his backyard in the company of the Shalom contingent. I sent him your fustians but the secretaries redacted what they supposed was a strong steganographic component, and the manifold blank spaces pricked his suspicious mind."

Tess seated herself at her desk. "I'd expect a slightly less adversarial attitude than the one Nevada seems to have copped." She swept her hands through her hair. "They have practically the same stake in climate change that we do."

Natty Phil bared his teeth. "You're aware how suave and slick Fleming and the Nevada people are. Cocktails will undoubtedly be served." He traced his temporal scar with the shoehorn. "Remain mindful that the leverage of a beverage can deliver one to the dreadmill of indissoluble regret."

The celebrity nodded. "I believe it was the Greek philosopher Atrocites who called freely flowing alcohol a situation no less perilous than skydiving without a helmet."

Ledbetter gently prodded the celebrity with the shoehorn and followed him to his cubicle. The celebrity helped the D.C.I. negotiate the webs of red barrier tape that decorated his work station. He spotted a suspicious pair of tan suspenders hanging from his garment hook. He tossed the suspenders into the wastebasket and began transferring his possessions from his desk and cabinets to the boxes.

The director examined a double-barrel directed energy launcher. "Throughout the interminable ascent of human progress, Ahab, you can rest assured that not a single item of enduring value was ever achieved by an individual while laughing." He hiccuped. "Are you about finished, rampike-breath?"

The celebrity slid his ray gun to the D.C.I. and displayed his telescopic bear-claw back-scratcher with the camouflage handle. "Tess gave me this." He placed the item in the box and piled his artificial sensitive plant on top of it. "All right, Big Sir, every scrap I haven't gathered I ungrudgingly donate to the Studio." He collected his briefcase and boxes and waited outside the cubicle as Natty Phil sealed the surrendered articles and picked his way back through the barrier tape.

The celebrity followed Ledbetter through the cubicle honeycomb. He adjusted his load rounding a corner and lost two stress balls. "A little help, P.L.?" The director backtracked, retrieved the errant objects and replaced them in the top box. He let the celebrity precede him to the subdirectorate door.

"This is where we part company, Unique Agent Oobops." Ledbetter cleared his sinuses. "From here you are to consider Radmilla your duly endorsed personal custodian. Please accord her the twin courtesies of compliance and tolerance." He opened the door. "Keep compaction of your timeline a priority. Climate change is the greatest challenge ever faced by our civilization."

The celebrity proceeded to the elevator and headed down to level six. He found Radmilla in the employee lounge seated at a table adjacent to the men's room. "Finally," she huffed, rising to meet him at the lavatory door. He arranged his load on the carpet. She removed a lidded paper cup from her medical bag and handed it to him. "You'll find a packet containing a disposable antiseptic towelette inside. I just verified that the restroom is empty. You know the drill. Go to it." She planted her elbow against the wall and propped her head in her hand.

The celebrity strode into the men's room, headed to a urinal, sanitized himself and started filling the cup. "Oobollix." A voice over his shoulder induced him to lift his head in time to see a bright blue flash against a black background. Stunned, he felt himself drop and gag, unable to breathe. He choked and flailed his limbs against the sensation of drowning. He shed the water tank that had enveloped his head and launched a protracted coughing jag.

"Mr. Oobops," Radmilla's voice tooted, "what are you doing in there?" The celebrity struggled to regain his feet and collapsed. "Oobops, are you all right?" He elevated himself to all fours, crawled across the wet tile floor, shouldered open the door and contacted Rad's knees with his nose. "Ahab, what have you done to yourself?" She stepped back. "Where's your specimen?"

"Aowhh, did you catch the attacker?" He gasped and coughed. "Record his escape?"

"Attack?" She took another step back. "The water delivery boy was the only person to enter the restroom while you were inside, and he was only in there for a moment. I thought his hooded raincoat was odd and you might be trying to cheat. He attacked you?"

Pazzionette stood beside Rad holding a wooden bell and giggling. "Aren't you guys supposed to be ready at all times for anything?"

Radmilla sashayed into the men's room and returned with

a nearly empty water-cooler jug. The celebrity staggered to his feet and observed that one side of the item had been gashed open. "You're going to have to produce another specimen." She expelled a confounded breath. "You can try again at a later date when you complete your coursework."

The celebrity leaned against the wall over his boxes. He coughed and checked his image in the corner high-angle shoplifter's saucer of the lounge. His face appeared blanched and his disheveled hair resembled a hailstorm-damaged wheat field. His suit coat and crotch were saturated. He zipped up his fly. He crouched and employed the close close-up mirror app of his Qilroy to restore his scalp to order.

"How bizarre would that be if a man actually drowned inside a water jug?" Raddy wondered.

The celebrity inhaled deeply. "Are we good to achieve escape velocity?" He teetered as he lifted his boxes.

"Security can grab your crap and store it." Radmilla placed her medical bag atop his boxes. "Let's move on. I have a profound regard for the tradition of the disgraced former employee's walk of shame. Pazzionette will trail us ringing the wooden bell." She tapped her glasses. "If you can manage not to give us any trouble, I think I can guarantee that this video won't end up on any social media sites."

The celebrity grabbed his briefcase and started down the corridor with Radmilla at his right elbow and Pazzionette directly behind him. Pazzionette rang the bell over his head as the procession encountered passersby, but the spectacle elicited scant attention. Pazzionette burst into laughter. "The water boy beat the shit out of Oobops!"

The celebrity coughed. "Viva Big Sir's delightfully daffy distaff of frightfully fetching fizgigs."

Rad eyed him warily. "Mr. Oobops, I sincerely hope that you don't believe you're babbling for my benefit."

The celebrity winked. "Mrs. Eisenstadt, you rock. You have a gneiss head on your shoulders, and I understand your extraordinary effort to roll it over me." He rubbed his mouth. "I know that beneath that taut professional deportment and stiff androgynous attire beats the heart of a horny sponge." He wiggled his pinkie in a gesture of caress. "Won't you please indulge me in this charged moment by spreading your straps and exposing your zygomatics for me to admire in all their bulging fullness?"

"Is that supposed to be a joke?" Radmilla clutched her glasses with her left hand to enhance her pinprick cyclops cam.

"It's supposed to be a clue." He filliped his forefinger against her ample diamond ring and scoffed. "I didn't know they still made Cracker Jack."

Radmilla hissed through clenched teeth. "Mr. Oobops, you remind me of a camp I attended when I was a girl. I recall I rode a gimpy mule named Otis."

"From bridal to bridle." The celebrity coughed. "For your last anniversary, I'll bet your husband gave you a dried avocado pit and a fire extinguisher. If I were he, I'd give you a zirconium-studded brank."

"Develop some self-awareness, you walking bag of swamp gas," Pazzionette chimed in. "The other day you smelled like dead gulls. It's a wonder you don't set off air pollution index alarms all over the complex!"

The celebrity pivoted to eyeball Pazzionette and continued walking backward. "You jazzy, sassy snapdragon." He blew her a kiss. "I demand an accommodation for my behavioral disorder." He faced forward and straightened his posture. "I like to make fun of the secretaries, and I'm addicted to fun."

Radmilla brandished her diamond ring. "I won't worry if you think this is inadequate, Oobops. The Bureau has offered me a $350,000 settlement for the exposure I've suffered to your steady abuse, so you'll in effect end up buying me a bigger one."

Raddy's hard heels clomped distinctively as she conducted the celebrity down the south stairwell. "You will be issued visitor's tags and assigned a temporary work station when you return. I'll do my damnedest to see that you're placed by yourself on level ten. Your clearance will remain the same and you will serve on deferred status at the discretion of the D.C.I. until you are ultimately released or – ugh – reinstated." The strut of shame extended all the way to the corner spot in the fortified underground parking structure beneath the O Building. The celebrity climbed into his Duryea Statement and waved goodbye from Checkpoint Chico before he drove off the Prosecution Complex.

One hour and one minute later, he received a directive from Ledbetter: "Report to Bob Hope Airport at 1600 hours today. You are to escort Unique Agent Tohnyin to Nevada Intelligence Bureau headquarters in Carson City for interrogation."

Outbound. 1820 PST Monday 3 April.

"You overmining air-drawn dagger of a woman, this flashy iron glider is actually your personal property?" The celebrity couldn't conceal his shock that the flirtation silver Chrysler Empyreal jet hybrid volantor in which he was flying belonged to Unique Agent Tess Tohnyin. "You must've come into some good fortune, or–"

"Or vice versa?" Tohnyin raised her headphone-equipped aviator goggles to her hairline. "I confess an admirer favored me with it; I can barely afford the monthly maintenance."

"The donor isn't Jerry Mercowitz?" The celebrity scratched his head with polite naivete. "I know that guy in the sniper unit is always trying to take you out."

"Men give me presents in grotesque disproportion to their significance in my life." The party in the California state airplane had lifted off without the CIB crypto-crats, and Tess had volunteered the vehicle she'd brought to the Burbank airport as substitute transportation. "I refer you, as an example, to Tycho Shalom and his father's Albert."

"I sometimes imagine that your to-do list consists entirely of men's names." The compact hydrogen-powered high-performance Empyreal could only accommodate two close acquaintances with extreme bobsled-style cramming, and she reclined atop him in the universal seat that they shared.

"There's a couple of women, just for the variety." The auto-navigator posted a close-craft warning, and she manually adjusted the flight vector. "The purveyor of this Ianto is not someone you know, Ahab, and it's not someone whose identity you need to know, so you can stop poking for clues."

He clicked his tongue. "The sniper was Gunnar, wasn't he?"

A wan smile flickered across her lips. "The sniper was Magnus, and he dropped me several months ago."

The noise in the cockpit could barely compete with the heat. "I'll bet he still misses you." She wore white short shorts and a black bandeau bra that strained to contain her plump, heaving bust.

Tess rechecked the image of the celebrity and herself in the mirror. Her hair carried the scent of salvia and felt like velvet when it brushed against his face. Even as her weight on his lap grew unsettling and painful, he found a tonic in the form of her firm, slender limbs. She cleared her throat, and he realized that he was ogling her. In the mirror, he discerned soft, tranquil curls at the corners of her mouth. She possessed complete confidence in her ability to control any social situation, and the attention that he couldn't resist paying to such a voluptuous creature pleased her. "Ahab, we're dealing with extremely cramped quarters." She turned her head. "You're a trained professional, so keep it down back there!"

The celebrity interlocked his fingers behind his neck. Tess turned her head again and nearly caught a faceful of forearm. "What are you supposed to be?" She adjusted the position of the interior mirror. "Prisoner of Zenda?"

He smiled affirmatively. "In the wilting words of sundry superb actors before me, I don't know what to do with my hands." He dropped his arms to his sides so his hands rested lightly against the silky skin of her outer thighs.

"Just make sure I don't have to tell you what *not* to do with your hands." Tohnyin flipped her goggles back over her eyes. "No more gnarly personal questions either, okay, lewd dude?"

"Mnhh," he grumbled. "I wish you hadn't reported the amount I won at the craps table in Vegas. After we returned to our rooms, I couldn't sleep, and I snuck out again."

She nodded. "I heard your door open and close. At first I presumed you'd engaged Lisa."

"I ventured down the strip, played a little more and lost almost everything I'd previously won." He snickered with disgust. "P.L. apparently remains oblivious to my financial downturn. I trust no one here will make any quick, loud moves to draw his attention to it."

"You let his little lobe modification cloud your estimation of his managerial prowess," she charged.

"Your basic loyalty gene is admirable." He playfully lifted her goggles. "I suspect ol' Handsome Dan was only lobotomized after Radmilla misunderstood when the quantum computer directed her to phlebotomize him."

Tohnyin snapped her goggles back into place. "I believe his lobotomy was designed to be as much as anything else a vasectomy." The Empyreal rolled and climbed. "You shouldn't have made that crack about his daughter Heidi in the Islands. He's going to deduce that she's compromised."

He inadvertently slid his arms over her ribs. "What went askew with Magnus the sniper?"

She sighed. "We both got what we wanted and decided to call it a relationship."

"And you were looking for what?" His darting eyes collided with hers in the mirror. "A steady spine-jangling adrenaline surge?"

"That sounds like him." The afterburners in Tess's grimace tightened the celebrity's pipeline curl. "So are you and Raddy like liver and onions, or can you relate to what a pompous, tetchy, overentitled disfunctionary she is?" She turned her head to study him over her shoulder. "You're aware that Natty Phil is disturbed by the flat hierarchical structure of the Bureau and envisions a bold reorganization inaugurating two geographic Operations divisions under him both headed by women. The power struggle for one of the appointments could very well come down to me versus Rad." She raised an eyebrow. "If a Studio schism is brewing, you can trust the notion you'd be doing yourself a huge favor by supporting me."

"Anything for you, princess, if you could just slide down a bit." The throbbing pain in his neck superseded his brattoo discomfort. "I hope your promotion won't be merely titular."

Tohnyin lamented the Empyreal's "700-kilometer leash" and struggled to repress a mild bout of range anxiety. The celebrity spent the remainder of the journey embracing the power pop surf sounds of Gary GlassPacks Beltz in *Beltz Outa Tune* and *Do or Die Over*. After nearly two hours in the air, the craft landed on Highway 395 and proceeded without a hitch to Nevada Intelligence Bureau headquarters on Roop Avenue in Carson City. The complex appeared to be a converted high school campus flanked to the south by a gazebo-size guardhouse in the shape of a flashlight aimed into the ground.

Tohnyin rolled the volantor to a jerky stop in a dark, vacant recess of the ungated back lot. She unfastened the harness and climbed out of the craft. The celebrity unlocked the seat, reclaimed his luggage and joined Tess on the chilly blacktop. From beneath the cockpit, she extracted a long tray lined with lights and packed with enough insulation for a trip to Venus. She produced a company towel and wiped her damp body. "Can you tell that a woman designed this lanto?" She shivered and brandished a black knee-length cocktail dress with subtle gold beading. "Presented to me by a different gentleman admirer." She smiled archly. "A very different gentleman admirer in Wardrobe."

"Classic Oscar de la Rental?" He doffed his shiny green silk mesh performance tank top. He borrowed the towel and tossed it back to her.

"I have to admit I've been panting for another opportunity to wear this dress." She plucked a clear bag containing shoes and trinkets from the tray. "It's an original Max Yardley." She intensified the tray lights. "Walk, turn and give me good shield, Ahab."

"Did you promise Max you'd never disclose the location of the concealed zipper?" He ambled to a respectful distance and slipped back into his olive-stripe dress shirt and black blazer.

She smiled demurely. "Would you approve?" The open-shoulder dress revealed the navel as the epicenter of a tie-shaped exposure, and her pearl-and-diamond earrings matched her navel ring. Her twisted gold bracelet and anklet also matched, she wore a pearl necklace, and her platform stiletto-heel shoes glowed like onyx to complete the outfit.

He smoothed his wrinkles as he circled her. "I suspect you'll throw a rod and a cone here and there." He set his suitcase on the Empyreal seat and shut the hatch. She returned the tray to its in-flight position and locked the craft.

The celebrity and Tohnyin strode to the nearest door and rang for entry. Tess stood squarely in the eye of the surveillance camera. "California Intelligence Bureau here by fraternal order to see Principal Fleming," she announced. The buzzer rang and admitted them through the outer door.

The compact corral of an anteroom was paneled with mirrors and became flooded with intense light. "Please present your bona fides," a metallic voice requested. The visitors raised their lapel badges and Qilroys. Strobe lighting replaced the steady glare, another buzzer sounded and the inner door clicked.

The celebrity and Tohnyin staggered through the door. "Welcome, esteemed amigos after dark!" A stout man with a kind, roguish face raised his arm and extended his hand. He wore a large tag on his maroon T-shirt bearing the printed phrase *HELLO, MY NAME IS* with the word "Classified" scrawled beneath it. "I'm your inside man Ariel Adair, NIB Public Relations Director. Follow me to the Hawk's nest. Call me Bugsy."

Outfitted with visitor's tags, the celebrity and Tohnyin hustled up three flights of stairs behind Adair. "Hawk's anxious to meet you," Bugsy chirped. He led his guests a short distance down a hallway to a stark office and guided them across the room to a glass panel which overlooked what appeared to be a converted gymnasium. About a hundred roisterers infested the floor beneath streamers and balloons. "Our twentieth anniversary party, with an old-fashioned blood-drive motif, is under way in our Center of Excellence Hall. If all goes well, maybe we'll hop down there. We can always use some fresh blood."

Bugsy pointed to a tall African-American man in a tuxedo holding a microphone on a small stage. "That's Hawk on the dais." Behind him, a jumbo screen simultaneously transmitted his close-up. "He just presented Vladimir Mathis with the Distinguished Service Award, and now he's going to toast him." A man leaner and paler than Tohnyin after a polar retreat emerged from behind Fleming on the dais.

"He looks like he could use it." The celebrity pressed his nose against the glass. "What was his distinguished service?"

"It's classified." Adair activated a speaker and the din of the celebration enswathed the office. "Hawk will give you the lowdown."

After a short, irreverent presentation, the jazz stylings of Mankruel charged the air. Bugsy squelched the sound. "Hawk," he squawked into his Qilroy, "the cream of your California crop has arrived." He paused. "A cheeky twosome: a Tohnyin and a Oobops." He paused again and terminated the connection. "Follow me, please. We're to meet him in the wiggle room."

Adair ushered his visitors through what should've been a

closet door to a spacious adjacent room with elegant tan curtains and luxurious brown carpeting. The room contained two centrally located grey booths and a windowed control station in the corner. A few minutes later, Hawk Fleming emerged from behind the curtains wearing his lacy white shirt with baggy leopard-print lounge shorts and scuffed athletic shoes. "Good evening, I'm Edgaron Fleming, Director of Nevada Intelligence." He exhibited a gracious grin and proceeded to Tohnyin. "Agent Tess Tohnyin? Your reputation precedes you." He shook her hand. "You may call me Special Ed or Hawk." He rapidly turned to the celebrity and extended his hand. "So nice to see you."

"Ahab Oobops." The celebrity pumped Fleming's hand. "I appreciated your toast. It would seem that the highest calling to which government can aspire is indeed to fix damage previously wreaked by government."

Fleming snickered. "I'm pleased that we understand each other." He stretched and gestured to the booths as Adair headed to the control station in the corner. "I've got a few short, simple questions for you two about your previous visit to Nevada, and in particular your activities in Las Vegas. In the interest of attaining the most uncorrupted product, if you wouldn't mind, I'd like you to each take your position in a separate hospitality booth and remain there throughout the interview process. You'll be able to hear some of your partner's responses, but others may be distorted."

"Distorted?" The celebrity opened the nearer booth and examined the door construction of fiberglass lined with convoluted foam. "What if we do mind?"

A perfunctory smile flickered across Hawk's face. "Then your spymaster Ledbetter X. Aldred will receive at this inconvenient hour a most disagreeable call in which I castigate his underlings for being obnoxious, nong-assed good-for-nothings." He rolled his eyes. "The booth doors don't even lock."

"Surf's up, Ahab." Tohnyin strode to the far booth, opened the door and entered.

The celebrity emitted a heavy breath. "See you in Steamer Lane." He climbed into his booth and closed the door behind him. He seated himself in the rocking recliner, and the booth became bathed in brilliant light. A mic clicked to open position.

"What's going down, quislings?" Fleming's voice sounded. "You crumblers succumbed to our pomander poison gas yet? Don't worry, the end won't come until we boil you in sunflower oil."

"I'm searching for a pulse," Tess reported.

"Could you turn up the lights?" the celebrity requested.

Hawk chuckled. "We have to make sure you stay alert while we sweat you."

"Ahab," Adair's voice invaded the booth, "I'll need you to remove your blazer and roll up your sleeves. We ask that you both firmly press the bare skin of your forearms into the microbristles on the armrests of your recliners." The celebrity readily followed procedure but found Qilroy network access denied when he attempted to contact Tohnyin. "Thank you for allowing us to monitor your perts."

"Away then, let's get right to ripping you each a new one." Fleming cleared his sinuses. "What were you doing last Saturday on Nevada sand?"

The celebrity rocked slowly. "We came to execute a scorched earth policy and found the earth already scorched."

"You want to provide specifics?" Adair directed.

The celebrity began breathing rapidly. "We're here to burn your streets right down to the bedrock, to commit mayhem against your power grid, to inflict pollution carnage by releasing your stored carbon and spent nuclear fuel, to foment tensions that'll topple government institutions, and in between maybe catch a show, slip in some shopping and try our luck at a little gambling."

"Thanks for sharing, Ahab." Hawk emitted a querulous breath. "Don't expect any straight answers from us, either."

"You keep proving that you don't hold our organization in very high regard," Bugsy charged.

"Confidentially, gentlemen, Ahab and I are perplexed by the missing sense of community we've encountered here," Tohnyin remarked. "The environmental adversity wrought by climate change will impact you to about the same degree as it'll whack us in California."

"We appreciate the greenwash, Tess," Adair snipped. "You're extremely effective at your job, especially when your job is escorting everyone involved hopelessly off point."

The faint duet of a dental drill and a radial saw hummed over the audio system. "You've made direct contact with WIO in Wisconsin," Fleming verified. "You're aware, of course, that Wisconsin hosts one of only three universities in the U.S. with a nuclear reactor that has the capability to manufacture weapon-grade uranium. The FBI informs us that a party of interest has indicated a willingness to become a customer. You wouldn't know anything about that, would you?"

"Public universities are always claiming they need more funding." The voice belonged to Tohnyin but the speech cadence seemed alien.

"I honestly have no room in my garage for a nuclear weapon," the celebrity professed, "and even more honestly, I can't believe that CIB has any use for one, either."

"U.W. also possesses the only helium reactor this side of the moon," Fleming stated. "You'll recall that last year a scientist working with it was killed, and the cloud of sabotage lingers over it."

"California envy?" Tohnyin prospected. "Some of our analysts suggest that WIO sabotaged a friendly reactor in an effort to further stigmatize and emasculate alternative power, and to keep the coal and ethanol burning so the greenhouse gases keep accumulating."

"Our analysts suggest that extremists in California are set to radicalize the green movement," Fleming asserted, "to the point that it becomes delegitimized and exhausts its popular support." He hissed. "At the *People's Globe Science Awards*, were you looking to pick up a particular scientist?"

The celebrity waited for Tohnyin to reply but only heard the background whine of the drill and saw. "We were just playing through," he offered, "following the links, hoping the misunderstood son might unmisdirect us to the misguided father."

"We've been sitting on Tycho for some time," Hawk disclosed. "We're watching his residence, keeping a tail on him. But since he's now leaving us for Wisconsin, we load him with incentives to play the Lad, and who should stroll in and crash that bash but you, Oobops?"

"Great trench artists capture the same political contours," the celebrity submitted.

"Great bureaucrats tap the same public trough," Adair countered, "and they siphon off the efforts of other bureaucrats."

"You cleaned up remarkably well at the trough of the dice table, didn't you, Oobops?" Fleming's snarky tone carried a monitorial tumidity. "You hit the same prop bet three times in a row and walked away with a cool $350,000, hmm? Do you generally consider yourself a pretty lucky slug?"

The celebrity smacked his lips. "Like a deep taproot in a shallow mudslide."

"You repeatedly accuse us of being the poor neighbor," Hawk contended, "the weak operational unit on the project team. I'm going to lay open the classified venture that should prove how deep our commitment runs, but if I find it's somehow become declassified, you crapulent interventionists, I swear you'll find an endless bloom of medical waste contaminating the area around the Santa Monica Pier."

"Clouds open to show riches," Tess interjected. "I cried to dream again."

Fleming emitted a heavy breath. "Vlad, our chief resident tool-and-die maker, just won an award for engineering dice with an inner molecular structure that can be rearranged by radio control. As it turns out, the mass can be redistributed just enough to influence the result of a toss."

"Shaving is outmoded anyway." The celebrity felt his brat-too pain spike. "So now you're putting a magnum force of stick people through pit school, Special Ed, so they can introduce the enhanced dice at opportune times?"

"They've already been introduced," Fleming reported, "and you've shaken hands with them. The Gaming Commission pressured the Aladdins III casino to enter Vlad's 'kinetic kismetic' dice into a game, and management capitulated on the condition that we compensate the casino and any affected customers for all losses sustained while the ki-ki dice were in play."

"Once the Gaming Commission honored our behest," Adair advised, "Aladdins III agreed to collaborate on our project for reasons beyond gaming license peril. They didn't believe the technology would work. And to an extent, it didn't, because a shooter has to hold the dice for a few seconds to enable the transformation, and Shalom Jr. picks and tosses dice in practically one motion. But you, Ahab, roll them around in your palm before you throw, so you filled the bill as the perfect test pilot."

"Our idea," Hawk explained, "was to influence the game so Junior won big because people who win big tend to broadcast the fact big." He grunted. "Particularly to someone like a skeptic parent."

The celebrity rubbed his chin. "Such intricate operations have little chance for a positive outcome, but it was a worthy effort."

"Thank you, Oobops," Fleming snarled, "I'll consider it something next to a favor when you hand-deliver the NIB invoice to Ledbetter for the $350,000 that got redirected to you in the course of the enterprise. CIB might be disappointed that those discretionary dollars aren't really there, but they obviously can't be yours to keep."

"Are you wrestling Bugsy for that last special brownie, Special Ed?" The celebrity felt a grimace grip his face. "If you're serious, I'd surmise that significant impairment has already occurred."

"You can't honestly refuse to return your ill-gotten windfall." Fleming's tone turned decidedly officious. "You're getting off damned cheap. We're absorbing the $117,540 we had to reimburse the Lad for the winnings of the other players at your table, not to mention the $26,600 they sent Tycho to cover his losses even though the ki-ki dice only influenced his play adversely when he bet against you. We're only asking for the return of the ridiculous net that you personally took away through our interposition."

The celebrity felt his gnawing concern about Tohnyin's welfare intensify. "That's going to be a problem, Hawk, because I lost most of my winnings at several other neighborhood gaming spots. I'll provide you with a list. Recover it from them."

"Ahab, I'm already drained and I'm getting irritable," Fleming snapped. "That money wasn't yours to squander, so which coat pocket you can find it in now is an internal matter for you to settle with Ledbetter. The alternative is to refer the matter to a federal judge, in which case you'll likely end up paying the amount of the house's gross loss plus punitive damages."

The celebrity began rocking. "When an agent of legitimate government suggests that we retroactively nullify my good-faith wagering, I call that corrupt."

"You're in denial, Oobops," Adair charged. "Would you like me to review the record of your wagers and rolls? There'd have to be something seriously wrong with you not to have realized there were serious incongruities at play."

"I was denied fair play," the celebrity contended. "Don't you agree, Tess?"

"We have an old craps table in the evidence room," Hawk submitted. "I'll have it brought down, and if you can roll even three hard eights in a row, we'll withdraw our claim."

"The flow of the game is lost," the celebrity objected. "That point in time had its own singular momentum, which can't be recreated. And the game we're playing now is over, too! We want to withdraw, don't we, Tess?"

"Your booth babe is under a temporary gag order." Fleming snickered sardonically. "You'll be finished here when you record a statement in which you personally endorse the transfer of $350,000 from CIB to NIB to replace the money that you took from the table at our manipulation."

"You wouldn't be personally offended if every third word is 'duress'?" The celebrity rocked more vigorously.

"If you refuse to comply," Adair advised, "Ledbetter is to understand that CIB can expect below zero cooperation from NIB on all climate change projects."

"Ahab, endorse the transfer!" Tess's voice pleaded. "I feel a health problem emerging in here!"

"I demand that we be released from these cooking porta-cells immediately!" The celebrity induced swaying of his booth.

"You plonk-stompers aren't locked in your cages!" the director asserted. "You can take the coward's way out anytime you like."

"You made my bets; you sleep with them." The celebrity flipped the three available levers, which he expected to include the internal release mechanism, but the door remained closed. "Tess, can you escape?" The sound of packing tape ripping layered an irregular bass-line beneath the squeal of the drill and saw. "Tess, can you hear me?" He pounded on the door. "Hawk, the exit is jammed!" The background whine of the power tools reached the level of a low shriek. "Bugsy!" His brattoo pain seemed to run the length of his body. "Fleming!"

"Relax!" The response came from an indeterminate source.

The celebrity waited. The power tool noise ceased. He heard the mic close. The lights were extinguished. He sat expectantly in the dark for another two minutes. "Let's go, you liver-chewing buzzards!" He rocked his booth violently until he flipped it onto its back. He kicked the door but it resisted the blow. He kicked it harder and it flew open.

"What the hell are you doing in there, Ahab?" The female voice carried a vague familiarity.

The celebrity popped his head out of the open hatch and found an individual in a Guy Fawkes mask and magenta beret releasing Tohnyin from her booth. He grabbed his blazer and climbed out of his cell. "Tess, are you in one piece?" The control station in the corner appeared vacant.

The liberator wore a V-neck taxi dress that matched her beret. A huge prop syringe protruded from her buckram-padded shoulder. Isis Ingersoll removed her mask and swept her tongue over her teeth. "So nice to see your flabbergasted faces again. And now that you've reinforced our coalition, who knows how soon we might be working together." She smirked. "How do you love my darling little party outfit?"

"It's a head-turner." Tohnyin surveyed Ingersoll from beret to pink shoes. "I can see why it comes with a mask."

"If nothing else, Tess, I've always admired your bravado." Isis sailed her mask at the celebrity.

"I'm sorry, Ahab." Tohnyin exhibited a frazzled mien. "I recorded a personal statement to vouch for your debt. The Natty man can honor or disregard NIB's *beheist* as he sees fit." She brushed her hair back. "I just had to get out of the wringer."

"Your Tess-timonial won't be regarded as legit." The celebrity slipped back into his blazer.

"Bugsy delegated me to come up and personally escort you off the premises." Ingersoll smiled balefully. "Are you two hungry? There's a little food left downstairs."

"We caught a whiff of your onion dip on the way in." The

celebrity smacked his lips. "It smells like a wash rag that hasn't seen the laundry bag in yonks."

"I gather you own hordes of those." Isis adjusted her decolletage. "Eyes on my face, Ahab. As an irregular conflict attorney, I can't help but wonder whether that pipeline curl is an attempt to cover a self-inflicted head wound?" She resituated her beret. "It could affect your sense of smell."

"I need something to munch." Tess headed for the door to Fleming's outer office. "Just a roasted garlic appetizer would be fabulous."

"I'm sure we can sate a kefir-quaffer." Isis unlocked the door. "And maybe a little crushed ice along with that as part of a mescal smash?" She led the visitors through the director's unoccupied office and down the hallway.

"On Wisconsin." The celebrity descended the stairs beside Ingersoll. "Any particular reason besides to run us off your turf you'd point us to the dry hole of a water park?"

The attorney swept her tongue over her teeth. "To gauge the limit of your intel." She expanded her perky chest. "The fact that you went up there forthwith demonstrated you were lost and stalled. But the Hoot *is* a WIO hotbed with a well-deserved reputation for selling access to video surveillance that isn't supposed to exist."

Isis led the procession past some giddy partiers on the hall floor to the food bar. "You're all dolled up like some mogul's moll, Tess, and yet you appear so fresh and clean."

"Did you think you spied lint in her navel the other night, too?" The celebrity drew vexed looks from both women. "She's as fresh-scrubbed as her two previous missions," he attempted a smooth extrication, "and clean as a brand-new horn."

"Forever Ahab." Ingersoll pressed her tongue into her lower row of teeth. "Looking for laughs in all the wrong places."

Tohnyin played with her necklace. "You've apparently discovered that Ahab has a slight attitude problem with women."

"You don't mean to say he's beyond indelicate." Isis handed

plates and napkins to Tess and the celebrity. "Did some woman demolish you in a past love-life?" She adjusted his collar. "What you need is misery regression therapy. Let's round up the usual suspects: the mother, the first serious girlfriend, the former wife? Who tap-danced all over your fragile little psyche?"

"There is no ex-wife." Tohnyin worked her fingers up his neck. "There may never have been a serious girlfriend, and in fact, I have my doubts that he had a mother."

"What then?" Ingersoll grabbed another plate. "Was he raised by wolves?"

"Whenever our agency needs hazardous duty performed," Tess asserted, "Ahab ends up being volunteered." She surveyed the nearly empty tubs of catered fare. "So it's my supposition he was raised by guinea pigs."

"I thought contemporary psychology was fixated in the moment," the celebrity challenged Isis. "You should be concerned with bad biochemicals triggered by cold-blooded coworkers." He pinched Tess in the shoulder.

"Could I have misevaluated you?" The attorney scrutinized the celebrity. "Describe yourself in a single word."

He claimed a prized celery heart. "Complex."

Ingersoll exhibited a tight-lipped smile. "Maybe you have a small amygdala, which equates to a stunted sex drive. You should think brain morph."

"Lysistrata would have no hold on Ahab." Tohnyin plunged a chip into the onion dip. "But there's no influence to blame for the way he is. He's above all intentional."

"Maybe he has an understimulated orbital prefrontal cortex." Isis placed the heel of her palm against the celebrity's forehead as if to check for a fever. "Or maybe his body produces a low level of oxytocin so he doesn't get the euphoric rush than normal people feel during sexual activity."

The celebrity offered a wry grin. "As a psychologist, Solly, you must view sexual dysfunction as slightly more self-effacing than death." He crunched his celery.

Ingersoll pointed to the jumbo screen, which featured an image of Tohnyin toweling off beside the Empyreal in the parking lot. "Full frontier nudity!" an impassioned pleasure-stalker on the floor cheered the imagery.

"You diddlers both owe me a public viewing of the brat-toos I seared on your sore asses." Isis loaded the last scoop of cheesy garlic broccoli onto her plate. "But I'll waive that obligation, Tess, if you'll join battle with me again." She puckered her lips. "If you win, neither of you myrmidons will be required to peel off your panties. If I win, you are both bound to bend over, drop your ragtags, grab your ankles and wag your bobtail brattoos up on the dais so every grunt in the room can appreciate my flair for the dark ops." She pointed to a pitcher filled with pale yellow liquid surrounded by mugs. "We'll craft the contest to see who can consume the most mescal smash the quickest. In fact, I'll compete against you both. We'll jam gavage horns down our respective throats to preclude cheating."

"We'll play your flash mob in the parking lot." Tess grabbed a shrimp.

Isis pointed at the celebrity. "Let the imbecile decide for once." She seated herself on the edge of the table, brought a knee to her chin and straightened her black fishnet stocking. "Whether you're soundly defeated and you're a loser per se or you refuse to participate and you're a loser per quod, you're still a loser."

The celebrity smiled complaisantly. "In the interest of establishing a rapprochement between our quarreling agencies, kissing-cozen, why don't we just join you for one cool, refreshing farewell cocktail in a thoroughly non-competitive environment?" He puckered his lips. "Let's drink to an easy atmosphere of high-end détente."

"Don't be such boorish detainees." Ingersoll rose and squeezed the celebrity's biceps with a pitying expression. "Play to display your desecrated flesh, Pantagruel, or in a moment, we'll post the nude candids of you and Winterhalter twirling your batons in the lift car on the way up the hill at Hootenan-ny's." She turned back to Tohnyin. "You still demur? Liberate your spine, Fearless Tess, and slam down some mescal with authority; you'll never respect yourself if you just race back to your little cloud-blisterer and retreat over the border."

Tess bumped the celebrity. "He's convinced me we've over-shot our welcome."

"Your mind is made up, and it's that simple?" Isis employed the long cinnamon stick in the pitcher to stir the contents.

Tess clutched a carrot. "You should equip yourself with a little cloud-blisterer, Cissoid."

Ingersoll snatched a mug and filled it. "I'm a terrestrial girl who'd rather own the road than the sky. I drive a Mustang GT with a stick. I like the control." She took a swig of her cocktail and eyed Tohnyin. "I'll bet you can't even drive a stick."

"Do you start your car with a crank, too?" Tess comman-deered a mug. "Why don't you get yourself a weaving loom, you little warp beam? That might give you some control over your tacky clothes." She poured her drink.

Isis nearly drained her mug. "You're implying what you're almost wearing there isn't an impulse grab from the back rack of the Trash Corral?"

"Tess is considered a fine sports car of a case officer because of her superb handling," the celebrity attempted to keep the repartee light and civil.

Ingersoll hissed. "The producers, the techies – California men as a breed are the most lecherous wussies in the annals of biodiversity, and if California women had any strength or smarts, they'd have taken advantage and been running the state long ago." Her annoyed eyes flitted around Tohnyin and settled on the celebrity. "Exhibit A here is a freak."

"The fleet of fully equipped men who aren't obsessed with sex doesn't exist anywhere, I-bags." Tess thumped the celebrity on the back of the head. "Even he can't be cited as an exception. He's just an inhibitionist, and the subtle rumblings of an ultimate breakdown are discernible when placing him under high pressure."

"Thank you for corroborating my initial assessment." Isis pointed to her face. "Eyes up here, Ahab."

Tess rocked back with hands on hips. "If you're violated by his hard focus, why don't you do a better job of protecting your cover?"

"Honest, I feared your Freudian slip was showing." The celebrity grabbed a depleted snack platter. "Who needs an ostentatious butter cracker?"

Ingersoll smoothed wrinkles on the celebrity's blazer. "Why do you give me the distinct impression of a painfully diffident man devoting considerable effort to eluding a personal problem far deeper than a puerile fixation?"

"You were well-counseled to ditch the bench for the couch, Icicle." Tess sipped her smash. "Because you seem blessed with the natural ability to escalate incidental remarks into full-blown psychological profiles."

Isis finished the wings. "You'd have limitless potential if you pursued the more refined end of couchcraft, Tess." She smiled primly. "You have an intuition of the same caliber as the rest of your feminine attributes, and you have the face of an intelligent woman when you remain expressionless."

Tohnyin cocked an eyebrow. "Can you repay that last compliment in a slightly less encrypted manner?"

Ingersoll's smile grew broader. "When you converse, you have a tendency to curl your lip and squint as if in anticipation of being intellectually overwhelmed, which becomes more self-explanatory the better I know you." She turned to the celebrity. "She's doing it now, isn't she?"

Tess sneered. "It's so hard to impress a girl who worked her way through school eating fire and swallowing swords."

"Why are you women all so keen on teasing each other?" The celebrity stepped between Tohnyin and Ingersoll, placed a hand on the outer shoulder of each and turned them away from one another. "What could make an adolescent schoolgirl more popular than the advertised ability to swallow a sword, hmm?"

Isis crisply removed the celebrity's hand from her shoulder. "His lack of discipline is dangerous." She speared Tohnyin with her gaze. "You should be concerned that an enemy interest will dangle a woman under his nose and make dogmeat out of him. I suspect he *is* headed for an ultimate meltdown. On his way home from work one night, he'll probably assault a synchronized swim team, but that's beside the point."

Hoots radiated across the floor. The jumbo screen showed Jerry Mercowitz with a digitally scrambled face paddling a nearly naked Tess Tohnyin with a digitally scrambled pelvis. Tess discharged a mouthful of mescal and sustained a coughing jag.

Ingersoll visibly struggled to mitigate her glower. "How negligent of us not to post 'No Spitting' signage around the spread."

"Let's take the podium, pay what we owe and take off!" Tess abandoned her cocktail on the table and took the celebrity by the hand. She conducted him and Isis onto the dais.

"Attention, everyone!" Ingersoll grabbed the microphone. "I'd like to introduce two of our froward California neighbors from CIB." A smattering of boos reverberated through the hall. "Unique Agents Tess Tohnyin and Ahab Oobops! I believe they have a message for us."

Tohnyin leaned into the celebrity. "Loosen up, Ahab, and imagine yourself plunging into Half Moon Bay." She clamped her hands on his hips and turned him so they both faced away from the floor. She hiked up her skirt, bent over and dropped her panties. He winced mightily and followed her lead in brattoo baring. He was struck by a blast of jeers, a swarm of peanuts and a makeshift boomerang.

Ingersoll hopped between the exhibitors and gave each

a sharp spank. "That's my parting shot across the bow!" The celebrity caught a cake stand in the back as he straightened his posture and pulled up his pants. Isis hustled her charges down the dais steps and past a phalanx of fractious faces. Someone withdrew her prop syringe. "Slide out the side door," she directed. A close-up of the identical brattoo pair appeared on the jumbo screen. The trio scrambled through an emergency exit and down a flight of stairs to a deserted basement corridor. "You stumblebums couldn't let me set up the act?"

"Does Nevada appreciate how lucky it is to have California creating momentum for progress in climate action?" Tess asserted. "Or is appreciation such a scarce resource around here that you just don't mind letting us take up your heavy lifting even when it's for crisis abatement?"

Isis emitted a bitter sigh. "Your moral superiority is struck in the same vein as your hedonism. California culture, in all its precious dynamics, is an ode to 'what makes me feel good.'" She led the ground floor corridor march. "Your drastic environmentalism pays homage to your spiritual narrative and serves as an occasion to play the blame game. If it weren't for a core group of concerned atheists, *Sex Is god* would be your state motto and a flying phallus would be your state flag."

Tess's gait grew stiffer. "Decrying the manners, morals and sexual politics of California is some reach coming from a daughter of the play-for-pay capital of America."

"Prostitution in Nevada is statistically no more prevalent than anyplace else," Isis maintained, "just more honest and less complicated."

"More honest and less complicated?" Tess snickered. "As a lady lawyer, you ought to be doubly outraged. And doubly threatened."

"I don't threaten as easily as you, Tess." Isis shortened her steps. "*Tu vole comme une hirondelle sans tete.*"

Tohnyin cocked an eyebrow. "How frustrating that standard English isn't big enough to hold you, I-beam. Are you one of those stilted sublinguists who needs to make herself feel superior by lacing her speech with insider jargon and spiking it with terms borrowed from other languages?"

"It's called an education, you callipygian *clochard*." Ingersoll strode around the empty guard station to the main exit anteroom door and opened it. "What's the matter, Tess, don't you speak any other language besides Fresno?"

"Some women emphasize the mellow playfulness in their eyes by crossing their legs." The celebrity tugged Tohnyin through the inner exit. "But for Isis it's just the opposite." He offered Ingersoll a complaisant smile. "Good night, Irene, let's hope our two agencies can establish a more rarefied common-ground of coherent best practices-"

Ingersoll slammed the door shut. "Work on yourself, Ahab!" She waved through the Plexiglas. "When you think you've restored some semblance of your manhood, come back and I'll try to identify signs of it!"

The celebrity posed in a fighting stance. "I'll keep my guard up for you!" He followed Tohnyin through the outer door as strobe lighting commenced. "Your desire to negotiate an accord seemed to wither abruptly toward the exit of that interview."

Tess raised her eyebrows. "She kept evading my mondos, and I concluded that the intel she's holding isn't worth anything." The CIB crypto-crats fixed their focus on their Roop Avenue surroundings and started around the NIB edifice toward the parking lot. "I foresee her degenerating into one of those bizarre hoarder women who collects exotic children from around the world. 'Let's see, I adopted a Fijian last year, so now I'm ready for a sub-Saharan African, or maybe I could trade my Latino for a Laotian.'"

The celebrity expelled a relieved breath. "Did you suffer a touch of claustrophobia up in the tanning cell, Tess?"

"Considering the tuck position we assume in the lanto, I don't know how you could speculate I'm subject to such a raw weakness." She furrowed her brow. "I just had one bad moment."

He clicked his tongue. "There are a lot of those going around. I had one when I anticipated the need to leap into my rescue boots."

She elbowed him in the ribs. "Don't ever feel that you're obligated to protect me anywhere except from public scrutiny when I'm changing my spywear."

He rubbed his side. "I had another when I considered the possibility that her mescal smash might be a knockout punch."

Tohnyin increased her pace and checked her Qilroy. "Fleming sent us a parting message. It concludes: 'We look forward to a more proactive, reasoned and collaborative approach in surmounting the hurdles which borrow and blend to corporealize the global challenge of climate stabilization.'" She and the celebrity approached the Empyreal. "At least my smart-armor says they didn't try to tamper with the vehicle." She disarmed the alarm and opened the hatch.

He grabbed his suitcase and opened it. "Same passenger rules apply?" He unfastened the top buttons of his dress shirt.

She nodded. "You can lose your shirt if you're wearing something beneath it."

He patted a leg. "Yes, you see I'm wearing pants." He dangled his sweat-sopped mesh tank top.

"Threat of a clammy sensation against my back?" She contemplated the bedraggled undershirt. "I'll let you ride shirtless this one time." She tapped him on the forehead. "Just don't pick tonight to stop being a gentleman, chaplain." She withdrew the garment tray from beneath the cockpit. "Stand directly between me and that overbearing flashlight tower."

He shuffled diagonally and doffed his wrinkled blazer and shirt. "Let's see if we can melt their batteries." He waved both garments. "*Au revoir*, NIB, if only in your dreams!" She changed into a periwinkle halter and matching short shorts.

He packed his excess clothes and stowed his suitcase beneath the universal seat.

In short order, the Empyreal rolled back into the light Carson City traffic and headed several blocks to the Dragon-Fly Exchange, the only all-night hydrogen fuel station outside Clark County in Nevada. The celebrity and Tohnyin disembarked and linked the high-pressure pump to the tank. "You're not quite dressed for it," she observed, "so I'll go in and pick up some supper."

"Gas station pizza is the moist!" he raved.

"I suspect the differences between the food and fuel here are very nuanced," she agreed. "I think I'll try the self-fried eel drowned in wasabi sauce."

"Would you bring me some beet sludge and ginseng ale?" He smiled complaisantly. "That's what I've been eating for lunch, and I'm convinced it's nearly doubled my capacity to hold my breath."

"Practice shamanic breath work and you'll find some real staying power." Tohnyin proceeded to the dining counter and returned promptly with a Hunan cuisine sampler platter. The crypto-crats shared the exotic fare in the heated outdoor booth at the back of the lot. At the end of the meal, the celebrity demonstrated his ability to hold his breath. Tess prevented him from tumbling off the bench. "You nearly broke the four-minute mark!" she scoffed.

Refueled and recharged, the Empyreal pushed north another kilometer and lifted into a vector connecting to the Skyway 80 corridor, which curved southwest to Sacramento. "Our visibility keeps diminishing." Tohnyin wiped a corner of the windshield. "Ahab, is your heavy breathing deliberate?"

"I'm practicing mindful awareness." He worked his fingers lightly over the nape of her neck. "If you don't mind my saying so, it feels like all the tension that left with your drink has returned."

She swept her hair back and sighed. "I was affected in the

hospitality booth by an episode that occurred on our Wisconsin campaign."

He lent her a supportive shoulder slap. "It might benefit you professionally as well as personally if you reviewed details with someone from the Studio outside of the company shrinkworks."

"I doubt it." She raised her goggles. "The drug Dennis slipped into my drink apparently worked more effectively than the one I placed in his, because there's a time gap between conversing at the hotel bar in Madison to finding myself confined in WIO's den of iniquity."

"He held you there?" The celebrity strained to sound impassive.

Tess nodded. "I remember three attendants: besides Dennis, there was a brusque guy named Omar with a big head of thick, dark curls, and a woman who wore thongs with padded heels. She had a high, squeaky voice and went by the name Noragreta. At first glance, I thought she might be a preteen."

He felt a dull brattoo itch. "A connected intern, a junior ideologue, a political prodigy."

Tess shook her head. "I suspect she's been eligible to vote longer than you and me put together. And they literally did 'hold' me in their converted gym overlooking a climbing wall about seven meters high that had twisted nails and bent spike-tips protruding all the way down to the scuffed wooden floor below. Very hard wood, they assured me, despite the warming temperatures. Wisconsin jack pine."

"That's your first recollection of your captivity?"

"'Welcome to the Y,' Dennis greeted me when I regained enough of my senses to hold together a coherent state of being." She leaned left and eyed him over her right shoulder. "They were all firing off questions about the California program to counteract global warming, and I really don't recall how I answered, but whatever I said didn't improve my situation. 'You are encouraged,' Omar told me, 'to raise your tractability quotient.' He grabbed me by a leg, Dennis took the other one, and scraping the skin of my back and butt over the rough surface of the wall, they thrust me upside-down over the side and suspended me there in your basic Y-position for several minutes." She offered an indignant smile. "When they switched me back to a seated upright position, Noragreta poked her fingers into my belly and swept her hands over my legs. She asked me what I thought those rusty corkscrew pins would do to my 'mild baby skin' if I slid over them all the way down the wall."

The celebrity wiped the back of his hand over his mouth. "You mean they'd taken all-"

"Exactly, Ahab." Tess grimaced. "She had fuzzy caterpillar forearms, and I suggested as a matter of comfort if not aesthetics with the climate heating up that she nix the limb hair. They ran my fingers over the spikes at the top, which must've been real because they cut me." She scrutinized the nicks on her right hand. "They dangled me again, and this time they released me. I recall hitting spike shafts and the floor, but none of the impacts was as jarring as I expected. I lost consciousness again, and that must be when they switched me to V-R."

"WIO was allegedly the brainchild of their Senate Committee on Higher Education and Tourism." He patted her wrist. "How did this group get so militant?"

"Their medical plan must not cover rabies shots." She snapped her goggles back over her eyes. "When I came around again, I had an awful headache, I could only move my neck a little, and I couldn't move my arms or legs. I was on a floor mat, something wet collecting around my lips, and I was gazing at a black flag mounted on a wall – a black flag with a black X in the center surrounded by a white circle and a red circle."

"They couldn't really be fascist fanatics." His eyes met her goggles in the mirror. "It must be their official terrorist prop."

She paused to check the instrument cluster. "Omar was

standing over me in his open dark blue Hawaiian shirt. He said, 'Are you back with us, Tess? You seem to have suffered some spinal trauma and an extradural brain hemorrhage. I don't think your spinal cord is severed, so you can expect to regain arm and leg function eventually. But you should get prompt medical attention for your head injury, or that'll come to a bad end. The gouge on your face looks a little nasty, too.' He smiled affably. 'We didn't intend to enable such an unfortunate outcome, but we need to optimize your strategic value as an expedient resource. Once you fully describe your anti-climatic activities, we'll relay you without delay to an appropriate medical examiner.'" She caressed her cheek. "I kept channeling what they taught in the resistance-to-interrogation course at the Mission. I denied the predicament, but I grew, ah, almost-"

"Terrified?"

"I don't like that word. I don't get terrified."

"It's nothing to be ashamed of."

"I don't get ashamed, either. Remember?" She raised her goggles and flexed her fingers. "Omar peppered me with questions about the drivers of climate change and actions to combat them. He pinched my hands and feet with pliers, and all I felt was tingling. I noticed the blood dripping down my chin was blackish, and it appeared to be coming from my eyes and ears as well as my nose and mouth."

"That beats my rough day at the office." The celebrity attempted to couch his empathy in cordiality. "I wish I could fix you a Vin Mariani."

Tohnyin re-engaged her goggles. "When I regain my wits the next time, Omar's gone and Noragreta is hovering over me with Dennis hanging in the background. Full feeling has returned to my extremities, little blood seems to have been actually shed, and it becomes apparent that the entire previous ordeal, including my 'brain hemorrhage' was a V-R fabrication." She swept her hair back. "I ask them to return my clothes. Noragreta snaps, 'Are you claiming someone took them from you forcibly?' I admit, 'Dennis and I were playing a goofy adult game and somehow I lost track of them.' She and Dennis exchange scowls, and she turns back to me with a hiss. 'If they turn up, we'll see that you get them.' Dennis leaves, and Noragreta puts her head beside mine and caresses my shoulder like an assisted-living nurse. 'Look, Tess,' she confides, 'I don't think you're so rotten to the core as a little misguided. If you'd just spill what insignificant information you have, we'll be done with you and discharge you honorably. Otherwise, there's going to be a strong sentiment around here to deactivate and reinvent you, a process that you would not find pleasant.' She stands back up. 'You better cooperate before Omar returns. He can be determined to the point of ruthless. You'd never guess that in a past life he was a distinguished professor of law, would you?'"

"Those who cannot sue," the celebrity suggested, "teach."

Tohnyin shrugged. "Noragreta powered down a bit and engaged me in mundane conversation about contemporary culture, politics and my life in California, but then she suddenly speculated on how things would change if I were in fact crippled or my face got carved up so bad that no one recognized me. 'Friendships will disintegrate into guilt-ridden patronization,' she predicted. 'Respect will turn to pity, as people who don't care to be reminded of your affliction go on with their daily lives while your memory fades dimmer and dimmer.'" Tess drew a heavy breath. "Whatever she wanted she wasn't getting, because she just started ranting as if she's losing her mind right before my eyes. And I think, 'They're going to stash me in a nuthouse with this split banana as my suite mate.' Finally, she exhausts herself. She looks at me, looks around and points to the exit. 'Get out of here before I lose my temper! Go to hell! Go anywhere! Just go!' I gather myself, and I stagger to my feet unable to believe my good reversal of misfortune. I don't even think about my clothes. Like the lady said, I just go!" She emitted a chortle and paused. "I throw open the door and run smack into the carpet of chest and belly hair poking out of Omar's open aloha shirt. 'Where do you think you're going, tsarevna?' He holds me by the shoulders. '*I'm leaving!!*' I practically shriek into his face. 'She told me I could go!' I gesture toward Noragreta, who says, 'Dennis was going soft on her, and it's pretty obvious she doesn't have anything useful.' Omar snickers. 'She's not going anywhere.' He takes me by my arm and swings me back around. 'You underestimate our fair Tess.'"

She took a deep breath and checked the instrument cluster. "Omar says, 'Unless you start cooperating beyond your wildest expectations, Tess, you're going to be our restless, little honored guest here for a long, long time.' I appeal to Noragreta, who responds with a sneer. 'Whatever you make of her,' she tells Omar, 'clean up afterwards because I don't want to have to deal with it.' He says, 'Instruct Dennis that she's mine. I'll require some time alone with her.' Noragreta leaves in a huff, and Omar folds his thick arms against his expanded chest like a pair of pet pythons. 'Get down on your mat,' he directs me. 'I find myself short on options so I comply."

The celebrity patted Tohnyin's shoulders. "Even the best enemy combatants fall for the fake luau."

"So I'm sitting there clutching my knees, and I say, 'If you're in charge, could you please order my clothes returned to me?'" She shuddered. "He says, 'What's the matter, Tess, do you feel naked without your burka?' I say, 'If you won't demonstrate the decorum of a gentleman, won't you at least extend a little professional courtesy in the form of something like a goodwill blanket?' He grows furious. 'Aren't you comfortable with your body, Tess? That's not the back-story we get about you. Besides, it's hot in here and getting hotter.' I say, 'If I've gained a national reputation, then you should appreciate we're both American patriots of a sort.' He scoffs, 'I'm an American; you're an intruder. Did the hag inform you I'm a quarter Indian?' I said, 'The hag told me you're not even a nice guy for a lawyer.' That got a sardonic chuckle out of him. 'Lie flat on your back!' he commanded. No better idea occurred to me so I complied, trying to conceive of some way to turn these piacular cacodemons against each other. I said, 'Is she right, or, brother, could you spare a blanket?' His dark eyes grew darker, and he snarled, 'I'll trade you an Indian blanket for some firm, reliable intel.'"

The celebrity felt a brattoo twinge. "Considering the circumstances, the high muckamuck could've offered to toss in some beads."

"Let's keep our comic thrusts north of the belt." Tohnyin sighed. "Omar started pacing around me, strafing me with questions and accusations about our business, and I countered with some of my own. He plucked a stogy out of his pocket and jammed it into the corner of his mouth. 'Got a light, Tess?' He produced a wooden match and struck it against his boot. 'It's time for a fireside chat.' He lit his cigar, puffed heavily on it and flicked the burning match onto my lap. I whisked it off, and he forced a mean laugh. 'Brush fires,' he remarked. 'You people decide to throw a war, and you never figure there'll be any casualties on *your* side! How many of your California spaced invaders are here, and what are your objectives?' He continued pacing. 'You'd better think twice about occupying my land, Tess, when your land is as fragile and vulnerable as you are.'"

"'You harm the chusks right off of the corn.'" The celebrity took Tess's wrist and smacked his fist lightly into her open palm. "We'll work up a reprisal for Omar set to the music of *Maim*."

"'Unique Agent Tess Tohnyin,' he challenged, '*unique agent* signifying you're each supposed to be an army of one?'" Tess hissed. "'That's an interpretation I approve of,' I told him. 'Who are you here with?' he snapped. 'My tour guide,' I said, 'is a civilian from Illinois.' He groaned and said, 'How are you using Charlton Shalom? How are you going to try to manipulate weather patterns?' I shrugged, and he placed the heel of his boot on my forehead. 'Let's start a stream of consciousness, Unit Tess, to reveal what's really on your mind.' I can't let this exchange get any more physical before I resist, so I demand a bathroom break. He snickers and says, 'Pollute yourself, and the hag will rub your nose in it.' He shouts, 'N-Gret, come back in here! Let's instill in our Tess a better appreciation for fossil fuels!' I separated his foot from my forehead and sat up. I said, 'Don't touch me again, chief.' He laughed and said, 'You don't get to use that line too often, do you, overnight bag?' Noragreta returned wearing a greasy smock and toting a large, red bucket. She approached Omar and said, 'Dennis will take another turn with her.' He knocked some ashes onto my hip. 'How are you set for firewater humor, Tess?' And Noragreta doused me with the contents of the bucket. 'It's a chemical blend,' she advised, 'mostly gasoline and alcohol.' My chest and belly stung a little, breathing became tougher and my eyes burned terribly. I said, 'You brickbat, we wouldn't treat a bomb-throwing insurgent with such cruelty in California!' I wiped the inflammatory agents from my eyes and fixed my blurry glare on Omar. 'If you're really a law professor,' I told him, 'you're the one who should be sitting on his pampered ass in his ivory tower wringing his manicured hands outraged about precisely this sort of abuse!'"

"He's a disgrace to the Sue First Nation." Clasping her hand, the celebrity felt Tess's pulse racing. "You should've called him an urticating, atavistic Phaethon and called her a coeval crisis-enabling chulo."

Tohnyin freed her hand and responded to an air space alert. "Omar said, 'That's right, pail-face, *we're* the savages. Ask your unmentionable colleague Unique Agent Ajax Oobitts what he did to my operative Paige Eiffel over Islamabad. Just in case he claims it's classified, he drew caricatures of the Prophet Mohammed on her naked body and tossed her from an airplane over an open-air market and then tossed her parachute out after her. How's that for California moral high ground?'" She held her gaze on him in the mirror. "Care to comment, Mr. Oobitts?"

He winced mightily. "You know why Eiffel's called 'the White Death.' We have provocation off the charts for anything we'd do to her. But I promise the reason that her parachute left separately was because she tried to take me with her. Let's leave the rest of the prophet-sharing in Pakistan."

Tohnyin sighed. "Omar crushed his cigar in his hand and bounced it off my crotch. He said, 'You're finished as a spy, Tess. The only question is whether you're finished as a woman and a functional human being, too.' Dennis reappeared, and he conferred with Omar for several minutes. 'Are you desperate to leave, Tess?' Omar panted. 'Thank you for your time this evening. Dennis is going to take you up in our open aircraft so you can see up close that there's nothing wrong with the atmosphere. He's going to ask you basically the same core questions I've asked you, and if your stock answers aren't more satisfactory, we'll not only allow you to leave directly, we'll insist on it.' They walked me out to an unlit courtyard and fastened me to the back of their all-purpose winged chopper, where you spotted me when we caught up with you in flight." She twisted and eyed him over her shoulder. "I'd be more grateful for the rescue if it didn't appear you're indirectly responsible for WIO placing me in that position. I'd say we're about even." She slapped his knee. "I trust you can now appreciate why my confinement in the NIB tanning booth left me a trifle rattled."

The celebrity felt his brattoo pain spike. "I get the impression that during your interrogation you stubbornly resisted giving up Jerry Mercowitz by name, too. Do you have a line on exactly what flavor the Mercowitz connection to WIO is?"

Tess emitted a protracted breath. "I don't believe he's simpatico with the climate science deniers. Funny thing about

Jerry – you have kind of a nice feeling right after interacting with him, but as time passes, the memory turns a bit sour."

"That's the tell-tale residual effect, as he'd put it, of a genuine phony." The celebrity reinserted his earbuds. "He's probably still up; keep your firewalls stoked."

The celebrity and Tohnyin exchanged speculation about how much Studio incentive to locate Charlton Shalom hinged on the inability of the Q.C. to accept the prospect of a prominent individual successfully dropping off the grid. "Do you ever consider how much of the climate crisis is politically user-friendly?" he asked her. The Empyreal crossed into the Skyway 5 air vector, and the unique agents gradually turned their attention to their respective Qilroys.

"Isis Ingersoll sent me a Memorandum of Symbiosis," Tess broke an extended reticence as they approached Los Angeles, "in which she acknowledges the need to 'recharge the strained aquifer of alliance' and apologizes for being even surlier than we were. She hopes you never discount your special value to the team, and she suggests that at our next *pas de trois*, she and I each grab a nut and make a wish." She chuckled and tossed her head back, bumping the celebrity's eye. "I must admit I'm impressed by the passion you seem to have inspired in her."

The celebrity rubbed his eye. "You may inform Narciss we'll entertain no further bone of contention." He grinned through her groan, which seemed to linger until she dropped him and his suitcase at his car in the Burbank Airport parking lot. "Give my regards to Long Beach," he bid her safe passage home.

> *Kit and Caboodle were fused at the loin,*
> *The twin sons of two mothers who were them-*
> *selves conjoined.*
> *Kit and Caboodle time-shared a left hip;*
> *When Caboodle lurched upright, it sent Kit in a flip.*

Kit and Caboodle breathed three-legged dance;
When they entered a contest, no one else stood a chance.
Kit and Caboodle honed cosecant strut;
They could move in a groove that no others could cut.

The half-brothers clung to opposing perspective,
A complement laced with both praise and invective.
Kit, Caboodle snorted, you're clever for a moron.
Caboodle, Kit retorted, you're tough for a wimp.

Kit and Caboodle caught wind of a threat:
The El Nino Connection come to repay a debt.
Kit and Caboodle ex-Dandy-Dance Coach
Had developed a dream team with a scorched-
floor approach.

Kit and Caboodle trained till they were gassed;
They discounted the conquests which had fashioned
their past.
Kit and Caboodle butt heads for who leads;
What Caboodle called bold style drew Kit's insecure screeds.

The half-brothers pulled for control and dominion,
The greater good crushed by indulgent opinion.
Kit, Caboodle complained, you always take top billing.
Caboodle, Kit explained, you best stay on my wing.

8TH MOVEMENT

Inbound. 0615 CST Wednesday 5 April.

"The world is a wonderful place from a distance." The celebrity recalled his previous trek from Los Angeles to Chicago as he responded to Guy Noyce's homage to night flight and the concomitant light show below. The quantum computer had selected the model placing 110328A/404 in the Lake Geneva, Wisconsin vicinity as its most credible, citing catchwords in darknet dispatches to Tycho Shalom from a bistro on Wrigley Drive called Non-Pub as its leading indicator. The Studio had deposited Unique Agent Tess Tohnyin on a cargo plane bound for the Windy City the previous afternoon and assigned the celebrity to a commercial red-eye flight. Tohnyin had rented a van at O'Hare XX Airport and driven directly to Lake Geneva. The celebrity had cobbled an arrangement with the photo-opportunist for a lift. "I can't thank you enough for picking me up at this ungodly hour, Guy."

Noyce tipped his captain's hat. "As I related yesterday, I was just about to leave Whispering Willowwacks when you called." He guided the sun-emblemed Sparrow onto the I-90 expressway. "I'm becoming quite comfortable there. Madelyn got up with me this morning and made me breakfast."

The celebrity flashed an astringent smile. "You two are getting on pretty swimmingly."

Guy grunted sleepily. "Four straight days with your two

mad ladies. I carried them to Baraboo Saturday so we could visit I.B. at the hospital, and we made it a three-day affair about the Dells wolfing buckets of chicken and ice cream. I tucked them back in their old Batavia crib Monday night, and we passed most of yesterday playing Flopsy and Mopsy."

The celebrity leaned forward on the padded thwart. "The two ladies?" He wondered whether the owl man's full meadow of body hair had been extirpated.

"Madelyn and her 8-year-old daughter Madison." Noyce turned his head and narrowed his eyes. "We found a favorable familiarity in the tender clutches of Mishy at Hootenanny's. I'd fight off the advances of Winterhalter's top-heavy harridan each night and then we'd hop over to Baraboo to give our mate a loud wave each morning." He chuckled. "Madelyn asked me to apologize on her behalf for abusing you so spiritedly the last time you chatted her up. She'd been under stress and eating sugary foods, so naturally she was edgy."

"You're a true grenadier, Guy, a man of chivalry, honor and distinction." The celebrity smiled complaisantly. "I can appreciate that she'd be a redoubtable stimulus in the steamy spa air."

The photo-opportunist grimaced. "You do realize I'm no egg-beater?"

The celebrity nodded. "I don't know what that means."

"Rawytt, I'm staunchly gay!" Guy spun his hat sideways.

"Madelyn never even mentioned her child during my stay with them," the celebrity muttered. Noyce snickered. "I.B. mentioned you're to be awarded full caretaker responsibility for the two Mads." He graciously upgraded the music offering to "Mendacious Rider" by Five Clydes.

The Sparrow reached a vertiport, and the owl man lifted the volantor into the Flyway 12 northwest corridor. Lumpy cumulonimbus clouds hindering low-altitude personal aircraft travel filled the sky, and the craft rolled unsteadily through a patch of wind gusts. "A harbinger of the geopolitical turbulence I'll be facing in Wisconsin," the celebrity remarked.

"Before you consume yourself with that thaumaturgy," Guy submitted, "let's take the issue under consideration of how you might help rectify my vocational grievance."

"I'm aware that my agency is running up a bill." The celebrity sorted through disguises in his tactical bag. "I do appreciate these favors, and your net worth will reflect it."

The photo-opportunist rotated his hat so it sat atop his head properly. "I thought we agreed the price of a ticket for this junket is that you'll direct the project we've spoken of previously."

"Not against What's-Her-Name?" The celebrity groaned. "You don't want to waylay a girl, Guy, even if it's just long enough to publicly disgrace her." He patted his tender eye. "I'd be willing to lead you in an exercise of guided imagery by which you can sublimate your desire to exact revenge." He smiled archly. "How often are ideas best relegated to the realm of fantasy, where short-term impulses pay much better long-term dividends?"

Noyce hissed. "That won't cut it, kinky. In fact, I'll no longer settle for a junior prank where Giselle's jog-togs go missing. If clandestine ops are your special calling, Ahab, then heed your call to duty. In terms of personal validation, I'll furnish her and you finish her."

The celebrity leaned back and rubbed his neck. "You don't want her stoned but you'd like her pea-graveled."

The owl man slapped the heel of his palm against the side of his head. "The architecture of the undertaking should be up to the exacting standards of your agency business. Let's give it a working name. How about Operation Mockers?"

"How about *Fantasia in C Minor Opus 35*?" The celebrity emitted a heavy breath. "What kind of operating budget are you planning to put behind it? You're not proposing to fund such an ambitious rumble with the money you've earned as Madelyn's wagonmaster, are you, Guy?"

Noyce turned and sneered. "So now you'll try to shirk your commitment through some logistics waffle? If that's not just a convenient excuse for a numbat with nothing in the tank, prove it rawytt now with some schematics."

"Provide the capital backbone," the celebrity challenged, "and I'll stage Mockers with a virtuoso elegance. You'll get a weaponless, fastener-free extraction." He experienced a brattoo twinge. "We'll install some non-standard equipment on her vehicle: a master circuit rigging all the controls so they can be overridden remotely. You'll be given the magic transmitter, so she'll effectively be your passenger prisoner. Please hijack her responsibly."

"How useless an act would that be?" Guy adjusted the position of the Sparrow so it avoided a cloud. "She has drivers, an entourage. Even with stellar surveillance work to catch her in a reckless moment when she goes shopping or clubbing sans hangers-on, her luxury car is likely to be hardened against just such an incursion." He hissed. "Even if you're able to arrogate her auto, where would we send her? The initial expression on her face when she thinks her vehicle has gone bumptious might be delectable, but who'll see it? And a moment later, she'll just call for help."

The celebrity winced mightily. "We might place a con-cealed camera or two in the vehicle, and you can spotlight her with your favorite tracking drone, so Giselle's haywire hayride can be shared with the world. We'll also turn her car into a soft shell, so we can jam or edit any inbound or outbound electromagnetic transmissions. When she gets on her sourcerer and screams to her personal assistant that her car is possessed and has trapped her inside, we can stifle that communique and alter the reply to, 'You must've *misactivated* the auto-nav, you self-obsessed, little bimbo!'"

"That should sink her into the abyss of a new dark age,"

Noyce scoffed. "Oobops, you blowfly, you're just clueless on how to proceed, aren't you?"

"Giselle is driven to an abandoned warehouse," the celebrity persevered, "where she's greeted by a band of loyal joy-boys wearing dishtowels who inform her that she's been anointed as the martyr from Oz to carry the message of destruction to America. Even better, she learns that she will be a 'recyclable martyr' because this particular cell of feisty firebrands has devised an exploding corset able to direct the total force of the blast outward while the wearer remains unharmed. To demonstrate, she is taken to a window overlooking a test site, where an android in a bandicoot suit loaded with explosives is surrounded by melons. One of the shabby envoys employs his Jatakar to remotely detonate the explosives, and the melons are massacred, but the dummy sustains loss of an arm and part of a leg. The exhibition is reset, the bandicoot suit explosives are detonated again and the android is liquidated as thoroughly as the melons. In the charmed third performance, only the melons are mutilated, and Giselle receives congratulatory pats on the back from all of her anonymous boosters. '*Atta girl! Atta girl!*'"

Noyce cringed. "What's the common refrain that echoes from both the sidelines of a ping-pong match and the balcony of community theater?"

"'Crash boom bang!'?" The celebrity gestured that the photo-opportunist should return his attention to piloting the craft. "'Let some air out of it!'? 'Don't let your discouragement show!'?"

Guy shook his head. "Try: 'The play is taking too long to develop!'"

"Wait for the kicker, prickwinkle." The celebrity slapped Noyce's headrest. "Among the slaps of confidence our fair Giselle receives is a friendly needle poke that segues her into the hazy world of V-R. And the fade-in to her altered sensibility plows her smoke-spewing car into the midst of a ubiquitous

California Earth Day rally. As the angry mob of global good-will Jaycees surrounds the pollutant-belching vehicle, Giselle's prerecorded message of doom plays and her jacket explodes!" He emitted an evil chuckle. "For a spell, Giselle is left parked in the parallel V-R universe under the delusion that she's the narcotic-tonked vessel of terror who just wiped out a festive gathering of concerned citizens."

The photo-opportunist snorted disdainfully. "For all the support I've rendered, Oobops, you stick me with a naff scenario too expensive and convoluted to execute. Your grand theft auto device alone is too spiffy and iffy."

"We can rework that aspect with some old-school artisanship." The celebrity clung to the luggage pile as the volantor banked left and hard right. "We trick out an exact duplicate of Giselle's car except that it has built-in remote-control capability, and while she's shopping or clubbing, we collect her car, and we replace it on the spot with our duplicate."

Guy thrummed his hat. "Even if this operational vision worked to the perfection of your derangement, it'd only serve to make Giselle a more sympathetic figure to the great muddled masses."

The celebrity snarled at the back of the owl man's head. "You're supposed to be a Royal Air Force logistics whiz. If money is the remora, canvass your paparazzi brethren for crowdfunding. You're fighting *their* feud, aren't you?"

"It's not a *feud!*" Noyce huffed. "I want a completely different scenario, something rugged, an operation without the plisky-puller dynamic!"

The photo-opportunist repeatedly turned and glared. The soundbars filled the cabin with shrill, vulgar contemporary music. The celebrity emitted an exasperated breath. "You really want to ruin Giselle, Guy? Star her in your flash-bang project for summer laughingstock theater."

The volantor began a rapid descent. "I'm setting us down short," Noyce announced, "as you need an emergency head-clearing." The road gear thumped twice and caressed Highway 12. "I was going to suggest that you take a hike around the lake, especially since there's an easement that allows the public to stroll the entire encompassing shoreline." The craft stopped in the gref lane, and Guy opened the door. "But I've decided the highway might provide better inspiration."

The celebrity laughed incredulously. "You're putting me off on the highway?"

"Just like you've put me off." Noyce rubbed his brow. "Contact me, Ahab, when you devise a layout to fulfill your mandates."

The celebrity dropped his suitcase and briefcase to the gravel. "I turned a staunchly gay man morose." He climbed out of the craft clutching his tactical bag.

"Oobops, you're a squeak and a squirt masquerading as a roar and a gulp!" The Sparrow door closed, and Noyce saluted indecorously. The volantor pulled away and rumbled up the road.

The celebrity strode along the shoulder pleased to have escaped from the photo-opportunist without proposing an acceptable measure that would expose Giselle to further peril. Droplets of rain began pelting him, and he coifed his head with his mullet cap. He sent an alert to Tohnyin: "I'm stranded ten kilometers south of Lake Geneva alongside Highway 12." He attached his coordinates.

"Wow," she replied instantly, "you continue to achieve the unthinkable."

"If you come and get me," he croaked, "I'll explain how I come to be in this position."

"Of course I'll extract you." She smiled magnanimously. "But I just stepped out of the shower, and it'll be at least an hour." She wrapped a towel around her wet hair. "I got us adjoining cabins on the *Janesy*. There's a World of Magnets show onboard the ship this afternoon that Charlton supposedly won't be able to resist."

"Is the source of that intel," he probed, "the younger Shalom or the older Mercowitz?"

"We can expect to catch Jerry later at the Slop Chest," Tess confirmed. "I've also been in contact with I.B." She rubbed her eyes. "I called him at the hospital yesterday to inquire about his condition. I would've mentioned that was my intention, but I wasn't sure you'd approve." She chuckled. "I wouldn't make a very good spy if I didn't get an extra little thrill out of going behind people's backs, would I?"

"I've been in contact with Noyce, and he indicated that Winterhalter will likely be moved to Santa Monica early next week." A northerly breeze harassed him. "But for now, I'm waiting on you."

"I'm sure you're counting the minutes." She draped another towel over her bare shoulder. "Look for an ultra violet van. Keep dry and stay native." She terminated the connection.

The celebrity climbed over the fence bordering the highway and took refuge beneath the protuberant eaves of a utility shed. Consulting his Qilroy, he reviewed keyword associations that the quantum computer had selected to project that the Shalom inner circle maintained a southeastern Wisconsin hub. The threads of an anonymous darknet exchange originating at the Non-Pub cafe on Wrigley Drive featured: "Mako," "Lamarr," "mesonic temple," "Albert," "linear polarization," "Schwinger limit" and "Tess." The celebrity withdrew rations from his tactical bag and allowed himself twenty minutes to munch almonds and drink noble grape juice. He returned to the highway and scrambled through busy traffic to be in position on the southbound shoulder to receive Tohnyin.

Forty minutes later, he received another call from her: "Ahab, I'm at the Non-Pub bistro across the street from a shuttle boat dock. I just disembarked from the *Janesy*, and I espied an eldster entering here in a yellow safety vest with his arms spread like an 'A.' There's a strong biometric match.

I believe I am at this moment staring across the lounge at the back of the prized head of Charlton Shalom."

"That's the way to start the day." He noticed the attenuated condition of his Qilroy battery. "Stay on him, buckarina. If nothing else, my morning jog should put me up there in eighty minutes."

"See if you can raise Guy Noyce to give you a ride." She fluffed her hair. "Target is on the move, so I have to get to work." She terminated the connection.

The precipitation rate increased until it qualified as a downpour. The celebrity lugged his suitcase along Highway 12 with his briefcase tucked beneath one arm and his tactical bag clenched overhead. He reached the intersection of Highway 50 at the edge of the village of Lake Geneva and followed it another kilometer west. He recognized a sanctuary opportunity and entered the Lake Geneva Community Center & Library.

He removed his mullet cap and headed to the restroom. He found it locked, but a sign directed prospective users to *See Librarian For Key*. He proceeded to the Information Desk and requested the instrument of passage. "Another man just took it," the woman with a furrowed brow reported. "You can have it when he brings it back." Her frown became a glare, and he realized that he was dripping liberally on her desk. He benevolently stepped back. She puffed out her cheeks. "I thought they said 'partly cloudy' for today."

"I guess the forecast was only partly clear." He met her stoic comportment with an arch smile.

"Nature is a spoiler," she agreed. "Climate is what you expect and weather is what you get."

A middle-aged man in a tie-dyed shirt appeared at the Information Desk. "Yes, I'm back."

The celebrity extended his hand. "I'll take it."

"What?" The tie-dyed patron scowled and pointed to a pod of media terminals. "That guy keeps waving his arms now!" A bearded, dark-haired man in a black leather jacket continuously fluttered his hands beside his ears. "Disturbing me and everyone."

The librarian sighed. "I'm sorry, there really is no rule against waving one's arms. He's been instructed to keep quiet, and as far as I can tell, he's doing that."

"I'll take it outside with him!" the tie-dyed patron snapped. "I'll take it outside with you!"

The librarian rose and gestured to the celebrity. "This person can vouch for why that's not sensible. Wait here a moment." She marched to the troubled pod and accosted the man with the restless hands.

"Pod-buster." The celebrity smiled complaisantly.

"I'll take it outside with you, too!" the tie-dyed patron offered.

"Someone should remain undisturbed." The celebrity shook more moisture loose. "When I complained, she dunked my head in the toilet." He fluttered his hands beside his ears.

A diminutive elderly man in a yellow photoluminescent vest with a rich deposit of powdered sugar girding his lips stepped between them and set a card attached to a large brass ring on the desk. "Is that to the men's room?" the celebrity ventured. The man fluttered his hands beside his ears, nodded and ambled away.

The celebrity snatched the key but kept his eyes on the elderly man. He tapped the card on the desk and released it. He grabbed his luggage and followed the man to the door of the "Makerspace" at the rear of the building. A poster beside the door touted *ZEBRA MUSSEL SHELLS AVAILABLE FOR CRAFTS*. Stationing himself at the door, the elderly man turned and surveyed the celebrity. "Moving in?"

"Musseling in." The celebrity dropped his bags and pointed to the poster. "I'm actually waiting to be picked up."

"I'm afraid you're too massive for me." The elderly man fluttered his hands beside his ears.

The Information Desk librarian rushed at the celebrity. "Here you are." She flashed a tight-lipped smile. "Sir, did you understand?" She extended the card on the brass ring. "This *is* the key to the unisex restroom."

"Change of plan." He patted his damp ballroom jeans. "I decided to perform my Kegels, so I won't be urinating all day."

The librarian exhaled disgustedly and eyed the elderly man. "Mr. Chutz," she chirped, "you said you recovered your Dewar flask? You have everything you need for the cryogenic volcano?"

"That's about to be determined." He brushed back wisps of white hair.

The librarian returned to the front of the building. "Does the output of a scientist change as a function of being observed?" the celebrity challenged. The elderly man grimaced, but the expression melted into an engaging grin. The celebrity stepped forward and extended his hand. "Dr. Shal-" A tall woman in a trench coat with a blonde pixie shag haircut brushed past him and grabbed Charlton.

"I'm sorry, Chutz, I forgot and went to Non-Pub." The blonde kissed Shalom on the forehead.

"I stopped off there myself." Charlton clasped both of the blonde's hands. "An aggressive, thuggish woman recognized me and chased me out of the place."

"Ah, Professor Shalom, it's a profound honor." The celebrity backpedaled so he could extend his hand again. "Sorry to interrupt, but I feel as if I've searched every curve of space for you." The elderly man exhibited an irritated glare. His hand still extended, the celebrity abashedly turned to the blonde. "Say, where do I know you from?"

Shalom rolled his eyes. "Have mercy on us all, professor of ignorance."

"Oh, hello, Mr. Oosblop?" The woman nodded to the celebrity. "The rented tux couldn't save your presentation?" Tiffany the Parallacts masseuse had cut her hair short. "This man covered my ass at the office, Chutz." She twisted herself into a sweetheart dance position. "Show him a little love."

Shalom reluctantly released the masseuse and shook hands with the celebrity. "You are become Death, destroyer of worlds, you state-sponsored monitor lizard."

"You've been expecting me?" The celebrity wiped his mouth. "Well, I bring good vibrations. Respectfully, sir, the name is Ahab Oobops of the California diplomatic corps working relationship committee."

"Ahab Oobops." Shalom rolled the syllables off his tongue. "Isn't that a species of bird?" He stroked the arm of his preferred blonde companion. "Tiny bird noted for its distinctively harsh racket."

"My colleague Tess and I met your son Tycho following the *People's Globe*s in Las Vegas." The celebrity produced Tohnyin's photo on his Qilroy. "She has something for you."

"It's a warbling, persistent song." The gravitron theorist strongman twitched in rumination.

Tiffany admired the Qilroy image. "I rubbed Tess in at Parallacts." She patted her hair. "Her pro look inspired me to go short."

The celebrity aimed his sourcerer screen at Shalom. "Doesn't she remind you of Hedy Lamarr?"

"Hedy Lamarr?" Shalom snorted. "Aren't you referring to Mata Hari?" He tilted his head. "She looks like the lady of the lake who came after me at the creamery."

The celebrity smiled tartly. "Hedy Lamarr was one of the inventors of spread spectrum sonar, an acclaimed actress and all-around twentieth century fox."

"Of course!" The three-peat Nobel laureate slapped himself in the forehead. "I'm something less than bothered with proper names."

"Tess is something less than bothered with proper manners." The celebrity patted Shalom on the shoulder. "I'll control her, but we need to gain some insight on what designs you have up your sleeve in the test environment for climate influence. The world throbs with unreasonable people who believe you're dangerous."

"And you'd be one of those?" Charlton felt the material of the celebrity's blazer collar and hooked an affable arm around his neck. "I'm sweet 76, Nathan, and an atmospheric scientist in only the most vestigial sense. I'm now mainly interested in cellular hygiene and evolutionary biology, so my *meshugener* son shouldn't look like such a *shmegigi*. Why won't he simply learn to breed vector-proof mosquitoes? I no longer publish or pass secrets, and I'm no threat to anyone."

"Professor Shalom, Tycho must've told you that Tess is holding your Lifetime Achievement Award." The celebrity experienced a brattoo pain spike. "You'd strengthen the positions of all parties involved and purchase a prodigious amount of political capital if you'd hear our propaganda."

"Put yourself in my place, Napalm." The elderly trainer of extraordinary particles gestured to the masseuse. "I'm looking for no interruption, so I can show this woman an eruption."

"Give us some time," Tiffany advised the celebrity. "Be at the water's edge on Riviera Beach with Tess this afternoon, and we'll get together for a little face-off. I'd like to show her my haircut and have a heartfelt talk about trench coats."

Shalom shrugged with affectionate annoyance. "I'll consent to a weak interaction."

The celebrity smiled complaisantly. "I can wait on the other side of the library."

"I'm too old for a babysitter and too young for a pallbearer." Shalom shook the celebrity's hand again. "Demonstrate that you can respect our privacy, Ned, and vacate the fallout area. The only thing I hate worse than a leader is a follower. If we see you or your grainiest surveillance detail before our appointed summit, I'll have nothing more whatsoever to do with you."

Tiffany flashed four fingers. "Private beach party for

four only." She followed Charlton into the Makerspace and slammed the door behind her.

The celebrity collected his bags and strutted out the front door of the library. Delighted to discover that the rain had abated, he strolled east to Wrigley Drive and stopped inside the Non-Pub cafe. He ordered a hazelnut frappe and took advantage of the free gadget supercharge. At eleven, he sent Tohnyin a message: "Lose something?"

Twenty minutes later, Tess's troubled face framed by a purple poplin rainhat appeared on the celebrity's Qilroy screen. "How did you guess?" she uttered. "Gnarly Charlie gave me the slip. He *must've* come aboard the ship. That's where I am now. If nothing else, I hope to reconnect with him at the World of Magnets."

"Maybe I can help you out, kid." The celebrity flashed a sly smile. "Because I have our mutual friend at the Lake Geneva Library. He's bent on demonstrating some volcano model. He's with Tiffany the handmaid, and if she isn't wired with WIO, she's all Anti-Alyce."

"You have him?" Tess exclaimed. "You have him restrained? Are you quite positive, Ahab, because this setup carries all the earmarks of a WIO ruse! They might be concerned we're getting painfully close to the primo domino." She sighed. "You've vetted him? Does he need to be flipped? Let your Shalom talk to me now."

The celebrity rubbed his sore eye. "They requested some breathing room and pledged to rendezvous with the two of us at the water's edge of Riviera Beach."

"You relinquished visual contact without tagging him?" She pulled her rainhat over her eyes. "What's the point of the shoreline venue? Was that your suggestion?"

"It's my impression they're concerned we might marshal forces, and they want to retain the marine escape option." He clicked his tongue. "I'd advise you to locate yourself on Riviera Beach-"

"You should be concerned *they* might marshal forces." She readjusted her hat. "What time is this powwow tentatively scheduled for?"

"Time is a tangled construct for Shalom. I was pleased to get a rough six-hour window."

She expelled an aggravated breath. "I'd advise you to go cagily stalking after them. Take charge, charm-buckle, and enlist locals as correspondents, if necessary." She looked off-camera. "If you haven't fallen for a fraud, he and Tiffany are apt to show up here. The matinee symposium starts at two, and I'm not going to evacuate my post. Better luck to us both." She terminated the connection.

The celebrity carried his luggage out of Non-Pub and started back through the drizzle toward the Riviera Pier. He headed out over the sparsely populated beach and gazed at the energized waves. He slapped moisture out of his mullet cap and traded his warm-up pullover and blazer for a dry sweatshirt.

The wind and rain intensity increased. A woman with a note of familiarity emerged on the shoreline carrying a white umbrella and smoking a cigarette. As she approached, he recognized the Information Desk librarian. "Info pro!" He tipped his mullet cap, drawing a perfunctory nod.

"I appreciate the extra effort with the key." He shambled alongside her. "But you could really do me and yourself a huge favor. The library has a slush fund, doesn't it?"

She eyed him circumspectly. "We have a rainy-day fund."

"How appropriate." He flashed his most enticing grin. "How would you like to convert some basic information into a thousand-dollar bump for your rainy-day account? All I ask is that you search the library building and advise me on the whereabouts of Chutz the vulcaneer." She furrowed her brow. "He should be leaning on a tubular blonde and easy to identify."

"Snooping is not information." She took a drag on her cigarette.

He imbued his countenance with more confidence. "How about if I sweeten the endowment with an additional thousand-dollar supplement payable to you personally?"

"Do I really need to call the police?" She pivoted and headed back toward the library.

"Will you reconsider if I slay you with a cute library joke?" he shouted after her. "How do you tell the staff at a public library from the street vagrants therein? The vagrants don't go on break!" She cast a beleaguered glance over her shoulder and kept walking. "I'll take your silence as a refusal, Mum, as well as a proclivity."

The celebrity stood at the shoreline in the pounding rain with his arms folded. Occasionally, he sang surf songs. Each time the *Janesy* cut through the mist and passed Riviera Beach, he sent Tohnyin a message: "Abandon ship!" He considered the interpretation that Tiffany had designated four as the appointed hour of the face-off. He was certain that Tess would've notified him if she'd found Shalom among the flux lines. The four o'clock hour passed. The precipitation diminished and ceased.

At 1650 hours, a black speedboat containing two figures in dark, hooded ponchos cruised toward the beach. The pilot cut the motor, stood and waved. "Ahoy, Mr. Oobops, is that you?" Tiffany tossed back her midnight blue headgear. "I'm so glad you didn't abandon us for the heavy elements!" She pitched her coil.

The celebrity waded into the chop and grabbed the line. "It was a torrential drizzle." He towed the craft ashore and helped the masseuse transition to land. "How did the volcano pan out?"

"It was so sweet," Tiffany cooed. "Chutz built an ice volcano that ejected a cryoclast of frost flowers."

"We're missing Delilah?" Shalom fussed.

The celebrity extended his hand to the hardscrabble world-class astrophysicist. "She was left with the impression that you'd be drawn to a show of magnetism onboard the clipper." He deposited Charlton on the beach and purged himself of a little moisture. "I expect your absence there to result in her presence here."

Shalom stiffly extended his arms away from his sides. "To what else did my whimsical space probe of a son alert you?"

The celebrity fluffed his waterlogged ballroom jeans. "He hailed you as quite the aficionado of mid-20th century mediocre cinema."

Charlton nodded petulantly. "You're probably aware that my first wife is an educator and an author. To think I knew her when she was nothing but a teacher and a writer. Her favorite form of torture was forcing me to watch chick flicks." He cringed. "European chick flicks."

"It's my understanding, Professor Shalom, that when your atmospheric theories ran afoul of your contemporaries', you were shut down while their specialist verified that you suffered from exhaustion." The celebrity watched Tiffany kick off her sandals and dig her toes into the wet sand. "At the insistence of the convalescent center staff, you were immersed in Second-World-War-era escapist fare so you could better appreciate how people removed from the actual theater of conflict removed themselves even further."

"*You're* quite the theorist, Nathan." Shalom slapped the celebrity on the shoulder. "In the end, the specialist conceded that it was not I but he who suffered from exhaustion! In order to preserve some humanity through the course of my asylumization, I acquainted myself with certain classic feature films and their standard-bearers, such major talents as Bogart, Garbo and Elizabeth Hepburn."

"Come sit by me, Chutz!" Tiffany shed her poncho and spread it beneath her. "Let's plan a sailing adventure."

The celebrity smiled intently as two gulls flew overhead. "If this seems like the point in a French film where you'd walk in, put your arm around the clinging girlfriend and tell your life story to a complete stranger, Doctor, please feel free to relate. I got the sense earlier at the Makerspace that I interrupted your climb of spiritual self-discovery, and in my capacity as company chaplain, that's the last thing I want to suppress."

"Chaplain." The eminent titan of the magnetosphere fixed the celebrity with a gaze at once contrite and astringent. "I don't think I believe in God, but I really like church."

The celebrity nodded. "I don't believe in exercise, but I really like the pain."

Shalom snorted and shook convulsively. "I quote my first wife there, Ned. She's a non-practicing atheist." He led the celebrity to a spot beside Tiffany, took her hand and seated himself.

"That's Jeanine," the celebrity verified. "Or Jenny? No, Janet, Janice. Not Tycho's mom."

"Heather mother of my children was a nice, pudgy Catholic girl of prime breeding stock," the annihilator of supersymmetric properties acknowledged, "fabulous with kids. She was fabulous because she talked to everyone, not least of whom me, like she was telling a 6-year-old a bedtime story. She arranged for my grant to post-doc at a private retreat under the sun here in Wisconsin, where they take a serious interest in cultivating a high-yield funny farm."

"So you feel a syrupy sentimental connection to the state of Wisconsin?" the celebrity gathered. "Aside from the fact that they just gave your son a job?"

"You're questioning why I reside in Lake Geneva?" Charlton sneered. "Walking the hallowed ground that was once Yerkes Observatory allows me to connect to my first telescope."

"My former fiancé left me Gold Coast beachfront property," Tiffany added.

The celebrity snickered. "Nobody at Parallacts knows you two are associating?"

"You are a pettifogging politico, Nate!" Shalom doffed his poncho.

The celebrity removed his cap and shook more moisture loose. "I imagine you're particularly disgusted by the politicization of science."

"I'm disgusted by the politicization of politics." Shalom mussed his wild, unruly hair. "Cool today, hmm?" He rolled up his poncho. "What do you need to decide: whether someone like me is liberal or conservative? Here's how to tell: a conservative misinterprets progress as outrageousness, and a liberal misinterprets outrageousness as progress."

"Environmental concerns are one of the last bastions of geopolitical alignments." The celebrity smacked his lips. "And these typically harbor a hierarchy of regional culture conflicts which serve to obfuscate the actual ecological dilemma."

Shalom shifted his weight uncomfortably. "So you and your incipient supercell established a Midwest front and descended on Parallacts?" He smirked. "Didn't the pablum of the profiteers on the panel find a home in your heart, no-see-um?"

"No more, I'm certain, than it did in yours." The celebrity moved behind the baron of the ionosphere. "Thus, you abandoned the stage of the global elite and rode your trike into the sunset."

"They could use less activists and more thinkavists, but McGuay generally served as my buffer with such agencies, so they never bid-up my blood pressure." Shalom stiffly extended his arms away from his sides. "The main exception is when the feds caught me doing my own research on ARPA's dime and submitting fabricated metadata. I took their advice to be a good noble gas and not interact with any other sinister singularities, to get lost deep in my own anomaly zone."

"Not to shovel shade on the shroud, Dr. Shalom," the celebrity prodded, "but do you have a concern there was something suspect about Worbley's fatal accident?"

"You were just a consultant slamming shade on their sham models, weren't you, Chutz?" Tiffany rubbed Charlton's shoulders. "Lincoln was an officer fiddling with the volume control knob."

"Sooo predictable." The arch amplifier of gravitational lensing shook his head. "McGuay was a natural resource. Another wind-powered seawater desalination plant that he designed just came online off California. A thinking entity might hijack a resource like that but would never destroy it."

"California isn't a thinking entity," Tiffany suggested. "It's a feeling entity."

"Debate that with Caltech." The celebrity squatted. "What was the nature of the errant diddling you were doing beyond your ordained Defense or Energy bidding, Doctor?"

Shalom turned to view the celebrity and toppled onto his side. "Give me a place to stand, Newt, and I can move the Earth!"

Tiffany pointed to the speedboat. "Mr. Oobops, would you retrieve Chutz's seat cushion?" The celebrity dutifully recovered the requested item, and the masseuse fixed him with the gaze of a coyote as he delivered it to the canceler of the cosmological constant. "Mr. Oobops, you look so tense. Lie face down on my poncho, and I'll walk on your spine."

The celebrity raised his hands defensively. "I have a fear of being trampled and a low frustration threshold." He seated himself opposite Charlton. "The good folks at Parallacts obviously believe that you still have a stranglehold on an effective climate change solution stronger than side effects or money."

"Isn't this Tess?" Tiffany peered over the celebrity's shoulder and curled her elegant fingers into binoculars. The celebrity turned his head, grudgingly dismissed his angular momentum and rose. He helped Shalom to his feet and signaled Tohnyin with a beckoning wave.

A smiling Tess approached in her purple rainhat and a salmon trench coat carrying a marbled, champagne-colored oblong box festooned with a golden bow. "Be still, my nucleus accumbens," Charlton remarked. Upon arrival, Tess exchanged semi-hugs with Tiffany.

"Dr. Shalom!" Tohnyin extended her hand like a quintessential physics club compeer. "I have this gift for you from your son Tycho." She transferred the package in the same motion that she shook hands. "We've met. I'm Tess Tohnyin of the California diplomatic corps for global sustainability."

"It's lovely." Shalom jogged the box. "A tesseract from Tess." He crouched with the item and shuffled back as if he'd taken a snap from center. "Go deep, Ned!" He whirled the package around like a hammer and lofted it over the waves. The celebrity stumbled in the sand but splashed into the water and plucked the box out of the air. "Abad, you catch on quick!"

The celebrity returned to land and shook his feet. "The name is Ahab."

"See what I mean?" Charlton clapped his hands. "As long as you rescued the thing, why don't you appropriate the privilege of opening it?"

Tohnyin seethed like wet barbecue. "Go ahead, Ahab. You're so adept at pulling strings."

The celebrity dismantled the ribbon, lifted the cover, brushed aside the tissue paper and exhibited a mint-condition People's Globe Lifetime Achievement Award Albert. Tiffany dashed to the celebrity and took possession of the item. "It's magnificent, Chutz!" She caressed it.

"Tycho must've had it in for you to stick you with such a servile, thankless task, Tess." Shalom rubbed his shoulder. "I wished to name my daughter 'Tesla,' but my interloping wife persuaded me it wasn't feminine enough, so I settled for 'Nikola,' and *we* settled for 'Elealeh Bardeen.'"

Tess offered a smile of resignation. "I like the name 'Tycho.'"

The quantum gravity whip grimaced. "She resisted that, too. She speculated it would cause the boy to be teased mercilessly, but I convinced her he would be teased mercilessly anyway."

Tohnyin raised and lowered her eyebrows. "A rose is well that blooms by any other name?"

Shalom tilted his head. "Indeed, my wife and I got divorced, my contumacious daughter and I are estranged, and I am my fribbling son's apologist."

Tohnyin nodded. "The cruel world has done a pretty sorry job of repaying you for all you've contributed, but there's time to change that tone, and to that end, I'd like to conduct the radical experiment of employing some candor." She gestured to the Lifetime Achievement Award. "Only one who really appreciates the full systemic problem of climate change can really appreciate the solution. We the people of California need a heating and cooling expert to change our planetary furnace filter."

Shalom grunted. "And it's yours truly you truly want to employ?"

Tess swept her hand through her hair. "With a past poised between dedication and enslavement to the study of the atmospheric forces, Doctor, can you really look me in the eye and convince me that you've abandoned the field for the safe space of an indignant leisure bubble?"

"Mother Nature is a wicked painted lady." The universal negative pressure cooker whisked sand at the celebrity. "By the time I'd reached school age, I was already committed to throwing her down, stripping her naked and wresting her secrets." He gestured to Tiffany. "I concede that I fell far short and I've had to settle for the next best thing." He shook with mirth. "In all candor, I calculated how the most arcane forces in the universe jive, and in the process, I upended the precious, hard-manipulated models of my high-strung contemporaries, thereby establishing a paradigm for a lifetime of bad public relations. But that's acceptable because a theoretician is always primarily driven by immanent reward."

The celebrity let his gaze settle on the Albert Award. "Yet, what richer way to frost your cake could there be than to force the people to stand back, bow their collective arrogant heads and admit they'd unjustly delegitimized you?" He beat sand from his jeans with his cap. "We believe you have a better chance of diagnosing what's happening with the polar shield than anyone else. And in California, you'd be invited to enjoy a host of research perks that'll positively shame anything that this maroon state can confer."

"And it's a more clement climate." Shalom folded his arms defensively. "Perhaps I've had too much freedom to succeed, and I might benefit from a glut of bright-eyed regimentation with a periodic sanity check to keep me honest."

The celebrity received a sharp elbow in the ribs. "Ahab gets himself too worked up." Tohnyin patted his side. "He obviously could never have found you, Dr. Shalom, if you didn't want to be found. We wouldn't be enjoying your company if you didn't feel connected to our cause. Work with us, and our agency will post you anywhere you choose and run interference against any agenda-driven barriers you may confront in the interest of restoring planetary sustainability."

"Tess suggests that you look distressed, Ahab, and we tend to agree." Charlton snorted. "Flop on your belly and let Tiffany walk up your back."

The celebrity adopted the grin of a man being garroted. "I thought we'd already discarded that idea as recipient-averse."

"Flop, Ahab!" Tohnyin slid her heel down his shin and tugged on his shirt front.

The celebrity squeezed Tohnyin's arm. "Take whatever Tess says with a grain of sand." She kicked him in the ankle. "She's a real piece of play." He hissed and dropped to a prone position.

"I'll tenderfoot you, Mr. Oobops." Tiffany leapt onto his scapulae. "We want our high-impact relief to penetrate to your core." She strutted down his spine and returned. "Try not to talk or pass out."

"You high-security-clearance landscapers promise me a compass rose garden," the quondam king of the plasma scientists submitted, "and I can't help but smell the underlying fish emulsion that fosters it. No entity reveals its true nature in a recruitment pitch."

The masseuse stepped on the celebrity's brattoo, and he coughed spasmodically. "You probably feel awkward, Mr. Oobops, but don't you feel better?"

"He's far more fragile than he looks," Tess contended. "Step up your treatment. Put some hair on his chest."

Charlton tapped his toe in the sand as Tiffany retraced her nerve-center crossing. "My first wife demanded that I take a keen interest in government works and political functions in order to do my part to build a world we can all proudly share." He snorted. "So I slipped into my concerned civvies and watched meritless, burdensome bickering slide across the enervated path of least resistance while official squabbles found funding with my blood, sweat and treasure. I concluded that the only thing of value that government is qualified to offer is entertainment."

"Glad to provide ground support." The celebrity pounded his fists in the sand as Tiffany twirled therapeutically on his lower back.

"Dig out a handful of mud, Oobops, and sling it!" Shalom summoned Tiffany back to earth. "What I propose is a poetic polemic. I want a representative of your agency to face off against a Wisconsin foe in a duel of wit, wisdom and insults – a flyting. And I'll be wide open enough to being coopted by whom I judge to be the winner to sign a letter of loyal intent." He retrieved his cushion and poncho. "Don't come armed with some political speech or courtroom spiel. I abhor a vacuum but adore a dysphemism. I'd encourage you to go directly after your adversary, challenge authority and hammer without restraint. Forge a verbal onslaught so clever, eloquent and relentless, it'll reduce your enemy to a shattered clam. Craft your darts carefully, and sling them so deftly that you ride your competition right off the stage on your raillery."

"Precisely when and where, Doctor?" Tohnyin sidled between Charlton and Tiffany.

"Your undertaking may be a little trickier than the sport designed by the skalds because you'll want to stay loosely faithful to your political platform, so I'll allot some lead time." He threw his poncho over his head and appeared to contemplate the lake. "Be ready to be real and mean to be seen for a date this Saturday night." He pointed over the diminished waves. "At the crest of the Coat Of Arms on the *Janesy* at astronomical dusk, and I'll arrange a venue for a private audience from there."

Tiffany returned the Albert to its box and grabbed her poncho. "I'll relay the invite among some dangerous people outside Madison who'll be interested in ensuring you'll have a worthy opponent."

Tess raised her eyebrows. "You mean WIO?"

"What's WIO?" The masseuse smirked as she slid her feet back into her flip-flops. "A bunch of accountants, isn't it?"

"Attend the flyting, and you'll find out," the celebrity predicted. He resituated the Parallacts masseuse and the Planck-walking stretcher of the spatial gauze in their respective seats and shoved the speedboat back into the water.

Shalom waved. "Sharpen your shtick, lynchpin, lest you lose your lease." Tiffany triumphantly shook the boxed Albert over her head. She started the engine, and the speedboat bounded toward deeper water.

The celebrity slipped Tohnyin an approbative smile. "That's bringing it, Camembert."

Tess rubbed her brow. "Ahab, where did you ever learn to entertain a prospective asset?" She sighed. "You look like you've been pumped out of a sump."

He jammed his mullet cap into his tactical bag. "I must admit I *am* impressed that the lab could reverse their stark statuette desecration."

"They couldn't." She exhibited a smug smile. "I ascertained the identity of the designer of the fabulous trophies for the *People's Globe* and contacted him. I was persuasive enough to skate around their exclusivity craptrap and procure an unattached sample."

The celebrity retrieved his luggage. "I can't believe we both overlooked Tiffany."

"You sure looked her over." Tohnyin removed her hat and basked in a slight break in the clouds. "Jerry told me he'd been urging her to scare up bigger ambition, so she asked him about me and my work, and she's now serving an internship for him hoping to land a comparable position with Illinois intelligence." Tess pointed to the Riviera Pier. "Let's catch the *Janesy* when it comes around, so those of us who need to get groomed over can move forward on that project."

He trailed after her. "I think *I'll* ask Jerry about you and your work."

Outbound. 1310 CST Friday 7 April.

"When this is over, chum, I'll take you snorkeling in the shark-infested waters off the Channel Islands." Unique Agent Rondo Bracey displayed a predatory smirk from his seat to the right of D.C.I. Philander Ledbetter in the secure conference center on the top floor of the Santa Monica P.C.

The celebrity glared at the teleconference wall screen from the austere confines of a rented comfort zone on the sundeck of the *Janesy*. "It's evident, Rondo, that you distinguished yourself at the FBI in Operation Duck-and-Cover."

"Schedule the duel to settle your personal differences for a time after you've both retired from the intelligence service." Seated to the left of Ledbetter, Strategic Lead Analyst Leland Montoone punctuated his admonishment with tony British notes.

"Let's give Rondo some accommodation, Ahab." Dressed to impress in saffron stretched velvet, Tohnyin rubbed her neck and kicked the celebrity lightly in the ankle. "Stay off his hiss list."

"Don't flatter yourself, Tohnyin, that flirting with me is anything but a waste of time for us both." Bracey sucked in his cheeks. "Let's just hope that you two path-losers have stumbled onto the true target, and he can be transferred to competent hands."

Tohnyin smiled diplomatically. "Neither of us has a doubt after vetting him in depth that he's the real Shalom," she insisted. The celebrity fluttered his hands beside his ears.

The D.C.I. traced his temporal scar with his finger. "I believe, Oobops, you'd begun providing your baseline assessment of the man."

"Charlton seems to be a free spirit as much as a free agent," the celebrity asserted. "I feel he fed the feds falsified findings primarily for the opportunity to conduct personal research, although he may be collecting a nominal stipend from Wisconsin, Illinois or a Midwest alliance."

"Seems to be," Bracey mocked, "may be, could be, possibly."

"The upshot is he wants us to throw him a flyting," Tess reported. "California against Wisconsin in a duel of wit and applied insult. The outcome of the contest will decide who merits his allegiance."

"We," Montoone held the word on his tongue, "are well aware that he means to test us." In contrast to the two cukes to his right, Monty fidgeted almost rhythmically. "Would you consider Charlton a charlatan, Oobops? Encapsulate your take on our prospects. With what region, country or movement do his deepest sympathies seem to lie?"

The celebrity leaned forward. "I wouldn't label Charlton a citizen of the world because it's too restrictive, but he's an existentialist, not an ethnocentrist. He's a dimension or two above geopolitical jostling, and we'd be well-advised not to insult him by extending him standard-protocol patronization."

"Existentialist," Montoone scoffed. "That's a pastiche term for someone intellectually and morally adrift."

"Oobops is an existentialist," Ledbetter interjected. "Aren't you, Ahab?"

"Oobops is a real man," Bracey snarled, "all five-alarm hot sauce and power-chord reverb drip. He's nothing a split lip and a concussion wouldn't improve."

The celebrity rose. "Charlton champions the Tchaikovsky-Schopenhauer paradigm of social autarky. The last place you'll find him is in lockstep with any large, organized program: corporate, religious or political."

"You don't know that," Bracey charged. "All these two intellectual runts have acquired is the projected vision that they were subliminally fed at the inception of their inclusions in the operation."

Monty whisked invisible detritus from his shoulder. "Am I aware of what you're referring to?"

"Unit Bracey provided the quantum computer with the totality of our information on Charlton Shalom, and the Q.C. returned a scripted prediction of how an encounter with 110328A/404 should unfold." The director cleared his sinuses. "It was to serve as a template for Oobops and Tohnyin to reproduce when they finally found and interacted with the Nobel strongman."

"I felt that we established a hearty rapport in our personal interaction." The celebrity reseated himself. "As spiritual emissary, I believe I reached Charlton on a visceral level."

"Religious emissary!" Bracey scoffed. "Ahab doesn't praise the Lord; he appraises the Lord."

"You've examined our fustians." Tess leaned on her elbow. "Did we satisfy the Q.C.?"

Bracey shook both forefingers. "Exactly what is the nature of the personal research Shalom was conducting? Where are Lincoln Worbley's notes on the polar shield? Hell, you croutons haven't even shaken out the thought process behind

Shalom's hate tweet to humanity. Did you pressure him for it or even reference it?"

Tohnyin shifted her gaze from Santa Monica to the celebrity. "Did a wry guy like Charlton strike you as the type to keep a diary of personal justification?"

"In the unlikely event he had, it wouldn't be germane to the result we're trying to achieve now." The celebrity returned to his feet. "With the personal connection we've made, I know I can stand up and deliver our payload within the framework of some well-placed jabs and precision counter-punchlines."

"You certainly look like you're no stranger to the sucker punch," Rondo granted.

The D.C.I. bared his teeth. "Oobops, you misinterpreted Shalom's attraction to Tess and transferred it to yourself."

"Amazingly, no," Tess conceded. "Charlton and Ahab appeared to bond like quarks of a spin."

Montoone nodded. "The crunch-point for gaining an inside advantage on this flyting is finding a combatant who can appeal to Shalom's unconscious biases. I believe we have two top candidates: Brandon Rosenthal in C.I. and Myra Applebaum in cyber-command. They've both bolstered their degrees with minors in physics and spent time living in Israel."

Ledbetter traced his temporal scar with his finger. "Reports I receive indicate that Myra cuts it up around the water cooler."

Tohnyin rolled her eyes. "You stuffed bucks aren't sincerely suggesting you'd appoint neither Ahab nor myself as the gladiatorial delegate? Ask the Nobel Committee how well patronizing Charlton Shalom plays."

The director stretched his collar. "You're saying we're being too transparent?"

"It won't be too transparent when it succeeds." Monty tapped his chin. "A flyting contestant enters the ring with a presenter who warms up the audience with a brief preamble and sets the tone of the takedown. Should we now declare a consensus that Tess serve as the presenter, we can instruct her to invest her introduction with a cantankerous remark delicately balanced to initially appear anti-Semitic and anti-geriatric but be neither. It will be cunningly calculated to divert Shalom's attention from the idea that our side might exploit a little good, reliable, solid-gold pandering."

The celebrity chortled. "You want her to give Shalom a shot that's not a shot, something in the spirit of 'I'm always drunk in San Francisco, but I don't drink at all.'"

"Oobops, how can someone in this line of service be so politically naïve?" Montoone's wiry grey hair always stood puffed slightly beyond what gravity should've tolerated. "As chaplain, you might promote the sentiment that we should seek to cheat in moderation, but ultimate victory by any means possible is the only legitimate goal."

Ledbetter pressed his thumb and forefinger against his brow. "Let the motion carry that Unit Tohnyin is our presenter."

Bracey emitted a low growl. "Why don't we agree instead, P.L., to insert a team with specialized credentials that can avoid this distasteful business of ethnic baiting and incendiary slur-meistering in its exchange of hostilities?" A supercilious smile flickered across his lips. "The fact that it became necessary to rely on me to re-energize the deteriorating arc of the op leaves me well-positioned to evaluate ideal deployment, and I nominate myself as presenter for frontman Unique Agent Nefrorius M. Al-Keypone."

"Al-Keypone?" Monty leaned forward and fixed Rondo with an incredulous gaze. "He views everything through the prism of identity politics and racial tension. As easily as he bruises, he would seem to be a person of primary colors black and blue."

Bracey folded his arms. "You've never talked to the man, so you know nothing that's not stamped on his resume. You don't realize that he has a background in battle rap."

"Big Daddy Black Ice Al-Baghdadi?" Montoone straightened his tie.

The celebrity stood, sending his chair tumbling over backward. "You might direct Radmilla to form a search committee to find Shalom an interpreter."

"Al-Keypone's very stage presence will compromise the Wisconsin offensive." Bracey crowded Ledbetter with vehement gesticulation. "Shalom should be seized with guilt at the prospect of not deciding in our favor. WIO will be left to tightrope an enervated path on eggshells to keep from tripping bottom layers of high-minded diplomatic taboos." He exhibited a toothy sneer. "I cite as glowing precedent for this decision an incident from the year 1937 in which African-American singer Marian Anderson performed at Princeton University but was denied lodging at the Nassau Inn, and no less a global player than physicist Albert Einstein sought to rectify the situation by taking her into his home."

"This sort of undertaking would seem to be in Hawk Fleming's wheelhouse." Tohnyin rose. "Why don't we solicit his participation?" She flipped the celebrity's chair upright.

"This campaign will remain to every degree possible an in-house proposition," the director decreed. "You're aware, Tess, that Mr. Fleming just submitted a dubious bill to CIB for $350,000 to cover Ahab's gambling debt on your most recent excursion to Las Vegas."

Bracey and Montoone gasped. "Oobops," Rondo snarled, "you swill-biscuit, why won't you flush? I take meds so I don't kill people like you."

"Ask your pharmacist for a carminative that'll make you kill yourself without disturbing anyone else." The celebrity dropped heavily into his chair and invited Tess to warm hers by tugging on her gown.

Ledbetter studied his Qilroy and hiccuped. "As we the people of this crisis summit are incapable of reaching the most fundamental accord, the Q.C. proposes that Unit Tohnyin serve as our putdown presenter and Unit Al-Keypone represent the state as our prime combatant." He bared his teeth.

"Tess, make it a point to cite the historical tidbit about Einstein and Marian Anderson in your prolog."

"Only Ahab has the flyte stuff to embody the offensive spirit that we covet." Tess jabbed an emotionally supportive knuckle into the back of the celebrity's hand. "If he pledges to channel his lampoons within the boundaries of social propriety, Big Sir, won't you reconsider and send him into the flyting behind me as our featured striker?" She exhibited a pouty smile. "Frankly, to commission Unique Agent Al-Keypone as skald plays like a reactionary shaming strategy fit for WIO."

The D.C.I. traced his temporal scar. "This renitent attitude that you and Ahab share, Tess, compels me to spiral this production audit into a rutted roundabout of reproach." He stretched his collar. "By the quantum computer's count, Oobops has represented a clear and present menace to CIB personnel within Prosecution Complex walls three times just since the start of Operation Shalom: in the commissary; at the secretariat desk; in the elevator. Therefore, Ahab, by resolution of the Q.C., you are to receive a Memorandum of Dereliction, which carries a minimum unpaid three-month suspension to be served immediately. As such, you are officially disqualified from serving as our flyting skald."

"That pay gap will cripple Ahab," Rondo remarked. "He's struggling as it is to support two or three prostitutes by himself."

"The public employment premium is the least of his problems." The director hiccuped. "Ahab, I have no idea how you'll palliate this scandalous setback when the select tribunal of review convenes to consider your case for reinstatement."

"Don't sulk over your personal power outage, Ahab." Montoone brushed imaginary phages from his neck. "Sooner or later, everybody dumps on you, don't they?"

"What's the matter, slick?" Bracey pounded. "Aren't you functional unless your stir-crazy straight woman sets you up?"

"Go bitch-slap yourself, swagger-stick." The celebrity folded his arms insularly.

"Ahab is effective because he's learned by experience to distrust people." Ledbetter pressed his thumb and forefinger against his brow. "He will retain a vital role in the op as our supreme decoy and ultimate gofer. Your exposure to the Anti-Alyce network, Ahab, will invariably lead WIO to prepare to engage you as the featured California performer. Imagine how hoodwinked they'll feel when they're instead confronted with Nefrorius." He bared his teeth. "The Q.C. warns that Wisconsin would cite our use of a state government jet to transport Al-Keypone to the flyting as evidence that our commitment to combat carbon pollution lacks a certain integrity. Ergo, I will instruct Radmilla to book Units Al-Keyone and Bracey on a commercial red-eye flight that will arrive at Chicago O'Hare at 0500 hours tomorrow. Serving as our security point-man and official greeter, Oobops, you will meet and escort the new arrivals to the Batavia safe house for provisional maintenance and ultimately to the Lake Geneva stage for expression of hostilities." He hiccuped. "I will arrange for your memorandum to be filed slightly askew so it must be refiled and cannot take effect until late Saturday."

"You've rented the 'jackwagon' we requisitioned." Montoone elicited a nod from Tohnyin. "So you'll be ready to extract the team from the O'Hare bus shuttle center as soon as Ahab summons you."

"That allays the sum of my concerns," Bracey scoffed.

Natty Phil eyed Rondo. "I trust that you'll utilize your extended travel time to prep Unique Agent Al-Keypone for the tournament at the highest possible level." He shifted his focus to Lake Geneva. "If there are no further squabbles or wobbles to stabilize, we'll leave you now to block micro-strategy."

"Keep your fustians current." Monty terminated the connection.

Tohnyin flashed an astringent smile. "Are *you* moved to

dance with the choreography we were given?" She opened the curtains and allowed sunlight to fill the comfort zone. "I fear for our friend Charlton, but we have our orders. I have a rental van to trick out as a hotel shuttle."

The celebrity reveled in the sight of a clear blue sky. "How long before the Sconnies count on this unseasonably warm weather?" He consulted his Qilroy. "It's going up to 16 degrees. Let's tackle our own micro-strategy around the pool shell."

"Maybe I'll catch you there after I complete my sordid assortment of personal errands." Tohnyin left the celebrity in the comfort zone. He followed her at a distance until he reached the Slop Chest. He entered hoping to spot Mercowitz and make inquiries about Tiffany. He kept the sparsely populated lounge under a two-drink surveillance and ranged to the Heart O' Gold. He conducted a thorough search of the casino, but Jerry wasn't appearing anywhere accessible.

The celebrity returned to his cabin. He donned his trunks, sandals and CIB terry cloth long robe, and he proceeded to a chaise at the edge of the empty pool on the lonely sundeck. He converted the long robe into a bivouac tent by tossing it over his head, and he studied his more obscure files on WIO. He determined that the flag featuring the black X that Tess had observed in enemy company was a political symbol of the Progressive Party, which had originated in Wisconsin. Two hours later, he received a barefoot kick in the ribs. He shed his robe shelter and found Tohnyin standing beside his chaise offering him a cup of steaming cocoa. He sat up, took the drink and slurped a sip. She plunked her body onto the adjacent chaise, swallowed a sip of her own drink and set the paper cup on the cement. She opened her white fleece robe to reveal her fabulous figure in a pink bikini with black borders. She hesitated. "I think it's a little chilly for me."

"Adapt." He savored another sip.

She raised her eyebrows skeptically. "How, by growing numb?" She discarded her robe and reclined. "The doors of our pick-up van are now officially customized with *Hotel WisconSin* decals and counterfeit tags. I even added puny *WIO* decals with ghost flames at the bottom to create a little confusion should any interested agents exercise malevolent designs on us."

"Onlookers will infer it's a kitsch niche radio station sponsor." He took a swig of cocoa and burned his tongue. "Closer to home, cup-barer, are you vying to bump and grind into Jerry?"

She forced a facsimile of a smile. "I last spoke with him shortly after we charmed Charlton. I surmise he's taking some blowback from his Parallacts peers because the in-house masseuse outflanked him to achieve their objective."

"Bless his raconteur racketeer heart." The celebrity set his cup on the deck, wadded his robe into a pillow and reclined.

Tess swept her hands through her hair. "I just completed a private conversation with P.L. I suggested that he employ his mood surgery as a convenient excuse to expunge the David Blair incident from the quantum computer's memory. If you had only two transgression credits, you could be slapped with a Memorandum of Delinquency, which doesn't carry a mandatory suspension."

"Who is David Blair?" He offered a bewildered smile.

"Who is John Galt?" she retorted. "The twerp that you allegedly assaulted in the elevator?" She chuckled. "What kind of inner junkyard mutt do you unleash, Oobops? Apparently, Blair called Natty Phil and demanded that the Studio sever all ties with you at once, and the D.C.I. told Blair that if he wished to prosecute a vendetta against you, he should be man enough to carry his own water. Anyway-"

"Those were the exact words he used?" The celebrity rubbed his neck. "I should've left that clout-spout lying in the elevator wearing nothing but his suspenders."

She narrowed her eyes. "I'm sorry I wasn't irresistible enough to crush the Big Sir's resistance."

The celebrity rolled onto his side to face Tohnyin. He felt drowsy and found it nearly impossible to follow what she was saying, but he analyzed her posture. She kept her knees slightly flexed, and the sun highlighted the straight lines of her shins. A polished glow appeared to flow from her legs over the rest of her skin. Her supple wrist dangled a hand over the frame of the chaise, and her nails gleamed like Wilshire Boulevard. A photographer might've spent an afternoon perfecting such a pose, and she'd just flopped that way. He respectfully raised his gaze beyond her to an illuminated poolside globe light and slipped into a state of unconsciousness.

He awoke sweaty and itchy in his cabin bed. Local time stood at 2320 hours. He retrieved the message that Tohnyin had left on his Qilroy nearly three hours before: "You're comatose. You've been complaining you're too tired to sleep so I didn't want to disturb you. I've gone to meet Jerry. Rest easy. Catch you when I come back." He rolled off his mattress and hit the floor. He wondered if Tess had already returned. He heard no movement in her cabin. He felt immoderately light-headed. He attempted to increase his heart rate by performing crab-walks. He wished he'd been shifty enough to send a surveillance bouquet to Tohnyin's quarters. He staggered to his feet and worked vigorously to unlock their connecting door. No sooner did a soft click announce that he'd succeeded than her main door opened and a light engaged.

He sent her an immediate message: "What ever happened to the girl next door?"

She sighed into her Qilroy. "Are you verifying that I'm alone, Ahab, or is this some drill bit?" He rapped on the wall. "Put a deeper dent in your sleep deficit." She appeared to be back in saffron stretched velvet. "Jerry alerted me there's a massive WIO counterinsurgency effort afoot. He heartily recommends we remain secluded in our respective cabins, so let's consider ourselves under strict curfew." She slipped the cocktail dress strap off her shoulder. "Please lock the door connecting our cabins, chaplain. I'll call for you in approximately three hours." She terminated the connection.

The celebrity couldn't get back to sleep. He crab-walked up and down the hallway, but the fatigue he induced didn't lead to slumber. He met Tohnyin with heavy eyelids at 0255 hours. Each crypto-crat carried only a tactical bag, and he declined her offer of a mephedrone capsule as the shuttle boat arrived with small complimentary coffees and conveyed them through the cold, black mist to the Big Foot parking lot. The commercially camouflaged dichroic puce van encountered no trouble with the repaired parking facility gate and headed onto Highway 12 for a trip that the autonav estimated at 85 minutes. "When we've whisked our hometown mugs to the safe house," Tess suggested, "we'll have Madelyn prepare us a breakfast banquet. If she won't, I will."

"You'll love the kitchen." The celebrity checked his booking on the 0700 flight to Washington that would serve as a decoy and gain unrestricted access to the gate area. "Did you drag me back to my cabin yesterday?"

"I arranged for a pair of deck hands to convey you down there on your chaise like Cleopatra." Tohnyin bared her teeth. "Ahab, Natty Phil called me yesterday afternoon because Rondo persuaded him that you needed to be cut out of the op straightaway. I argued, and he tasked me to deliver the order. So I fortified your cocoa with tiletamine." She flashed a wan smile. "Just before I left to meet Jerry, I called P.L. back to argue further. He insisted you really deserve a 'Memorandum of Treachery.' I submitted that proves you're a superb spy. He didn't know how to respond, so he reinstated you for this morning's rendezvous."

The celebrity experienced a natural energy spike. "If I receive a Memorandum of Treachery, I'll forward it to one far more deserving." He patted her wrist. "The flyte team is now projected to arrive at Gate C9 at 0610 hours, just 35 minutes late."

The van reached O'Hare International XX Airport Terminal One at 0450 hours. "I'll be waiting for your stage call five minutes away from the bus shuttle center," she confirmed.

He hopped out of the vehicle and slammed the door. "Break a leg." He tapped on the roof and watched her speed away. "Over someone's head, if you have to." He shuffled into the terminal building, checked in and toted his tactical bag through the airport security gauntlet without a hitch. He arrived at the appointed gate at 0525 hours and established an invisible security perimeter. He scrutinized the few lethargic travelers and laborers, peered beneath seats and searched around waste receptacles. He identified the positions of surveillance cameras and inspected doors and corners.

At 0538 hours, the celebrity received a call from Bracey. "The seagull has landed," Rondo announced. "Where are you?"

"Staring at your arrival gate." The celebrity smiled complaisantly. "You would appear to not only be in ahead of schedule but ahead of your airplane."

"You abscess." Bracey expelled an annoyed breath. "We caught an early H.S.C.T., which brought us in exactly 50 minutes ago. Did you really expect us to broadcast our preferred flight, especially to you?" He waved dismissively. "We've retrieved our luggage, and we're waiting for you at the bus shuttle center. Might you hurry up and haul your low-performance ass over here so we can proceed?"

"Left right left, right?" The celebrity started on a brisk march to the bus shuttle center. "Follow the red arrows, repeat?"

Bracey sucked in his cheeks. "While Unit Al-Keypone is in the men's room, let's review your instructions."

"He's in the bathroom?" the celebrity objected. "You don't want to leave him unattended for an instant!"

Rondo rolled his eyes. "We walked through together and checked it out. Would you have busted up the plumbing to make sure no bad guys are concealed in the pipes?"

The celebrity shook his head. "If you don't believe that people can find places to hide in the bathroom, then you're deeply deluded passing for merely mistaken."

"Shut it off!" Bracey snapped. "That's first. You are to greet Mr. Al-Keypone with a terse formality and then refrain from flapping your yap further in his presence." Rondo looked over his shoulder. "Otherwise, you'll try to prove how culturally attuned you are and offend him with some flatline faux pas like 'Black people should lighten up.'"

The celebrity boarded the elevator. "Is Nefrorius still in the lavatory?" He cleared his sinuses. "What's he doing in there, Bracey, seeking asylum from you? Check on him." He lost Bracey's scratchy transmission when he received a call from Tohnyin. "The seagull pulled a fast one," he informed her. "The talent is in timeout mode." He started down the lower level corridor. "But it's time for us to move into position."

She winced. "Glad I interfaced. Give me seven minutes to reach the rendezvous point."

Bracey re-established his connection. "Oobops, you refugee from a junior high playpen, did you deliberately drop me?"

"Tess is on the way, Gulliver." The celebrity realized that Rondo had terminated the connection.

The celebrity arrived at the boarding lounge of the bus shuttle center. The bank of seats facing the street was populated with four travelers. Bracey emerged from the men's room and stood facing the outside door with arms akimbo. The celebrity strode up to him and dropped his tactical bag. He tucked his left fist behind his back and extended his right hand. "I'm into leather."

"That's the way to get your jaw fractured, Priscilla." Bracey pointed to a huge canvas bag. "Instead grab Al-Keypone's duffel and break your back." He nodded toward the men's room. "He's experiencing a little problem with dysentery but he'll be right out. Where's the freewheelin' floozy with our ride?"

"Tess is on the expressway driving against traffic to hit

your mark." The celebrity retrieved Nefrorius's heavy canvas bag. "The lady would be pleased, Rondo, if we signed off on a nonaggression pact."

Bracey sneered. "That's a good poodle. You stay in the shadows with your head down, do no more or less than you're directed, and we're besties." He looked over his shoulder.

Al-Keypone emerged from the men's room in a khaki derby. "How are you doing, Malky?" Rondo welcomed him. "You advised me you've never worked with Oobops? He's used principally to infiltrate white supremacist groups because he has such a natural aptitude for it."

"White supremacist groups like CIB?" Nefrorius nodded perfunctorily. "Unit Oobops, I've seen you around."

"Unit Al-Keypone." The celebrity smiled complaisantly. "Did you have a pleasant flight, or were you seated beside Rondo?"

"A little stomach upset." Al-Keypone patted his abdomen. "Circadian irregularity." He wore a finely tailored dark suit like Bracey's but an open plum shirt. "I expect I'll recover by and by."

The celebrity nodded. "Did Rondo mention how many black belts he holds?"

A subdued umbrage filled Bracey's eyes. "Zip it, Oobops, or I'll hold the leather one I'm wearing around your neck."

Al-Keypone scanned the premises. "Where's our travel agent?"

"Progress report, Oobops?" Bracey hissed. "Never mind; I'll call her myself." He worked his Qilroy and paused. "Closing." He shook his head. "Three minutes." He retrieved the set of two grey valises and one jumbo suitcase behind the lounge seats and set them beside the celebrity. "I won't tolerate a nanosecond of slack in our bull-rush to the van, pumice-head, so you better be at that rear bumper one count after she stops so you can hurl yourself with all your baggage in the back, or we'll be a blur and you'll still be here. You can handle these as one load, right?"

The celebrity secured the straps of his tactical bag between his teeth. He picked up the rest of the bags and held them for three minutes. Rondo expelled a heavy breath. "Can't she get her lithe rear in high gear?"

"Where the rubber meets the road, she leaves us exposed," Nefrorius grumbled.

The celebrity dropped his bags. "If you two fob-gobs ever discover free verse, you'll be deadly."

Al-Keypone fixed the celebrity with a wry grin. "Pray you never discover how deadly."

"Let's step outside!" Bracey eyed the celebrity coldly. "You're making us conspicuous in here." The celebrity gathered the luggage with a disgusted grunt and followed Rondo and Nefrorius out the door. "Tohnyin is probably in the wrong place waiting for us two blocks down the line." Bracey assessed the landscape and thrummed his Qilroy. "I'll call her again."

The celebrity let the bags drop to the sidewalk. Al-Keypone paced slowly back and forth. A colony of ants had exploited a crack in the cement, and Bracey began stomping and scraping them with the edge of his shoe. The celebrity stepped on Rondo's toe. "Why don't you leave them alone, Bracey?"

"What's your crisis now, Oobops?" Bracey pushed the celebrity back with a forearm to the chest. "Ant advocacy?" He appealed to Al-Keypone with a head gesture to the celebrity. "Can you believe this goofy bork-wuss? He's moaning because I squashed some ants."

Nefrorius stared blankly. "They aren't black ants, are they?"

Rondo exchanged tense, uncertain glances with the celebrity. "Tohnyin doesn't respond." He stopped killing ants. "If I have any pull in the Studio, Unit Oobops, you'll undergo unprecedented psychological trials in order to have the remotest chance of retaining your job."

The *Hotel WisconSin* shuttle van appeared and skidded to a stop. "Our suckle-bucket has arrived." Bracey extended his arms like a crossing guard as the front passenger's door flew open. "Wait!" He dropped to a crouch. "Everyone back inside! Obey orders! Move!" Al-Keypone accompanied him into the building, and the celebrity followed with the full load of luggage. Rondo peered through the glass at the idling vehicle as the rear doors popped open. "What's that on the side? It's a WIO vehicle!"

The celebrity lost his tooth-hold on the straps of his tactical bag. "That decal is attached for our identification purposes and to further confuse any undesirable dinks."

Bracey's glower oozed with distrust. "Try on this inside joke, tampon-squeezer. Before we go out again, you visually make the driver."

With the recollection of misidentifying Isis as Tess in the Heart O' Gold casino gnawing at his subconscious, the celebrity contacted Tohnyin on his Qilroy. "You're 200 milliseconds late. So some members of the team need to examine your full body of evidence to verify that we're not mobilizing our opposition group."

Tohnyin stationed herself at the open passenger's door. "Are you guys sniffing airplane glue, Ahab?" The iris scan virtually confirmed her authenticity if the attitude didn't.

The celebrity discarded Rondo's luggage and ambled out the door shielding himself with Nefrorius's heavy bag. "Seriously, Tess, to improve commando morale, would you please exhibit yourself in the open air, turn and walk to the rear doors?" She sighed and removed her hands from her trench coat pockets. She lengthened her neck and strode to the rear of the van.

The celebrity summoned Bracey and Al-Keypone, planted his free hand on Tohnyin's shoulder and tossed Nefrorius's bag into the rear of the van. He accepted both valises from Rondo and hurled them into the vehicle. Nefrorius tipped his derby as he filed past, hopped into the passenger's seat and slammed the door. A mustard-yellow *HAZ MAT* straight truck with a high cab rolled up the road and stopped ten meters behind the van. The celebrity shook Bracey's heavy suitcase. "Bringing Shalom cement flippers?" Tohnyin grabbed the suitcase, flung it into the vehicle and climbed in herself.

The celebrity headed back into the building for his tactical bag. The *HAZ MAT* truck engaged its strobe light and pulled ahead to a position where its box rested parallel to the van. A strapping man in a hard hat, safety goggles and a glowing chartreuse vest jumped out of the truck cab. The driver's door of the van slammed shut. The celebrity noticed two dull forklift blade tips protruding from beneath the passenger side of the van. He darted out the door. The tires of the van were lifted off the road. Lights flashing, the *HAZ MAT* truck started forward carrying the van alongside it.

"Out, everyone get out!" The celebrity lunged between the rear doors of the rising, tipping van and grabbed Tohnyin's foot with his free hand. Al-Keypone slid into the driver's seat. Bracey's suitcase smacked the celebrity's arm and he lost his hold on Tess. The celebrity tumbled into one of the doors and took a punch in the solar plexus from his tactical bag. Clinging to the door, he clinched the straps of his bag between his teeth as he opened it. The truck gained speed and tilted the van to a 45-degree angle. He produced his Swainson's Thrush kite and activated it. The engine of the van roared and its wheels spun furiously in the air. The celebrity pulled himself up and gained a tenuous foothold on the rear bumper. The man from *HAZ MAT* labored to pin doors shut as Bracey engaged him atop the van. Bracey appeared to slip. The celebrity targeted the *HAZ MAT* man's hard hat and launched the weapon. The Thrush clipped Rondo's brow as he lunged at the adversary. The *HAZ MAT* man boosted Bracey over the passenger's side of the van. A kick in the side of the head from an unseen source on the truck sent the celebrity plunging to the concrete.

The celebrity absorbed a kick in the sole. He held his head and rolled onto his back. He didn't believe he'd ever lost consciousness because he recalled the sound of screeching brakes, blaring horns and heated cursing. Bracey stood over him holding the headless Thrush. "Take your feathered friend back, you doddering oaf!" He hurled the kite off the celebrity's shoulder.

The celebrity moaned. "How long-"

"Since we lost our transport?" Rondo snarled. "Ten minutes."

The celebrity sat up. Bracey's left eye looked swollen. A bus approached, honked and swerved around them. The celebrity staggered to his feet, snatched his kite and tactical bag and hobbled back toward the bus shuttle center. He had multiple cuts on both hands, and the pain in his left elbow and hip overwhelmed him. He plunked himself on the curb and placed his head between his knees.

Rondo stood at the side of the road thirty meters away jabbering into his Qilroy. Ten minutes later, he limped to the celebrity and stood over him. His eye appeared stark red and was highlighted on top by a gash. "I anonymously reported the abduction to the cops. They transferred me to two different departments. They wanted too many details." He hissed. "I've been trying to reach Ledbetter but have so far not succeeded." He wiped his eye. "Have you been doing anything over here besides crying?"

The celebrity emitted a vexed breath. "It's apparently accomplished as much as you."

"The rendezvous would've unfolded cleanly if you hadn't come along," Bracey uttered. "We would've been out of here if Tohnyin had been prompt."

"We would've been on our way if you hadn't herded us back into the building when she pulled up." The celebrity rose. "But if WIO took this much trouble, they probably had more roadside assistance in place to intercept us farther along our course."

"You seem to have a lot of information about their operational procedures," Rondo charged. "You're the disgruntled employee who'd figure he could salvage his reputation by this sort of debacle, so it wouldn't be shocking to learn you were complicit."

The celebrity received a call from Tohnyin. "Oobops, old buddy," a vaguely familiar voice greeted him. "Are you okay? You hit the road like a lead balloon! We're still falling down laughing!"

"Identify yourself!" The celebrity hoped his timbre didn't convey the extent of his tension.

The man exposed his face to Tess's Qilroy cam. "Recognize me now, comrade?" He snapped the eye patch which accented his dark hair and mustache. "Your slingshot put my eye out." He coughed and snorted. "Call me Ishmael."

The celebrity surveyed the image. "Devil's Lake. Dennis!"

"Boo-rah, Ahab!" Dennis nodded vigorously. "That's one hellacious aim you've got on you. Hopping on one foot in the pitch dark with the seat down, I'll bet you hit nothing but bowl!"

"If you don't use your head, somebody else might." The celebrity wagged a grim forefinger. "You've arrogated her Qilroy. Where is she?"

"Poor, sad Tess." Dennis chortled. "As you'd expect, the whore turned easy." The contempt flickered palpably in his unimpaired eye. "Even quicker than the gangstar. Both of your diddly-squatters are in protective custody."

Bracey grabbed the celebrity's arm. "I'm Unique Agent Roald Bracey, and from here you're dealing exclusively with me." He glared into the Qilroy cam. "You're the pukes who van-jacked our personnel carrier?"

Dennis stroked his mustache. "I'm the engineer who put new meaning in the term 'pick-up truck,' and your Tohnyin and your Al-Keypone have had their threat-status significantly downgraded by the experience."

"So where does our argument stand now?" Rondo challenged. "What's it all really about: climate change, Charlton Shalom, money?"

"I'm offended by the suggestion that money is our motivator, Roald, but we'll accept two billion dollars to defray the cost of our security operation." Dennis adopted a pouty demeanor. "In the meantime, to demonstrate that our side is the reasonable one, we'll release high-maintenance Tess in short order." He smirked. "We'll release Nefrorius after we win our little dispute with California tonight in Lake Geneva and you arrange a capital transfer of two billion dollars to our treasury."

"These issues are far greater than any particular one or two individuals," Bracey insisted. "Even two *million* dollars would be out of the question. Your lack of environmental awareness will have grave consequences for you as well."

Dennis expelled an annoyed breath. "You're too materialistic, Roald. You're a brutish lout incapable of symbolic thought. Going forward, I'll only negotiate with Oobops."

Bracey snickered sardonically. "I'm sorry you feel that way, claim-jumper, because you're stuck with me."

The celebrity shoved Bracey away. "I'm back in the picture, Dennis. Where do we find Tohnyin?"

"Let me tell you about Tess, Ahab." Dennis exhibited a wry grin. "During her last visit, we cut a little fashion teardrop into her cheek, and beneath that flap of skin we inserted a device that allowed us to track her movements and monitor her communications. The device also introduced free lithium ions into her system which may have made her less perky and more pesky." He rubbed his face. "Now we removed the lithium gun portion of the original device and replaced it with a nanobomb on a passive circuit that we can detonate remotely anytime we please by just dropping our signal. It's not designed to kill her – it'll just blow off half her face, probably taking either an eye or an ear dependent on how the explosive charge settled." He fidgeted with his eye patch. "The medics are optimistic that they can craft me a new working eyeball within two years, so I'd figure Tess's face can be reasonably reconstructed within five. We'd expect her usefulness in the industry to be satisfactorily diminished by then."

"How do we, ah, save face?" the celebrity demanded.

Dennis grunted. "Keep out of the state of Wisconsin and its business. And if the rest of your high-minded carbon-mongering doom-promoters don't stay the hell out, I forecast you're going to start losing people like Tohnyin and Al-Keypone in a manner that has nothing to do with a standard climate model. We'll enroll Nefrorius in Hostage University for instructions on how to safely deactivate Tess's personal explosive device. Monday morning when our weekend transactions have been successfully concluded, we'll send him back to you with your staff vehicle, and your final warning will be complete."

Bracey clutched the celebrity's Qilroy. "What assurance do we have that you'll carry through with that promise?"

The engineer scoffed. "There are no guarantees in life, gents, but you win the long game by playing the percentages. You have some micro-explosives experts in California, but we've rigged the bomb in a way that'll make it nearly impossible for someone who doesn't know exactly what they're doing to disarm it with an acceptable outcome." He smirked. "That's *our* inside edge. I should also point out that Tess isn't aware she's carrying a blast-bolt in her cheek, so I'll leave it to you whether or not to spill our dirty, little secret. It might ruin her weekend." He sneered. "Do we have an understanding?"

The celebrity strained to remain calm. "We'd best humor the mechanic," he uttered, "who gunned down I.B. Winterhalter."

Dennis guffawed. "You're the wisest ass in the West, Ahab. I have other lives to impact, so I'll leave you to arrange an instrument of money transfer and customize your playbook for tonight's performance. With any luck at all, there'll be no weather event or carrier glitch that might interrupt the signal, and our Tess can stay connected. Wait for *us* to contact *you*, or she won't make it."

The celebrity felt as if his head and stomach were spinning in opposite directions. "Hurt her, Ishmael, and I'll call you a hearse, because that's what you'll need."

"Will that be all, Ahab?" Dennis snarled. "Does Nefrorius rate an equal threat, or do the elitist Forniars reserve reprisal privilege for someone like Tess?" He terminated the connection.

"Nice." Bracey displayed a minatory grimace. "In the standard course of hostage conservation, what you said there might've gotten her head blown off." He received a call and straightened his posture. "We've encountered a complication in securing personnel at Chicago O'Hare that may require an across-the-board reassessment of our strategy." Rondo ran his fingers over his gash. "Unique Agents Al-Keypone and Tohnyin were abducted and our transport was commandeered by enemy combatants." He mumbled briefly and gestured to the celebrity. "I have the D.C.I. in Santa Monica. He wants you linked so we don't have to repeat everything more times than usual."

The celebrity joined the call, and a disheveled, shirtless Natty Phil appeared on his Qilroy screen. "P.L.," he interrupted Bracey, "we have a desperate situation with Tohnyin. The flywheel who shot Winterhalter and calls himself the state engineer contacted us and announced that Tess's release is imminent, but he added that they surgically implanted an explosive device in her head."

Bracey scoffed. "It sounds like a load of horseshit."

The celebrity winced mightily. "Right, that's not your winning smile on the line, is it, headbutt?"

Ledbetter pressed his thumb and forefinger against his brow. "It's demoralizing that Illinois has evolved into such a rogue state. At least in Wisconsin, you know what you have."

Bracey rubbed his eye. "Natty Phil, I had just about repelled the ambush when Oobops shot me with one of his birdie kites and knocked me off the moving vehicle. I can't prove it was deliberate, but he and the WIO shakeshaft chatted like they were old cellmates." He grunted. "My eye socket is loose."

"If we can stop beating ourselves over the head with shaky allegations, we'll trade credit and blame shares later." The D.C.I. patted his hair. "I'm attempting to have the somatags of both Tohnyin and Al-Keypone tracked as we speak, but we're being jammed or the devices have been disabled."

"The WIO officer believed to be named Dennis Blount," the celebrity persevered, "informed me they'd advise us of Tess's location when they release her. He said they'd train Nefrorius to disarm Tess's 'blast-bolt' and then release him once we forfeit the flyting in Lake Geneva tonight. But I don't trust them. You need to send the bomb disposal squad ASAP."

The director traced his temporal scar with his shoehorn. "I'll assemble the backup flyte team and dispatch them to O'Hare on an H.S.C.T. That roster will include Kahn Vanderslenk, arguably our best improvised bomb disposal tech. If you're able, Ahab, remain handy. Rondo, you seek medical treatment for your injury. Should we prevail in the flyte tonight, we can expect some modified negotiation offer. They'll probably attempt to swap Al-Keypone for Shalom. If there are no further faults to flaunt, we'll leave this channel open to alert one another of any developments." He terminated his connection.

"I trust we have a consensus," the celebrity submitted, "that it would be counterproductive at this point to advise Natty Phil of WIO's ransom demand."

"That noise about money wasn't serious, you pathetic dupe." Bracey hissed. "He was deriding the idea of climate compensation. Do Tohnyin a huge favor, Oobops. If they contact you again, forward the call to me for further negotiation." Rubbing his eye, Rondo strutted out of the bus shuttle center.

Local time stood at 0658 hours. The celebrity paced anxiously. He purchased two energy drinks and consumed one. He developed a theory that the hostages remained on the airport premises. He lingered around the baggage carousels. He consumed his reserve energy drink. He received a call from Bracey at 1030 hours: "Word from WIO?"

"Nothing." The celebrity decided to confide in Rondo. "Killing time is killing me."

"You are the most self-centered bozo I've ever met." Bracey had acquired a bulky eye bandage. "I was just treated for a cracked orbital bone, a detached retina and a concussion."

The celebrity smiled complaisantly. "I hear bee venom therapy is good for optic nerve trauma, Rondo, if you're man enough to endure a little stinging."

Bracey emitted a heavy breath. "I shouldn't even be back on the street."

The celebrity nodded. "I presume that the backup team is in the air."

Rondo eyed the celebrity peevishly. "There's a maintenance problem with the aircraft in California. They're also having trouble deciding who to bring in as Al-Keypone's replacement." He tapped his bandage. "I'm sure you're under the impression you might still be inserted as skald but that's not happening. You simply lack the scientific background to be an effective combatant. You have the same major weakness as Nefrorius without any of his strategic advantages."

"What," the celebrity challenged, "makes you think *you're* qualified to rate whether *I* am or not, you high-powered bellows?"

Bracey sucked in his cheeks. "Listen, stooge, when I was in high school, I excelled in the natural sciences to the degree that Caltech rewarded my aspiration to be an aerospace engineer with a merit scholarship offer. But what I encountered when I toured the campus were clusters of nimrods roaming around barefoot, which struck me as so uncivilized that I shifted my priorities to law and government." He shook his head. "Shalom's dossier indicates that he entertained a similar sentiment."

"Do you mean to suggest, space cowboy, that except for a

missing crate of wingtips, you'd now be assiduously pedaling a solar-wind craft toward the Crab Nebula, and we wouldn't be dedicating precious bandwidth to patronizing your foolish conceits?"

"Now hear this." Rondo terminated the connection.

At 1205 hours, the celebrity received a call from Lucas Galachel. "Ahab, it's me." Tohnyin appeared on his Qilroy screen, her countenance dazed and vacuous.

"Tess, where are you?" He attempted to put a tracer on the call origin location. "Are you hurt?"

"I'm a little under the radar." She flashed a forlorn smile. "They separated Nefrorius and me. They made me ingest all the drugs I was carrying: a methaqualone, mephedrone, Copioids cocktail. They thought I passed out – or passed away. I escaped, hitched a ride and *borrowed* a sourcerer."

His guarded relief overwhelmed him. "Let me fetch you–"

"Ahab, I just spoke with Natty Phil." She held her trembling fingers over her cheek. "I started picking at my little war hickey, and he alerted me to the deeper personal problem associated with it." She patted the cut. "I'm going to remove the in vivo ordnance myself before WIO blows me up."

"Tess!" the celebrity snapped. "Kahn Vanderslenk is on his way to help you!"

"Just remain calm?" Tohnyin forced a chuckle. "I'm surprised Kahn's still with us as often as he slips up." She sighed. "Moreover, I won't risk having anyone else harmed by my mini-mine."

The celebrity flattened his pipeline curl. "Tess, please wait for Kahn! At least wait for me!"

"If you need to collect me, Ahab, I'm in Kenosha, Wisconsin, at a dumpster in the alley behind the Druid's Mart beside the bus station on Highway 50 next to the freeway." Tess raised her eyebrows. "Stay with me online, chaplain, and say a little prayer if you got one. I need a few minutes to get my mind right."

The celebrity raced out of the terminal building and engaged a semi-private floe blue NG Gurnard gref to convey him to Kenosha. "Tess, I'll connect you to Kahn so he can direct your procedure remotely."

"Too dangerous," she decreed. "I took two minicourses at the Mission on micro-explosives. I'd hate to think that time was wasted."

"Don't become living proof that a little knowledge is more dangerous than none." The NG Gurnard crawled onto the expressway, entered the gref lane and began passing other vehicles.

"Ahab, attend me in silence." She stared stoically into the sourcerer cam for twenty minutes.

Shortly after the gref entered Wisconsin, the celebrity accepted a call from Ledbetter: "Has Tess come in yet?"

"I have her on my other line. She insists she's going to perform the blast-bolt excision herself."

"Prevent her self-mutilation by any means possible, Oobops." The director cleared his sinuses. "Our replacement team of Brandon Rosenthal and Kahn Vanderslenk has been conveyed to Bob Hope. They should be dropped into Wisconsin by 1600 hours CST. I am currently pursuing diplomatic channels to match brinksmanship with WIO queenpin Llewellyn Morse. If this reprehensible organization contacts you again, forward the call to Unit Bracey." He terminated the connection.

The celebrity returned to his Tohnyin connection. "Are you still with me, Oobops?" She set her sourcerer on a compost bin. "I'm about to go into delivery."

"Tess," he pleaded, "I'm not ready! I have things to say to you!"

"Magnifying mirror function applied." She displayed a small knife and tweezers. "Manicure instruments sharpened and sterilized." She held the blade against her face for several minutes. "I'll always think of you, Ahab, as having an unnatural regard for decency." She sliced into her cheek and grimaced, drawing a ribbon of blood. She inserted her tweezers. He gasped silently. She gently probed and prodded for several more minutes. With a twist of the wrist, she withdrew the tweezers and held her knife hand over her cheek. "It's ouwwwt," she cooed. She stepped back and held what looked like a tiny diode attached to a thin wire against the sourcerer cam. A pop and flash ended the transmission.

"No, no, no, no!" The celebrity clutched his temples. "Faster," he shrieked at the driver, "faster, please!" The gref exited I-94, raced three blocks west and cut off two motorists pulling into the Druid's Mart parking lot. The celebrity leapt out of the craft with his tactical bag and dashed behind the building. He found a glassy-eyed Tohnyin crumpled on her knees beside the dumpster, slowly rubbing her trembling hands against each other. Her punctured cheek and her collar were smeared with blood. She looked up and offered a tortured smile. "Little cut on the bias. Operation successful."

He dropped to his knees and put his arm around her. "You must've had a real blast."

She emitted a series of deep breaths and ground her teeth. "My hands burn." She moved her fingers lightly over her face. "My nose still stings!" She emitted a guttural cry filled with both angst and ferocity. "When I get through with Dennis, the only state job he'll be qualified for is palace eunuch!"

"You're still bleeding liberally." The celebrity opened his tactical bag and removed his survival kit. He pressed a disinfectant strip against Tohnyin's facial wound and electrocured the laceration. He applied a hydrocolloid dressing to the blistered backs of her hands and helped her to her feet. He contacted the D.C.I. and let Tess announce her state of revitalization.

The D.C.I. hiccuped. "We can agree that the Bureau owes you a debt of gratitude, Tess, for enduring adversity beyond common reckoning."

"Then pay it off by sending Ahab into the flyting behind me as our skald," Tohnyin demanded.

"You've also been replaced as our presenter." Ledbetter pressed his thumb and forefinger against his brow. "Recognizing that the planet could share your destiny as 'damaged goods' if we fail, Unit Bracey has heroically volunteered to resign as the lead of our Hostage Locator Task Force in Chicago and suck it up to serve as presenter tonight for Brandon Rosenthal. Upon further reflection, I grow more comfortable by the moment at having installed Rosenthal as skald and weaponizing the ethnic identity and derivative cultural values he shares with Shalom."

"I thought we also agreed," the celebrity asserted, "that Shalom wouldn't appreciate being patronized like a humorless, witless twinkie beyond the reach of rational analysis."

"Tohnyin's recovery does alter our situation." The director traced his temporal scar. "I now have complete confidence that Morse can be persuaded to facilitate Al-Keypone's release, perhaps as early as tomorrow. Our main objective tonight is to put up the token resistance of a presence so Wisconsin doesn't become even more dangerously emboldened. You two are to reappear in Lake Geneva as our super reserve force, and you will troubleshoot the event as official stand-ins until relieved of duty by Rosenthal and Bracey." He bared his teeth. "If you pledge to prevent this from becoming the ultimate night of tipping points, I'll leave you to debouch." He terminated his connection.

"Aw, hell." Tohnyin sighed. "Let's drag our smoked butts back to the *Janesy* and clean up."

"I doubt that my ride from Chicago is still waiting." The celebrity looked west as he led Tess around the building. "If you're up to hoofing it, we'd have a 50-kilometer shot straight down Highway 50 to Lake Geneva. The overseers at the Mission trained you to run a marathon backwards in high heels, didn't they?"

"That sounds like a program designed exclusively for you." Tohnyin narrowed her eyes and followed the celebrity's gaze. The Gurnard remained in the Druid's Mart parking lot with its engine idling and the driver seated on the hood stuffing his face with junk food. The CIB crypto-crats uncomplainingly paid the steep downtime fee and accepted an express ride back to Lake Geneva.

The celebrity and Tohnyin caught the shuttle boat from the Riviera Beach pier and were conveyed to the *Janesy*. They headed directly below to their respective cabins for a brief rest and recovery including wardrobe change. At 1830 hours, the celebrity received a video message from Tess's plundered Qilroy showing Unique Agent Nefrorius Al-Keypone being loaded onto an airplane. The accompanying text read: "Carbon capture returned to Sacramento source in better condition than when received. Be smart and follow suit."

The celebrity and Tohnyin re-emerged at 1900 hours and arrived at the Coat Of Arms forty minutes before astronomical dusk. The celebrity wore his tan blazer and dressy slacks while Tess commanded a strapless confetti-print white sundress. As he admired the superb makeup artistry she'd displayed in covering her cheek wound, a familiar voice greeted them. "This ain't the dude you were with last week." Doorman extraordinaire Burl unclasped the velvet rope.

"I.B.?" The celebrity pulled Tess to the entrance jamb. "We found him in an alley. The medical examiner's report established his cause of death as malnutrition."

The celebrity disabled his sourcerer. He and Tohnyin found the luxurious lounge packed with too many tourists to fit comfortably on all of the furniture. "Where's Rondo and crew?" Tess wondered. A girl in Jacqui boots cruised through the room on a hot-pink recumbent bicycle, and Tohnyin gestured to her. "That's Noragreta, my WIO detainment camp counselor." A closer look ascertained that the rider in the plaid vest was a small middle-aged woman. "And there's Omar." Tess pointed to a stocky man with dark curls in a green aloha shirt seated at the end of a couch on the other side of the room.

Noragreta and Tess locked glowers. Noragreta scooped a crumpled piece of plastic garbage from the floor and tossed it into a recyclotron. "Look at me, look at me!" she squealed. "I'm saving the planet! I'm a friend of the Earth!"

"The next time you make a deposit," Tohnyin growled, "don't let go."

Omar rose and approached. Noragreta continued her weaving and split the celebrity and Tess. "We're honored by your company again, Tess." Omar bowed. "How many of your fellow presiders over the last gasp of civilization flew their private crafts in to support you in shaming us for our gratuitous abuse of the environment?" He extended his hand to the celebrity. "And you would be, uh, Roland?"

"I certainly would not." The celebrity reluctantly shook hands.

A smattering of applause rippled through the lounge as Charlton Shalom entered in a pith helmet, canary yellow sweater and baggy safari shorts. He carried a riding crop. The reaction intensified as Tiffany appeared behind him wearing a celestial blue evening gown and diamond necklace.

"Everyone's acquainted?" Shalom inferred. Noragreta parked her bicycle and joined the scrum. "Glad you could complete us, kiddo." He turned to Tohnyin, observed the knot in her cheek and noticed her burned hands. "'The sweet face of a young girl is blistered by the scalding rain.' Is that the subliminal message you're angling to put out, Tess?"

Tohnyin fixed Omar with a smile that dissolved into a sneer. "It's the aftermath of surgical improv to remove a subcutaneous explosive charge planted by our Wisconsin settle-it-with-violence mongers."

"Was that your big idea?" Charlton questioned Omar. "One should be violated so she'd sneeze and blow her little mind?"

"I hadn't heard of that." Omar rubbed his hands through his thick hair. "Of course, I can't be held to account for the abuses perpetrated by the more militant factions of our counteroffensive." He folded his arms. "A project was recently proposed in which a mood-enhancing passive electromedical device would be embedded to manipulate the energy state of lithium ions, thereby causing chemical reactions in the subject's body, which might manifest themselves as depression and disgruntlement." He chuckled. "Metallic particle resin was to be smeared in the subject's hair to make it serve as an antenna as well as really shine. It sounded like an experiment your son Tycho might design."

The polymath bender of gravity waves shook his head. "Reprogramming someone's brain in such a fashion makes for shoddy P.R., doesn't it?" He clapped his hands. "But save your salvos. If no one needs a battlefield comfort stop, let's shift this shootout to the stage."

"Come out with gums blazing for the flyte of the century!" Mercowitz appeared between the celebrity and Tohnyin. "Pillory with abandon; bulldoze the opposition to oatmeal!" He dispensed shoulder slaps of encouragement. "Then if, as forecast, this bash turns out to be a futility rite, we'll be here for you in your period of moaning."

"Pleased you could cast us off, X.O." Shalom saluted the Parallacts associate and gave Tiffany a farewell wrist clasp. With a head nod, he sent his four combatants through the door and into the narrow hall that led to the lunar lounge. But he conducted the quorum through a side door, and they descended a ladder. "You're going down in a submersible, skalds, where we'll suffer no interference from the curious, the spurious or the furious."

The submarine sat on the rollers of a stern ramp and looked like a miniature bullet-train tube car. An attendant in an intrepid blue jump suit held open the hatch. "Everything is sub standard, sir," he reported. He confiscated sourcerers and frisked the players for weapons.

Shalom led the charge through a cramped engine room passageway of pipes and cables into a spacious saloon. "Here's the flyting pit." The cool, dim, stuffy venue featured a stage which purported to be an unfinished pyramid. Two crossed lances decorated the wall behind it, and a twinkling bright grey eye filled the ceiling. A tartan floor cushion and set of bagpipes lay on a tatami mat before the stage. The Nobel recidivist straddled the pipes and gestured to the stage with his crop. "I know it's a challenge for government personnel to understand something plain and simple, but you are each to occupy one of the four yoga mats arranged in a horseshoe pattern up top, presenters inside. Please maintain a loose lotus sitting position with legs crossed and palms cupped upward throughout the match. Leave the mat, lose the match." The combatants climbed the pyramid and took their places.

"I'm going up front to conduct the launch." Shalom stood erect. "My regrets to the California contingent that the sub isn't Los Angeles class, but it does have a roll stabilizer, so if I can press buttons in the correct sequence, I should be able to trim us without flipping us on our heads or shredding us in the screw." He exited through the forward bulkhead door and shut it tight behind him.

Noragreta winked at Tohnyin. "When you visited, some silverfish might've migrated into your open sores and cavities. I hope you're not experiencing any peculiar internal sensations."

"She's too tough for that," Omar contributed. "She's a peculiar agent."

Tess grinned unflappably. "If you don't slaughter these two onagers, Ahab, I'll slaughter all three of you." She kicked his funny bone.

"So this is Oobops," Omar cooed. "Our reports indicate that Ahab thinks women don't count."

"Give the storm-tripper some credit," Noragreta chided. "Oobops doesn't count on women thinking."

A resounding thump preceded a series of vibrations. The sub pitched violently and swayed, scattering the flyting combatants over the sides of the pyramid. The skalds regathered themselves on stage, and the illumination above the spotlight eye increased. A smooth sensation of floating ensued, and Shalom returned with a tea service. "Now that we've achieved neutral buoyancy, the contest begins with a formal tea ceremony. And any supporters you might have aboard the *Janesy* can watch you live in the lounge." He furnished cups and saucers and poured each skald a steaming cup of matcha.

Omar offered an effervescent smile. "What's this boat's capacity?"

"It seats five comfortably, and I like to be comfortable." Shalom proceeded back to his floor cushion and cradled the whining bagpipes.

"The sub has an electric hybrid propulsion system, hmm?" Omar sipped his tea with a raised pinkie. "Is that the only reason it's so much quieter than you'd expect? How long can it stay submerged? That is, when does the oxygen supply become insufficient to support life?"

"I'm glad you asked about that," Shalom responded, "because I'm tired of answering your silly questions, and I can't answer those." He pointed the riding crop at each flyting combatant in turn. "This baton is to serve as my bumper crop to designate a new speaker. When I recognize that you're rambling, brown-nosing or you have otherwise overextended your claim to the floor, I'll end your turn by waving this stick as a prelude to drowning you out with a blast on the pipe." He blew a strained sour note. "In the words of astute existentialist ringmaster Martin Buber, 'No thing reveals itself except through the reciprocal force of confrontation, in the lightning and counter-lightning of encounter.' This flyting is dedicated to the throngs of witless wonders who've exchanged their sense of lively fair-playfulness for a self-indulgent self-righteousness and choose to puff themselves up by taking offense to anything under the sun: Have yourself a feast." He pointed the baton at Noragreta. "Fire when ready!"

Noragreta flipped her ash blonde tresses over her left shoulder. "Good evening, honorable grand adjudicator Dr. Shalom and concerned ladies and gentlemen." She nodded to the celebrity and Tohnyin. "I'd take the opportunity to welcome our distinguished invaders from California to the great state of Wisconsin if they weren't already in the process of attempting to welcome themselves to it. I'm Noragreta Haggarty, publicist for the Department of Sustainability and Emergency Government, here to introduce Professor of Law Omar Bardot, expert in environmental affairs. For all the good eggs breaking beneath the pressure of the doom cloud that descends with the coastal elite, the cure is WIO, and the doctor is the lawyer." She tapped Omar on the knee.

"Thank you, N-Gret, I'm pleased to participate in this humble execution." Bardot eyed the celebrity and Tohnyin. "We know our opposition by reputation, of course, and I've been looking forward to opening a dialog with you, Ahab, since I found the talons of some of your projectiles in my colleague's vertebrae." He smiled tartly. "We've enjoyed playing host to his presenter Tess, who's on a one-woman mission to disprove the old adage that 'Nothing's as easy as it looks.' Tess developed her tools of influence early. On the morning of her fifteenth birthday, her braces came off, and in the evening, so did everything else. Since then, she's spread her erotic capital on an ever-inosculating trajectory, and she now expresses her efficiency and resourcefulness by wearing bra straps sealed with an easy-open pull tab. She's convinced considerable important, powerful men of her property value-"

Shalom blew a croak on the bagpipes and pointed the baton at Tohnyin. "Good evening, Lake Geneva," Tess opened over the dissipating drone, "how are you doing tonight? I observed an awfully good-looking crowd in the ship's lounge, so we must have a lot of out-of-state visitors. I tease, naturally. Wisconsin women are as attractive as any in the country, or at least no more than a diet and a shave away from it." She snickered. "We're Tess Tohnyin and Ahab Oobops, humanitarian aid workers from California on a course to enable the deep pockets of socially and environmentally conscious activists around Madison, as we remind the nodding countryside of our worsening environmental dilemma. As a process bonus, we hope to ascertain how high-placed, self-styled enviro-shaman Omar can remain blissfully oblivious to a festering ecological catastrophe and so willingly abdicate any responsibility to make the world a more habitable, secure place."

Noragreta waved her arms and received consent of the crop. "Most of the world would gladly trade their local climate woes for California's troubles." Her features blazed with affability. "Travel to sunny California, meet someone with a warm, welcoming smile, and you can be sure you're interacting with a fellow tourist."

Tohnyin vigorously tapped her cheek. "You're off the laugh meter, cheese-bag. In the same vein that you misrepresented me, why don't you comic thrusters bang away at air quality deterioration, weather pattern instability and increased storm severity leading to resource allocation destabilization and infrastructure damage, ecosystem imbalance-"

Shalom blew a protracted note on the bagpipes and pounded the riding crop like a gavel. "You've discharged a thankless task, presenters." He pointed the baton at Bardot. "Let's refresh the fight on the front line."

"Think of the reservoir as half-full, Tess." Omar flashed a tight-lipped smile. "Imagine how many furriers and tanners rising global temperatures will put out of business. Less heating fuel will have to be consumed." His demeanor became solemn. "California might relieve the chronic stress of its intellectual drought by learning not to view science through the politics of green-tinted sunglasses. They exaggerate the environmental threat of manmade emissions and conveniently neglect to mention the beneficial impact of a warmer climate in areas like the upper Midwest. They need to wrap their salted-in-the-shell West Coast brains around the erosion of their traditional turf privilege. More federal tax dollars wash over the Golden State than any other biosphere in the union. We've bought into their wind and water projects, and in return, they offer an organic fear-mongering service and seek to gridlock our lives in an onerous minefield of regulatory claptrap and procedural gobbledygook. As a proud Native American, I retain a close, transcendent connection to the Earth, and as the father of two wonderful, precocious children, I carry an overriding interest in preserving a healthful environment for the future. I resent any suggestion by these krummholz to the contrary, and I'm outraged-"

Shalom sounded the bagpipes and signaled the celebrity. "Ready to sail boldly into the crucible, Avery?"

"Aye, windjammer." The celebrity let the drone subside. "That's our code in the nautical and aviation capital of the U.S. for anything that stops a lawyer dead in his yaks. And it's a particularly welcome relief when Omar's dictating the diatribe because his remarks inspire a poor sap spoiling for a phytonutrient with the sensation of biting into putrid produce."

Bardot snickered sardonically. "I'll proceed slowly, Ahab, and explain things more thoroughly. We know you thought the call for improved fencing at the border entailed claymores."

"Of war paint and wall paint." The celebrity thrummed his abdominal muscles. "Omar's prime duty in his day job is to decide which of his interests to cheat, and in this case, he split the difference and betrayed both his past and his future." Bardot raised his teacup. "I accept that we're placed at a serious disadvantage in this parley by Omar's professional experience in aggravating tensions. When he was in law school, he collected spare coin at funerals heckling the eulogist on behalf of clients who didn't care for the deceased." The celebrity raised his cup and took a sip. "It was a natural progression. Like Tess, Omar discovered his calling early. Dubbed by tribal elders as Running Mouth, he recognized that his proficiency as a noisemaker and his appetite for public service must lead him to become an attorney or a singing butler. Unfortunately, he was too tone-deaf to carry a tune and too clumsy to carry a tray." He grinned complaisantly. "If musical instruments were morals, Omar would be a contrabassoonist. If they were manners, he'd play a heckelphone."

Shalom pointed the baton at Bardot. "I believe we're being treated to a demonstration," Omar opined, "on why California has a higher rate of mental illness and commitment for insanity than any other state in America."

"It's because under Wisconsin law," the celebrity pounced, "body snatchers and cannibals are repeatedly deemed to be as sane as the presiding judge at their trial." He exchanged scowls with Noragreta. "Wisconsin might attract more federal tax dollars if most of its major construction projects weren't a century behind everyone else's."

"Ahab seems unsteady, rather insecure and unsure of himself." Bardot offered a smirking sneer. "He needs to drink less. Or more. Or he needs his mommy. The reason he doesn't still live with Mom is because her trailer doesn't have a basement."

"We're able to determine that the woman Omar lives with is his wife because he'd have far more personal autonomy if it was his mother." The celebrity presented his hands as if to be cuffed. "Omar customarily refers to his wife by the honorary tribal name he's given here: Yes Deer. He's edgy tonight because Her Nibs blew town and left a lock on the fridge. Omar strives to be the dedicated husband and conscientious father by taking meals with his family at least five times a day."

"You're routinely rejected by your imaginary friends, you invisible carbon fart-print." Bardot exhaled heavily. "People who've been previously subjected to him warned us about his puckish wit, and now that I've been exposed to it, I concede I'd like to whack him with a hockey stick myself."

"You might have to work up to that one, gym rat." The celebrity smiled balefully. "When Omar trains, his favorite exercise is the sit-out. His booby prize of a spouse regards the thick lump inhabiting the pumpkin shell on his shoulders as his most impressive muscle, but if he picks his nose, his head implodes. A windlestraw of a woman, the wife was charged with crimes against nature and humanity when their son was born with a father-favoring head the size of a soccer ball. The obstetrics team initially though it *was* a soccer ball, inserted into the womb by Omar to give the boy a head start on sports."

Bardot rolled his eyes. "Are you so anti-family, Ahab, just because you couldn't find a happy camping ground for your own minihaha? Allow me to give *you* an honorary tribal name: Crying Wolf."

"Omar's daughter is the pride of the tribe," the celebrity persevered. "She's a cloying pestle of a girl who's heavily into diversity like her soccer mom but with a multiculturalist verve that appropriates Italian and African-American popular arts. Her name is Arapaho."

Bardot scoffed with sufficient gusto to generate spit. "Enough crap about my kids, Oobops, you chip off the old gorgon. We're all grateful your environmental consciousness extends to not polluting the gene pool with your own pro-creation." He raised his cup of tea. "Your looks could gag a maggot; your face would make an ichneumon fly sick!"

The celebrity nodded. "You, on the other hand, cold-truth denier, have a smile as lovely as the wart between a baboon's glutes. I've seen cuter faces than yours rise from a set of rattles. If a shipment of 21 cadavers included Omar, and each anatomy student in a class of 20 could select one, Omar would be the odd specimen out."

Bardot shook his head. "Ahab is obviously the product of a troubled childhood, watching his neo-hippie methane-head of a mother roam the roundabouts in sagging underwear, blowing the hair out of her face and making love to a bottle of Cutty Sark. Oblivious to everything except offsetting her personal carbon count against the sizzle tally, she finally shaved her head so solar rays striking her proportionally flat scalp would bounce harmlessly back into space."

"The scars of Omar's origin are bigger than all blame." The celebrity held his gaze on the stoic Shalom. "When his father first sighted his mother naked in the woods, he agonized over whether to go husband or hunter on her. What a trophy rack! 'You'd best not be Godiva,' he brayed, 'cuz you ain't no lady!' Only history will decide the wisdom of his choice that stuck society with another blood-sucking, prevaricating squid of a high-lacquered lawyer, whose thick crust of a persona begs a serious bakeover."

"Am I a codger, a tosher, a rotter?" Bardot chuckled. "None of Ahab's insults are anything but an empty exercise in generic name-calling; the only meaning his words carry are what they say about himself."

"Are you calling me a name-caller?" The celebrity bared his teeth.

"What I'm going to break through the white noise and call you, blue belly, is an eco-bigot." Omar folded his arms authoritatively. "Ahab's signature strike is a glib assault on my ethnic heritage and my family. He may be the sort of benign pest who does busy little favors nobody needs, but deep down he's a racist, a sexist and a homophobe, and that's on a slow day."

The celebrity slapped his thighs. "I remind you, snow-job, you're the one who introduced your family as political props and came out of the chute wielding the geno-shield as a sword. You're the one cooking a recipe for environmental disaster that'll flush your huddled masses of climate refugees into the ultimate storm." He clutched his throat in a choking gesture. "You insinuate that the battle is beneath you but in fact it's beyond you. Omar would be a much deeper dipstick if he chafed less with cultural sensitivity to personal dismissals and more with climatic sensitivity to manmade emissions."

"Your climate shift needs a paradigm shift," Noragreta interjected. "You're cooking the data for environmental disaster. You're a flawed meat thermometer!"

"He's a thermophobe." Bardot grimaced. "Even if I were the sort inclined to pick targets with unacceptable properties like your ethnicity, Oobops, service demand doesn't require me to work up to nameplate capacity and attack nerve centers that aren't fair game." He looked askance at Tohnyin. "The bottom line is that we the Great Lakes Region can find better uses for our disposable income than to keep us from freezing our asses off. Keep your overcrowded, overtaxed California lifestyle to yourselves. Grapple with your own local environmental fits and starts come what may as we've always had to."

"Spoken like a true law doctor," Tess quipped, "like a bad medicine man, a primitive political parasite, a cartoonish cross between a medfly and a barfly. Of course, red Wisconsin's idea of high culture is playing with their greasy food before they eat it-"

"*Sure'n'begorah*, the green people look so renewed and smell so clean!" Omar fixed Tess with a sneer and turned it on the celebrity. "'Tis a relief to know their hearts aren't set on stealing our water, only our minds. They make me want to slip into my body stocking, grab my sippy cup, mount my bikey and ride boldly ride because when simple air use requires great personal expense and complicated accounting measures, I'll need to keep moving to stay warm."

"Go European!" Haggarty rooted. "That was the epicenter of global turmoil last century, and their laws and cultures would provide the perfect setting again!"

"You should provide your native sons and daughters with such a dystopia," the celebrity scolded. "The thicker the safety net, the fewer players you lose."

Noragreta scoffed. "It's puzzling that a man of your

perspicacity wouldn't have noticed how poorly such elegant-sounding systems tend to translate to the real world."

"Hollywood has always gotten it." Bardot held his focus on the celebrity. "I can ashk him," he channeled screen legend Humphrey Bogart, "accushe him, shall I, of being shecret Ashkenazhi?"

"Was toleranche the problem with your firsht wife, sholishitor?" the celebrity responded with his own Bogart impression. "Shpeak up or shut up." He espied a proto-smile in Shalom's eyes. "Backlot background. Near the end of filming the picture they all shtill talk about – *Cashablanca* – azh would be expected, the Bergman broad and myself developed an acute case of the hotzh for each other. But I knew it would never work out. For her part, she already had two or three rich boyfriendzh in addition to her two or three rich husbandzh. For my part – well, Bacall never did let me keep pets. Sho I delivered a parting shpeech that made the one in the picture look lame by comparizhon. I informed her, 'You're a fine-looking Shcandinavian dame, Ingie, and I'd love to take you around the block for a tesht drive, and kick your tirezh and toot your horn. But my heart belongzh to the Jewish gal because she has nagging down to an ahrt form. It givezh us an excushe to shlap each other around.'" He pointed to the grand slam scientist. "You can imagine the sense of urgency with which the Hollywood icons of the day like Bogie, Kate and Jimmy would view the climate change peril."

An explosion rocked the submarine and heaved it onto its side. The overhead eye cracked and crashed to the stage at the front of a massive deluge. Knocked to the bottom of the ruptured pyramid steps, the celebrity attempted to gulp air as the roaring torrent pinned him atop Tohnyin. He managed to grab Tess's wrist in the enveloping darkness. Struggling to maintain consciousness, he imagined his head would explode as pressure and more thundering pressure pounded down. His chest grew tight as he twisted and tried to rise against the crushing force. Pressure in the saloon equalized. He thrashed and kicked.

He reduced his task to the immediate act of escaping the shell of the craft. Disoriented, he knew only an excruciatingly cold, blurry black, and he feared he hadn't survived the explosion. His desperate need to breathe and the sensation of Tess punching his arm and kneeing his groin assured him that he remained alive. He tried to follow the path of the bubbles he expelled to the surface of the lake. His thoughts degraded to reaching and kicking.

He surfaced, towing her after him. He inhaled air and ejected water. Gagging and retching, she struggled to breathe. Their enervated muscles fought to tread water in the numbing grip of the frigid lake. A wave overtook them. She resurfaced a short distance from him hacking furiously. A corner of the unfinished pyramid stage surfaced. "Tess," he gasped.

"Go back!" She coughed violently. "For them, for Shalom!"

The crippled submarine blew to the surface, creating a wave which flipped the pyramid so about half of the structure protruded above the water. Lit by emergency lights flashing amber and red, the craft listed radically. A spotlight shone on the sub. Shalom waved from the uncompromised cockpit of the vessel. The top section of the saloon had been ripped away, and a streamer of bluish vapor rose from the rear. The source of the spotlight was a rapidly approaching yacht. The yacht spot beam probed the pyramid, which bobbed in the chop about ten meters beyond the submarine. It then found Tohnyin and the celebrity struggling to stay afloat in between.

"You murdering bastards!" Bardot appeared at the most ravaged section of the saloon wielding one of the decorative lances. "This is precisely what we should've expected from the goddamn filthy Forniars!" He slammed the sharp end of the lance into the water in front of the celebrity.

"*We* didn't order take-out, sumac!" The celebrity shook to dislodge water from his ears and mouth.

"You're the one who benefits from the disruption!" Omar raised the lance again. "You're the one who'd need a reset! If it wasn't you, it came from the Alice corps wing-nuts you were sent to incite!" He slammed the end of the lance into the water a short distance from the celebrity. "Same difference! You blew Noragreta's leg off!"

The celebrity lunged for the lance but missed. "You're the ones with the fear of flyting; you're the charge-planters!"

"They don't have any trouble wasting their own planet, do they?" Tohnyin stabilized herself halfway between the celebrity and the pyramid. "Be grateful," she advised Bardot, "all your victims made it back to the surface!"

"Is there any call to idiocy you airheads don't heed?" Omar plunged the lance into the lake and attempted to employ it as an oar. "There're oxygen masks on the wall. To broadcast in real-time, we couldn't have been very deep, and you must know the craft automatically blows to the surface in an emergency!"

The submarine drifted close to Tohnyin, and the celebrity propelled himself beside her. Bardot jabbed his lance in a threatening gesture as the yacht arrived. "I promise if you don't get N-Gret medical attention immediately, you'll both be bleeding as lustily as she is!"

"Ahoy, curds!" The voice on the bullhorn at the ship's bow railing sounded disturbingly familiar. Deck illumination increased to reveal the speaker as a man with an eye patch. It was Dennis.

Tohnyin raised her eyebrows and emitted a gasp that seemed more disgusted than astounded. A stunned, hangdog expression flickered across Bardot's face. "Haggarty's hit!" he shrieked. "I couldn't close the wound! Take her aboard for medical treatment!"

"Kerfer's on board." The state engineer tossed the end of a rope into the tilted sub saloon. The two vessels aligned themselves with a hard bump. A black-suited figure jumped into the saloon and helped Omar pass a moaning Noragreta to Dennis and another deckhand on the yacht.

"You had him!" Dennis upbraided Omar. "You had the climate shifter shifting narratives, and all you had to do was point out that's all the alarmists can ever do, but your ego couldn't just let everything he was babbling roll off! No, you started to swap impressions!"

"Szhtockholm szhyndrome!" the celebrity roared. "We threatened to become an untidy unity!"

"Shut up, schmuck!" Dennis turned to his black-suited compatriot. "Bring us around so I can deal with these billet-heads!"

"Thanks for the smoke-show, Tess!" Shalom saluted from the sub saloon. "It made for a good time had by all." He boarded the yacht as it pushed around the sub.

"Trigger warning!" Straddling the bow railing, Dennis trained a black pistol with a suppressor on the celebrity's face. "What's that old adage I'm so fond of?" He snapped his eye patch. "Aye, 'an eye for an eye.'"

"Dennis, *please* don't!" Tess thrashed desperately. "I'll do anything you want! I'm a higher value-"

"You'll give us a communal golden shower?" Dennis glanced at Tohnyin and squeeze-cocked the front grip strap of the handgun. "Feed the crappies, Angelenos-"

Another explosion issued from the cockpit of the submarine, and the celebrity plunged beneath a wave as Dennis fired a shot in his direction. He clawed furiously for depth. He thought he heard one more close gunshot and another distant one. He surfaced at a side of the pyramid obstructed from the yacht. The stench of burning electrical circuitry hung heavy in the air, a thin plume of smoke drifted overhead and the shadows of flames lapping the sub fazed him. He was relieved to hear a muffled series of coughs emanate from the adjacent, dark side of the platform.

"Come on out, CIB!" Dennis's grating voice echoed.

"We'll just take some propaganda shots and release you!" Some expletives and a pause ensued. "Ram the pyramid! Crush the reefers!"

"Don't be a damned fool, Blount!" Omar voiced the objection. "The sub is nearly sunk. No fate could be more fitting for them than hypothermia, especially after I so diligently guarded our moral high ground in handing Oobops his beatdown!"

Dennis laughed maniacally. "If they cling to that lumber-pile, they might make it to shore!" He fired two bullets into the pyramid. "You hear me, Awax? You concede that Heavy Duty here kicked your ass in the flyting?"

"The real kicker, bellicose veins," Omar bellowed, "is I'm not one part Native American! The gross majority of your thrusts were not only illegitimate but irrelevant!"

"We intercepted a transmission from that Rondo joker!" an unidentified voice shouted. "He's put out two search-and-rescue boats!"

"Let's shove out of here!" Omar commanded. "Ahoy, California crybullies, we're going to leave your outcome to the lake's idea of natural selection! If you survive, you'd better advise your handlers to let civilization evolve without systemic interference, or we'll show up Santa Monica for the outrage mob of hateful, hypocritical, bottom-up, sweaty-assed swamp donkeys that it is!"

"You know what's the real pisseroo?" Ishmael wailed. "If those leaster-bunnies have to be replaced, chances are their jobs will be outsourced to someone marginally competent!"

"The worst thing if they don't make it," Bardot argued, "is their offal remains will acidify our fine freshwater resource!"

Two more bullets were fired into the blast-vented pyramid. The yacht extinguished its lights and spun the stage-works as it glided past. The celebrity dived and resurfaced on the side of the platform facing the burning submarine. The capsized vessel was largely underwater. "Ned!" The slumping figure of

Charlton Shalom clung to the pyramid. "I had her, but I lost my grip! I'm not sure she was breathing-"

"Tess?" The celebrity dived beneath the platform. He flailed through a quadrant of liquid darkness in panicked futility. When he thought his heart would burst, he resurfaced gagging. The bagpipes floated on the water along with a few small chunks of burning debris, and a speedboat buzzed in the distance. "Tess! Oh, God, no! Tess!"

He thought he spotted an irregular bump on the surface that disappeared beneath a wave about seven meters away. He filled his lungs with air, knifed into the chop and swept numbly across the distance. He clawed deeper into the water and started back toward the platform in a zigzag. He collided with an unresponsive Tohnyin. Laboring for every bit of muscle control, he dragged her to the surface and hauled her back to the stage-works.

Shalom switched on his pith-helmet light. "I was trying to use my leg to hold her up-"

The celebrity pinned Tess's shoulders against the pyramid steps. He thought he felt a carotid pulse. He tilted her head back, pinched her nostrils, placed his mouth over hers and provided a rescue breath. He couldn't discern any chest rise or air flow. He coughed for a few seconds and gave her a second breath. He checked again for a pulse and found none. He awkwardly boosted her higher on the platform and felt their weight drive the stage-works lower in the water. He gave her thirty chest compressions and two more rescue breaths. "*You won't leave me like this, Tohnyin!!*" A wave lapped over them. He performed another cycle of compressions and breaths. "Tess, *please!*" A trickle of blood ran down her forehead. He roared in agony. She gurgled and twitched. She coughed weakly. "That's it!" She coughed with more vigor. "That's it!" He wiped blood off her face and discovered a gash beneath her hair. He checked on Shalom and found him submerged to his neck, his features contorted with distress. "You hang with us, Professor!"

Tohnyin hacked and retched for several minutes. The celebrity kept his hand pressed against her head wound and patted her lightly on the shoulder. She finally moaned, gasped and slapped his hand away. "Enough," she uttered in a weak, scratchy voice. "Where's Rondo?"

The celebrity hissed tenderly. "Were you grazed when Dennis fired into the platform?"

Tess rubbed her cheek and held her head. "I slipped underwater. When I resurfaced, I must've banged my head."

A wave separated Shalom from the floating pyramid and left him bobbing in the water with his arms angled stiffly away from his sides. The celebrity dived into the chop, grabbed the luminary-at-large and pulled him back to the stage-works. "Sorry to be a burden, Abner, but I was shot below the knee."

"Shalom's shot in the shin?" Tohnyin verified. "Can you tell how bad?"

Charlton raised his gaze. "Noctilucent bands herald Auriga, Perseus and Cassiopeia." He pointed overhead into a haze with no discernible stars. "We started a kilometer out on the west side of the lake." He gestured over his shoulder. "I calculate our best chance is to try to push due north."

The celebrity shivered. "That's the way to Tiffany's house?"

Shalom rubbed his chin. "Here is where it really pays to be smart enough to win a Nobel Prize in physics, Nathan. I love Tiff, but I have no desire to place my life in the hands of a flaky romantic partner fifty years younger than me."

The celebrity attempted to promote sensation in his lower extremities by extending his legs out of the water in fan kicks. "Speaking of qualifying as a quantum master, Doctor, I'm certain we saw you wave from the ravaged sub and then board WIO's yacht." He smiled deferentially. "Are you really capable of being in two places at once? Or how is it that you can be here now?"

"You saw Genghis Novotny board their ship," Shalom submitted, "a battle-hardened veteran of community theater, who bears an uncanny resemblance to anyone who looks like me." He paused to wipe his face. "I postulated that whichever side lost the flyting was likely to demonstrate its idea of fair play by attempting some illegitimate post-match recruitment tactic. That's why we held the event in the sub. I kept my body double concealed in the cockpit in the hope that we could execute a switch just prior to the dirty abduction attempt. Naturally, it worked, although I didn't expect anyone to go so far as to blow up the whole shebang. I got swept adrift by dumb luck."

"I refuse to believe that anyone who belongs to our side could bear responsibility for these detonations." The celebrity pointed to what seemed to be due north. "I think I can discern skyglow. If I can rip a few boards loose from the platform for oars, is everyone up to helping me try to nudge the stage-works to shore?"

"I have little vim left in my limbs," Shalom moaned, "only ache and cold."

"Don't sink us, Ahab," Tohnyin objected. "Let's take turns huddling together for warmth out of the water at the top of this life-buoy." She slid down and took Charlton by the arm. "Come up higher, Chutz, and let's see if we can't check your wound." The celebrity helped Tess resituate the slayer of sub-atomic hydrae beside her. She draped his arm around her neck and directed his pith-helmet light over his knee. "It doesn't seem to be bleeding profusely. There's an exit wound." She rubbed his leg. "The *Janesy* should be coming around soon, shouldn't it? Maybe we can orient ourselves to its path."

Shalom readjusted his pith helmet. "Is the fog dense, or is it just me? We must've drifted far enough toward the middle of the lake that the ship could pass without our knowledge – except perhaps for a series of monster waves."

"Then waiting to be rescued is the best we can do." Tohnyin reclined on her elbows. "The paramount thing is to stay mentally engaged."

"Perhaps Oobops would regale us," Charlton challenged, "with another vintage vignette from the screwball cult of golden Hollywood personalities?"

The celebrity wiggled his toes. "Were you awareh," he channeled the breathless staccato of a mature Katherine Hepburn, "that I once scheduled romantic trysts independent of one anotheh with film director John Ford and aviator Howard Hughes for the same time on the same evening at the same place? I strutted inside the It Café, spotted them seated back to back at adjacent tables and instantly realized my faux pas. Well, what could a poor girl do? To avoid discovery, I ducked into the phone booth in the lobby, where I produced the number for the hottest escort service in town, which I'd found rifling through the pants of screen legend Spencer Tracy, and I ordered their two best girls to hit the It at once. I then waited and watched with glee as the vamps arrived and each in turn picked up and left with one of my intended suitors. The next day I took great delight in berating John and Howard both for standing *me* up the previous evening."

"Recall, Ahab," Tess remarked, "the last time you performed an impression, the theater was firebombed. I'd hate to see what happens if you ever play *MacBeth*."

The celebrity felt a sly smile cross his lips. "My Bogey sealed our victory in the flyting, didn't it, Dr. Shalom?"

"When I asked for an encore, Aman, I was introducing a note of sarcasm." Shalom removed his pith helmet and rubbed his brow. "You offered a respectable resistance in verbal combat, but you lacked the law professor's gritty, working-class edge. A desperation wafted up around your effort to be cute."

"He was too slick and prepackaged, too plastic and polished, too affectedly unctuous," Tohnyin reasoned. "Please recognize that Ahab isn't representative of our organization and realize that you share our values and opt to work with us regardless of the match outcome."

"Tess was a cheerleader in school," the celebrity observed.

Tohnyin swept her hands through her hair. "How would it sit with you, Doctor, to go to work for Wisconsin but really report to California?"

Shalom studied his pith helmet. "Call me red-shifted; Wisconsin won the flyte. I'm predisposed to sympathize with their climate snooze-alarmism anyway, but I do resent being shot. Even by accident."

"Accidents don't happen in a vacuum," Tess suggested.

A series of waves rocked the board-works, inundated its occupants and twisted it a quarter-turn, knocking Charlton to the bottom of the platform. He shivered violently. "I could use relief from this raw spring in the land that global warming forgot."

Tohnyin extended her hand and helped the titan of the magnetosphere crawl back beside her. "Chutz, you've contended that the Earth maintains its energy balance like a living organism, that through its natural feedback loops, it'll self-mend. Do you honestly subscribe to some sort of Gaia theory? Do you really believe that climate shift poses no significant threat?"

"It's my Goyim theory," Shalom asserted. "Climate change is like football Saturday, with some winners, some losers and a few upsets. It's a discipline worthier of an economist than a geophysicist."

"It's more like *casino* Saturday, isn't it," Tess maintained, "with far more losers than winners?"

"As Buber would say," the celebrity contributed, "'The radiation of the force of the You penetrates the ordered world and thaws it again and again.'" He executed rhythmic kicks. "Through the years, Dr. Shalom, you've taken conspicuously contrarian positions on a host of scientific issues-"

"Like atmospheric carbon provides a stabilizing influence?" The Nobel Prize recidivist shifted his weight uncomfortably. "Check the gradual decline of extreme weather events throughout the previous century up to now. The scientific community is too scared, lazy and arrogant to commit real science and consider alternatives to its parochial speculations. You climatologist criminologists ought to learn the difference between correlation and causation. Saving a degree and a half was always an overreaction to an overcorrection. It should all be subsumed under acclimatization." He coughed and snorted. "The biggest benefit of the polar shroud is psychological. Society wants to lawyer its way out of the problems presented by climate shift when it could much more elegantly engineer its way around them in unforced increments. According to my toy climate model, the most dire change that diminished caps might bring is a disrupted ocean heat conveyer system in the Atlantic, weakened and run amok due to an influx of fresh meltwater. The upshot could be a much harsher climate throughout Europe. To underscore the talking points put out by your opponent, Europe has such a distinguished history of destabilizing the globe that it seems strikingly poetic that the globe should destabilize Europe."

The celebrity shrugged. "Most wars start because some empowered dink is stumped for a clever comeback."

Tohnyin crawled down the platform to the water's edge. "Huddle up and warm up with Chutz," she instructed the celebrity. She plunged her lower body into the lake. His feet practically numb, the celebrity clambered up the board-works to the world-class astrophysicist. "What in Washington happened with ARPA and DARPA, Doctor? You were active in a Project CatchDrift, which appears to have involved high-power transmission of radio frequency energy into the upper atmosphere for the purpose of manipulating air currents and holding particles in closed contours."

"Heed this public service announcement, Avery, just in the event that I go deep." Shalom wiped his face. "You must be familiar with the maxim 'There are no enemies in a snowstorm.'"

The celebrity grunted. "I may be too bipolar to buy that optimistic a take on human nature."

"When I was held over at one of my rest stops," Charlton persevered, "the idea occurred to me that the Middle East might benefit from a protracted cold front. I decided I'd try to manufacture one and hoped in so doing I might numb down a few hostilities endemic to that hotbed of hotheads. So armed with the resources of the U.S. government to explore radiative forcing for the purpose of fortifying the polar cap shroud, I conducted research on blasting radio frequency energy into the sky through mobile high-power transmission antennae arrays called space heaters developed by Lincoln Worbley. We exploited pressure points in the jet streams that enabled us to exert control over flux of wave activity and wave strength and to influence local cloud formation and surface temperature. Upon discovery by my overseers that I was pursuing a personal agenda which meandered significantly from the U.N. proxy agenda they'd engaged me to support with federal tax dollars, I readily confessed that I'd merely fabricated the manipulated data they were expecting. DARPA unceremoniously discharged me and ordered me to stay a statistically significant distance away from all further scientific endeavor."

"I can relate." The celebrity smiled complaisantly. "You'll recognize you made the right decision in joining us when you read the inscription beneath the statue at the center of our Boohenge labyrinth."

Tohnyin displayed a loose piece of wood. "Ahab, join me back in the drink! Let's try to propel this lifeboat toward the shore!" She began employing her board as an oar.

The buzz of an approaching speedboat stifled the conversion. "Have they been watching and waiting impatiently for the lake to swallow us?" Shalom moaned.

"That must be our colleague Rondo Bracey!" Tess stopped paddling. "We're secure!"

A light from the speedboat washed over the board-works.

"All that's secure," the celebrity contended, "is your martyr's star on the karmamentarium wall!"

"Don't fall for Ahab's fables," Tess comforted Charlton. "Rondo will be your Studio body man, and his integrity is intact."

"Rondo's a howitzer barrel of fun if you're ready for some heavy recoil." The celebrity rotated the board-works so a corner faced the oncoming speedboat.

"Tohnyin, is that you?" The speedboat helmsman wielding the microphone wore an eye patch. "Tess!" He increased his cockpit illumination. "Code in!" Rondo Bracey had replaced his bulky eye bandage with a green eye patch.

"*Rainbow!* Rondo!" Tess waved as vigorously as buoyancy would permit. "Show a little faith, chaplain," she chided the celebrity. "We trusted we'd be extracted!"

"We traced your somatags." The speedboat drifted beside the floating pyramid. "This canoe can only hold one more person, but I'll try to take two. Oobops can wait for Rosey to pick him up."

"Rondo, reassure me that you didn't wreck us!" the celebrity demanded.

"We were delayed at the hospital," Bracey snarled. "As a timesaver, the team jumped out of the aircraft over a field in Batavia, but Rosey's chute tangled in some oak branches. Kahn climbed up to rescue him and fell out of the tree. They're keeping him overnight for observation." He eyed the grand slam scientist. "Dr. Shalom? It's an honor, sir, but I'm required to certify your identity. Your son Tycho told one of our agents you taught him a tongue-twister as a toddler which only you'd be able to recite."

"*Vhaaa?*" Charlton sighed heavily. "I recall a verse we chanted as we converted our leaf blower to a rocket launcher because his peewee science-fair project was due the next day: Warden Warren Warchetz worships warship workshops."

Rondo smiled affirmatively. "You're the manitou." He

extended his hand to Tess. "I'm going to have *you*, Tohnyin, kneel dead center behind the seats. You'll cling to me and the Doc for support."

"The slightest false move lands your bad finger in his good eye," the celebrity exhorted Tess.

Charlton rubbed his pith helmet. "What'll your bottomless bureaucracy do to me, Ned?"

"Subject you to the equivalent of a bottomless life-insurance pitch," the celebrity speculated, "until you agree to cooperate with us."

Tohnyin clutched Bracey's arm. The speedboat nearly capsized as he hauled her aboard. "I'll swing around to the other side of the raft to collect Shalom," he announced.

Charlton leaned closer to the celebrity. "Keep your eyes glued to the sun, Ahab. Earth climate has been influenced recently by changes in the magnetic field of our favorite star, but what's important is ARPA neglected to cut my access to their complete data. They'd prefer that you not know knots at the poles indicate we're moving into a period of diminished solar stimulation, so all the resources spent on the big cool is a big waste. Increasing carbon emissions is what may damn well save us."

She was a harlot and a half,
Not even wholesome for a party girl.
I sat me down and did the math;
The child she bore's not my bambino.

It was a doggle of a boon,
Not even prudent for a crazy man.
A full endowment from the moon,
Your data dance the Hopscotch Polka.

There's trending danger in the flue:
'Tis not a theory but's in fact a fact.
When wise men jeer for peer revue,
Their working numbers get stochastic.

CODA

"Up the post creep some of them *spydahs*, them red, long-legged spydahs, the type that spoon incessantly till they've sucked the bodily juices out of their suitahs." Seated beside Unique Agent Tess Tohnyin in the luxurious downtown L.A. office of Philander Ledbetter's intrepid golf partner and plastic surgeon acquaintance Dr. Dorian B. Cloney, the celebrity spotted a tiny transmitter behind her armrest. A small fountain gurgled softly in the center of the rarefied anteroom, its opaque shell peppered with the evanescent silhouettes of darting koi. Resplendent mixed-media beachscape renderings by artist D.B. Cloney decorated the apricot walls overlooking plush couches and chairs. And a triad of octagonal tables displayed glossy, hard-copy collector's-edition popular magazines arranged in fans. Prominent among the mags lay the current edition of *The WHO*, which touted excessive pictorial coverage of its lead item: *Teen Victim Princess Giselle Engelhart Romps Nude On California Beach!!!*

"Are the magazines poised to revive you in case you inquire about the price of a procedure?" The celebrity chuckled with frustration as he entered personal information on the medical form filling his Qilroy screen. "I better start prioritizing. My insurance plan isn't going to cover half of what I need."

Tess grimaced. "In a profession as ticklish as ours, truant-wit, you took the cheap insurance? You're not even at Tier Two?"

The celebrity stiffened his neck. "I once was a Tier Two-tin' denizen, but getting the boot busted my medicine. When one goes on termination appeal, he must negotiate a series of fiery hoops in order to maintain his health benefits. I detest the clerical work so much I thought I might try traveling light for a while."

Tohnyin rubbed her palm against her forehead. "I can't work with you knowing you still have that abomination welded to your butt." The dark-haired caryatid of a receptionist evaluated her with a vigilant gaze. Tess modified the celebrity's medical form information, electing a program of radical laser brattoo eradication microsurgery and revising his "Single" status to "Married."

He casually crushed the armrest transmitter. "I might violate one proscription a day to remind myself I'm alive, but I'm not going to try to get away with skulduggery of that magnitude."

"You're not getting away with anything if your rear is covered by my Tier Five plan." She sighed. "We could both use a little break. When we're through here, you can escort me to Vegas and treat me to a night of victuals and nuptials." She fixed him with a penetrating squint. "I've considered taking an action like this for some time. I'm so weary of men hanging all over me like mydas flies."

He emitted stuttering noises. "You sound serious. What's more, you sound sober." He flashed a perplexed grin. "Of course, you do have a great poker face." He restored his "Single" marital status.

Tess swept her spiky bangs off her forehead. "I have a great face period, which under the circumstances, you should be pleased to observe. When the doctor finishes with me, it should be perfect. As to Vegas, I'm perfectly serious." She restored his "Married" status. "We'll wed in secret, and the news will leak, creating a shock wave which should, so to speak, give my hounds pause."

A dizzying surge of emotion crashed across the tail of the celebrity's flat, quotidian breakers. For a shining moment, he basked in the soft, tranquil smile that possessed her lips. "I wonder, ah, I feel-" He found his fingers caressing her wrist, and he recalled a sonnet he'd written or lifted long ago for his beloved Tina. "Should our hearts know not a day of roles undreamed but as charade, of pinioned wings, a humbled tongue, from shaded branch to hope's lamp run-"

"When you get squared away with the Studio again, you can opt into the thinking person's insurance plan yourself, and we'll have the marriage dissolved." Tohnyin offered a wry pout. "If we just register as domestic partners, we'll be investigated, and I don't want to have to keep a drawer full of your socks and underwear in my house." She freed her hand. "I'm doing you a professional favor with the expectation that in the near future you'll reciprocate." She raised her eyebrows. "You didn't think I was inviting you into bed with me, did you?" She snickered. "Did you think I was offering to bear your progeny?" She thrust her head back and laughed heartily. "Mrs. Oobops!"

"Mr. Oobops." A nurse hovered over the celebrity. "Mr. Oobops, the doctor will see you now." He leapt to his feet and followed her. Before entering the inner sanctum, he glanced back at Tess. Their eyes locked and her laughter became more ebullient.

The nurse guided the celebrity into a tiny room which held an examining table. He was startled to find another rigid patient joining him before he recognized his image in a full-length mirror. Folded on the table was a recycled-paper polka-dot gown. "Please remove your clothes," she instructed, "including your Qilroy, and put on the gown, opening to the back. You may leave your socks and shorts on."

He nodded. "Keep only the nasty stuff." She left him with his troubled thoughts. "What *is* wrong with me?" he muttered. "What could I have been thinking?" Tohnyin was a capital tease. She'd dangled herself in front of him and he'd gullibly snapped at the bait. Even if her offer had been genuine, how far over the edge of insanity would one have to tumble to entertain the prospect of *marrying* Tess? She'd probably toyed with him as revenge for his concerned investigation of her DNA. The only friction he'd ever know with Tohnyin would be wholly acrimony.

He stripped to his socks and shorts. The upscale gym lighting in the room enhanced the cuts of his muscular physique in the mirror, but it also increased the shadows cast by his nose, eye circles and depressed scars. Subliminal commercial persuasion seemed to be everywhere. He donned the polka-dot gown and boosted himself onto the examining table.

Dr. Cloney entered shortly. "Hello, Mr. Oobops," he stated in the rich, comforting baritone of a skilled surgeon. "What can we do for you today?" He glanced at the celebrity and reviewed his medical chart in his Jatakar.

"Life has left me a little frayed at the edges, Doctor." The celebrity shifted his weight. "I'd like some of the scars expunged." The doctor parked his Jatakar atop his impeccable thick, black hair and extracted a small laserscope from the bulging breast pocket of his lab coat. He squinted through the lens at the area under the celebrity's right eye. "My hobby is trash-talking street gangs."

Dr. Cloney flinched, switched yellow light to blue, leaned forward again and tracked the celebrity's cheek topography. "Your superior informed me you cut a rough swath through Wisconsin."

He neatly palmed the scope and examined the contours of the celebrity's cheeks with his fingers. "You'd like the scars on your arms and chest excised, too?" He split the paper gown down the longitudinal perforation and tossed it aside. He again squinted through the scope and made a cursory torso survey. "And you had some complaint about your body art?"

The celebrity smiled deferentially. "Ah, moving on down, I have a fresh brattoo on my buttocks that I'd like removed."

Dr. Cloney nodded. "Would you stand up, drop your shorts and show me?"

The celebrity rose from the examining table. "I would think if you can remove brattoos, you'd be able to easily excise a temporal scar like Phil Ledbetter's."

"We could if we wanted to deface a state landmark." Cloney sighed impatiently as the celebrity turned to display his brattooed side, clutched his waistband and lowered it to his knees. "Still some residual oozing?" The doctor slid his fingers over the outer ridges of the brattoo. "You have a veritable bas-relief back here, don't you?" The celebrity gazed at his veritable full-frontal nude image in the mirror. "Body art eradication remains the second most popular procedure that we perform, but there's considerable labor here. Do you have coupons?" He chuckled. "Is there anything else?" A mellow flourish of trumpets signified a Jatakar alarm. "Pardon me momentarily, please." The doctor checked his sourcerer. "I have to address this." He administered a light spank of resolution, and the celebrity raised his shorts. Cloney executed a perfect military pivot and crisply strode out of the room, authoritatively slamming the door behind him.

The celebrity lowered his shorts again. He was above the sleazy flash of morphing a body part to attain some cosmetic hegemony, wasn't he? A light behind the mirror engaged, and the spectacle of Director Phil Ledbetter appeared. "Having trouble with your containment strategy, Oobops?" the D.C.I.'s inquiry issued through a room speaker.

"Natty Phil!" The celebrity hiked up his shorts. "Why, I, ah, seem to be having a bit of an image problem." His humiliation crystallized as anger. "How is it that you happen to be lodged behind the mirror in my doctor's examining room?"

"I'm here to have a mole removed." Ledbetter pressed his forearms against the back of the mirror. "Privacy is aberrant, but questions about my medical status are not open for public discussion." He leveled a stern gaze. "I have completed my review of your fustian on Operation Shalom. As an opening footnote, your allegory framing our secret operation as a symphony or musical theater replete with act-closing mood ditties that you thought you'd redacted was recovered." He bared his teeth. "Remind me how you rated your performance in the flyting."

"I took a verbal cheese grater to Omar," the celebrity asserted. "It was a blowout."

Ledbetter cleared his sinuses. "How do you account for the stark divergence between the fustian I received from Unique Agent Bracey and the ones you and Unique Agent Tohnyin submitted? Rondo reported that your performance was far from inspiring, although it was better than anything he expected."

"Is that supposed to be an endorsement?" The celebrity stepped away from the examining table. "Or his charming way of saying that I suck?"

The D.C.I. patted his hair. "It's his charming way of trying not to say it."

The celebrity nodded. "When Rondo speaks, his *ignoscente* becomes pronounced."

"Then how do you account for the fact," Ledbetter challenged, "that Operation Shalom resulted in Bracey and Al-Keypone receiving special honors along with pay grade increases?"

The celebrity clicked his tongue. "What starts with 'P,' ends with 'L' and means preferential?"

The director fingered his temporal scar. "Is it your wish to initiate a specious counteroffensive impugning my executive integrity?"

The celebrity approached the utility mirror. "You're the fairest of them all, P.L."

"I'm better than fair, Ahab." The D.C.I. pressed his thumb and forefinger against his brow. "I'm the one responsible for encouraging your Studio support personnel such as I.B., Radmilla, Tess and Rondo to subject you to sharp derision for the duration of Operation Shalom. The quantum computer predicted that the mission would lead to some sort of highly charged political verbal battle. And the hazing that you sustained from the CIB apparatus served not only to prime you for the ultimate showdown but to fortify your resolve and clarify your appreciation for your unique position within the organization." He cleared his sinuses. "The more something costs, the more it's valued, and this is never more ineluctably the case than where cost equals discomfort that one endures for a cause."

"I haven't noticed any recent deviation from the mean in the treatment I've received from Radmilla, and if anything, Rondo has grown more gracious." The celebrity eyed the director intently. "That includes denying me a seat in his speedboat on Geneva Lake. My attitude is my caretaker, Natty Phil. How do you reach the conclusion that my dedication needs a boost?"

"Oobops, your nescience is indictable." Ledbetter rapped on the mirror glass. "You've been thoroughly vetted in regulatory compliance with the standard protocol of our agency control module." He hiccuped. "How have you failed to hack into the quantum computer to ascertain the misconduct code behind your termination? 'The poet is by definition a subversive agent always in revolt.' The Q.C. determined that since you're really not with the program, you shouldn't really be with the program."

"You're not serious!" The celebrity winced mightily. "Please forgive me, Natty Phil, but I can't understand how I could be offboarded purely on the brittle logic of artificial intelligence."

"Let me count the ways." The D.C.I. traced his temporal scar. "The CIB might abide your eristic overexposure to nihilistic currents of self-indulgent rogue-wave literature, but you've come to embody toxic individualism, assuming political postures unsanctioned by the social consciousness of the

Bureau. In the course of Operation Shalom, your preference for a spiritual explanation over a molecular one blinded you to the potential serviceability of a double-duty independent agent named Alec whose hostile recruitment attempt might've provided you with a mixed-agenda link deep inside Wisconsin."

"I sensed that shoat had a collateral agenda." The celebrity headed for the chair that held his clothes clump. "I missed the connection that the Parallacts masseuse could've provided. Yet the fact is I ultimately delivered the scientific asset of the century to our no-excuses, results-only agency."

"You're fortunate that he wasn't delivered to the bottom of the lake." Ledbetter cleared his sinuses. "Tohnyin cites her source Mercowitz as reporting that the foreign agent 'Deshi Bud' finagled access through 'Burl' the club doorman and has claimed credit for placing the bombs in the sub. When in the course of the flyting you resorted to the opinions of Hollywood entertainers to validate your cause, Bud thought you were panicking and on the verge of surrender." The director patted his hair. "A savvy streetfighter keeps a wary eye on all bystanders."

"Dense smoke advisory, P.L." The celebrity thrummed his abdominal muscles. "I'm still being denied post-op access to Shalom."

"He isn't clicking as seamlessly as we'd expect," Ledbetter complained. "He doesn't seem appropriately threatened by the climate change crisis and doesn't work with any sense of urgency to impact the environment." The director traced his temporal scar. "I've mentioned to him in passing how pleased I am with my lobotomy, extolling the benefits it's provided in my professional as well as my personal life."

"Give the new laureate on the block a chance." The celebrity repopulated his pants. "Conversion comes by degrees. I'd-" He heard muffled voices in the next room and pointed. "They can hear us through the wall."

The D.C.I. hiccuped. "Dr. Cloney's office is an emergency directorate of operations. He's holding an information forum here two weeks from tonight, and the select tribunal of review will convene to hear your reinstatement appeal directly afterward. As a condition of the Bureau's settlement with the secretariat on their panoply of grievances against you, I've authorized Radmilla to name the seven tribunal justices. She's selected herself and her two undersecretaries, D.D.O. Montoone, Unit Bracey, Chief of P.C. Security Havatas Wahlberg and H.R. Senior Compliance Analyst David Blair."

"Couldn't you fit Paige Eiffel into the rig?" The celebrity laughed. "They'll vote to fire me off Cathedral Peak in a runaway railroad."

"Apply the force of gravity as an ally, trub-ball." Natty Phil bared his teeth. "By the bylaws of the Bureau, if the tribunal cannot reach a unanimous verdict, it is declared void, and another tribunal with seven new members convenes at a time subsequent to the end of the current state assembly term." He kneed the mirror. "Can't we all rest assured there's reason for knee-jerk optimism that you'll take the onus of obstruction to previously unplumbed levels, and *tamperarily* rejigger their nefarious brew in a manner to undermine it with your own?"

The celebrity smiled complaisantly. "Independent of the planet, the people who inhabit it just grow warmer and warmer."

Let's cheer our strong, swift lads
As they put on the pads.
Roll, team, roll!

Salute our future moms
As they light up our proms.
Shine, line, shine!

Support that big brown bear
As the first cabin there.
Wave, rag, wave!

Secure our legacy
As the mark you can't see.
Rave, wag, rave!

ABOUT THE AUTHOR

Richard Fendry lives in Wisconsin. When he's not exercising his literary chops, he's an avid horticulturist. He believes that untold health issues can be linked to not spending enough time outdoors.